DANIEL PLAINWAY

 OR

THE
HOLIDAY HAUNTING
of the
MOOSEPATH LEAGUE

VIKING
75 years

Daniel Plainway

 OR

THE
Holiday Haunting
of the
Moosepath League

Van Reid

VIKING

VIKING
Published by the Penguin Group
Penguin Putnam Inc., 375 Hudson Street,
New York, New York 10014, U.S.A.
Penguin Books Ltd, 27 Wrights Lane, London W8 5TZ, England
Penguin Books Australia Ltd, Ringwood, Victoria, Australia
Penguin Books Canada Ltd, 10 Alcorn Avenue,
Toronto, Ontario, Canada M4V 3B2
Penguin Books (N.Z.) Ltd, 182–190 Wairau Road,
Auckland 10, New Zealand

Penguin Books Ltd, Registered Offices:
Harmondsworth, Middlesex, England

First published in 2000 by Viking Penguin,
a member of Penguin Putnam Inc.

1 3 5 7 9 10 8 6 4 2

LIBRARY OF CONGRESS CATALOGING-IN-PUBLICATION DATA
Reid, Van.
Daniel Plainway, or, The holiday haunting of the Moosepath League / Van Reid.
p.   cm.
ISBN 0-670-89171-1
1. Portland (Maine)—Fiction. 2. Maine—Fiction. I. Title: Daniel Plainway
II. Title: Holiday haunting of the Moosepath League. III. Title.
PS3568.E47697 D3 2000
813'.54—dc21   99-057672

This book is printed on acid-free paper.
∞

Printed in the United States of America
Set in Janson Text
Designed by Kathryn Parise

To Maggie

All I write is first written for you

❧ CONTENTS ❧

from the *Eastern Argus*, October 22, 1896   1

PROLOGUE
November 27–December 2, 1896   5

1. THE EMPTY HOUSE, Thanksgiving 1896   5
2. A VOICE BEFORE DAWN, November 28, 1896   8
3. HOW THE NEWS WAS READ IN GILEAD, December 2, 1896   13

BOOK ONE
December 3, 1896   22

1. NOT TO BE CONFUSED   22
2. MEETING THE *CALEB BROWN*   28
3. THE MAN WHO WOULD NOT COME ASHORE   32
4. THE ASSEMBLED LEAGUE   36
5. THE HAT AND THE HACK   39
6. THE COVINGTON GOAL   43
7. THE MEMBERS WERE DISARMING   48
8. THE PORTRAIT AND APPLE PANDOWDY   51

BOOK TWO
December 4, 1896   56

9. SEVERAL PEOPLE RECENTLY MET   56
   Daniel's Story (1874–1891)   60
10. A TALE FROM OTHER SEASONS   63
11. INCIDENT ON A TRAIN   69
   Daniel's Story (1877–1891)   75
12. THE QUIESCENT INCARCERATION OF TOM BULL   77
13. STARTLING CIRCUMSTANCES AT THE ABODE OF MR. THOLE   80

14.	Emulating the Chairman	88
15.	The Reason Why	97
16.	Calling Capital Gaines	101

BOOK THREE
December 5, 1896
107

17.	Lovely, Dark and Deep	107
18.	John 19:27	112
19.	The Undisclosed Motives of Roger Noble	115
20.	Frantic Whispers and Pointed Dispatch	124
21.	Beyond the Forest of Fallen Trees	131
	Daniel's Story (May–June 1891)	135
22.	Stones in the Lake	139
23.	Speech at Midnight	143
24.	The Tor	151
25.	Others Lost Their Hats as Well	155
26.	The Banks of Lake George	163
	Daniel's Story (July–November 1891)	166
27.	The Span Between Trains	168
28.	More Sense of a Letter	175
29.	Number Two in a Series of Three	181
30.	Advice Did Not Come Cheap	191
31.	The Ox at Plow	196
32.	The Third Crash	198

BOOK FOUR
December 6, 1896
210

33.	Gifts	210
34.	Advanced Uses for a Hat	214
	Daniel's Story (November 1891–April 1892)	218
35.	The Last of the Wawenocks	222
36.	The Battle of the Smoking Pine	227
37.	Curier and Therefore	234
38.	-Athians and -Ashians in Flux	241
39.	Several Parties Not Necessarily Looking for One Another	242
	Daniel's Story (April 1892–April 1893)	248
40.	Two Hearts	253
41.	Two More	257

BOOK FIVE
December 7, 1896   263

42.	BETWEEN TALES	263
43.	UNCLE FRANCIS NEPTUNE	268
44.	THE RUNE AND THE WORM	272
45.	BETWEEN GRANDFATHERS	281
46.	UNFINISHED KNITTING	283

BOOK SIX
December 9–18, 1896   292

47.	SEVERAL ATTEMPTS AT TYING UP LOOSE ENDS	292
48.	BUT SOME WERE DOUBLE-KNOTTED	296
49.	AND WE WERE SO SURE THAT WAS THE ANSWER	300
50.	MUTUAL CONCERNS	302
51.	PERSISTENCE	306

BOOK SEVEN
December 21–22, 1896   310

	Daniel's Story (Mid-December 1896)	310
52.	LULLABY	314
53.	SOMEONE COMING BACK	318
54.	PARLEY'S PLAN	322
55.	EXPECTED SENTRIES SLEEP	325
56.	A SOLSTICE CAROL	327
57.	WHAT THEY DIDN'T KNOW INSIDE	332
58.	MORE ON SEVERAL RELATED POINTS	336
59.	ONE FINAL SCOUNDREL	338
60.	ONE POSSIBLE ANSWER	343

BOOK EIGHT
Christmas Eve–Christmas Day 1896   346

61.	THROUGH THE KITCHEN DOOR	346
62.	TWO MYSTERIES	350
63.	HAT IN THE RING	356
64.	CONFESSION IN A CHRISTMAS KITCHEN	360
65.	LIGHTLY I TOSS MY HAT AWAY	367

66. SPHERES IN TRANSIT 368

67. NUMBER SIX IN AN ONGOING SERIES 371

EPILOGUE: THE OCCUPIED POCKET
New Year's Day 1897 377

AUTHOR'S NOTE 380

Daniel Plainway

or

The
Holiday Haunting
of the
Moosepath League

from the Eastern Argus
(Portland, Maine)
October 22, 1896

A Mysterious Portrait

The Search for a Kidnapped Child

A Gunfight on the Sheepscott

NEW MYSTERY!
READERS ARE ASKED TO HELP

by Peter Mall

Shore dwellers in Wiscasset and Edgecomb were certainly wakened one night last week when a series of gunshots rang out over the otherwise quiet waters of the Sheepscott River—gunshots that marked the end of a strange and fearsome pursuit.

Readers may recall a small item in this journal, nearly two weeks ago, which related the disappearance of a boy of about four years. As it happened, other events, including the search for the schooner *Loala*, eclipsed the news of the child, the more so since little was known about him and no relations came forward to play the part of the bereaved and anxious family.

It is perhaps a mark upon our own selves that any tale of a lost innocent could so quickly and completely vanish from the public consciousness, and certainly a double badge of honor to those who have taken it upon themselves to secure that child from the brutal circle into which he had fallen.

First among these is Wyckford O'Hearn, known to Port-

landers as the Hybernian Titan for his exploits upon the
baseball field. It was Mr. O'Hearn who rescued the child,
known now only as Bird, from bad company in an ancient
cellar hole beneath Commercial Street.

Since then several people have acquitted themselves gal-
lantly by taking on the boy's guardianship, though criminal
elements gave every indication of wanting the child back
among themselves. In particular Mr. Matthew Ephram, Mr.
Christopher Eagleton, and Mr. Joseph Thump, who are known
to our readers as the charter members of the recently formed
Moosepath League, jeopardized their own safety by disdain-
ing the gang's nefarious intent and whisking the boy from
harm's way.

Many adventures, which may someday be described, followed
fast upon the heels of this flight, culminating in the kidnapping of the child and a gunfight upon the Sheepscott
River during the night of the 14th. Sheriff Piper of Lincoln County and Colonel Taverner of the United States Customs Agency led the final pursuit, which was punctuated
with exchanged shots. One Adam Tweed, known among the denizens of the waterfront as something of a thug, was apprehended after he deliberately and with malice aforethought
threw the child into the cold night waters of the Sheepscott.

The child, as has been mentioned, was rescued anew, and
Tweed himself was brought down by a very timely shot from
Mister Tobias Walton of Portland, who is also the chairman
of the aforementioned league. Tweed's wounds were not fatal, however, and he is now in the custody of Wiscasset's
jailer, pending trial.

Mr. O'Hearn was among the wounded as well, but after
some worrisome moments, he appears to be on the path to
recovery, and patrons of the game in Portland can look
forward to hearing the crack of his bat once again.

The authorities still have an interest in speaking to a
man named Eustace Pembleton, who is greatly involved in
this matter and who is believed to have escaped from their
net on Wednesday night. One Tom Bull, something of an instrument to Pembleton, was captured on the morning of the
15th, along the eastern shore of the Sheepscott near the
Boothbay town line. Bull, who was perhaps not born with that

name but acquired it by dint of his size, gave a fearsome struggle, and ten men were required to subdue him.

Those involved on the law's side of the chase are simply glad to have the little boy back in the arms of safety.

In securing the child from his kidnappers, however, a new mystery has been discovered. Among a thieves' cache found near the fort on Davis Island in Edgecomb was a portrait of a young woman who bore so strong a resemblance to the little boy, that no one who looked at the two together could deny a relationship between them. Indeed, Mister Walton is sure that the portrait is a likeness of Bird's mother, and he has, at his own expense, commissioned an etching based on that picture, the results of which the reader will find printed in conjunction with the present article.

It is hoped that by disseminating the unfortunate lady's likeness in this manner, some soul will recognize her and come forward with information regarding Bird's parentage and birthright. Any such intelligence will be kindly forwarded to the editor of the Eastern Argus, and a happy sequel may yet be added to this child's curious and harrowing tale.

PROLOGUE

November 27 – December 2, 1896

1. The Empty House
Thanksgiving 1896

It had snowed for an hour or so that morning, and the large, wet flakes still coated the windward side of trees, lined the bare branches of oak and maple, and formed a speckled fleece over the evergreens that guarded the carriage drive to the Linnett house.

On the way home from Fryeburg, Daniel Plainway pulled the horse and trap up before the stone columns at the end of the drive. He and his sister had been celebrating Thanksgiving with friends, and the snow had actually made it safe to leave later than they had planned, as the road glowed in the dusk, and the tracks of other wheels and horses described the way in dark lines and pockmarks before them.

Martha Bailey complained just a bit (in a wordless groan) when her brother stopped before the Linnett property. They had just crossed the town line into Hiram, and she looked forward to a fire in her own hearth; but to tell the truth, she was snugly wrapped in several throws, and the soapstones, warmed in their host's kitchen oven, still radiated comfortingly beneath the quilts at their feet.

"Do you mind if I take a turn up?" asked Daniel. The expression on his face was almost childlike, though not untouched by a self-realizing humor.

"No," she said. "You've been thinking about it since we came the other way this morning."

His chuckle was almost unheard as he shook the reins and the brown mare turned her head between the tilting columns.

The house itself was not visible from the road, and the ancient pines lining the drive hid the gray sky and darkened the atmosphere beneath so that one trusted to the instincts of the horse. There were several turns in the way, and one dip over a tiny running brook before they came to the first row of hedges and the manse itself rising out of the knoll ahead of them, amorphous in the shadows. Not half a mile away was Clemons Pond, glazed with ice, a dark presence in the fields beyond and below.

As they neared the house, a small breeze stirred the hedges.

"Oh, hurry," said Martha. "This place gives me the chills."

He passed her the reins, untangled himself from the throws, and climbed down. The wet snow gathered on his boots and crunched in the stiffened, uncut grass. Martha could see footprints appearing behind the man more easily than she could see the man himself, giving her the shuddery impression of an invisible being approaching the house.

The steps to the porch complained of Daniel's progress; the key sounded dully as he turned it. The air within, when he opened the door, was colder than the November evening. He had known the people here, had handled many small legal businesses for the Linnetts in his capacity as a lawyer, but had spent most of his time among these walls as a guest and a friend.

Daniel stopped in the hall and peered into the gloom of the parlor, remembering the lights and the voices. Nell often played the piano in the evening when they gathered here, and everyone but Linnett himself sang, he being too concerned for his local fame as an old grouch. It had been an undeserved reputation for the most part, until the last year or so, and even then his great rage was the product of a broken heart.

Daniel Plainway was not sure that he believed in ghosts, but he didn't think he would be frightened if he met one here. *There's more to be feared from the living than the dead,* his parents had told him more than once. He looked up the dusty stairway and thought of Nell descending there: a child, a young woman. She had been dear to Daniel's heart, like a lovely cousin who brings the holiday with her.

The holidays he remembered best of all: the grand Thanksgiving feasts, the Christmas candles throughout the house, filling the rooms with light on the eve before like the very grotto at Bethlehem. Old Ian Linnett never tired of his annual Yuletide jest: On the night of the winter solstice (Doubter's Day, he called it) he would arrive with a tiny spruce—barely three feet high—and teased everybody by announcing that *this* was the tree; as soon as he had cajoled the laughing and complaining crowd to decorate the whimsical thing, the real tree would make its entrance upon the backs of sturdy men, and Linnett was never satisfied unless it scraped the ceiling in the front hall.

Daniel craned his head back to look at the ceiling where daylight might have revealed the scars left by the topmost branches of long-forgotten trees.

Standing in the door to the front room, across from the parlor, he did not need a light to discern the shapes of furniture covered in sheets and throws or to remember that Nell's portrait was missing from its place above the hearth. Other things were missing from the house these past three years. He was pretty sure he knew who had taken them. "If I had just seen it all coming," he said aloud, and he shivered to think that perhaps his voice was unwelcome there.

Then he heard it again, a soft sound like a young woman's voice, but as from some irrevocable distance, and almost the notes of a simple melody; no doubt the wind was in a chimney or playing against a cracked eave.

Daniel closed the front door and locked it, feeling a small regret for having come here again. He stood on the porch and thought, *It's almost as if I still believe they'll all be here.* After the gloom of the house the strange patterns of snow on the lawn seemed to give off a light of their own. He could see Martha, waiting patiently in the carriage. It was important that he not appear melancholy when he returned, which meant just a moment more to regain his bearings.

He stepped around the corner of the house and looked over the pond. Everything seemed frozen, pitched in a single moment of discovery, and the sensation was so strong within him that he was startled to see the footprints leading from the back of the house.

The kids have been up here again, he thought as he walked the side lawn. *Well, as long as they don't harm anything.*

But there was something about the footprints that did not suggest a youngster had made them. There was only the one set, for one thing, closely spaced and weaving slightly, and they came from the house, and stopped at the edge of the pond. Daniel had thought that he would be fearless in the face of a phantom, but the prints touched him with an apprehension that rose to a vague dread as he followed the tracks to a place overlooking the water. The impress of a body marked the snow.

Old man Linnett had come from the back of the house with that same halting, weaving gait. He had collapsed and died in this place more than three years ago; Daniel could almost vouch for the exact spot.

"Is there anything the matter?" asked Martha when he returned to the carriage.

How could she know in this dark? he wondered. "I only wish they were still here," he said.

"*I* wish you wouldn't come."

"It's all right," he said, patting her knee through the throws wrapped about her. He covered himself up as well as he could and shook the reins, hoping that he didn't appear to be in a hurry. "Something hot when we get home," he suggested.

She looked at him in the dark but could see nothing of his expression.

The horse, surefooted and undaunted by the prospect of ghosts, pulled them past the hedges and through the guardian pines to the road home.

2. A Voice Before Dawn
November 28, 1896

Lydia O'Hearn was not too proud to half dress herself beneath the covers, a practice she had observed, on cold mornings, since her husband first brought her to his farm in Veazie. Sean O'Hearn used to laugh and make her laugh whenever she hauled her things on in bed, sometimes with the blankets over her head. These days, without her husband to help warm the sheets (a warming pan was not the same thing by any stretch), there was all the more reason to snatch her clothes and scramble into them beneath the covers on a morning like this. It was dark, with the curtains closed against the chill, but when she did climb out of bed, she could see her breath in the room.

She hadn't been too avid about farm life, or country life for that matter, when she arrived with Sean thirty years ago; she hadn't been too avid about the life when he died twenty-two years later, but she stayed, and she ran things with the help of her daughter, Emmy, and son-in-law, Ephias Ostertag, and somehow had developed some fierce feelings for it all. Her other children—those who survived the rigors of life to become adults— had separated like geese that fold away in flight to light upon their own fields or ponds. One of these, her son Wyckford, had returned for a time, and she was glad to know, rising that morning, that he was there to help fill the house again.

Once dressed and on the landing above the front hall stairs, she looked out the octagonal window that Sean had put in for her as a birthday present the year before he died. It faced east and was often her first view of the day. A hint of dawn shone through the single frosty pane this morning, with what Lydia considered to be a lack of conviction.

She didn't know why, but it occurred to her that she should write to Mister Walton. Then she remembered that she had dreamed of this man she had never met and that he had been telling her about Bird's mother.

Once she had said good morning to the dog, Skinny (a fat black animal of amiable disposition), it did not take her long to shake up the coals in the kitchen stove and get some kindling blazing; with two large sticks of wood and the flues and drafts open she had the firebox roaring and the oven ticking. She put the kettle on and rattled some pans so that everyone would know that Mother was up. Closing the damper, she could feel the heat from the stove almost immediately. There was paper, pen, and ink in the cupboard drawer, and she arranged these on the table, set a chair by the stove, and opened the oven door. The light in the kitchen was yet pretty dim, but she could see to compose a letter.

Dear Mister Walton, she wrote. He was all but a stranger to her, and yet because of everything he had done, particularly what he had done for her son Wyckford and for Bird, she had no difficulty addressing him as *Dear Mister Walton* with all sincerity. She paused only to wet her pen, before continuing.

> You will be pleased, I know, to read that Wyckford has improved greatly since I wrote you last. The cold weather gets into his wound, and he still has difficulty moving his arm more than an inch or two, but he is not in such constant pain and is able to face the day with more hope.

Hope was the important notion here. Wyckford had been shot in the shoulder last October, and the bullet had done untold damage. Lydia's hope was that her son would be able to work again; she knew that a man unable to wield some sort of tool to make a living was not much valued by society and soon despised by himself. Wyck's own hopes were more specific, and less likely. For several years, during the warmer months, he had played semiprofessional baseball in Portland, and uppermost in his mind was the fear that he would never again be able to swing a bat.

Lydia heard small footsteps on the stairs, and she put down her pen to wait for the attendant feet to enter the kitchen. After a quiet interval a head of brown hair and a pair of brown eyes, three feet or so from the floor, peered around the jamb. There was the look of humor in those eyes, a little mischief even, which pleased her. "I hope you're not in your bare feet," she said, knowing that he was.

The little boy, known to them only as Bird, showed himself and his bare feet. Here was the object of Wyckford's efforts, and the efforts of

Mister Walton and many others, the single small life that had precipitated a kidnapping, mortal chase, and her son's near loss of life. She had quickly grown to love the child.

"You get over here!" she said in mock anger.

He grinned as he hurried, socks and shoes in his hands, to the table, where she pulled out another chair. He sat down, and she grabbed up his sweet, scarred little feet and began to rub them vigorously.

"Oh, they're like ice!" she declared, which pleased him more.

This had become a ritual with them, and no one could have guessed who looked forward to it most. When she had chafed his feet warm and dressed them, she got up and washed her hands under the pump—an icy reminder of the day—then pulled down some plates from the cupboard. The kettle was already rumbling. Something occurred to her then, and she said, "I was just about to write Mister Walton about you." With a thought of what to write next, she sat back down and took up her composition once more.

> Bird seems to enjoy the farm more and more, and even Ephias doesn't mind him following about while he does the morning chores.

It was true. Though Ephias Ostertag was the unfortunate picture of a taciturn Yankee (what Emmy saw in the man, Lydia would never know) and though he seemed as stony as a New England field, he had warmed to Bird considerably and hardly growled when the boy accompanied him as he fed the creatures in the barn and milked the cows. But once Lydia's son was up and about, moving stiffly after another wakeful night with his splintered shoulder, the little boy was Wyckford's constant companion.

> You will understand, I think, Mister Walton, when I confess to you that it will be difficult to see the boy go, if ever his mother is found.

Emmy appeared in the kitchen, exchanged good mornings with her mother, and informed the boy that her husband had decided to lie abed and let Bird do the chores. Bird looked game. Ephias was not long behind her, though, and he had overheard his wife's quip. "He's already milked some and gathered eggs," said the man, and this intelligence was meant as praise, despite the growl in which it was couched. The man sat down and stretched an arm toward the dog. Skinny made a grunting noise while Ephias stroked her head.

Emmy returned from the pantry with a slab of bacon, and soon thick slices of the stuff were snapping in the pan and scenting the air with smoke and spice. Ephias sat at the table and packed his pipe, which would hardly leave his mouth the rest of the day.

"What does an owl in the night mean?" wondered Emmy.

"Probably that there is an owl nearabouts," returned her mother.

"Granny used to say something about an owl at night," insisted Emmy.

"A dog howling after dark is not considered fortunate. It's all superstition."

"No, I'm sure it was an owl she used to go on about."

"You would hardly hear one during the day, I think."

"I've heard one three nights in a row," said Emmy. "He woke me up last night. It's a strange sound when you're half asleep."

"It's sitting in the apple tree by your window," said Lydia. She was surprised that an owl would take up residence at this time of year but said nothing.

Wyckford came down the stairs. His tread was the heaviest in the house, the more so since his wounded side had thrown off his gait. He was a man of some altitude, though no longer the splendid "Hybernian Titan" who had spent so much ink in Portland's sporting press. He looked gaunt and drawn these days and older than his thirty years. There were strands of gray in his bright red hair. He was uncomfortable with his function (or, more aptly put, his *lack* of function) in the household.

Ephias, who said nothing about Wyckford's presence, was nearly as discomfited as Wyck. Ephias, it was suspected, had always considered Wyckford to be capricious and unreliable; playing baseball, it would seem, was no way for a man to make a living, even for some fraction of the year. The adventure that had led Wyckford to rescuing Bird and coming to physical grief was only a symptom of an irresponsible nature.

But Wyckford had labored in his time—as a line tender for the railroad and demolishing old buildings to make room for the Portland sugar refinery—and the inactivity of the past month and a half had told upon him as much as the wound that had caused it.

He might have left, if not for Bird. There was a powerful bond between the redheaded giant and the little boy that had been immediate and hard to explain, but if Bird had unintentionally led him to these straits, his presence was helping to lead him out of them.

This morning, however, Wyckford did not linger on Bird, who was sneaking a piece of bacon to Skinny. "Where's that ax?" Wyck asked his mother, by way of good morning. Someone had given him an ax, hoping that the use of it would duplicate the swing of a bat and bring his arm back to life. Of all the chores that Wyck hated, while growing up on the farm, none had been so onerous to him as chopping and splitting wood. He had spent many an hour contemplating that ax and (not insignificantly) the person (that is, the young woman) who had given it to him.

"It's in the shed, I think," said Lydia. She didn't think Wyckford should be swinging an ax. It had been too soon since he'd been wounded, and she feared he would do more damage to his shoulder, not to mention the danger of chopping off a toe. Nothing else was said. Ephias didn't look any happier, lighting his pipe. Emmy did not turn around from the stove. But when breakfast was on the table, Wyck put some food into him.

He needed help getting a warm coat on, and Lydia couldn't see how chucking an ax was practical or even very smart. Bird was ready to join him and forgo the morning chores, but Wyckford clearly needed to approach this test alone.

Lydia touched Bird's shoulder and without a word shook her head.

Wyckford trundled out into the cold morning, looking ungainly but determined. They did not watch him, except for the little boy. As he stood below the kitchen steps, the man's breath came in great puffs of steam. Beyond him the backyard was bleak with frost.

"Ephias," said Lydia when the door was closed, but Ephias had his coat on already.

"I can see the woodpile from the barn," was all Ephias said. He gave a reverse nod to Bird, which was as much invitation as the little fellow had ever gotten from the flinty man. Bird hurried with his coat and hat and followed him out.

Perhaps it wasn't so strange that Bird could enjoy the morning chores with Ephias, neither of them ever said very much. Ephias's lack of words, however, was the weight of rocky fields and broken fences; Bird's silences were bright, the silences of someone who truly listens, like that of a man in a bird-filled wood. Bird followed Ephias, and Skinny waddled after Bird; they were an odd trio.

When they were gone, Lydia said to her daughter, "That was nice of Ephias."

Emmy was thinking she would cook an apple pie for her husband. "He'll surprise even himself some days."

Lydia didn't like to think of Wyck swinging an ax with his broken shoulder but knew somehow that it was necessary. She thought of the person who had given the ax to Wyckford and decided to ask Mister Walton if he had heard from her.

"Who are you writing?" asked Emmy. She had the dishes in the sink and was working the pump handle.

"Mister Walton." Lydia dipped her pen and considered the letter. The sound of her writing was large in the kitchen.

Emmy poured some hot water from the kettle in after and nearly had the dishes done before she spoke again. "Tell Mister Walton," she said, "that the boy is spoken for."

3. How the News Was Read in Gilead
December 2, 1896

The Grand Trunk Railway ran through the center of Gilead on its course through the foothills of the White Mountains, and it is there that the train deposited Daniel Plainway on Thursday morning, the second day of December 1896. It had snowed in the night, and a white dust lay over the roofs and porches along Gilead's Main Street. A sack of mail was deposited in a coach waiting outside the station, and the town postmaster and the porter exchanged greetings and speculations about the weather.

Daniel was the only passenger to get off this morning at Gilead. He carried a small leather case, which contained certain legal papers, a ham sandwich, an apple, and a change of shirt. "Good morning," he said to the man in the carriage.

"Looking for someone?" asked the postmaster. He wore a dark cap, and his large gray mustaches waggled when he spoke.

Daniel considered the overcast sky as he spoke. "Gerald Pinkney," he said. Plainway was a pleasant-looking fellow, with wide brown mustaches; he was dressed well, and there was a large gold chain arched across a stomach that was something below portly.

"Gerald will be up to his uncle's," said the postmaster. "What a time he's had!"

"So I understand."

"Come up with me to the post office, if you can wait, and once I've sorted the mail, I'll take you up. There'll be a stop or two on the way."

"Thank you," said Daniel. "I would like that."

The use of the carriage seemed a strange formality since the post office was but three or four doors up. Daniel was a little surprised when they stopped, but he got out and gratefully caught the smell of coffee as he stepped inside. Mr. Beals, the postmaster, called to his wife—the post office took up the parlor of their house—and she met Daniel and hurried off to get refreshments.

Several people wandered in to watch the sorting of the mail, and Daniel greeted each of them. He stood in a corner with his coffee, leaving the straight-backed chairs for the elderly folk. There were six or eight of them before long. They were interested in him and curious to hear about the town of Hiram, where he hailed from, some forty miles away as the crow flies. Only the parson among them had ever stopped there, though one old fellow thought he had passed through, years before, on his way to his brother's. Several of them remarked that Gerald Pinkney had had quite a time, and Daniel said that he had understood this to be the case.

Talk was not much different from what one might expect to hear in the post office back home; Daniel knew the familiar tones, the voices quiet and measured in the converted parlor. The Bealses kept track of the talk while they sorted, a process they lingered over. The day was young, and the mail was a high point for most of these folk; there was no need to rush things.

A good deal had been happening in town. Mr. Garnish had discovered a perfectly good turnip in the garden behind his house that he had previously overlooked. "Frost never got to it," he explained, several times.

Evidently something like this had happened before; someone said to Mr. Garnish, "You have a rare gift for finding harvest out of season." Those in the room looked to Daniel, as if for outside comment.

"I'm often amazed at how many people have rare gifts," he said.

"And do you have a rare gift, Mr. Plainway?" wondered an elderly woman.

"I could whistle before I was three," he answered, and this seemed to satisfy them; the conversation moved on to other matters.

Mrs. Feeney had lost a button off a coat sleeve, and the cat had knocked it beneath the stove. She was waiting for her granddaughter to come by and fish it out for her. She showed the wanting sleeve to her audience, and talk fell upon her granddaughter, who was well thought of.

"I like a child that smiles," said Mr. Garnish.

"She's a nice girl," admitted Mrs. Feeney, who allowed others to forward most of the praise.

Daniel was not surprised to discover, through further conversation, that Mrs. Feeney's granddaughter was twenty-two, with a child of her own. He had the pleasant sensation of not having gone anywhere at all, unless it were back to his own youth.

"What's doing in your neck of the woods?" asked Mr. Trace.

"Neck of the woods!" said Mrs. Feeney, as if she'd never heard such talk, and in front of a stranger! "Edward!"

"Well, sir," said Daniel easily, "we have a fellow down our way who is looking forward to a grand harvest of Christmas trees."

There was a "You don't say!" and at least two "Good heavens!" and other such exclamations.

"Where'll he sell them?" wondered Mr. Garnish.

"Oh, he'll head for the coast," said Daniel, "drop off a few along the way, and do the main part of his business down at Portland. Ten cents a foot, right out of his wagon."

The old folks were delighted. In their lifetime Christmas had been transformed from a day during which people celebrated by firing off a few guns to a majestic holiday of holly and fir boughs and visits from Santa Claus. Only twenty years before, many churches were still debating the propriety of celebrating what was considered a pagan holiday, but even the parson, sitting with them, smiled to hear of all those Christmas trees.

Mr. Garnish admired (what he considered) the pure Yankee cussedness of it. "Selling little trees!" he said. "They'll be selling rocks out of their yards next."

The light outside had increased or changed in some way, so that Daniel could look out the parlor window and see between two houses across the street. A narrowed vista of distant mountains rose above the river valley of the Androscoggin.

"Mrs. Feeney," said the postmaster. He had a single bit of mail in hand. The elderly woman brightened to see it, and she hurried over. Two or three others among them were blessed with a letter or a package, and soon Mrs. Beals was left in charge of things and Daniel was ushered out into the chill.

"Usually I head east first," said the postmaster, "but I'll do things in reverse today and baffle everybody."

"Gerald's uncle's, I take it, is west," said Daniel.

"It is." The road rose and fell with the land, and with it the view of the Presidential Range, off in New Hampshire. "It'll be the sleigh in another week, I warrant," said Mr. Beals. "Don't like to let go of the carriage," the postmaster was saying. "It means winter and sleighing till snow breaks."

Daniel knew that snow breaking meant the mail was delivered on foot till mud cleared or not at all.

"You're a lawyer," said Mr. Beals.

"I am," said Daniel.

"Thought so." This was enough for a minute or two. They pulled up before the first house outside the village, and Mr. Beals hopped out with his delivery. Daniel waved to the woman who came to the door, and he could hear the postmaster explaining who he was. "Gerald has had some time!" said the gray fellow when he climbed back in.

"So I understand," said Daniel again.

The old Pinkney place had been a tavern long before, one of the resting places and watering holes that led travelers into the White Mountains. Since then Gerald's uncle Pughe had lived there for twenty years by himself, and the place had not been very well tended. It looked abandoned, slouching above the road, its front porch gazing to the west and the blue and white heights. There were two wagons parked in front of the old house, and Daniel stopped for a moment to consider the oddities piled therein.

"Daniel!" came the familiar voice of Gerald Pinkney, and a stocky fellow stomped onto the porch. "What a time I've had!"

Daniel smiled. "Have you?" He looked to the postmaster, who had gotten from his carriage and followed him.

Mr. Beals shrugged. "Been a pleasure meeting you, Mr. Plainway," he said then. The postmaster shook Daniel's hand and politely left them to their business.

"If I could be sure there was a smidgen of truth to what they all say," said the man on the porch, "I'd take it down stick by stick!" Gerald Pinkney and Daniel Plainway had known each other since their days at Colby, and Daniel had always thought of Gerald as a slightly antagonized bee.

"You won't sell it in pieces," said Daniel. He stood and looked up at the old creation.

"That's just it," said Gerald. "I believe I do have it sold." He led them up the steps and into the house, which felt cold and empty. Daniel was reminded of the Linnett estate and not for the first time worried about those strange marks in the snow by the pond. There were three other fellows, young men, with Gerald, who were helping him clean out the place. They stood in the front room, where a stove did its best against the constant opening of the door.

"I've taken up floorboards," Gerald was saying. "I've looked between walls. We've wandered from room to room, *thumping* on the walls, and all we found was an old musket in the partition between the kitchen and the pantry."

"Unloaded, I trust," said Daniel. Then he asked wryly, "No digging in the cellar?"

Gerald was taking it all very seriously, however, and he shook his head. "Couldn't find any sign of recent digging, but we sunk a hole or two. There's an old siege well down there, and we sent one of the neighborhood kids down it with a lamp." Daniel was chuckling now. "Laugh you may!" said Gerald, who was not really angry. "But Uncle Pughe sold his investments in five ships before he chased off here, and as far as I can tell, he didn't spend much!"

"He might have lost it," suggested Daniel, who understood the vagaries of the market. "He might have given it away."

Gerald made a low sound, like a growl.

Daniel looked about the front room. Only the dining room would be larger in an old tavern, but the ceilings were low, and chairs stood in three of the room's corners, as in older days. There was a bed in the fourth corner, against an outer wall (which seemed chilly), and Daniel walked over to the old headboard and considered the yellowed clippings from newspapers and periodicals that covered the walls above the mattress.

"We opened the mattress, of course," said Gerald.

Daniel leaned forward, fascinated by the panoply of faces and figures before him. Both walls from corner to nearest window were covered with drawings and etchings of women. There were fashion advertisements and comic panels, portraits of famous ladies and domestic scenes; there were women at their needle and thread, cooking, playing the piano. There was nothing that was not demure and pleasing to the eye—handsome dresses and handsome figures within them, large eyes and Cupid's bow lips.

"That's quite a gallery," said Daniel pleasantly. He could imagine Gerald's uncle finding comfort in all these fine ladies when he woke each morning.

"Yes," said Gerald, his mind briefly taken from his hunt. "My wife was a little scandalized. Not that there's anything in particular; it's just the sheer weight of it."

"It's a great lot of work," agreed Daniel. He chuckled again, but his eye had been taken by a particular portrait, which seemed itself to be the copy of a framed work of art. There was something in the young woman's eyes, expressed therein, that harkened to Daniel.

"What I need to know," Gerald was saying, "is there such a thing as a stipulation in a selling agreement that says if something valuable is found after the transfer of the building, it must be turned over to the previous owner?"

Daniel leaned closer to the wall. The clipping didn't seem as old, or as yellowed, as some of the others. There were two small lines of print beneath the face of the young woman.

"Of course," continued Gerald, "that presupposes a degree of honesty on the part of the buyer."

The portrait discovered beneath Fort Edgecomb, now in the custody of Mister Walton, read the legend beneath the picture. The woman was beautiful despite what Daniel suspected was an imperfect rendering. He considered the eyes and the almost sad smile.

"Daniel, are you listening to me?"

"I'm sorry, Gerald. I am not."

"You want to take that wall with you?"

Then Daniel knew. "Gerald," he said, his head buzzing, "I know this woman!"

Gerald and the young men crowded around to peer at the picture. "This one?"

"Yes. My word, it's Eleanor Linnett!"

"An old flame, Daniel?" asked Gerald.

"Not at all," said Daniel Plainway. "Simply a dear friend. She died four or five years ago."

"I am sorry."

"But you see," said Daniel as he reached out to touch the piece of newspaper, "this picture of her—well, the picture that this is copied from disappeared, along with her son."

"Did he take it with him?" wondered one of the young fellows. They were all ready to be wrapped in Daniel's sudden mystery.

"Not by himself," said Daniel, hardly hearing himself. "He was only a year old." He felt out of breath, his mouth was dry, almost with fright, as if he had seen a ghost.

Gerald saw that his friend had grown pale, and he forgot about business for the moment as he suggested that Daniel sit down.

"We've just wondered so about the boy and worried about him," explained the lawyer. "I knew the family well, and there was a man intended to be the boy's tutor. I'm not making much sense, I know—" He touched the picture again. "May I take this?"

"Of course," said Gerald, and Daniel carefully eased the picture from the wall. It had been glued there, but the glue was stiff and came away without damaging the clipping.

"What paper do you suppose this came from?" asked Daniel.

"Who knows?" said Gerald. "There were hundreds and hundreds— stacks of papers—all through the house!"

"I wonder if I could match the type," said Daniel.

"We threw them all out," admitted Gerald.

Daniel read the legend beneath the portrait again. *The portrait discovered beneath Fort Edgecomb, now in the custody of Mister Walton.* Who was this Mister Walton, and what business had he taking custody of Nell's picture? Daniel, who liked most people, felt a vague irritation with this Mister Walton. If only the accompanying article had been saved, but the wall boasted of nothing but pictures of handsome females. "Edgecomb," he said. "That's near the coast, I think."

Gerald hoped to bring Daniel's attention back to the difficulty regarding Uncle Pughe's missing fortune. "That's quite something, finding that here. What say we have a bite to eat? We've been keeping the kitchen going. Then maybe you can help me decide what to do."

Nothing but handsome females, Daniel was thinking as he looked from the piece of print in his hand to the place on the wall where he had lifted it. *Except for that green tinted picture of Silas Wright there.* Daniel stepped up to the bed once again and leaned forward to peer at the government engraving peering back from the surrounding femininity. Beside the late statesman were the bold words *Treasury of the United States—Fifty Dollars in Gold Coin!*

"Gerald," said Daniel, "have you looked behind these clippings?"

He had begun several letters, though he was not sure to whom he intended to send any of them: *To whom it may concern*, perhaps. The clock in the hall tolled eleven, but he did not think that he could sleep yet. He had been here most of the evening, arriving after dark from Gilead, and having explained to Martha what had happened, he bolted a quick supper and sequestered himself in his study.

On the desk before him was the newspaper portrait; on the floor beside him lay the *Atlas of the Maine Railway System.* Finding Edgecomb on a map had been the first order of business, and half a dozen times he had returned to the book to trace the lines of roads and railways, hills and coastline, attempting to descry from those charts the manner in which Eleanor Linnett's portrait might have found its way to that riverside town and into the hands of the previously unheard-of Mister Walton.

The portrait discovered beneath Fort Edgecomb, read the legend beneath the picture, but what could that mean?

He thought he heard something in the hall and looked over his shoulder. A brisk wind, coming down from the mountains, rattled at the west end of the house. The hall was dark, and Martha startled him by appearing in the doorway of his study.

"I thought you had gone to bed," he said.

"I did," she said, "but you were making so little noise down here I couldn't get to sleep."

There was a certain inversion to Martha Bailey's sense of humor that Daniel welcomed. It meant, he hoped, that she was not entirely unhappy living in her brother's house. She had married more than ten years ago but had lost her husband to a logging accident within a year of their wedding. She had been with Daniel ever since. There was a picture of Edward Bailey in her room, above the headboard of her bed, like a patron saint.

Daniel himself had always thought marriage a pleasant idea and had even known someone to whom he had contemplated a proposal. He was reticent, however, in such matters, and life was permitted to interrupt his intentions. She had married the year after Martha and moved away.

Their own family—parents, two brothers, and a sister—had all gone before them, and it was not strange that Daniel had allowed himself to become an adopted uncle at the Linnett house.

"I think I will go to Edgecomb," said Daniel to the curtained window before his desk.

"You said yourself that a telegram would serve as well," said Martha.

"I did, didn't I."

"I wasn't sure at the time whom you were trying to convince."

Daniel picked up another item on his desk, the fifty-dollar bill that Gerald Pinkney had pressed on him. He had been embarrassed to accept such a gift, atop his fee, but Gerald was so delighted with Daniel for discovering (however accidentally) Uncle Pughe's stash, papering the parlor walls beneath the mass of feminine portraits and newspaper clippings, that he would not have taken no for an answer. Gerald was not a greedy man and had made similar gifts to the young fellows who had helped him in his search. "If you thought I was crazy all this time," Gerald had said, "you never let on."

"Maybe I'll use this to travel with," said Daniel to his sister. The bill still had traces of wallpaper paste on one side and felt stiff and unreal when he waved it. The truth was that he had already earmarked the bill for Christmas.

"You should keep it," said Martha, "and take yourself fishing with it next spring." She made her way across the floor and stood by his desk, looking down at the picture of Eleanor Linnett. The engraving failed to do justice to either the woman or the original portrait, but it harkened enough after both to revive memories, which were not all sad. "She *was* lovely, wasn't she," said Martha.

"Yes," replied the brother. "And never knew it—or, at least, never thought about it."

Daniel was both wise and mild, but Martha knew there was still much of the child about him, and she worried accordingly. She half suspected that her brother, in his own *un*suspecting way, had been in love with Nell Linnett, and she would not have blamed him. But if Daniel displayed reticence to the world in such matters, it was not a signal of any lack of self-awareness; he *had* loved Eleanor Linnett as a friend, or a cousin, or as another sister perhaps. He had looked forward to her happiness with some young fellow and to watching her children grow.

Though the happiness with some young fellow had been skipped over somehow, there was (or had been) a child. This person—a boy, who could be no more than four years old now—was the true reason for Daniel's troubled heart. He looked at the picture again and read the words beneath it. *The portrait discovered beneath Fort Edgecomb, now in the custody of Mister Walton.*

What could it mean? And if the portrait was in the custody of this Mister Walton, where was the child? Where was little Bertram Linnett?

"How will I know if he's taken care of?" she had asked. "You'll let me know," she had said. As always the memory seemed to obstruct Daniel's ability to breathe.

"Mr. Lyatt is coming tomorrow," said his sister.

Daniel let out a sigh as he remembered this long-standing appointment. "Yes, of course," he said. "Thank you. I'll leave Friday morning, then." He hardly thought he would sleep between now and then, but once he had come to this decision, a yawn rose up and overtook him. "I could be sending telegrams and letters back and forth for days with who knows who," he continued when it had passed, "and meanwhile, where is the boy?" *Nell's boy must be a sweet little fellow,* he was thinking.

Martha surmised the boy was beyond *any*body's reach by now but said nothing. Daniel would have to find the truth or discover more questions on his own, and it was not for her to sow his heart with darker fears. She kissed him on the top of his head and said good-night.

Daniel put away his pen. He folded the half-finished letters and tucked them into the wastebasket beneath his desk. He looked again at the maps, figuring his itinerary. Then he sat some more, listening to the wind and considering the past and the possibilities of the future. The clock was striking two when he came awake with a start in his chair. He turned out the light and went upstairs to bed.

BOOK ONE

December 3, 1896

1. Not to Be Confused

"**A**m I very much deceived in thinking that the object above us, just now, is a hat?" said Aldicott Durwood.

"If you *are* deceived," said Roderick Waverley, "then I am every bit as deceived for thinking you are correct in thinking that that object above us, just now, is a hat."

"And I equally deceived in my agreement," said Humphrey Brink.

One would not guess from their indifferent, almost weary tones that a great deal of excitement surrounded these three men. On the upper bank of the Eastern Promenade in Portland, Maine, an army of revelers (not all children) were plummeting the white slope on sleds and toboggans and vehicles unnamable of every shape and size; more figures made the long trudge back to the top, and the air was large with shouts and laughter. The brilliant remnants of a perfect December afternoon seemed willing to linger, even as shadows lengthened and the sun reddened over the western ramparts of the city.

To the south, at the mouth of Portland Harbor, the sails of an incoming schooner caught this radiance, and many at the top of the slope paused to watch this vessel round the northernmost point of Cape Elizabeth. It was identified, at first, as a three-masted vessel, but by the time a tug met her, it was clear to veteran seamen and armchair sailors alike that she was of the four-masted variety, limping into port without her full complement of sails and rigging. Soon a flag was raised at the observatory to indicate the ship's business connections, and several people spoke the name of the *Caleb Brown*, which was overdue.

But Durwood, Waverley, and Brink were oblivious of the drama evidenced by these sights, even as they were inattentive to the general gaiety about them. Hands clasped behind their backs, they peered up at the floating hat so that each seemed to be playing the identical role in a formal tableau. "It does seem to be staying up there a very long time," continued Durwood, who was darkly handsome, with a pencil-thin mustache. "For a hat," he added.

"It isn't some sort of kite, is it?" wondered Waverley, who was lighter, taller, clean-shaven, and every bit as handsome.

"I never saw a kite like it," asserted Brink, who wore a close-cropped beard and winged mustaches. He was the shortest of them and perhaps the most dashing.

A great shout went up as a toboggan race commenced. More people arrived at the crest of the hill, and voices rose in pleasure and surprised greetings. Durwood, Waverley, and Brink, however, were oblivious of everything but that single object.

"Is it a very nice hat?" wondered Durwood. "I might like to have it if it is a very nice hat."

"I think not," opined Waverley. "It looks to me like a very lowly hat."

"It's very high for a lowly hat," said Brink.

"I hope you thank me for making that so easy for you."

"You meant nothing of the sort, I am sure."

"Who do you suppose belongs to it?" wondered Durwood.

"I'm not in the habit of recognizing people by their hats," informed Waverley. "I have enough difficulty recognizing most people, if you must know, and sometimes I confuse the two of you."

"Confuse the two of us with what?" queried Brink.

"Is the hat descending?" asked Durwood.

"Blast the hat!" said Waverley.

"No, really," said Durwood, "the hat *is* coming down." And so it did, right into his hands.

"And here, I think," said Brink, "is the attendant—or, as it were, nonattendant—head approaching us now." Brink snatched the hat from Durwood and stuffed it under the back of Waverley's coat.

They took note of a hatless fellow who was hurrying along the ridge of the hill and excusing himself as he weaved through the crowd. Just ahead of the bareheaded man, there was a younger man (still in possession of his own headgear) who appeared to be searching the sky for the truant hat. "He has a friend, I think," said Durwood.

"Ah, yes," said Waverley. "Perhaps his friend will lend him *his* hat."

Durwood, Waverley, and Brink took such interest in these two that the younger man addressed them with a "Good afternoon."

"Hello," said Durwood. It was a greeting that had gained some vogue, since the advent of the telephone.

"There was a hat," said the young man, even as the hatless individual caught up with him.

"A hat?" said Durwood.

"Was there?" said Waverley.

"A hat and no head?" wondered Brink.

"The head is here," said the bareheaded fellow. Indeed, he was bareheaded in almost every sense of the word, for without a hat he was left with only the slightest fringe of brown hair; a portly man of middle age, he wore round spectacles that sat at the end of his nose. He smiled as he pointed to his bald pate, which shone rather handsomely in the light of the westering sun. "It is a head that must harbor some aversion to hats," he admitted, "since it does so little to hang on to them." He laughed as several young children nearly bowled him over in their hurry to reach the hilltop.

"You have lost hats before," said Durwood.

"The very same, in fact," said the jolly fellow. He extended his hand and introduced himself. "Tobias Walton." There was some need to speak above normal tones with such a raucous crowd about them.

"Durwood," said the man who had caught the hat. "Aldicott Durwood."

"Roderick Waverley," said the man who had the hat beneath his coat.

"Humphrey Brink," said the man who had put the hat where it presently resided.

"I am Mister Walton's gentleman's gentleman," said the young man.

"He is my good friend," said Mister Walton, indicating good-humored disagreement with his companion.

"Sundry Moss," said the young man.

Durwood, Waverley, and Brink did not formally beg the young man's pardon, but their frowns made it clear that further elucidation was necessary.

"My *name* is Sundry Moss," explained the young man.

"You don't say," said Durwood.

"He did," said Waverley.

"Do you speak to your parents?" wondered Brink.

Sundry smiled with one corner of his mouth.

"Do you know his parents?" asked Waverley of Brink. He was a little concerned that the shaking of hands, prompted by these introductions, would loosen the hat from beneath his coat.

"I confess to an unfamiliarity with mosses in general," said Brink, who was wondering how he might actually *cause* the hat to drop.

"Walton," Durwood was saying. "The Walton whose family once owned the shoe factory?"

"Yes, indeed," said that man, who was doing his best to show polite attention to the conversation, though he was still concerned with the whereabouts of his hat and more than a little distracted by the flurry of activity around them.

Sundry had been watching the progress of an odd expression as it crossed Brink's face, and finally he asked, "Is something the matter?"

"There *was* a Walton, I think," interrupted Waverley, "who recently drew the chairmanship of a new society." He regarded his companions. "A club, in fact. The Beaverwood Guild!"

"No, no!" declared Brink. "It was a bigger animal than that, the White-Tailed Deer Society, I am certain of it!"

"No, no, no!" contradicted Durwood. "It was a moose, I am sure, the Moosejaw Lodge!"

"I have the honor of being the chairman of the Moosepath League," said Mister Walton, with a bow. "We meet on Thursday nights at the Shipswood Restaurant. You must drop by sometime."

"We have our *own* club, actually," said Brink dryly.

"Do you?" asked the hatless man.

"Do we?" chorused Durwood and Waverley.

"Our club!" said Brink, as if wounded by the question.

"Ah, yes!" said Durwood.

"Our club!" said Waverley.

Mister Walton and Sundry were more than a little suspicious by now. "And the name of your club?" asked Mister Walton.

"The name?" said Durwood.

"The name!" declared Waverley.

"We are the Dash-It-All Boys!" announced Brink.

"Good heavens!" said Mister Walton with a laugh.

"How very right!" agreed Durwood.

"Couldn't have said it better myself," said Waverley.

"Not the temperance group?" said Sundry.

"Not at all," said Brink, "that's the Dash-*Away* Boys."

"And you are?" said Sundry.

"The Dash-It-*All* Boys," said Brink again. "Not to be confused."

"We are very glad to make your acquaintance," said Mister Walton.

"Are you here for the commotion?" wondered Waverley. He waved a hand toward the activity on the slope.

"Alas," said the portly fellow with surprising sincerity, "we did not bring our sleds," and he touched his bare head to indicate that he must continue his search.

"I did think there may have been a hat," said Durwood suddenly. "It went over the slope, I think."

"Did it?" asked Mister Walton.

Sundry looked skeptical, but he wandered to the brow of the hill.

"I think Durwood may be right," said Waverley. "There *was* something floating about."

"Thank you for your help," said Mister Walton, and he reached up to tip his hat before remembering that it wasn't on its customary perch.

Sundry was considering the busy slope when Mister Walton joined him. "It would be hard to say," he opined. The hill was alive with swift sleds, overburdened toboggans, and mid-hill collisions. Dark coats peppered the snowy bank.

Mister Walton beamed at the sight of it all. "The breeze *might* have taken it down there."

"I'll go down," said Sundry. "Someone may have seen it."

"Look, over there!" said Mister Walton, pointing.

"Your hat?"

"No, a very sparsely populated toboggan! Quick, Sundry, we may be able to catch the train!" The portly man was hurrying along the ridge, past several groups of people readying their vehicles, to the place where two youngsters eyed the course of their imminent descent. "Boys!" he shouted. "Young fellows!"

The two children with the toboggan did not at first connect Mister Walton's shouts with themselves, but as he drew closer, they looked with alarm at his approach and would have fled down the slope if not for the absolutely pleasing smile upon his face. One of the *young fellows* in fact was a little sister, and after a gracious apology for his error he revealed his purpose in hailing them, saying with a laugh, "I was always told that a toboggan will run faster with more weight in the front. What do you say?"

The children gaped at the portly fellow. Sundry drew up beside his employer. "You want to take the hill?" wondered the brother. He could not have been more than nine or ten, his sister perhaps seven.

"I do, indeed," said Mister Walton, who was a little out of breath. "I have been told that my hat may have blown down there, and I should like to retrieve it."

"We'll get it for you," offered the boy.

"It is splendid of you to offer," said Mister Walton sincerely. "But I haven't ridden a toboggan in years!" Clearly the portly fellow thought this state of affairs had gone on long enough.

"All aboard!" cried out the little girl.

With surprising agility Mister Walton leaped to the fore of the toboggan and sat down heavily. The vehicle tipped a little at the crest of the slope. "Climb on, Sundry!" declared the older fellow. He resituated his glasses upon his nose. Several people in the vicinity shouted with surprise to see him take his place on the toboggan.

"Hang on," said Sundry to the children, who hunkered behind Mister Walton. Sundry took hold of the rear of the toboggan and gave it a proper shove before jumping on. The snow on the hill was well packed by now, and the toboggan was not long in realizing a startling velocity.

Mister Walton had forgotten the dizzying effect of skimming the ground with one's head leading in a flying dive for the bottom of the slope, and he let out a great joyful whoop. They were passing sleds and toboggans that had taken off before them, and the crowded slope suddenly seemed a more difficult path to manage. Occasionally they struck a dip in the hill that sent showers of white over their bow and prompted a series of happy shouts from them all, so that many climbing the bank heard them above the general din and leaped aside to clear the way.

Durwood, Waverley, and Brink watched all this from their position at the top of the hill. "They are showing a good deal too much energy," said Durwood, "when one considers the hour at which I retired last night." The sight seemed to give them all a headache.

Waverley led the way to their carriage, slipping the hat from beneath his coat. "It's not such a bad hat."

"It's a very wayward hat," said Durwood.

A cab was trotting past when they reached the road, and Waverley gave the hat a spin in the air. The hat met the head of the horse and bounced between the animal's ears, then slid to one side, only to catch on the buckle of the animal's browband. It made the horse, which was otherwise a rather ordinary creature, appear vaguely rakish. The driver, who had been turning into traffic, straightened in his seat and was startled to find his animal sporting a very neat homburg. Durwood looked after the chapeaued equine as if something in the sight made him melancholy.

"We never did find out if Mr. Moss speaks to his parents," said Durwood.

"The Dash-It-All Boys," said Brink.

2. Meeting the *Caleb Brown*

The toboggan continued to gain speed, and Sundry wondered if they would break through the drift of snow at the bottom of the long slope and find themselves merging with the traffic on Fore Street. They came to a hissing halt, however, some yards short of the snow heap but several yards further than anyone else had reached.

The brother and sister were awed with the effect of Mister Walton's mass on the velocity of their vehicle, and though his hat was nowhere to be found once they reached the foot of the grade, the bespectacled fellow was so very exhilarated by their descent that he suggested a second run. Fast friendships were quickly formed among this unlikely quartet, and soon every child with a toboggan was looking for a portly pilot. Not a few unlikely participants were encouraged by Mister Walton's example, and despite the lateness of the hour, the revelers upon the slope were galvanized to action.

Finally, at the foot of the hill (was it after the third or fourth run?), the two men bade farewell to the children; by this time the hill's population and the level of noise seemed to have tripled.

The eastern twilight had softened the brilliant hill to a dusky blue, fiery clouds of pink and orange hung in the west, and this last blaze limned the western ramparts of the city. But Mister Walton and Sundry's attention was drawn to the waterfront and the arrival of the crippled schooner at the Atlantic and St. Lawrence Wharf. They were not a great distance from this business, and as the fortunes of all seafaring ventures are of interest to those who live in a seafaring town, they joined the crowd gathered there.

Lamp and lantern light was gaining precedence on the wharf, and as the darkened sky drew down and the dockside buildings loomed on either side, Mister Walton and Sundry had the impression of walking into a vast room, the many voices echoing from walls and hulls lending credence to the notion. The damp harbor air formed a frosty mist as the temperature declined with daylight, and the surrounding shapes glinted with condensation.

The tug was easing the *Caleb Brown* along the wharf as Mister Walton and Sundry walked among the disparate figures common to the waterfront: businessmen and idle onlookers, old salts and opportunists. The crowd thwarted their view of the ship from the gunnels to the waterline, but the remaining masts rode by, as well as a mare's nest of lines and broken spars. A sudden gust blew past the crowd, as if the schooner had brought with her the very storm that had taken her mizzenmast and foresail; Mister Walton, with his bare head, was particularly chilled by it.

A gangplank was raised from the wharf, and as people moved aside to facilitate this work, an older gentleman turned slightly and met Mister Walton's eye. "Toby!" he said in surprise.

"Mr. Seacost!" replied the jovial fellow after only a moment's hesitation.

The two men shook hands with great warmth of feeling. Lawrence Seacost was taller than Mister Walton, unbent by his seventy-some years and evidently undaunted by the winter night. He had a grand beard, though no mustaches, and creases beneath his eyes that expressed (and had no doubt been caused by) an immense sympathy with all things. Mister Walton introduced the man to Sundry, saying, "I was a member of Mr. Seacost's congregation some years ago."

"I retired *many* years ago, Toby," said the older man.

"I am very pleased to meet you, sir," said Sundry.

"Without the able tutelage of my former parson," continued Mister Walton, "I would not have known a cedar waxwing from a tufted titmouse. He is an amateur ornithologist of extraordinary learning."

"We must have our hobbyhorses," explained Mr. Seacost to Sundry. "Men of the cloth most especially, it seems. I am glad to meet you, Mr. Moss."

"You will be glad to know, Mr. Seacost," said Mister Walton, "that Sundry has made a career, these past few months, of keeping me from trouble."

"Have you?" said the older man, as if this might be an extraordinary thing.

"When humanly possible," admitted Sundry.

"I shouldn't *be* surprised to find you here, Toby," said Mr. Seacost. "The papers have you everywhere and all about!"

"Oh, dear," said Mister Walton, abashed at this unintentional notoriety.

"Buried treasure," continued Mr. Seacost. "Rescuing children. Is Mr. Moss a member of your club then?"

"He is indeed."

"The Moosepath League," said the minister, almost to himself.

"Yes, sir," said Sundry with evident humor as well as pride.

The old man laughed. "Come, come. What I have to offer will pale before your recent adventures, but you will find worthy company in my friends who are just debarking now."

Several men whose concerns regarding the *Caleb Brown* were notably monetary had boarded the schooner and were talking with the captain at the rail, but the captain hailed past them to a man and a woman at the head of the plank, saying, "It's been a pleasure having you aboard, ma'am, sir. I pray our misadventure with the wind hasn't inconvenienced you."

The man at the gangplank tipped his hat, and the woman said something to merit a laugh from the captain. The man turned, after a step or two down the plank, and called out a name, whereupon a dog of fairly large parts bounded over the rail and trotted alongside them to the wharf.

"Here is a man after his own hobbyhorse," Mr. Seacost was saying as he stepped up to the end of the plank. "And his wife along, thankfully, to keep his feet in the stirrups."

"Lawrence!" said the man, once he had scanned the crowd and set eyes upon the retired clergyman.

"Frederick!" replied Mr. Seacost. "Izzy!" and he embraced the woman, who was first off the plank. He bent down to stroke the dog's head. "Ah! It was you, Moxie, dear, that I wished to see."

"I knew it!" said the woman with mock hauteur.

Mister Walton introduced himself when the man from the ship nodded to him, and the man took Mister Walton's hand, saying, "Frederick Covington, sir." He was of medium height, and his movement and firm grip evidenced some athletic ability and physical strength. He was somewhere between Mister Walton and Sundry—that is, between forty-nine and twenty-seven years in age. He wore a short round hat, but his clothes, including a fine cape, were black, with something of the cavalier about him that was contradicted only by the clerical collar at his neck. His eyes were dark, and when he took his hat off to greet Mister Walton and Sundry, he revealed curly dark hair and disclosed a good-humored, clean-shaven face from beneath the shadow of its brim. "This is my wife, Isabelle."

Mrs. Covington thrust out her hand and proved to have a strong grip as well, much practiced no doubt in the receiving lines outside church every Sunday. She had a humorous way of lifting her chin when she regarded a person, and Mister Walton found himself beaming back at her. Isabelle Covington had wide-spaced blue eyes and a nose that turned up handsomely at the end. Her complexion was fair, and her hair that darkened blond that accompanies near middle age, but her eyebrows were dark and expressive. "I am pleased to meet you, Mister Walton," she said, "and trust you are here to see someone other than our dog."

"I had no idea that I was going to see a dog," he admitted.

"That is all you need to say, thank you, sir."

Sundry was introduced to the Covingtons then, but it was clear that he was interested in their dog.

"And this," said Frederick Covington, "is Moxie."

Moxie was a large collielike creature with a beautiful white face and expressive black-lined eyes. She had regular markings of tan and black, though she was predominantly white from her spotless breast to her shining pantaloons. She sat and offered a polite paw to her new acquaintances. Sundry, whose family was famous for its numerous dogs, realized how much he had missed these animals, and he made a great deal of her.

Frederick meanwhile embraced Mr. Seacost and declared how pleased he was to be there.

"Let us help you with your bags," said Sundry when these arrived at the end of the plank.

"A rough passage?" Mr. Seacost inquired.

"We had our troubles," said the younger clergyman. "A squall off Cape Ann, the day before yesterday, carried away the mizzenmast at the masthead. Then, as soon as they had the rigging cut away, the rest of the mast between the masthead and the deck went. Captain Matthews put her before the wind, and we thought we were done with the damage till the foresail was carried off later in the day."

"Frederick thought a poor cook was the worst of it," said the woman.

"I will warn you, Toby," said Mr. Seacost, "that Frederick's *prime* hobbyhorse rides on a dining table."

"Hobbyhorses are we talking?" said Mrs. Covington. She pretended to pinch Mr. Seacost's shoulder.

"Man does not live by sermons alone," said the husband with an attempt to look serious.

"Then we are in accordance as regards our needs, sir," said Mister Walton, "since Sundry and myself are meeting friends at the Shipswood Restaurant within the hour."

"We wouldn't want to interrupt your club's arrangements, Toby," said the older man.

"Nonsense!" said Mister Walton. "I can't overstate what a pleasure it would be to have you as our guests!"

Mr. Seacost turned to his friends and apprehended, in the husband, a hesitant expression. "You had other plans perhaps."

"Not a plan of my own, actually, but a task I promised to fulfill, and perhaps I can further put upon Mister Walton to help me with it."

"Why, certainly," said Mister Walton, with only a brief glance toward Sundry. "I would be more than happy, whatever it is you need."

"I hadn't thought to get this done the moment I stepped from the wharf," said Mr. Covington, "but it seems a shame to lose the opportunity. There is another passenger on the *Caleb Brown* just now, quite an elderly man by the name of Mr. Tempest. His original destination *was* Portland, but for reasons he prefers to keep mysterious, he has decided to stay aboard and return with the ship to Rhode Island. That is all that I know of his story, but he has charged me with finding someone who would write a short letter for him, which he will dictate in his cabin."

"Why, certainly," said Mister Walton again, though he was a little confused that Mr. Covington himself could not carry out this duty, and the thought was as clear as if he had spoken.

"Frederick offered to help the man in this capacity," explained the wife with some delight, "but it seems Mr. Tempest's tolerant nature could not forbear the disrepute of my husband's vocation."

"Oh, my!" said Mister Walton.

"So it is no use your volunteering, Lawrence," said Mr. Covington to Mr. Seacost. "He'll have absolutely no truck with the clergy."

"Good heavens!" said Mister Walton.

"Bad habits will catch up with you," said Sundry. He maintained a bland expression as he reached back to adjust his own collar. "My mother used to tell me that."

"She is a wise lady," said Isabelle.

"He doesn't like the captain either," said Frederick.

"Every man with his own hobby," said Sundry.

"He sounds a challenge," said Mister Walton with more humor than trepidation.

3. The Man Who Would Not Come Ashore

The first mate of the *Caleb Brown* paused before a low door at the bottom of the companionway and knocked softly.

"Yes!" came a craggy voice.

"Mr. Tempest?" said the first mate.

"I haven't changed my name."

The sailor glanced at Mister Walton to see if he appreciated the seriousness of his endeavor. "There is a Mister Walton here to see you."

"I don't know a Mister Walton."

"Mr. Covington asked me to come," said the portly fellow, his voice clear and untroubled.

After some moments, during which the first mate and Mister Walton exchanged shrugs, the voice called out again. "Are you waiting for an invitation?"

The mate shot daggers at the door, but Mister Walton lifted a hand to indicate that he was up to the test. The bespectacled man's expression was mild as he opened the cabin door and stepped inside. "I was, actually," he replied, and seeing the mate's hesitation, he said, "I'm fine," before he pulled the door shut.

The room was small and dark; a lantern swung from the low ceiling. In a berth against the outer bulkhead sat an old man who glowered fiercely. "So what did the preacher send? Not one of his cronies?"

"I met Mr. Covington only ten minutes ago," said Mister Walton.

"You are not a preacher then?"

"I have not answered that calling, no."

"I couldn't bear people thinking I had some sort of conversion," said the old man testily.

"I will be pleased to inform anyone who is interested that that is not the case," said Mister Walton with a sort of steely humor. As his eyes grew accustomed to the dark quarters, he became aware of some trunks beneath the bunk, a writing table hinged to the wall to his left, a small mirror and personal tackle hanging in a net on the right. The lantern swayed and shadows shifted with the ship at anchor; there was the sound of movement on the deck above and the occasional rub of the hull against the wharf.

Mr. Tempest too was revealed in the lamplight. He was a large-boned man with outsized hands and feet. His features had been roughened by time and cast by temperament into perpetual night. He was well dressed; a tailored coat hung at a bunkpost. "You needn't fear me," he said. "I may be dying, but I'm not diseased, if that's what you want to know. It's just that my hand won't remain still." He raised his right hand, and Mister Walton saw it agitate the air.

"I don't fear you at all, Mr. Tempest."

"You will take a letter that I dictate," said Mr. Tempest, his tone only slightly less combative.

"That is why I came," said Mister Walton with a small nod.

"And you will deliver it."

"Here in Portland?" Mister Walton was wise enough to know the details before he made a promise to deliver personally some letter to Shanghai.

"The City Hotel," said Tempest.

Again Mister Walton nodded, his curiosity up. He went to the table, which was designed to accommodate a person sitting at the bunk; there was a hard-cased trunk beneath the berth, however, and for a seat he upended this, then lowered the hinged tabletop from the wall. Tempest had a small case of writing things at the foot of his berth, and soon Mister Walton was poised with pen and ink above a sheaf of paper.

"To Ezra Burnbrake, City Hotel, Portland," said the old man. Mixed with the creaking of the ship and the comings and goings of the crew above, there came the sound of a pen nib scratching its way through Tempest's words.

You were surprised when I searched you out for the purposes of securing certain holdings, and in fact I have been less than candid with you as to why those holdings are of interest to me. Suffice it to say that in the intervening days my interest has waned, and I should ask your pardon for causing you an unnecessary trip; you do have my assurance that this transaction was the makings of a queer deal.

There are others unnamed who will take up my intended mission and press you, when you might have needed no pressing before this letter, but from one whom you have never knowingly met, save by post and telegram, to one who has no reason to think of the sender as anything but a weak-minded old man, I suggest that you resist all overtures on the subject. There are many, unknown to you and me, who would benefit from your firm stance, and likewise lose if these other people acquire what they want.

If you find my motives elusive, I shall simply say that I tire of those unnamed and that your niece once did me a kindness that she will not remember. I am not interested in hearing from you and shall consider all business between us to be terminated. For all intents, and to all your purposes, I am dead.

What trepidation Mister Walton had not felt when he entered Tempest's cabin descended upon him now, and he wrote the last sentence hesitantly, as if it would only come out of the pen by way of gross labor. The words *I am dead* in particular fought his intentions, and the final letters shivered as they reached the paper.

He raised his face, feeling beads of sweat on his brow; his hand had cramped.

Tempest sat unmoving in his berth. His hand shivered before him. Mister Walton considered that he was observing some atavistic force, self-perpetuating and self-sustaining, yet barren.

"I have acquired an imagination in my age," said Tempest quietly, "and that has been punishment enough for anything I have done."

After a silence Mister Walton leaned toward the man slightly and said, "Am I to write that?"

"What?" said the man, as if he had not heard himself. "Let me sign it."

He shifted his feet, which thumped upon the deck, and bent over the table. His shivering hand took the pen from Mister Walton, and with some effort he scrawled an unreadable signature. "He will know who it is."

Mister Walton had never written anything so extraordinary, and though they were not his words, they had physically come from his hand, and they troubled him. Mr. Tempest troubled him as he leaned back in his bunk with a dark sigh. "Is there anything else I can do for you, Mr. Tempest?" he asked. He felt as if he had one brief moment to offer Tantalus a drink of cool water.

"Sympathy for a crazy old man?" said Tempest. "I can imagine that too."

Mister Walton took off his spectacles and peered at Tempest with great dignity.

"I can imagine it," said Tempest, "but I can't feel it."

"It is a beginning."

"Is it? One without the other is simply confusion. There is an envelope in the writing case there. You don't need to address it if you give it to Burnbrake personally."

"I understand."

"I was going to offer you recompense for your trouble."

"I wouldn't take it."

"That occurred to me. I trust Covington wasn't too offended."

"More amused than offended perhaps."

"Then I did him an injustice."

Mister Walton replaced his spectacles, then took an envelope from the little box and folded the note into it. His curiosity was not entirely assuaged; the note, though plain in its unhappiness, was yet cryptic in its details. But if the unhappiness of the man before him might linger, the letter of his words were all but forgotten before he reached the door.

"Didn't you have a hat?" asked Tempest.

"It was the loss of my hat that brought me here, sir," said Mister Walton.

Tempest's eyebrows raised. Curiosity, as Mister Walton could have told him, is not a low sensation. "I can't imagine *that*, but you look cold without it."

"I am Tobias Walton, Mr. Tempest," said the portly fellow with a cautious bow. "I live on Spruce Street, here in Portland, and I am at your service."

"Good-bye, Mister Walton. I trust we shall not see each other again."

Mister Walton was almost surprised that it was night outside. Then he remembered that Sundry, and Mr. Seacost, and the Covingtons were awaiting him in a carriage just off the wharf. The cold air above decks was welcome, even on his bare head. The stars were out.

4. The Assembled League

Mr. Pliny, owner of the Shipswood Restaurant on Commercial Street, was always happy to see Mister Walton and the members of the Moosepath League, for a single jolly customer is like the bit of sand around which the oyster grows the pearl. Most who knew him thought Mister Walton was himself a pearl, and good things did seem to surround him.

The members of the Moosepath League were unaware of the interest they had caused in the public at large. The papers had outlined their exploits, both in the "Affair of the Underwood Treasure" and in the mysterious "Gunfight on the Sheepscott River," and the small size of their club (which was imagined by many to indicate a sort of exclusivity) only increased the notoriety of each of its constituents.

Neither were they aware of bringing fame to the Shipswood Restaurant by making it their meeting place every Thursday evening at seven. Mister Walton, who was perhaps more cognizant than the three charter members, would not have presumed to imagine, and perhaps only Sundry Moss wondered at the increasing crowds and the moments of silent eavesdropping from nearby tables.

The unannounced purposes of the Moosepath League served only to heighten the mystery, and truth to tell, this lack of an express mission continued to be an issue of some trouble for the membership. Theirs was not particularly a sporting fellowship, though years ago one of their number had gone fishing in the Presumpscot River and very fortunately was pulled out of the stream just above the falls below Pleasant Hill. They did not share political persuasions, nor did they attend the same churches. They were not tradesmen or merchants. What they did share was a great goodwill, an admiration of Mister Walton, and unbounded curiosity.

This, as it happens, was enough.

Mr. Pliny, then, was pleased to see Mister Walton arrive some minutes before seven with Sundry Moss, two new gentlemen, and a lady, all of them as cheerful as they could be. A pretty air was singing from a pair of violins in the back of the main room as their coats and hats (discounting Mister Walton's, of course) were taken and they were escorted to the club's usual table. "I'll be back with more chairs and your menus," said Mr. Pliny with a bow.

Frederick Covington pulled out a chair for his wife, then sat down with a satisfied noise. The restaurant's atmosphere was redolent of good food as well as sweet music, and he had made no pretense regarding the state of his stomach.

"Then you are Portland's answer to the great detective himself!" Isabelle was saying. Mr. Seacost had been describing to her what was public knowledge of Mister Walton's recent adventures.

"Good heavens, no!" said Mister Walton, blushing. "We were very much accidental in our involvements, believe me."

"How do you like to snowshoe?" asked Frederick offhandedly as they received menus from Mr. Pliny, but the question remained in the air unanswered as other conversation was forwarded.

"I trust the remaining members will be here," the owner was saying hopefully.

"It is their plan, I believe, yes," said Mister Walton.

"I am anxious to meet these gentlemen," said Isabelle.

"They will be agog to have such a lovely addition at our gathering tonight," said Mister Walton.

Mrs. Covington did not blush, but she raised her menu before her, looking as if she had thought better of Mister Walton.

He laughed because she had no idea how accurately he had spoken.

It was Matthew Ephram who arrived first, and he *was* agog. A single male guest would have warranted great enthusiasm on his part, but to meet three new people and one of them a female raised the night's gathering to the level of the historic.

If the Covingtons and Mr. Seacost had expected a man of heroic aspect, then they were not disappointed in Matthew Ephram, who was tall and well-proportioned. He had dark hair and fine black mustaches, and he wore an impeccably tailored suit of gray herringbone. He held the day's edition of Portland's *Eastern Argus* beneath his arm. He carried three or four watches on his person at all times, and he consulted one of these, even as he shook Isabelle Covington's hand, which she had offered. "Three minutes past the hour of seven," he announced, as if to mark the very instant.

"Izzy's very interested to meet you and your colleagues, Mr. Ephram," said Frederick.

"Is he?" said Ephram. "I am sorry, I wouldn't know."

The clergyman hesitated. He and Ephram considered each other for a moment: Frederick with a look of near laughter, Ephram with honest wonder. "I'm sorry, I don't know either," said Frederick.

"Oh, please, don't apologize," said Ephram.

Smiling, Mister Walton had cleared his throat as preamble to sorting this out when there came another voice. "Good heavens!" it said, and the men stood again and Mrs. Covington watched with amusement as Christopher Eagleton was introduced. He shook hands with everyone, including Ephram, at least once, and Ephram was inspired also to shake Mr. Covington's and Mr. Seacost's hands again.

Though the oldest of the three Moosepathians (he had already celebrated his fortieth birthday), Eagleton looked the youngest, owing perhaps to his full blond hair and lack of beard or mustache. As was usual he wore a tan suit, and he held his customary copy of the *Portland Advertiser* in one hand as he shook with the other. He himself was agog at the sight of a woman at their table and expressed to her how unprecedented and how welcome was this circumstance. "Continued clear tonight," said Eagleton. "Overcast tomorrow, with possible flurries. Moderate temperatures foreseen." He was something of an amateur meteorographer, and it was not unusual for him to inform others of expected weather patterns.

"Five minutes past seven," said Ephram.

There was a sudden crash nearby, and all tables halted to see Joseph Thump (of the Exeter Thumps) pick himself up from the floor. There did not appear anything in his immediate vicinity that might have tripped him, so he may simply have been upended by the sight of Mrs. Covington. He was not a tall man, but very broad of shoulder, and his expression was difficult to read, since it was hidden behind a remarkable profusion of brown beard and mustaches. Wearing his habitual black suit, he carried with him the latest issue of the *Portland Courier.* Clearly he too was agog.

Another round of handshakes began, joined by Eagleton and Ephram; Frederick Covington thought he must have shaken Ephram's hand five times and could foresee doing so several times again before the night was out. The thought made him laugh.

"High tide tomorrow morning at five-fourteen," said Thump at a juncture that did not strictly call for this information. Weather prognostication and the exact moment in time (eight minutes past seven) were also repeated by Eagleton and Ephram, to the mystification of Mister Walton's guests.

Eagleton had no more than sat down (again) when he announced, "I met a dog outside the restaurant."

"As did I!" exclaimed Ephram, somewhat astonished at this coincidence.

"A dog!" stated Thump. He nodded emphatically, and after some discussion (which was so involved that others at the table had not the heart to break in) they decided that they had all seen the *same* dog, and this appeared to raise the coincidence (in the Moosepathians' eyes) to the altitude of the near miraculous.

"I suggest the pine bark soup," Mister Walton was saying, "for anyone starting with a hearty appetite. There are three kinds of freshwater fish in it!"

"I wonder what her name is," said Thump about the dog. Among his friends, his questions were known for their gravity.

"Moxie," said Frederick Covington finally. He happened at this moment to be lifting his water glass for a drink.

Thump directed his attention to the clergyman and thought about this. He knew that Moxie was a beverage—a nerve tonic, actually—sold at soda fountains and advertised in the *Portland Courier* with the picture of a man pointing assertively and declaring, "Drink Moxie!" (Thump had actually tried the drink once and liked it very much two or three weeks later.) The word had also recently come to mean "indomitable pluck and spirit," and now Thump thought it was being used as a toast, which he liked very much. He raised his own water glass to Mr. Covington and said, in his deep voice, "And to you, sir!"

"Moxie!" said Eagleton, who raised his own glass.

"Moxie!" said Ephram, following suit.

Mister Walton thought he heard a bark from outside.

5. The Hat and the Hack

"That creature is better dressed than you are," said Pearly Sporrin, of Sporrin's Livery, on the western end of Commercial Street. He stood in the gateway, the stem of his pipe half an inch from his lower lip, and observed Charley Hatch's horse and rig in the lamplight.

"It's none of my doing," said Charley Hatch, leaning forward in his seat to eye the object in question. He had made no move to detach the hat from Violet's crown since discovering it that afternoon but continued to view the homburg with vague suspicion. "I turned to shake the leads, and there it was."

"What? Did she grow it then?"

"For all I know."

"She'll be a hat factory next." Pearly patted the animal's muzzle. A breath of cold wind blew from the harbor; Pearly could glimpse the glint of light upon water between the buildings across the street. "Better than a glue factory, isn't that so, girl?" he said to the horse.

"What do you have there, Charley?" asked an aged fellow, stepping from the stable.

As Charley didn't immediately answer, Pearly spoke up. "He's foolish about that nag of his, Doc. Bought her a hat. It'll be a dress and petticoats tomorrow."

"That's a pretty fine hat," said the shaky old fellow as he approached the horse and cab.

All that anyone knew about Doc Brine was that nobody knew if he was a doctor of anything, but he could cure a sick horse as surely as any man in the city. He had been seeing some poor creature inside; now, as usual, he was in need of a drink. He had a way of laying hands on a horse or a dog, or even a cat—why, he'd cure a cat, if you asked him!—and that animal would let him do anything he needed to bring it to health. It took the stuff out of him, though—that's what he'd told Charley once—and he always needed a drink afterward. Someone had told Charley that Alexander Brine had been a horse doctor during the war and that he'd had to put so many disabled creatures down that it had ruined him.

"Don't know where it came from," said Charley about the mysterious hat. It *was* a nice hat, but he was not overfond of it. A body couldn't trust such a thing. He'd learn to wear that hat and learn to like it, and someday it would just up and be missing as quickly as it had appeared.

"How's the bay?" asked Pearly.

"Terrible congested," said Doc. "I got her up and moving. Only thing for it. Up and moving." Clearly whatever he had done, it had cost him. He was shaking badly, and Pearly knew that the owner of the bay was not at hand just now to pay the old man.

The liveryman fished in a pocket and came up with a coin. "I'll talk to Mr. Cleaves in the morning," said Pearly. He laid the coin carefully in Doc's palm so that the man would not drop it.

"Wish I had another of these," said the old man to the horse, waving the coin before him. "I'd buy that hat from you." He reached up to scratch her nose. Old Doc Brine didn't own a hat, and the few gray hairs left to him could hardly warm his head on a night like this. He thought no more about it, however, and wandered off in the direction of the nearest tavern, where cheap beer (or any beer) was sold against the law of the state.

The streets were shiny with snowmelt, and the sidewalks were spotted with white. Lamps and lighted windows along the street made halos in the low-lying bank of sea smoke that crawled from the harbor. The foggy atmosphere made strange shadows, and looking after Doc Brine as he moved against the light from a store, Charley and Pearly could almost swear they saw his bony form through his clothes. He shook, and he looked cold, even if Charley Hatch did know it was the demon shakes.

"Doc!" said Charley, and he leaped down from the cab. He was not a young man himself, but he was spry, and he snatched that hat from Violet's brow and hurried after the old fellow. "Doc," he called again, "you could use this a good deal more than Violet. If she wears that thing, she can't see out the corner of her eye. It makes her nervous."

Doc Brine laughed. "What? No, Charley, I was just having fun, is all."

"Well, I'm not," said Charley, and he thrust the hat at the old man. There was a brief impasse; then Charley said, "You got Violet back on her feet a couple years back, Doc. I haven't forgotten."

"Yes, but you paid me, Charley."

Charley Hatch laughed under his breath. "Violet didn't. It's her hat, you see." And he and Doc both laughed when Violet let out a sudden nicker.

"Well," said Doc Brine, "if she insists, I won't insult a lady." With obvious pleasure he took the hat and placed it on his head. It was a little large for him, but all the better to cover his ears on a cold night.

"If your feet are cold, put your hat on," observed Charley. "That's what my old pop used to say."

The peculiar thing was, Doc looked as if he'd lost the shakes; he stood before Charley like any other man, almost festive with that homburg on, and he took a deep, steady breath. "Thanks, Charley. It sure is a nice hat," he said. "My toes are warming already." But the truth was, his heart was a little warmed.

"Merry Christmas, Doc," said Charley. They both were old enough to remember when the old folk—the old Dutch folk—celebrated St. Nicholas Day on the sixth of December, only three days hence.

"Merry Christmas, Charley," said Doc Brine.

Feeling a little awkward, Charley scuffed back to his horse and rig and proceeded to lead them through the gate and into the stables.

Leaning against the gatepost, Pearly Sporrin let out a puff of smoke from his newly kindled pipe.

Doc Brine had not shuffled very far down Commercial Street before he met and greeted several people he knew, including the matronly figure of Dotty Brass, who ran a house on York Street that Doc had neither the money nor the inclination to patronize. He had cured her cat a year or two ago, and she gave him a sweet smile and happy regards as she hurried past. He tipped his new hat and breathed a sigh of relief when she was gone; he was a little afraid of her and her establishment.

He had just turned back to recommence his progress down Commercial Street when he caught sight of a dissolute-looking fellow who stood in the recessed doorway of an abandoned storefront. The old man took two or three furtive glances before he stopped again and said, "Is that you, Lincton?"

"Good evening, Doc," said the man in the doorway. He stepped down to the street, and Doc Brine could see he was in a bad way. Lincton was a young fellow, not yet twenty-five years old, who had until recently worked on the wharves, landing cargo. An injury had left him without work, and he had become a common sight lately walking the streets.

Lincton wasn't the young man's real name; his father, Jacob Washington, an imaginative and zealous veteran of the War Between the States, had christened the boy Lincoln N. The middle initial stood for nothing but itself and served only to unite his christian and surname in a sort of patriotic prayer whenever they were pronounced together. The boy was not very old, however, before some wag decided to shorten the whole *moniker*. The first syllable from one president and the last syllable from the other were combined, and the young man was dubbed Lincton, a nickname that adhered.

Doc Brine was already fingering the coin in his pocket when Lincton came out of the shadows. The hat on the old man's head was still working its warmth, and the look of hunger in the young man's eyes touched his conscience; here was a fellow in need of a sustaining meal. These days Doc could get by on crackers and canned herring, with the occasional bit of beef thrown in. Young folk, he told himself, required more.

"No work yet?" asked the old man. He suspected that Lincton had given up the search in a stupor of hunger and cold.

"I think the foot is getting better," said Lincton, though his limp was as pronounced as ever.

"You need a meal, young man," said Doc Brine, and before the other could reply, he had taken the single coin from his pocket and pressed it into Lincton's hand.

Lincton hardly registered the gift at first but stood in the wet street while Doc hurried off in awkward silence. Finally the young man blinked at the coin, which glinted dully in the gleam of a distant lamp. "Thank you, Doc!" he shouted. He could not see the old man, but he heard a response rise from the shadows.

Lincton was not a drinking man; but living along the wharves, a person learns quickly where a drink can be had, and contrary to his natural disposition, this is where he took himself. He had enough in the one coin for three pints of watery beer. In his rickety state, however, even this dilution instilled a sense of false courage. He began to contemplate his late father's government-issued navy Colt, lying cold and heavy beneath his threadbare coat.

6. The Covington Goal

"But the hat was not to be found," said Mister Walton when he and Sundry had finished telling how they happened to meet with Mr. Seacost and the Covingtons that evening.

"It was quite a hill," allowed Sundry.

The charter members could hardly get their imaginations past the point in the tale at which the toboggan had been commandeered.

"It's tremendous!" said Ephram. The meal before him and his attendant appetite were all but forgotten; even Mister Walton's lack of a hat vanished in Ephram's mind before the vision of the grand fellow standing at the bow of the runner and pointing onward, like Washington crossing the Delaware.

"I've never ridden a toboggan," said Eagleton. "And I would very much like to meet these fellows who came to your assistance," he added. "Durwood, Waverley, and Brink. The *Dash-It-All Boys!*" He liked the ring of the name.

Thump had ridden a toboggan—once. (Or had it been a sled?) At any rate, he had been a lad then and had slid down a short slope and run into a stone wall. His mother had called him in. Gazing over his empty plate, he felt nostalgia for this otherwise forgotten moment.

"I am sorry we did not meet you at the *top* of the hill," said Isabelle, who thought the adventure sounded gay.

"Good heavens!' said Mr. Seacost, who was trying to imagine himself on a toboggan.

"It is a fine season, there is no doubt," said Mister Walton. He looked out the restaurant window and admired the snowy scene as it was illumined by lighted lamppost and carriage lantern. "And in these days, particularly, when we anticipate Christmas and the Yuletide blaze, there is a delectable sense of mystery in the air."

"Mystery!" said Eagleton in a hushed tone. He had always sensed *something* about Christmas, beyond the obvious religious and secular festivities, but he had never realized that it was simply *mystery*.

"We tell ghost stories on Christmas Eve," said Sundry about his own family tradition.

"It is a British custom that you may be following, sir," suggested Frederick Covington. "Mr. Dickens himself put it to good use. The Christmastide has traditionally been rife with spirits."

"And the animals speak at midnight," said Isabelle, with childish delight in her eye.

"I wish now that I had gone to the barn to hear them," said Sundry.

"The genuine mystery of Christmas," expressed Frederick, "is that no one can partake of it all. Some of its prettiest pleasures are those that just graze our fingertips."

"But Mister Walton will try his best," said Isabelle, for she had gotten the cut of the portly fellow and thought he was a man who could keep Christmas well.

"Well, I have the toboggan behind me now," he admitted with a happy smile. "But there are many pleasures to be had when snow flies."

"I suppose we will be up to our waists in snow soon enough," said Isabelle, looking to her husband.

"My wife," explained Frederick, "is referring to our ultimate destination, which is Skowhegan."

"Are you expecting more snow than elsewhere in Skowhegan?" wondered Mister Walton.

"More snow in the woods than on the streets," said Isabelle. She was clearly having fun at her husband's expense, but Sundry, in particular, wondered if Mrs. Covington's energy and badinage was a means to cover something deeper—or even troubling.

"Is it a sporting expedition then?" asked Mister Walton.

"Sport of sort," she replied.

"I told you, Toby, that Frederick is pursuing his own hobbyhorse," said Mr. Seacost.

"Yes, you did."

"I am on a very important point of business," said Frederick with a glint of humor.

"My husband has been *making* it his business," said Isabelle, "to preempt Columbus's claims of discovery."

"Frederick's specialty of study," continued the older clergyman, "outside of his seminary concerns, is Old Norse."

"The *Vinland Saga!*" declared Mister Walton. The thought obviously pleased and excited him, and Ephram, Eagleton, and Thump were accordingly fascinated, though they were not sure yet about what.

"Yes, indeed," said Frederick with a smile. He could not hide his delight in knowing a fellow enthusiast.

"And you have found proof of Viking presence in the New World?" wondered Mister Walton.

"I have been called on several times to identify an artifact or to translate supposed runes."

"You are the expert then."

"I am the 'great disprover,' Mister Walton," said Frederick, with his distaste for this self-imposed title showing clear upon his face.

"Oh, dear."

"For myself, the *Vinland Saga* is proof enough—its descriptions of geography, of nature, of the native peoples."

"*Skraelings*, they called the people," said Mister Walton, refreshing his own memory.

Frederick nodded. "But it is important that I be harder on the evidence than anyone, if you understand."

"Of course. There are those waiting to ridicule any claim."

"You understand the problem then and the delicacy with which I must approach any possible evidence." Frederick sighed a little, for it was a subject of some dearness to him. "If there is any question—and so far there has always been, at the very least, a question—but any question at all, I must say no."

"It isn't easy for him, is it, dear?" said Isabelle, and there was a very real sympathy (*and again, a little trouble*, thought Sundry) beneath her soft smile.

"So you are going to Skowhegan," said Mister Walton, who himself sensed more to this story than was readily told.

"We will make a short stop at Augusta," said Frederick, "where the man who found the artifact has photographs of it. He discovered it in the woods near Skowhegan last summer but only recently got around to finding out who might tell him something about it. The artifact is too large to remove from the site, and he has no desire to return to the place where he found it while snow is on the ground. There is, as it turns out, some urgency to my mission, and I wish I had another contact in Skowhegan. Maps and directions are all very good, but it is better to have someone who knows the territory and whom you can trust."

"*I* know someone in Skowhegan!" said Mister Walton. "Someone who certainly knows the woods nearabouts, for he is a great hunter and fisherman."

Frederick Covington's expression brightened with this declaration. "Would he have any interest in such a harebrained business?" he wondered.

"I wager he would," said Mister Walton, amused by the clergyman's phraseology, "once it was properly explained. I could write a letter of introduction, or"—and here Mister Walton's own aspect glowed with sudden inspiration—"or we could go with you!"

"What a capital idea!" declared Mr. Seacost. "Frederick, you would have the benefit of two experienced adventurers, I promise you."

"I couldn't be such a nuisance . . ." began Frederick.

"Nonsense!" said Mister Walton. He was leaning back to make way for his bowl of pine bark soup, which had been ordered by everyone at the table upon the strength of his recommendation. The waiter placed the steaming bowl before him, but he was lost in the consideration of another expedition. Then his expression altered slightly, and he said, "But I *have* promised to deliver this letter tomorrow." He patted a coat pocket.

Ephram, Eagleton, and Thump had been as excited as Mr. Walton about the proposed trip, and each hoped that he might be included in the plans to accompany the Covingtons. (The notion of trekking about in the snowy woods had thrilling implications.) Now they realized, however, that they had a further duty to fulfill.

It was Ephram who spoke first. "Mister Walton, we shall be pleased to deliver the letter for you. The members of the club."

"Hear, hear," said Eagleton.

"Hmm?" said Thump. He was brushing back his beard in anticipation of his soup. Spoons were poised; the table napkins had been unfurled upon their respective laps.

"Thank you, Mr. Ephram," said Mister Walton. "But I hesitate to burden you with an errand that I took for myself."

"No burden at all, I assure you," said Ephram, who felt quite adamant about the issue now that the suggestion had been made. "What is our great pleasure could never be a burden."

"Bravo, Ephram," said Eagleton.

"Hmm?" said Thump.

It occurred to Mister Walton that the members of the club would have liked to accompany them on such a journey, but also that a smaller party would surely be less trouble for the Covingtons. "I thank you again then," he said. "The letter is to go to a Mr. Ezra Burnbrake, who is expected at the City Hotel." He lifted Mr. Tempest's letter from his coat pocket and solemnly passed it to Matthew Ephram, who very solemnly placed it in his own coat.

"It shall be delivered on the morrow," pronounced Ephram.

"Now," said Mister Walton, "I hope I haven't taken anything for granted, but we are at your service. And I will be there to explain to my friend, who would have probably jumped at the chance to accompany you in any case."

"Wonderful!" said Mr. Seacost.

"Isabelle?" said Frederick to his wife.

"Good company speeds the hour," she said, and again moved the entire table with a very pretty smile.

"Moxie!" said Thump, and Ephram and Eagleton raised their water glasses to join in his cheer.

"I should tell you," said Covington, hoping to avoid further misunderstanding and possible embarrassment. "Moxie is the name of my dog."

"How very wonderful!" said Eagleton, his glass raised. Ephram and Thump too thought it a fine name.

"Moxie!" shouted Thump again, and now they all raised their glasses and said, "Moxie!" amid much laughter.

"It's a wonderful toast," said Ephram, "though I've never heard it before tonight."

"I think it has been freshly coined," said Isabelle with a sympathetic smile.

The members of the club, who loved nothing better than to be at the cusp of new things, were delighted.

"Are you coming, Mr. Seacost?" asked Sundry.

"I think not, Mr. Moss, though I will be waiting, of course, to hear of your new adventures or read of them in the papers perhaps. Don't let them lead you into kidnappings and gunfights, Frederick."

"We will be very cautious," promised Sundry.

"I am nothing if not stimulated by the prospect of our chairman's expedition!" exclaimed Christopher Eagleton as they collected their hats and coats in the foyer of the Shipswood Restaurant.

"And that is not to mention the anticipation of delivering this letter!" said Ephram. He patted his coat pocket meaningfully.

"To say nothing!" agreed Thump. "To say nothing!"

"Hear, hear!" said Eagleton.

"Is Moxie coming?" asked Sundry of the Covingtons.

"Oh, yes," said Frederick.

Outside the restaurant the members of the club were amazed to discover that the dog they each had seen on the way in was in fact the Covingtons' dog. Coincidence was rampant!

Moxie shook hands with them all, delighting them, and once the Moosepathians bid the others good-night, they strode into the night with a cry of "Moxie!"

"Moxie!" came the nearly hilarious reply.

The dog let out a happy bark.

7. The Members Were Disarming

Lincoln N. Washington had been a steady, if not overly ambitious, worker during his days on the wharves. He had ingratiated himself with his fellow laborers rather than his employer, so when a crane rope broke and a crate of machine parts crushed his foot, he had been given an extra dollar by a sympathetic foreman and let go. A few days later some of his fellow workers had raised almost three and a half dollars among them and left it with Lincton's landlady, who kept it against the next month's rent. Two months later he was on the street.

Now, standing in an alley that emptied onto Commercial Street and the waterfront district of Portland, with the warp of three pints convoluting his judgment, young Lincton held his father's pistol shakily before him and considered the old man's self-proclaimed military glory.

The late Jacob Washington had been, if anything, less steady and certainly less ambitious than his son and had parlayed patriotic declarations and a minor wound into a life of homebound idleness. Lincton's mother, dead these ten years, had supported the family as a laundress, and Jacob had failed his children as an example, even as he railed against their inadequacies in the shadow of his ever-enlarged military accomplishments.

Lincton hardly understood what he was going to do till he heard footsteps and conversation growing out of the right-hand shadows of Commercial Street. He leaned around the corner of a brick building, just enough so that he could see three figures moving toward him, silhouetted against the streetlamp that stood across from the Shipswood Restaurant.

He pondered the heavy piece of iron in his hand, raising it a little to peer down the narrow blue gleam of the barrel at a window across the way. He felt oddly calm, for the moment, and though desperation lurked nearby, fogged slightly by drink, he had no real murderous intentions. It is significant that he did not cock the pistol.

He wanted to look out at the approaching men again, but forced himself to wait in darkness, trusting his ears to tell him when they were almost upon him. Then the realization of what he planned to do struck him from the top of his spine to the forward edge of his scalp; it jolted him like the touch of a cold piece of steel or a bucket of seawater.

The first of the three figures stepped into sight.

Among the Moosepathians, Ephram walked with the longest stride, and he occasionally outstripped his friends by a yard or two before holding back a step so that they might catch up with him. He was just halting for this reason when he reached the mouth of the alley and a shout came out of the darkness. What Lincoln N. Washington was saying, in the harshest tones he could muster, was "Give it over, now!"

What Ephram, who was in the midst of hitching back his stride, did was *double* hitch his stride. What Thump and Eagleton did was collide with their friend, and what they all did was slip upon the snowy sidewalk.

Ephram clutched for the only thing within reach, which was the young man who had stepped out in front of him. All that he managed to grasp, however, was a length of cold metal, which (quite by accident) he tore from the newcomer's hand. With nothing else to hold him up, Ephram fell to the sidewalk with a very loud exhalation.

The unseasoned bandit was in this process pulled from his own feet and forward, and Thump, who was reaching for Ephram's shoulders as a means to keep his own short stature upright, caught hold instead of Lincton's.

To Lincton's uncoordinated senses, one man had snatched his gun away from him, and the second was throwing him to the ground.

Eagleton managed somehow to step over the newly developing heap, but he placed his heel upon a bit of icicle that had fallen from the eaves above and slid two or three feet before landing on his most padded portion. He possessed a certain innate athleticism in his otherwise untrained limbs, however, and, by catching at the edge of a door stoop, was able to use the impetus of his slide to lever himself back into an upright posture. The effect, had anybody been watching, was not unlike that of a runner sliding into a stolen base, and no one could have been more surprised than Eagleton himself.

Young Lincton knew that he had flushed the wrong birds, and leaping to his feet, he turned about and ran into Eagleton, who had come into contact with another portion of the fallen icicle and who gripped Lincton's shoulders with a little more fervor than would a man grasp the rail who had been washed overboard. Lincton was caught, since he was utterly terrified by these men of action and could not at the moment move a muscle.

Ephram in the meanwhile was unconsciously imitating the progress of his Darwinian ancestors as he attempted to stand erect. With one hand he administered aid to Thump's similar postural campaign, and with the other he leveled the pistol toward Lincton's back, or rather, he leveled the pistol's grip to Lincton's back, since he was gripping the weapon by the barrel.

"Good heavens!" declared Ephram. He had never handled a gun before, but he knew enough to swap ends with the revolver by transferring it to his other hand. "Good heavens!" he said again. "Is this yours?" he asked of Lincoln N. Washington.

The young man closed his eyes and seemed ready to fall on his knees. "Oh, please!" he shouted. "I beg your forgiveness!"

"Good heavens!" said Ephram again. He found the grip of the revolver very awkward in his left hand and thought how best to get it by the grip in his right hand. The operation was not as complicated as he feared it might be, and a very pleasant smile lit his face.

"Oh, please!" said the young man, turning to face Ephram and Thump. "I never meant harm!"

"Never meant harm!" said Ephram. "Good heavens, lad! It was *I* who ran into *you!*"

"An unfortunate accident," rumbled Thump.

"Are you injured?" inquired Eagleton. There was enough combined illumination from streetlamps along the way that he was able to notice the young man favoring one foot.

"I beg your pardon?" said Lincton.

"I beg your pardon," said Ephram, who realized that he had been pointing the gun at the young man. The mandate against pointing anything at people had been ingrained in him since his earliest memories, and he quickly transferred the pistol, barrel first, to his left hand again. Thump, who had seen Ephram relocate the pistol—barrel in right hand to grip in left to grip in right to barrel in left—thought his friend awfully clever. "I do beg your pardon!" said Ephram again with great emphasis.

"I beg your pardon?" said Lincton again, who wasn't sure why his own pardon had been begged. He was confused, and not a little frightened by this mysterious solicitude.

"Not at all," insisted Ephram, not elucidating matters for the erstwhile bandit.

The next few moments were a blur to Lincton. Eagleton helped dust him off, while Ephram pressed the pistol back in his hand and Thump handed him several bills of generous proportions. Then Ephram saw some dirt on the fellow's sleeve and brushed that off, while Eagleton, who had been a little shocked at the condition of the fellow's coat, pressed several bills of generous proportions into Lincton's hand that was not occupied by the pistol. Then they all begged the young man's pardon again several times over, and while Ephram put into the young man's already well-moneyed palm several bills of generous proportions, Thump passed Lincton his card and assured him that they were looking for help at his family's shipping firm if he was in need of employment.

"Are you sure you are not injured?" asked Eagleton again.

"Terribly clumsy of me," said Ephram.

"Good evening," said Thump.

And they each raised their hats to him and continued on their way,

Ephram showing particular care whenever he approached the mouth of an alley or the corner of a building.

Lincoln N. Washington sat down on the nearby stoop. He had counted more than twenty-nine dollars when the events of the past few minutes caught up with him. He was shaking again. He looked up the street, after the three gentlemen, but they had disappeared beyond the next street-lamp. He considered Thump's card through a blur of tears, realizing that he had just tried to rob three men, and in return they might have saved his life.

8. The Portrait and Apple Pandowdy

Mister Walton was thinking of Phileda McCannon when he and Sundry arrived home at Spruce Street that evening, which is not to say that there was anything very different in his thought processes just then. He had hoped for the opportunity to see Miss McCannon again since escorting her to the Hallowell Harvest Ball nearly two months ago, but Phileda was in Orland now, tending an ailing aunt, and letters from her had been short and direct.

Phileda was a direct sort of person, to be sure, but Mister Walton had hoped to glean from these communications some sense of attachment be-yond friendship. He had been encouraged by their time (and the pleasant-ness of that time) spent together, and twice his (admittedly tentative) courtship had been cut short by happenstance and calls for help in other quarters. Their association was left unresolved; he had not heard from her in more than a week, though he had written twice.

As expected, Mrs. Baffin (the elderly cook who, along with her elderly husband, continued to watch over Mister Walton and his home) had left something in the warming oven: two large helpings of apple pan-dowdy. Mister Walton and Sundry could smell it the moment they entered the front hall; shaking the snow from his boots, Sundry volunteered to venture forth to the kitchen so that they might fortify themselves before packing.

Mister Walton hung his coat upon the hatrack in the hall and, return-ing to the front door to be sure it had been pushed to, caught a glimpse of light reflected against the portrait in the parlor.

Anyone who had observed Mister Walton in the past several weeks might have predicted what came next. He stepped into the darkened par-lor and turned up the lights. The portrait standing against the opposite wall by the bookcase troubled him. The lovely young woman with the soft expression gazed back. It wasn't proper somehow to relegate the picture to a closet or turn it against the wall, yet the notion of actually hanging the painting somewhere seemed presumptuous.

He had received three or four letters from Mrs. O'Hearn, written at her farm in Veazie, where she and her son Wyckford and other members of their immediate family were taking care of the little boy. Bird had "grown an inch," she wrote, and though he remained a silent child for the most part, she believed that he was coming out of his shell a little bit at a time. The child had gone through much hardship, and among the O'Hearns he was truly safe for perhaps the first time in his young life; Mister Walton was disquieted by several elements in the affair, but none more than the haunting suspicion that Bird might be better off *not* knowing his origins or anything about this beautiful young woman.

But the possibility that Bird's mother—and Mister Walton was certain that the portrait represented just that person—was alive and suffering for the fate of her child was enough to counterweight his apprehensions.

It had been a month and a half, or nearly so, since Editor Corbell of the *Eastern Argus* advertised an engraving of the portrait and printed three articles about the events leading to the picture's discovery. (These pieces were purportedly written by one Peter Mall, though Mister Walton suspected this to be a pen name for Mollie Peer, who was directly, if accidentally, responsible for Bird's rescue in the first place.)

In uncharacteristically (for the newspapers of the day) quiet prose these items related how Wyckford O'Hearn had snatched Bird from Eustace Pembleton's underground lair, how the criminal elements of Portland's waterfront had believed the boy knew the whereabouts of a wealthy cache, and how Bird had been rescued from further hazard. There had been the tale of the tunnels beneath Fort Edgecomb, to which Bird led them, and in which that troubling picture had been found. A reward had been offered for information about the woman, but in a month and a half, though several hopeful leads had been presented, they were no closer to knowing where (or even who) she was.

Mister Walton was a little transfixed (and not for the first time) by the large brown eyes looking out at him, the loveliness of the oval face, or perhaps simply the mystery behind it all. Sundry found him there when Mister Walton failed to show in the kitchen. The younger man was standing in the doorway, hands in his trouser pockets, leaning with a shoulder against the jamb, when the portly fellow realized his presence with a start.

"I was just wondering whom I most feared for," said Mister Walton, "the mother or the child."

"We know the boy is safe," said Sundry, echoing his employer's thoughts, "but the mother is perhaps beyond our concern."

"It is true." Mister Walton turned down the light in the parlor, and even then he could discern the outline of that face in the portrait. "I wish I could let her know that her child is in good hands."

"Perhaps you will yet," said Sundry.

Mister Walton moved into the hall and the younger man lingered briefly in the doorway. Sundry had spent some meditative moments himself, considering that enigmatic face.

"From the size of these portions," said Sundry when in the kitchen he opened the door to the warming oven, "Mrs. Baffin expected the members of the club to come home with us."

"There'll be cream in the icebox," Mister Walton reckoned aloud. Mrs. Baffin's apple pandowdy was a source of great comfort to him.

"Another expedition!" said Sundry happily.

"Indeed!" said Mister Walton, who realized that he was in want of distraction. "It has been quite an evening, what with the Covingtons' mission and Mr. Tempest's letter."

"Not to speak of the Dash-It-All Boys," added Sundry.

"I had forgot," said Mister Walton. "And what did you think of those gentlemen?"

"I think *that* club was invented for our benefit," said Sundry.

"I think you are right."

"My father would say that Messrs. Durwood, Waverley, and Brink could be trusted about as far as you could throw the lot of them at once."

"A wise man, your father."

"I was a little surprised," said Sundry, "when Mr. Covington mentioned that his trip to Skowhegan was urgent somehow."

"I took note of that as well," said Mister Walton. "Considering an object that may have remained in one place for several centuries, it *is* surprising that any urgency should be attached to reaching it."

"It did make me curious," admitted Sundry, "though it didn't seem polite to inquire."

"Perhaps he only meant that it was urgent he get back to his church," thought Mister Walton.

"That was probably it. I liked Moxie," said Sundry, as if he were ready to forgive the Covingtons for any mystery for the sake of their dog.

"She is a beautiful animal," agreed Mister Walton.

"It is too bad we *didn't* meet the Covingtons at the top of the hill," said Sundry. "I once had a dog that liked to go sledding."

"Did you?" Mister Walton was pleased with the image this raised.

While they indulged in Mrs. Baffin's apple pandowdy, Sundry reminisced. "Yes," he said. "I called him Plummet, he liked sliding so much. He wasn't a big dog, but he was all for it! He would take the front of the sled and stick his nose out, and his ears flapped behind him like flags in a wind." Mister Walton was chuckling now as Sundry warmed to his tale. "When we got to the bottom of the hill, that dog would take the rope in his teeth and pull the sled up, he was so eager to go it again.

"One day, in the middle of January, I happened to notice my sled had been moved, and there were dog prints all around it, which made me suspicious. The dogs all sleep in the barn, and that night I went out to feed them, and sure enough, Plummet wasn't among them. I went out and found the sled missing from behind the woodshed, and I followed a set of dog tracks and the marks left by the runners to the big hill behind our house.

"What do you think!" said Sundry, "but Plummet was out there sliding the hill all by himself. There was a bright moon out, and I watched him for half an hour from a stand of trees. He'd take that sled down the hill, drag it back up, and go it again.

"Well, it was a cold night, and I knew he would put the sled back more or less where he found it, so I left him and went inside."

Mister Walton thoroughly enjoyed this narrative, the more so since he understood that Sundry was purposely drawing his mind away from more melancholy concerns. These days thoughts of Phileda McCannon were never far away, nor did many hours pass before he glimpsed once again (in his mind) the portrait of the unknown woman standing by itself in his parlor. "You've said there were *many* dogs at your parents' farm," observed the bespectacled fellow. "Did none of them take up the sport once they saw what fun Plummet was having?"

"That's a story in itself," said Sundry, as Mister Walton might have guessed. "One night some neighbors showed up at our house, kicked their feet at the stoop, and came in to gather at the stove. There were sleds and toboggans missing at several houses nearby, and all tracks led to our farm, as it turned out. I knew immediately what had happened and led everyone up to the hill, where every dog for three miles was on the slope and having a sledding party."

"Plummet had been talking, it seems," said Mister Walton with something like a straight face.

"Word had gotten around, I guess. Everyone kept their sleds locked up, after that, which I thought was too bad. This is fine apple pandowdy!"

"It is indeed."

"My aunt put out a fire with a kettle of the stuff once."

"Did she!"

"It's where that old saying comes from, I think," Sundry was saying.

"I don't believe I know that 'old saying,'" said Mister Walton, and this time he laughed heartily.

Sundry's expression remained almost bland, but the light in his eye gave him away. "Well," he replied, "my uncle was always saying it. 'Great smoldering apple pandowdy!'"

BOOK TWO

December 4, 1896

9. Several People Recently Met

The sun had not risen above the ocean when Sundry set his feet upon the braided rug beside his bed, but the herald of the day, reflected from clouds out over the harbor, caused enough light to lift the snowy darkness outside his window to a gray-blue. He drew the curtain and leaned upon the sill. A small bird stirred below his window; the house across the way was silent and sleepy. He heard stirrings in the room across the hall while he splashed his face in the cold water from the bowl on his washstand. He considered his face in the mirror and wished it would give him more reason to shave or none at all; next to a prodigious growth, like that of Mr. Thump's, his crop of pale stubble was hardly more than chick down.

Sundry's mind pattered around several objects while he dealt with his cheeks and chin. He often considered the possibility of growing a mustache and thereby decreasing the area to be tended. Some small vanity would not allow him to begin such a project, however, when there was the promise of female company, and he added his upper lip to his razor's itinerary.

Uppermost in his mind that morning was not their forthcoming mission, but the morning routine at his family's farm in Edgecomb. It was yet early, but his father would be up soon, stoking the fire. He would start the bacon. Sundry's youngest brother would no doubt be up next, and then his mother. He was feeling homesick perhaps and he realized that it was the early hour of his rising that made him so; it was too much like farm hours, too much like country living from dawn to dusk.

He had shaken off the weightiest of this sensation by the time he had his shirt on, tucking in the tails as he knocked on Mister Walton's door. It opened quickly, and the portly fellow, himself at his morning ablutions, stuck a lathered face without spectacles into the hall. "Good morning," he sang melodically.

"Good morning, mister," said Sundry. It was a droll greeting and also one with some history between them since it was the first Sundry had ever spoken to Mister Walton.

"I was wondering if a compass was not a good idea," Mister Walton said.

"I think I packed one."

"Of course."

Sundry chuckled wryly; he hoped he never disappointed Mister Walton's faith in his abilities and foresight. "Breakfast?" he asked.

"It would serve very nicely," admitted the portly fellow. He had his shirtsleeves rolled up and his collar opened as he applied his razor. "I'll be right down to help you."

"Take your time," said Sundry, and he clumped down the stairs and out into the kitchen, where the stove needed refiring. The house was cold, and it would take an hour or so to make things comfortable. Sundry liked to have the stoves at least ticking before the Baffins arrived, but on most mornings he left the cooking to the offices of the capable Mrs. Baffin.

In the kitchen Mister Walton opened the oven door and sat before it while he put on his boots. "You don't think that I made an error giving over that letter to Mr. Ephram, do you?" he asked.

"Not at all," said Sundry. "I believe he was eager to be of service."

"Yes," said Mister Walton. "But Mr. Tempest said something to me, just before I left him, that has had me wondering."

"All night no doubt."

"Some of it." Mister Walton rose up and got the coffeepot. "He said something to the effect of 'I may have returned the favor'—that is, the favor of delivering the letter—'by introducing you to the Burnbrakes'—that is, the people to whom the letter is to be delivered."

"Yes?"

"I couldn't help wonder, when I thought of it, if he were being ironic."

"Meaning that he wouldn't be doing you a favor at all."

"Exactly."

"And therefore, you wouldn't be doing our friends of the Moosepath League a favor by passing on the errand."

"In a nutshell." Mister Walton did admire his friend's ability to understand.

"It seems that a brief explanation followed by the dispatch of the letter would constitute the most of their involvement."

Mister Walton chuckled as he dolloped coffee grounds into the pot. "I must say, I was curious about these people myself."

"Was there anything in the letter that indicated trouble for the bearer?" wondered Sundry.

"It is strange," said Mister Walton, "but I don't remember the contents of the letter very well. I wrote down the words and tried not to pay much attention to them. They were not very happy, is what I remember most of all, though they didn't seem to represent bad news per se. It seems weeks ago instead of last night." Sundry was working the pump, and Mister Walton went to the sink with the coffeepot. They heard the back door and knew that the Baffins had arrived.

"They're early," said Sundry.

"I'm not surprised somehow. I think Mrs. Baffin has premonitions."

"We are going to Skowhegan, Mrs. Baffin," said Sundry when the elderly couple entered the kitchen.

"Skowhegan!" said Mrs. Baffin as if this sounded like an outlandish place.

Mister Walton chuckled softly. "In search of Viking treasure."

"Goodness' sakes, Toby!" said Mrs. Baffin. "No more treasure, please!" When Mrs. Baffin got excited, the burr of her Nova Scotian childhood returned to her voice. "If my hair wasn't white already," she said, but her admonishments were not without humor.

"Perhaps we will meet the Vikings themselves," teased Mister Walton. He moved away from the stove so that she could stand before it and warm herself. Her husband was chuckling as he hung his coat by the kitchen door.

"A Lost City of Gold," said Sundry.

"The Northwest Passage!"

"We are poised for action!"

"I'll make you some sandwiches," said Mrs. Baffin.

The Grand Trunk Station, situated at the eastern end of Commercial Street by the Atlantic and St. Lawrence Wharf, had a sleepy aspect when Mister Walton and Sundry Moss arrived by carriage. The light of day was itself sleepy, casting a rosy sheen upon the snowy roof of the station and blue shadows in the surrounding streets.

The first train was waiting; the engineer and the fireman were firing her up, and there were lazy hints of wakefulness about the engine: a quiet huff of steam, a puff of smoke and ash from her stack.

Inside the station there was little sign of vigilance. The ticket taker sat frowning in his booth, another man looked as if he were resting upon his broom rather than applying it, and to complete the picture, three figures were stretched out upon benches and sound asleep. Mister Walton knew that many a stationmaster wouldn't have allowed vagrants a warm place on a winter's night, and he said as much to the man in the booth.

"They each gave him a five-dollar piece to leave them alone," said the man.

"Good heavens," said Mister Walton with a laugh. "It's a steep price for a bench and no pillow." But when he looked at the prone figures again, he realized that the cut of their coats did not suggest the frugalities of the hobo life.

Sundry took a closer look at one of these fellows and made a noise of discovery. "I believe it's the Dash-It-All Boys," he said.

Indeed, this seemed to be the case as one of them lifted his hat from his face and peered, with one eye, at the morning. The clock on the other side of the station did not encourage him. Humphrey Brink considered Mister Walton and Sundry and asked, "It is yesterday afternoon again?" He gave a kick with one foot and dislodged the hat of the man on the next bench.

The light disturbed Aldicott Durwood's repose, and he made a face.

"It's Mister Walton and Mr. Moss," said Brink.

"Then it *is* yesterday afternoon," said Roderick Waverley from beneath his own hat, and for some moments there were no further signs of his being awake.

Durwood sat up, however, and blinked. Clearly the Dash-It-All Boys had never spoken truer words than when they disassociated themselves from the temperance group the Dash-Away Boys; they had been in such a pickled state, the previous evening, that they had been unable to get themselves home. "Mister Walton has a hat," said Durwood, his tongue sounding thick.

"Then it is either before yesterday afternoon, prior to his losing it," suggested Brink, "or he has acquired a new hat or found the old one, which would make this the following day."

This logic suited Durwood. "It is tomorrow then," he said, and ceased to consider the problem.

"Good morning," said Mister Walton amiably.

"Thank you," said Durwood.

"Did you find your hat?" wondered Brink. His eyes were closed again.

"We didn't," said Mister Walton. "But I had a spare on hand."

"Very wise," said Durwood.

"I wish I had a spare on hand," said Brink, though he may not have been referring to hats.

"I trust you gentlemen had a good night," said Mister Walton, somewhere between a mild scold and a chuckle.

"We didn't want to miss seeing you off," explained Durwood, who hadn't known until this moment that Mister Walton would be going anywhere.

"It was very good of you," said Mister Walton, who was up to this.

The Covingtons arrived, and while Frederick waited outside with Moxie, Isabelle came in for their tickets. She was only too pleased to see Mister Walton and Sundry but accepted introductions to Durwood, Waverley, and Brink from a cautious distance. The three men stood for this honor, and Sundry was ready to catch any of them, as they were a little unsteady on their feet.

Mrs. Covington explained to the ticket man that she needed a freight tag for her dog, and soon—with all the proper tickets and papers and farewells to the Dash-It-All Boys—Mister Walton and Sundry escorted her out to the platform where Frederick and Moxie greeted them cheerfully.

"I trust you slept well," said Mister Walton as he shook the man's hand and the dog's paw.

"Not a wink, sir," said the clergyman.

"We'd all do with a nap on the train," said Mister Walton.

Inside the station the ticket man peered over the counter of his booth at Durwood, Waverley, and Brink. The three men stood uncertainly in the middle of the station. Waverley looked back at his bench longingly.

Daniel's Story
(1874–1891)

It had been raining all the morning and most of the afternoon on the day that Daniel Plainway first saw the Linnett house; but the western clouds had broken up as the day waned, and the sun blushed from behind the estate. The trunks of the great oaks along the drive were as dark as their shadows; their rain-wet crowns glowed in the late light. Ian Linnett himself greeted Daniel at the front door and led him to the back porch, where everyone was watching for a rainbow.

There was a cry of discovery as the old man and Daniel stepped out into the golden afternoon.

It had begun for Daniel Plainway only a few days before, when Ian Linnett first came calling; the lawyer had recently arrived in Hiram, and he was in the process of unpacking his books when a knock rang at the front door. Daniel was green from school and had chosen not to settle in his native Cornish since two attorneys practiced there already; conversely, the only other lawyer in Hiram was eighty-four years old and asleep most of the time. Daniel set up practice in his new home on the outskirts of the village and owed much of his success, in the end, to Ian Linnett's obvious trust.

But that first day he was daunted by the big man with the white beard and the dark, overhanging brow. Linnett was nearing sixty at the time and had already developed a reputation as the old oak of local society. He had a terrific rumble of a voice, and his most pleasing compliment or blandest observation sounded like the growl of a bear. There were only the two chairs in the study then, and they sat in the nearly bare room while Daniel worried that the tea was too weak and the pound cake his mother had sent him a little dry.

The old man took up half the room, it seemed to Daniel, and was graciously pleased with everything. Linnett had investments in lumber concerns (which had made his fortune), but he was a man to look ahead and was interested in turning some of this over into railroad stock. He had called upon Daniel, however, to invite him to dinner as much as to initiate business, and the next afternoon, after a day of rain, a nervous young man appeared at the Linnetts' front door on the appointed hour.

The Linnett estate was a fine example of the Greek Revival, with a large two-storied kitchen ell concealed from the drive by the broad facade of the house, as well as an unconnected barn. Four expansive rooms stood at the corners of the main building and as many others, longer and narrower, occupied the upper story of the ell. There were still servants in those early days, who were quartered in attic rooms.

That was a household then, and a stranger might not tell the friends from the family. All were welcome, and even the kitchen door was open for the men of the road and the less fortunate. It was a merry place, though Ian Linnett enjoyed playing the old gripe. Simple pleasures were prized at the Linnetts': lemonade on the back porch, watching the sun set over Clemons Pond on a summer afternoon; someone banging at the piano in the front room while everyone sang old tunes, or carols as Christmas drew near; long winter evenings by the parlor fire, watching the shadows dance and telling old stories to make one another shiver or laugh; walking the nearby woods with Ian and his grown son Bertram and their dogs. It was not long before Daniel felt at home there, and soon he was fishing with Ian and Bertram on a Saturday morning and eating at their table of a Sunday afternoon.

There was Ian (his wife, Elspeth, had died some years previous), Bertram (another son had left home under a cloud years before) and Bertram's wife, Gwendolyne, and more often than not there were cousins and aunts and uncles. And there was Gwendolyne's Aunt Dora, who often came to care for her niece whenever she took sick, as was often. When it became clear that Gwendolyne was expecting a child, the joy was muted, and Gwendolyne spent much of her confinement out of sight. Aunt Dora became a regular resident of the estate and was herself seldom seen by the rest of the family.

When Eleanor was born and Gwendolyne rallied from her ordeal, a collective relief was palpable throughout the house and the community. She died a year later, almost to the day of her daughter's birth. Aunt Dora continued on as the baby's guardian and nanny.

Daniel first met Eleanor Linnett when she was three days old and he had been the family's lawyer for four years. He had never held a baby before but looked remarkably confident, cradling her in his arms. Even then people sensed a sweetness about Nell that surpassed what a person finds naturally sweet in a child. As mild as May, her father said, which was the month in which she was born. Daniel was asked to stand up as her godfather, which honor he happily accepted. He became Uncle Dan, though to Nell he was always Uncle Daniel: she and her grandfather always employed his full name, a conscious expression of love and regard that is difficult to explain to anyone who doesn't already understand.

He was Uncle Daniel, and never was a visitor more happily received, or more delighted to be so received by, the lovely little Nell Linnett. How many times had he stepped into that front hall and heard her squeal of delight as she launched herself down the stairs and into his arms.

She was five, she was eight, she was twelve, she was too old and should have been too dignified to leap into his arms, and she delighted him the more by not caring. When one day he did look a little uncertain despite himself, she simply threw her arms around him and kissed him on the cheek instead, and though his back might have thanked her, he was a little regretful.

She would play his favorite songs on the piano. But then, *he thought without jealousy,* she plays everyone's favorite songs. *It seemed her great pleasure to please, and this trait, he was convinced, was unalloyed with any ulterior thought or motive. She could soothe her grandfather when nothing else would do.*

At Christmastide the population of the house increased; gifts were secreted beneath beds and in closets, Nell played carols in the evenings, and their voices rose in the beautiful, stately melodies of the season. On Christmas Eve the house was ablaze with candles and laughter and Nell. Sometimes Daniel saw her sitting quietly, beaming at the people she loved, smiling with tears in her eyes. She only pouted when the great tree was taken out on New Year's Day, though it would make a wonderful bonfire.

They were only human, of course, Nell included, and they did have their foibles and their travails. Daniel knew them all and counseled many.

When, in her sixteenth year, her father (the gifted, amiable, and somewhat idle Bertram Linnett) was killed in a riding accident, Nell held Daniel's hand through the funeral service and said almost nothing for weeks. Ian invited Daniel (among others) to supper almost every night in hopes that old beloved company might draw the girl out. It surprised Daniel a little. Nell had loved her father, that was plain, but the good-natured Bertram had never played a very large part in his daughter's life. Her quiet, dull sorrow "drew the lights from the house," said Ian. Everyone waited with patience.

Slowly she came to life again, with the spring, and something also seemed to come to light: the young woman budding out of the girl. Nell had always been beautiful, as a baby, as a child, as an adolescent; now an early grace was visited upon her, and the recent tragedy of her father's death seemed only to strengthen the lovely generosity of her smile, even if it had muted it with a touch of life's dark possibility.

One day she came down the stairs with an unpracticed poise, quietly, her eyes glowing as Daniel stood in the front hall. Old Ian was calling from the parlor that they should come in to him. Nell reached the bottom step and took Daniel's hands in hers, the small embracing the large.

"I am so thankful to God," she said to him, "every day I am thankful to God for you." There were tears in her eyes.

It was then that Daniel saw how well she understood that someday he might be gone, that she had, all those long weeks, considered the probability that her grandfather and her aunt Dora (a stern but much loved presence) and other people she cared for would precede her from life and that there were not enough hours in the day, or days in her lifetime, to soak them into her heart.

10. A Tale from Other Seasons

The first train came through Hiram before sunrise proper, and when the tracks veered south, Daniel could see the flush of dawn from his window. The snowy countryside was blue in the morning's twilight, pines rising like lances against the slopes. Daniel had hoped to use the time to think, but he found the processes of his mind to be fractured, making it difficult to keep the images of the day before (and what he hoped might happen today) in proper sequence.

Before the sun had actually peaked over a distant hill, he fell asleep, lulled by the cadence of the rails. He came awake with a deep breath and the realization that daylight, if not the absolute orb of the sun, had arrived. They were coming into a village, and the whistle blew as they approached a crossing. He watched for the station to see where they were.

"South Windham," said a man across the aisle. He had not been there when Daniel fell asleep. That and the distance of this station from Hiram told Daniel that he had slept for an hour or so, and deeply.

"I didn't hear the call," said Daniel, with thanks implicit in his tone. He nodded.

"South Windham!" came the cry of the conductor, as if the man across the aisle had needed corroboration.

There would be Westbrook next and a change of trains at Cumberland Mills before the short ride to Portland, where he would switch trains a second time. Then the litany of place-names would sound like Mother England with Yarmouth and Freeport and Brunswick and Bath, till they came to Wiscasset, a name that rang confidently with the tongue of the New World. Edgecomb, where the portrait had been found, was only the next town on, and Daniel had decided to stop at Wiscasset, which was a county seat and where (presumably) there would be some informed public officeholders. The sheriff, he was sure, would know something.

They came through Portland's northern neighborhoods when the day was still young, and his third train took him from the plainer side of the city, where the smudge of many fires made gray the surface of previous snows.

He had brought out some papers to read but found himself distracted by what lay ahead and by the changing face of humanity in the seats around him. The man who had first spoken to him got off in Westbrook, coming home from Canada for the holidays. He was replaced, once Daniel was heading out of Portland, by a drummer who tried to sell him a bottle of tonic, the primary ingredient of which was supposedly extracted from a plant found in the Orient. In volume, of course, the primary ingredient was extracted from a still, and this was one way to circumvent Maine's abolition of liquor, which by 1896 had been on the books for nearly forty years.

Daniel occasionally indulged in small beer, which was still permissible, or a bit of elderberry wine to close a legal matter, but little else. He thanked the drummer but refused even a free sample.

They were joined in Freeport by a family whose house had burned to the ground and who were traveling to relatives in Bath. They had lost everything but the clothes on their backs, and Daniel sneaked a dollar bill into the youngest child's pocket and put a finger to his lips to urge secrecy in the matter. A fellow with a cat and a mandolin got on in Brunswick, and he might have been talked into playing the instrument if the animal had not kept his hands busy.

The man with the cat, along with several other people, boarded the train for its ferry ride across the Kennebec, but man and cat got off in Woolwich across the river. They were well away from the higher elevations now, and glimpses of bays and inlets and little rivers had followed them since leaving Portland. These coastal lands were without forests to speak of; rolling fields and granite heights crisscrossed with hundreds of miles of stone wall, so that from a particularly steep slope the snowy terrain looked like a quilt of irregular white patches.

On the other side of Woolwich the conductor called out the county seat of Wiscasset, famous in the papers these days for a sensational murder trial that *reportedly* involved skulduggery among certain Waldoboro town officials and the falling-out of best friends. The papers, even as far as Hiram, had been full of the business, and the town was bursting with reporters and curiosity seekers, so that private individuals were renting out rooms to supplement the crowded hotels.

A stretch of field and the eminence of Birch Point fell past them, and the Sheepscott River came to view, cold and gray beneath an atmosphere speckled with large flakes. The houses above them and to the left grew large and grand, the shacks and boathouses below more numerous. Tucker's Castle passed by, the image of a Scottish estate copied stone for stone, its lofty windows gazing darkly upriver. The whistle blew, a bell rang, the train yard enfolded them, and the Main Street of Wiscasset appeared as they slowed with a burst of steam into the station.

Daniel had never been here before, and he was struck by the handsome buildings along its steep streets, the brick Custom House standing by itself at a riverside corner, the courthouse and a white steepled church looking down from the top of the hill. The day was dark enough so that store windows along the Main Street glowed cheerily, and several establishments were decked out with signals of the coming Yuletide.

He said good morning to the fellow at the ticket booth and asked after Sheriff Piper, whose name he remembered from the accounts of the ongoing trial.

"He's having his locks shorn," said the ticket man offhandedly. He was counting out change but took a moment to indicate the general direction that Daniel must take to find the sheriff. It didn't surprise Daniel that the sheriff's private business was public knowledge in a small town like this. No one had exactly got on top of a roof and shouted that the man was having his hair cut, but the ear-to-ear telegraph would be nearly as efficient, complete (Daniel was sure) with opinions on whether the sheriff needed a haircut, or perhaps he'd waited too long or needed to look particularly presentable for a day in court.

Looking up the street through a frosty window, Daniel caught sight of the barber pole, and thanked the man in the ticket booth. With his small leather case carrying not much more than it had carried the day before, he stepped out, tightened his coat collar a little, and walked up the street.

There were two customers being groomed at the barbershop, and three more waiting; an infamous trial was surely good for business and gossip both. Talk did not stop, or even quiet much, when Daniel stepped in—a sign of polite behavior his mother would have said. "You don't stop talking when someone walks in a room," she would say. "They will think you were discussing them."

"Good morning," said one of the barbers when conversation gave him a place to put it in.

"Good morning," said Daniel. "I'm looking for Sheriff Piper."

The man in the right-hand chair was being finished up with a shave. He opened an eye and considered the newcomer noncommittally. "How are you this morning?" he said.

"Well enough, thank you," said Daniel. "My name is Daniel Plainway. I'm from Hiram."

The sheriff considered his geography. "I think I know where that is," he said pleasantly.

"Malcolm Henry worked up that way at a sawmill," said the barber as he considered the planes of Sheriff Piper's face. He waited to see if the sheriff had anything else to say before applying his razor.

"Quite by accident," continued Daniel, "I came upon a newspaper clipping yesterday." He could see that everyone, including the sheriff, took it for granted that he was referring to the trial. "It was just an engraving of a portrait and a caption referring to Fort Edgecomb and a Mister Walton."

The sheriff opened both eyes now. The barber, sensitive to such subtle indications, pulled his razor back. "Just the picture and the caption," said the sheriff.

Daniel felt his skin tightening at the back of his neck. "There was nothing else with the clipping."

"And that brought you down here."

"I know the woman in the picture."

This colloquy was circumscribed by complete silence. The other patrons and the two barbers never looked from their tasks or their newspapers or (in one case) the scene outside the window, but none of them was missing much.

The sheriff leaned his head back and closed his eyes. "Give me a moment. I'll be right with you."

"Take your time, Sheriff," said Daniel quietly, belying his growing excitement. "I wouldn't want to hurry a man's shave."

"Forgive me if I seemed to be putting you off in there," said Sheriff Piper when he stepped onto the sidewalk with the lawyer. He had been revealed, when he stepped out from under the barber's sheet, as an amiable, rugged-looking fellow with rangy limbs and a square jaw. With the door to the shop closed behind him, he pulled the fur collar of his coat closer about his neck, feeling the lack of hair there, and crammed a round hat over his ears.

"Not at all," said Daniel.

"There was just the picture then," said the sheriff again.

"And the caption." Daniel had the clipping in a coat pocket, and he pulled it out to show the sheriff.

"It's an unusual matter." Piper glanced at the engraving before handing it back. "And not all of it has been conducted under the auspices of official business. Do you mind a walk?"

"I've been on the train all morning, so a walk would be fine."

Without saying where they were going, the sheriff led the way up the street, touching his hat to the women as he met them on the sidewalk, greeting the men with a reverse nod. Daniel thought that Piper was well liked among those who knew him, and was pretty sure he liked him too. High sheriff was the term then in use, but Charles Piper seemed content to walk on the same level as everyone else. "Last summer," he began, "there was a fellow who came into town, named Tobias Walton."

"He's not from Wiscasset then?"

"He hails from Portland."

"I was just through there," said Daniel, more or less to himself.

"He got into an interesting difficulty with some rusticators and an escaped bear—well, that's a story itself—but I met Mister Walton, and as it happened, he and a local boy, Sundry Moss, went with myself, and Seth Patterson, the jailer, and a customs agent, known as Colonel Taverner, to watch for smugglers at Fort Edgecomb." Piper cast an eye in Daniel's direction. "I told you it was an unusual matter."

Daniel smiled at the sheriff's rueful expression.

"We almost caught some—smugglers, that is—but what would concern you would be the presence of a little boy among them."

Daniel stopped. "About four years old?"

"You know him?" The sheriff turned when he realized that the other man had come to a halt. He paused a step or two away.

"I may know who he is," said Daniel. That tight feeling at the back of his neck came back, and he shrugged as if a chill had run through him. "This was last summer?"

"Have you ever known a man named Eustace Pembleton?" asked the sheriff, and when Daniel shook his head, Piper described the man.

"He sounds very like the man who disappeared with the boy," said Daniel. "Edward Penfen."

After that Piper interrupted his story only two or three times. Someone sweeping a door stoop or another person walking past would pause for a moment's conversation. Daniel and the sheriff turned up Federal Street, where there were handsome houses on either side and an old cemetery on their right. Daniel had an unpleasant twinge of fear, for just a moment, that the sheriff was bringing him to a graveside.

They were climbing a long slope then, and the sheriff's tale had skipped ahead to October, when as it turned out, the little boy known as Bird was rescued by the efforts of several stalwart individuals, not the least being a young woman named Mollie Peer and a baseball player named Wyckford O'Hearn, who was badly wounded during a gunfight on the Sheepscott River.

It was in a tunnel beneath the long since decommissioned Fort Edgecomb that the portrait of a young woman was found among a robbers' cache, and it was Mister Walton who first saw the striking resemblance between the little boy and the woman in the picture.

"It was Mister Walton," continued Piper, "who paid to have an engraving made of the portrait, though it is only a *fair* likeness."

"And it is Mister Walton who has the portrait."

"It is in his custody, yes," said the sheriff.

"Bird," said Daniel.

"Yes." Piper did not press him but glanced now and again to see how close they might be to getting Daniel's half of the story.

"There is some irony intended there, I think," said Daniel finally, and his voice did not indicate any humor.

"Irony?"

"It must be him." Daniel was a little lost with his own thoughts. "He disappeared when he was only a year old. Linnett was his family name."

"Linnett," repeated the sheriff. "That's where Bird would come in, I suppose."

"*Bertram* Linnett." Daniel was thinking of Nell and her baby boy.

"Bird," he said in a breath. It was not much of a name for a little boy to live by. "But where is he now?"

"At Wyckford's mother's," replied the sheriff. They had stopped near the top of the hill. "Up north somewhere. They have a farm, I guess. Mister Walton wrote me to say it was a fine place for a kid. I have to tell you that the boy and Wyck—that is, Wyckford—are pretty tight."

"I will tread carefully, Sheriff," said Daniel.

"I told you it was quite a story. Like something out of a book."

"No more than his mother's story, I promise you," said Daniel, but there was in his manner the indication that he was not ready to say more— *unprepared* was the feeling that Piper got.

"Here we are," said the sheriff. "There's someone inside you may be able to tell us something about."

They were standing before the county jail, a very cold and lonely-looking edifice on this winter day. The living quarters for the jailer and his family might have looked homely enough but for the square gray walls of the prison itself, directly attached. The only color on those plain walls was a rusty stain beneath the iron-barred windows.

"What do you do, Mr. Plainway?" said Piper as he led the way to the front door of the jail.

"I'm a lawyer."

Charles Piper hesitated only briefly, and Daniel knew that the man was casting back on his story and their conversation, wondering if he had said too much.

"I am the executor of the Linnett estate," said Daniel, "but I am here first and foremost for the well-being of Nell Linnett's child."

"Come on in," said Piper.

11. Incident on a Train

The train had already made two or three stops outside Portland, and the population began to rise in the car that had started with only their own party and two blond fellows (one of whom wore a large mustache), who sat with their backs to the Covingtons. The sun, as it distanced itself from the rim of the ocean, laid a blinding light across the snowy fields and treeless hills, so that everyone tended to squint away from the windows.

Pairs of seats faced each other, like benches at a table. Mister Walton sat near the window, opposite Mrs. Covington, and the sounds rising from his chest hardly contradicted the notion that he was catching forty winks.

Sundry himself stifled a yawn. A mother and child sat directly across the aisle; the little girl was singing a song as she combed the hair of an old doll. Several newspapers were unfolded, and more than one traveler was following Mister Walton's praiseworthy example. The blond fellows behind the Covingtons were sharing a large sandwich, and despite a good breakfast, Sundry felt hungry watching them.

"Does Moxie mind travel?" asked the young man.

"She's very used to it," said Frederick. The dog was in the baggage car and had made friends with the bag handler before the Covingtons had time to leave.

"It's a shame she can't ride with us," said Sundry.

"I could use her to warm my feet," said Isabelle.

"I rode on a train with a raccoon once," said Sundry. He had to repress another yawn.

"A raccoon?" said Isabelle.

"Just a baby, but he got loose and a woman mistook him for a rat and the end of it was we were kicked off the train."

"Mister Walton and yourself?" said Frederick.

"Yes, *and* the fellow with the raccoon."

"I wish we could promise you such diversion," said the clergyman.

"I had a duck once," said a man across the aisle from Sundry. "A fellow stole it and took it to Woolwich."

Since the conversation had hitherto avoided the subject of ill-gotten ducks, Sundry took a moment to consider this unexpected information.

"Did he live in Woolwich?" asked Frederick.

"The duck? He lived with me in Richmond."

"I was thinking about the man."

"I don't know where he lived. But they caught him in Woolwich. It happened last October. He was a good friend."

"I wouldn't think he was *too* good a friend if he filched your duck," said Sundry. "I'm adamant on the subject of stolen fowl."

"I was talking about the duck."

Sundry did not blink.

"He played the mandolin," said the man, and though they each wanted to, nobody asked the question that inevitably came to mind.

"You say he *was* a good friend," said Mister Walton. Curiosity must have wakened him. "I hope nothing happened to him."

"The duck?"

"I think that's whom I meant," said the portly fellow.

It was then that they heard a honk come from below the man, and as if in answer a yellow bill poked out of the bag between the man's feet.

"Careful he doesn't get you thrown off the train," said Sundry.

"He goes everywhere with me now," said the man. "I think he got a taste for trains when that fellow took him to Woolwich."

"I'm glad he's safe," said Isabelle.

It was between Freeport and Brunswick that Sundry opened one eye slightly and realized, with a start, that he had been asleep. He had only to listen to know that Mister Walton had returned to the Land of Nod, and immediately opposite Sundry, Frederick sat back, eyes closed, wearing a very reasonable and understandable smile; Isabelle was curled in her seat and had her head on his shoulder. Sundry was a little envious in a general sort of way, and his thoughts were sped to a young woman he had met the previous October, whose name he had never discovered, and another young woman, Priscilla Morningside, whom he had met the July before that.

A sigh escaped him, then a movement—or rather the sudden cessation of movement—on the part of the blond man directly behind Frederick Covington caught Sundry's attention.

Sundry watched from beneath his eyelashes as the blond head wavered strangely behind that of the clergyman. The man wore spectacles, Sundry noticed, and he seemed to be correcting the angle of his head so that he could see something properly. There was something mechanical about the movement, more like the manner in which a person would adjust a tool than his own appendage.

A small point of light flashed briefly in Sundry's eye, and he couldn't fathom its source. Then the flash came again, and Sundry understood suddenly that the man's spectacles had a little mirror attached to the back of one lens, that the man was watching someone behind him, and that the mirror had caught the light from the window.

Sundry had all he could do to keep himself from leaping up with a shout. What could the man be watching for? Sundry eased the one eye shut and barely cracked the other. The second man too wore spectacles and was presumably using a similar device to supplement the first man's purposes. But if they were watching the Covingtons and their companions, why observe them while everyone was obviously asleep?

Sundry realized that the two men must have an objective besides simple scrutiny, and this was corroborated by a furtive movement at Frederick Covington's coat pocket. The first blond man in fact was retrieving for himself a small envelope, and the pickpocket was depositing the object into his own coat when Sundry leaned forward and took hold of his wrist.

"Pardon me!" said the pickpocket indignantly, and the man beside him nearly jumped from his seat. "What do you mean?" said the man with the mustache when Sundry did not offer to let him go.

The Covingtons of course were up immediately, and Mister Walton, who must have been deep in the arms of Morpheus, roused himself with a yawn, blinking behind his spectacles. "Sundry?" he said.

Snatching the envelope from the thief's hand and returning it to its owner, Sundry said, "I believe this is yours, Mr. Covington."

The cleric managed to frown with his brow, while he looked at the envelope with what Sundry perceived as a wry smile. "It is," said Frederick in the mellifluent tones of a choirmaster. "Did I drop it?"

"Into this fellow's hand," said Sundry. He still had a grip on the appendage in question.

"I demand that you let me go!" said the man with the mustache, and his seatmate made a similar, if less articulate, sound.

"I'm not sure that you're in the position to be leveling demands," said Sundry. He did let go of the man's hand, however, before violence was offered or warranted. "I saw him reach into your pocket for that envelope," he said to Frederick.

"He is very much welcome to it," said the cleric without altering his smile. "I believe it is a laundry bill and a note explaining a new policy regarding the use of starch."

"I thought I was reaching into my own coat," said the thief.

"And do you have an envelope in *your* pocket?" wondered Sundry.

"No," said the man. "That's why I was so surprised!"

The commotion was of great interest to the other people in the car, and several shouted encouragement to one side or the other. The conductor had been called for at the first sign of trouble, and he arrived in the car with an official sort of frown clearing the way. "What's all this now?" he demanded as he approached the scene.

"I have been accosted by this man!" exclaimed the blond man with the mustache, which addendum waggled to complete the picture of agitation.

"What he is particularly annoyed about," informed Sundry, "is that I prevented him from picking Mr. Covington's pocket."

The conductor glanced from Sundry to the blond man and finally to Frederick Covington. Mrs. Covington seemed to think the entire business unamusing; Mister Walton watched the proceedings with concern.

"That is a serious accusation," said the conductor.

The first blond man thought, just then, to hide whatever evidence might be found against him, and he would have put away his spectacles if Sundry hadn't stymied his intentions again.

"That's a very interesting pair of glasses you have there," said Sundry, and by the element of surprise he was able to lift them from the man's grasp.

"See here!" shouted the man.

Even the conductor thought this more than was necessary; he grabbed hold of Sundry's wrist in turn and took the spectacles from him. "That is quite enough of that, sir!" he said.

Sundry was not to be daunted, however; he asked the conductor to take a closer look at the glasses, and when the man could see nothing strange about them, the young man carefully pointed to the inside of the right lens.

"What's this?" said the conductor.

The Covingtons leaned forward, their own interest piqued. The blond men's looks of outrage began to melt before expressions of a more desperate sort.

"It's a mirror," explained Sundry, "so that he can pick the pocket of whoever's behind him."

"Is it?" said the official. It wasn't clear whether he believed Sundry or not. "Did he take something from you?" he asked Covington.

"A laundry bill," said the clergyman.

"I thought it was *my* pocket," said the blond man again.

"That's not much to go on if you want to press charges," said the conductor. "What do you want to do?"

It might have seemed unusual that a man of the cloth would apply to another person in such a situation, but anyone who knew Mister Walton, however briefly, would not have been surprised to see someone turn to him for advice. "I am wondering what you think, Mister Walton," said the clergyman.

"I have great faith in Sundry's perceptive abilities," said the portly fellow, a keen light showing from behind his spectacles, "but more significant is my faith in his fair-mindedness. It seems to me that the telegraph companies are very much up on criminal activities, and when we reach the next station, we might find intelligence to corroborate Sundry's characterization of these fellows or give them the opportunity to exonerate themselves before a judge."

Mister Walton continued with the sort of expression one might give a wayward child to whom one meant to be merciful without making light of his misconduct. "Then again," he said carefully, "nothing of great value was at risk—if I understand correctly that you hold little sentiment regarding your laundry bill, Mr. Covington—and that of course has been recovered. Perhaps it would be best instead if these gentlemen chose to part company with us altogether and make Brunswick, which we are approaching, their immediate destination."

"There," said the conductor, clearly impressed, "that is as fair as it gets."

"At any rate," said Frederick, as if this had just occurred to him, "I *am* in the *business* of forgiveness."

"Frederick," said Isabelle quietly, if with a certain insistence, a hand on her husband's arm. Covington only needed to shake his head to cut short the conversation.

"I certainly am not going to travel with people such as these!" said the first blond man, seconded by further sounds from his companion. "And I *certainly* will report to the railroad regarding your conduct toward an innocent passenger!"

"I *certainly* think you should," stated the conductor dryly. There was a whistle from the engine in front of them. "And don't think *I* won't report this incident to the stationmaster, in case you decide to board a later train. Why don't you grab your bags and follow me?"

"Keep a hand on your back pocket," suggested Sundry.

"Enough from you, young man," said the conductor with a sternness that was not without humor.

The blond men looked indignant as they gathered their things, and Sundry might have regretted the accusation if either one of them had once looked him in the eye. Bystanders commented upon the incident as the conductor escorted the men from the car. There was another whistle, and they could feel the train slowing for Brunswick station.

"My word!" said Mister Walton. "How very lucky you were awake, Sundry. How did you ever spot them?" He gripped his friend's shoulder warmly.

"Thank you, Mr. Moss," said Frederick Covington.

Isabelle, her expression troubled, watched the blond men leave the car.

Sundry himself was feeling some doubt about what he had seen; to his mind, falsely accusing a person was just about the worst thing a body could do. "I hope I didn't jump to any wrong conclusions about those fellows," he said to Frederick.

"Nonsense," said the minister. "That was his third or fourth try. I was wondering when he would get hold of the thing."

Daniel's Story
(1877–1891)

The first time Daniel Plainway saw Parley Willum was briefly, as Parley came out of the woods with a shotgun in hand and something out of season slung over his shoulder; the sight of the sheriff, who had accompanied the lawyer to the Willum abode, stopped the man in an attitude of furtive surprise. He knew that these officers of the court were here to deliver a summons because of a threat he had made against another citizen in town. Parley turned about with his illegal game, unhurried, though with no wasted motion, and disappeared into the undergrowth.

"He has to come home eventually," said the sheriff, who made no move to pursue the man, "and when he does, the summons will be waiting for him."

Elizabeth Willum appeared at the door then, and Daniel was surprised to see such a comely woman, where he had perhaps expected a pipe smoking carlin wife. She had hardly inquired why Daniel and the sheriff were there before young Asher Willum wedged himself out between his mother and the doorjamb. Asher was nine or ten, eyes gleaming like a wolf's, dark hair hanging over his ears. Daniel had never seen such a young boy look dangerous, but he was unsettled by those hard eyes and the expression of disdain—disdain, not because here were a sheriff and a lawyer but because here was anything that was not himself. The boy flashed an expression, not altogether dissimilar, at his mother.

In most towns there were "Willums," folk who lived in a house far from the road, sheltered from sight like an animal's den, their children rising up, generally unnumbered by the community and rarely touched by whatever brief appearances they made at the local school. They would have certain wood skills, these people, but would carelessly leave a telltale bottle where they had been poaching and where the sheriff wouldn't otherwise find so much as a footprint. In some places people such as these would simply have been squatters, but in Hiram the Willums had secured their land down by Trafton Pond by other means, commonly thought to have involved a murder earlier in the century.

They were always up to something, plotting, yet they were not deep, only watching with suspicion and wondering where they might acquire something of another man's labor. Their yards were monuments to acquisitiveness, littered with useless objects jealously guarded. Their children wore bruised faces, knocked about by life, one another, and their parents.

In this yard there was a dog, half choked at the end of its leash, a plate of water just beyond its reach. "I'd say that dog was in need of a drink," said the sheriff, the lack of expression on his face indicating just how angry he was.

Asher Willum smiled, baring his teeth. There was no mistaking, he was a handsome lad. The mother simply said, "The kids will tease it," though she showed no inclination to do anything about either the dog or the children.

Then Asher's younger brother Jeram wormed his way out past the dirty faces in the doorway and scrambled down to the dog. He was a frail-looking child, the very opposition to his brother's wiry hardness, his face small and uncertain. When he bent down to slide the dish within the dog's reach, the animal let out a vicious snarl and lunged at him. Teeth snapped within an inch of the little boy's face, and he fell backward, barely pulling his feet away in time.

Daniel and the sheriff both jumped for the boy, and each caught hold of a shoulder to yank him back.

"You see what you did, putting your nose where it doesn't belong?" scolded the mother, who registered no concern for her son.

"It's no wonder the animal is mean!" said the sheriff, his anger now out of hiding. "You either treat it right or, if it isn't to be trusted, put it down!"

Daniel had Jeram in front of him, holding him by the shoulders. The little fellow looked up at him and said, "I'm all right, mister." He didn't thank Daniel outright, but his gratitude, and even a certain amazement, were clear in his voice. Not knowing what to say, Daniel simply patted the boy on the back and nodded.

The sheriff delivered the summons to Mrs. Willum, saying, "If Parley gets lost and doesn't see that in the next day or so, let me know. We'll go out looking for him." His voice was raised loud enough for Parley himself to hear, wherever he was hiding in the brush nearby. The sheriff gestured to Daniel, and they walked back to the road and the carriage left there.

Daniel had been practicing law for three years when he first saw the Willums, and he often thought of that first sight of Asher and Jeram years later, having more or less forgotten it for more than a decade.

The two boys stood out, in the larger sense of Hiram's community, for contradictory and even complex reasons. Neither was stupid in the sense of having been born without native wit or capability; Asher in fact conveyed a keen sense of humor ("the surest sign of intelligence," someone had once told Daniel), and though that humor was often simmering just below the level of cruelty, people occasionally saw a flash of something unsullied by the general course of Asher's dark nature. The boy was always handsome, and as he grew to manhood, he made no mystery of either his interest in the fairer sex or his intention to use that handsome face in his pursuits. Daniel would always think of him as a wolf, not simply the fairy-tale despoiler of maidens but a true creature of the woods: flashing teeth, wild ways, beautiful, dangerous.

The other boy was of a nature so contrary, even to his own clan, that some suggested Elizabeth Willum had been "jumping the fence." Jeram's manner was the butt of some humor, though he carried himself with a strange sort of dignity that Daniel admired. Aunt Dora at the Linnett house said Jeram was fey, and there was something otherwordly about him; he was slim and delicate in appearance, and even his features were too fine to be handsome.

Jeram was unaware of anything different about himself or consciously avoided thinking on it; instead he spent as much time in school as fate and his family would allow. He was an attentive student and soaked up his erratic studies; but one day he stopped coming altogether, and though the boy puzzled him greatly, the schoolmaster took it upon himself to inquire after Jeram at the Willum place. Parley Willum nearly took a stick to the man, claiming the schooling had made the boy strange and swearing that never would a "Willum darken the schoolhouse door again!"

The boy was seldom seen after that, though his brother was often among the layabouts on the village common or playing at jackdaws and mumblety-peg on the porch of the general store. As a young man Asher had the dash of an army officer swathed in anarchic energy; few women in town had not at least taken note of those clear blue eyes, though most were quickly taken aback by their clarity of intent. Two or three young girls soared too close to this son, and at least one had spent some requisite months with relatives in another town.

Daniel Plainway was busy in those years, increasing his practice, joining the cogs of town politics, spending pleasant evenings and Sunday afternoons at the Linnett estate. He thought very little about the Willum boys (or the Willums in general when there wasn't a pertinent court case pending) till the day Clayton Bond told Daniel he'd seen Jeram Willum and Nell Linnett sitting together beneath an apple tree down by Ten Mile River.

12. The Quiescent Incarceration of Tom Bull

Sheriff Piper led Daniel Plainway into the jail end of the building on Federal Street, and they were immediately enveloped by the breath of cold stone, though a stove banged and ticked away on the other side of the guard room. Daniel was a little surprised to find a woman at the door to the cells, a lamp on the table beside her and a book in her lap. There was a shotgun leaning in the corner behind her.

"Good afternoon, Charles," said the woman. She took off her spectacles. "Sir," she said to Daniel.

"This is Mrs. Patterson, Mr. Plainway," said the sheriff.

"I am pleased to meet you, ma'am," said Daniel.

"Seth's brother has been sick, and I sent him down with a bowl of stew and a poultice," she explained.

"This is Mr. Plainway, Laura. We've come to get a glimpse of Tom."

"He's not hard to sight," said the woman. She retrieved a ring of keys from the wall opposite the door to the cells. If she was curious about Daniel and why he wanted a look at their prisoner, she said nothing, which was just as well since Daniel was surprised that they wanted a glimpse of *anyone*.

As a lawyer Daniel was not unfamiliar with jails and their occupants—both the keepers and the condemned—but for all his experience he could not suppress a shudder whenever he heard the guard door shut behind him. They had entered a narrow, poorly lit hall, which was flanked by several heavy doors and barred apertures. Daniel heard someone humming a familiar tune. A stove burned with a reddish glow at the other end, and the heat it gave off was enough to ward off the cold if a person was bundled up or at physical labor.

"We have two guests at the moment," said the sheriff, his tone neither cruel nor bitter. Daniel knew that Piper was only speaking with a sort of practical wryness that allowed him to keep a certain essential distance from the men he had incarcerated. "How are you, Jep?" he asked of a fellow who sat in a chair by the aperture nearest the stove.

The man stopped humming to say, "Pretty well, Sheriff, thank you." He was indeed dressed in coat and hat. He held his hands quietly in his lap, and he stared forward, as if he were watching something of great interest. "Mr. Patterson's brother has been poorly, I understand."

"This is Mr. Plainway," said Piper. "We've come to see Tom."

"Oh?" said the man behind bars, and they might have been back at the barbershop, talking pleasantly, there was so little inflection in what they said. Daniel knew, from reading the papers, that this was the suspect in the sensational case presently on trial, a man who had been accused of murdering his best friend. Jep recommenced his humming, and Daniel listened as he tried to place the tune.

The first thing that the sheriff did was to check the stove and stoke it up well with coal. Jep merely nodded his appreciation, hardly blinking as he stared forward. On the other side of the corridor Piper approached another set of bars and peered in. Daniel stepped up to look past the sheriff.

He had expected a second man to be close to the bars as well, but what he could make out, after his eyes adjusted to the dark, was an enormous dark form in the coldest corner of the room. There was straw on the floor and blankets on a bench, which stood perpendicular to the hall. A low table and a stout chair occupied the center of the room. Beyond this there was only the dim mass of some large man, watching without apparent interest from the furthest corner of his cell.

"Good afternoon, Tom," called the sheriff. He turned to Daniel, as he was not expecting a reply (nor did he receive one). "They call him Tom Bull," he said to Daniel. "It took ten or twelve good men to catch him, subdue him, and bring him in. He's here till next spring, but I don't know that letting him out will be doing him a favor."

Daniel moved closer to the bars and peered after the man, feeling conspicuously like the patron of a zoo, not the least because the man inside the cell seemed like some great placid creature of the wild.

"You don't recognize him?" asked the sheriff.

Daniel shook his head. "Should I?"

"He was one of the crew from whom the boy was rescued," explained Piper.

Nell's little boy, thought Daniel, and something cold gripped his stomach. In his mind he tried to place a four-year-old child in the company of such a creature as this; there was something so strange and animallike about the man as he sat blinking at them. Jep, across the corridor, hummed his tune. Tom Bull startled Daniel by lifting a huge arm and scratching himself behind the ear.

"He wasn't the worst of them, by far," the sheriff was saying. "Tweed was the man to contend with."

"And this Mister Walton knocked him down with a single shot?"

"He did at that. Tweed is in Portland now, where he has some hard questions to answer regarding several other cases. Once we caught him, it seems everyone wanted him."

"And Mr. Bull?"

"Him they were happy to let us keep."

Daniel looked back at Jep for a moment, still trying to place the tune the man hummed. Returning his gaze to the man in the shadowy and cold corner of his cell, he said, "He seems calm enough."

"Like a sleepy horse ever since we got him here. He let us take him to the courthouse and back without a word or a struggle."

"Perhaps he didn't like the company himself," said Daniel.

"Don't be thinking too highly of him. He once offered to bust Sundry Moss's head with a rock. And he broke a piece of lumber over Wyckford O'Hearn's back."

"It's a wonder the man wasn't killed!"

"O'Hearn was good for it. He swung about and put old Tom on his knees with a single blow. That was in the cellar hole, where Wyckford first rescued the boy."

Daniel strained his eyes at the dark corner again and made out the face of the giant. That great placid face took on a more sinister aspect now. "I must meet these people," said Daniel. "So much is owed them."

"I think they feel paid up," said the sheriff. "But something tells me you'll be meeting them soon enough."

In the wordless moment that followed, the tuneful humming from the other side of the aisle gained precedence to the ear. The accused murderer had not moved from his seat or altered his posture.

"What is that tune?" Daniel asked of Jep.

Jep paused in his humming and thought. "I can't recall. But I've always liked it."

"I do too," said Daniel. "It's a lullaby, I think."

"Is it? I can hum anything that I've heard once," said the prisoner, "but I have a great talent for not remembering the name of a tune."

"Yes," returned Daniel, as if they all were back at the barbershop, having their hair cut. "I was just saying the other day how amazed I am at the number of people who have a rare gift for something."

13. Startling Circumstances at the Abode of Mr. Thole

By the end of the nineteenth century a swath almost fifty miles wide along the coast of Maine was all but deforested in the name of settlement and cultivation, shipbuilding and commerce, and nowhere was this more evident than on the line of the Maine Central Railroad as it followed the Kennebec. Small groves occasionally stood at the back end of a farm, and magnificent maples and oaks and elms lent character to homes along the way, but particularly during the winter the thousand hills and those valleys tributary to the great river lay, beneath their weight of snow, as bald as a plain and as white as the moon.

The sky that morning was uncluttered. The sun dazzled the white fields, and even in the car people were squinting.

There were many stops along the way, and as the stations fell behind, the male portion of the Covington party began to rouse itself from lethargy; only Mrs. Covington had remained wakeful. Hunger was not a small factor in this metamorphosis, and long before the hour of noon Mister Walton and Sundry had shared out some fine edibles from the hamper supplied by Mrs. Baffin. The Covingtons were greatly impressed by the woman, though they had never met her, and never more so than when Sundry produced a mince pie from the basket.

Other folk nearby were let in on some of this feast, and Sundry remarked how sad "those blond fellows" might be if they had only known what they were missing.

"It is punishment enough, I think," declared Frederick, but his wife said nothing. Indeed, Sundry wondered if her expression hadn't darkened at the mere mention of the pickpockets. All in all, with the bright day and the view of the river, not to mention the company, Sundry had imagined that the unpleasantness caused by those two fellows was all but forgotten.

Mister Walton was tempted to make a brief sojourn at the Hallowell station when they got there, if only to stretch his legs as an excuse to glimpse the riverside portion of town. Somewhere past Gardiner, however, he decided to forgo this indulgence; the thought of seeing Hollowell without the attendant sight of Miss McCannon was too melancholy.

Soon after this stop the dome of the capitol building made fleeting appearances, and when they climbed a short grade the entire building, as well as the Blaine House, came into view. There was a stop below these sights, but then, the train entered the residential ward of the city. The remains of lunch were hardly put away when the whistle blew and the train slowed for the next stop.

Here was the busiest station they had come to since leaving Portland. There were passengers departing and boarding, wagons waiting for cargo and mail coaches along the sidings. Sundry was the first of their party off the train, and once he had handed Mrs. Covington down, he led the way to the station house in search of a porter. Frederick Covington went directly to the baggage car, from which Moxie bounded with a happy bark as soon as the door was rolled open.

It was such a lovely day that Mister Walton and Isabelle pressed through to the street side of the station house and waited on the steps in the brisk air. Sundry joined them in a minute with news of their things, and a man walked up to them and asked Mister Walton if he were Frederick Covington.

"I have not that distinction, sir," said Mister Walton, "but this is Mrs. Covington."

"How do you do," said she, and put out her hand.

The man took her hand briefly and gave a slight nod. He was of medium height and very businessy-looking with a camel hair coat that was opened to reveal a dark suit and a handsome watch fob hung in a practiced loop. He wore a dark round hat and wore brushy mustaches that moved when he spoke. "I am Herman Thole," he informed them.

"Mr. Thole!" said the woman, obviously surprised. "I didn't expect you to meet us at the station."

"Didn't you?" he said, sounding surprised.

"This is the gentleman with the photographs," she explained to Mister Walton and Sundry.

Mr. Thole seemed more surprised still when a porter arrived with a loaded handcart. "Are these *your* bags?" he asked.

Moxie appeared around the corner of the station, quickly followed by Frederick. "Good morning," said Frederick on his approach. "It isn't afternoon yet, is it?"

"This is my husband," said Isabelle.

"Frederick Covington," said the clergyman, and he took Thole's hand firmly. "How nice of you to meet us, Mr. Thole," he said when the man was introduced.

"Nice?" said Thole, and his eyebrows nearly met over his nose. "Your telegram was nothing if not adamant that I *did* meet you!"

"Telegram?"

"Your telegram from Portland station this morning."

"I didn't send a telegram," said Frederick.

"This morning?"

"Not this morning, not from Portland station. My correspondence with you has been by letter alone."

"But the telegram," said the man. He found a piece of paper in his coat pocket and handed it to Frederick.

Covington considered this with a frown, a single sound of surprise.

"I've been here two hours," Thole was saying, and he did not sound happy about it. "Couldn't imagine what you wanted."

Frederick handed the telegram to his wife. "Good heavens!" she said when she had read it.

"You *didn't* send it?" said Thole. "But what does *that* mean?"

"It means that I might have guessed it," said Covington. Mister Walton and Sundry were startled by the almost bitter sound in his voice.

"But it says urgent," continued Thole.

"It is, I'm afraid," said Frederick. "We must get to your house as soon as possible."

"But that is what I thought you were going to do, before the telegram."

"I *didn't* send the telegram," said Frederick. "We must move quickly! Mister Walton, Mr. Moss?"

"Shall we come along?" asked Mister Walton.

"By all means, but please be quick."

"And our bags?"

"Let us leave them here," he said to the porter. Already he was hurrying down the steps of the station. "Do you have a carriage, Mr. Thole?"

"With the chestnut mare."

Even the dog seemed to understand the need for haste, for she was the first in the carriage. The mare turned her head at the odd sensation that Moxie's boarding caused through the carriage harness.

In another moment the mare was trotting up the slope of State Street, none too fast to judge by Frederick Covington's expression. Moxie lay at their feet, making a very pleasant foot warmer. Mister Walton, perplexed but quiet about it, sat opposite the man and wife.

"Our friends would perhaps like to know what was happening," said Isabelle, with that insistent tone returning to her voice.

"I beg your pardon," said Frederick. He had the telegram in hand, and he unfolded it before giving it to Mister Walton.

GRAND TRUNK TELEGRAPH COMPANY
Portland, Maine

DEC 4 AM 7:43

AUGUSTA, MAINE

MR HERMAN THOLE

14 CHURCH ST

URGENT YOU MEET WITH US AT STATION. ARRIVING 10:10 OR 11:40.

COVINGTON

"It is very strange," said Mister Walton.

"Yes," said Covington slowly, though he seemed to contradict himself with his manner. His wife glanced from Mister Walton and Sundry to her husband, clearly thinking that more explanation was due their companions.

"It's not far now," said Thole, who was driving. They passed handsome houses on either side, and a gray church occupied the corner where they turned.

When they pulled into the yard of a large colonial house, Covington was the first from the carriage. Thole had every intention of bringing horse and carriage into his barn till he glanced at the clergyman, who was waiting on the walk; then Thole hopped down and threw a rein over a hitching post. "Please, come in," he said, though uncertainly.

"The room where you keep your photographs," said Frederick.

They entered a wide hallway beside a flight of stairs. From the wall of the landing above glared the portrait of a hawk-nosed man. In the first elaborately furnished room they came to there was a stand in one corner, and the drawer in it was opened, to Mr. Thole's surprise. He considered this for a moment before shutting the drawer.

Thole led them to the next room but stopped short in the doorway. "What in God's creation!" he declared, a statement that in the presence of a clergyman (not to mention the clergyman's wife) might have seemed a little indelicate.

"Is it very bad?" asked Frederick as he reached the door.

Thole stepped into the room, moving like a sleepwalker, his head turning slowly from side to side. Isabelle let out a small gasp when she reached the threshold, and Mister Walton and Sundry hurried their steps.

The room was in shambles. Papers and pictures (mostly tintypes and photographs) were spilled all about, cupboard drawers had been pulled from their places, and these were tossed helter-skelter in the corners; furniture was heaped against the walls.

"They worked here in the middle of the room," said Covington, standing in the one bare spot on the floor, "and they simply tossed everything as they went through it."

"All my pictures!" Mr. Thole was saying. "My things!"

Sundry glanced at Mrs. Covington; the color had left her face.

"I don't understand," said Mister Walton, almost to himself.

"Nor do I, sir!" said Thole, who was beside himself with anger and frustration.

"Your wife is passed away, I know," said Covington, "but do you have no servants?"

"Why, yes," said Thole, just considering this. "Good Lord," he swore, and disappeared in the direction of the hall, calling out for "Winifred and Tim." Frederick bent down and lifted some papers from the floor, not to look at them, but to corroborate physically what his eyes had told him.

"It's terrible!" said Isabelle.

"Who could have done such a thing?" wondered Mister Walton.

"I fear I know only too well, Mister Walton," said Frederick. "But I couldn't have guessed it. They have never, to my knowledge, perpetrated anything so brazen."

Again Isabelle passed that look from her husband to their companions, and this time Covington nodded. They could hear Thole calling for his servants in another part of the house.

"These appear to be deeper waters than I had expected, Mr. Covington," said Mister Walton with great seriousness.

"Everything I told you and Mr. Moss last night," said Frederick, "was the truth, Mister Walton. This"—here he held his hands out to indicate the signs of plunder before them—"this I am shocked about, but perhaps I shouldn't have been surprised." The man looked to his wife for help.

"Frederick told you," said Mrs. Covington, "of the care he must take in investigating these artifacts."

"Yes," said Mister Walton.

"But to add to his travails," she said, "there are those who would destroy any evidence before he reached it."

"Dear me!" said Mister Walton. "Are there people so anxious to prove you wrong that they would destroy evidence?"

"There are people who are only too hopeful that I am right, Mister Walton," said Frederick Covington with a strange smile. "Twice I have reached the site of a possible artifact: runes found in a wood, in the one case; more runes dug up by a farmer's plow, in the other. In *both* cases someone reached the artifact before I did and destroyed it! Scratched out the runes!"

"Scratched them out?" said Mister Walton.

"The runes had been ruined," said Frederick wryly.

"Dear me!" said the bespectacled man again. "But if the people responsible were hoping for proof of the Norse discovery of the continent," added Mister Walton, who was speaking for Sundry Moss as well, "I don't understand why they would destroy possible evidence."

"We were mystified as well, sir, I can assure you," said Frederick. "But that was before we became aware of a small society that exists in Boston known as the Broumnage Club. Your servants?" he asked Mr. Thole, who had returned to the room.

The man raised his hands. "They are nowhere to be found. But there are things scattered about and drawers pulled all over the house."

Covington made a sound deep in his throat. "Mr. Thole, I heartily apologize for this."

"It wasn't your doing," said the man half-questioningly.

"Even without the telegram, it is obvious that your house has been ransacked because of your communications with me regarding the runes you found."

"It is *that* then," said the man.

Covington nodded. "Whatever the cost of setting things to rights, Mr. Thole, you must allow me to make good on it."

"Well, Mr. Covington, I don't know."

"I insist. I trust your servants are well . . ." He prepared to leave.

"I don't know that I trust them at *all* anymore!" declared Thole.

"I am sorry to hurry you," said Covington to his companions, "and I'm sorry to leave *you* in this situation, Mr. Thole, but it is imperative that I make the next train to Skowhegan."

"Don't you want to see the pictures of the runes?" wondered the man, his mystification only deepening.

"They will be gone, I can almost assure you, sir."

"Gone? But I have them with me."

"What?"

"I took them with me when I came to the station. When I got the telegram, I couldn't imagine what was so urgent, but I thought you must be passing through Augusta rather than stopping and wanted the photographs. I brought them with me. See?" He produced from a coat pocket an envelope in which there were several paper photographs.

"Mr. Thole," cried Covington, "you may have saved the day!"

"Really?" said the man. "Is that what they were after?"

Then something else occurred to Covington, and he said, with new alarm, "You didn't have a map about, showing the whereabouts of the runes, or anything written in a journal?"

"I didn't, no. I am out in the woods all summer, photographing up by Oaks Pond and Lake George, and I don't really need a map to remind myself where I found something. But they may have gotten the negatives for all I know." He began to cast about.

"But the only description you've written is the one you sent me by post?"

"It is, sir."

"That is a blessing! These photographs themselves are a triumph! May I take them with me?"

"That is why I brought them to the station in the first place," said Thole. "What is this all about?"

"I promise an explanation, sir, but in season. I suggest, and even request, that you do not move anything till the police have looked it over."

"I'll photograph it!" said the man.

"And if you would hurry us back to the station."

"But the police will want to know what you know!" declared the man.

"All I possess is speculation, I promise, however much faith I have in it. I shall be back to make a statement, but first I must get to Skowhegan! Mister Walton, Mr. Moss, if you still want to come along?"

"You couldn't keep me away, Mr. Covington," said Mister Walton, and Sundry appeared at least as game.

"Frederick!" said Isabelle then, and it was clear that she was near to bursting.

"Dear," said the clergyman, "I think you should take the train back to Portland and stay with Lawrence till this is through."

"You are not leaving me behind to worry about you," insisted Isabelle. Mister Walton and Sundry thought they heard the tones of a well-worn conversation, and she confirmed their suspicions by saying, "We have discussed this," her expression indicating that there had been discussion enough.

"There is nothing to worry about," said Frederick unconvincingly.

"And this?" she declared, her hands swept out to take in the overturned room. "If there is nothing to worry about on *your* account, there is nothing to worry about on mine!"

"Mister Walton," said Frederick, rubbing his forehead as if to promote thought. "Mr. Moss. Perhaps Isabelle and I should go forward without you."

"Certainly not," said the portly fellow. "We will go to Skowhegan as planned, but perhaps you should tell us more about this situation."

"Yes," said Frederick with sudden decision and a renewed sense of haste. "But on the way. Mr. Thole, if you would take us back to the station?"

They had no more than stepped out the front door than they heard a woman scream, and two people jumped down from a cab that was pulling up before Mr. Thole's home. The woman, dressed in dark clothes and with a simple shawl thrown around her shoulders, was first down the walk. She was of middle years, and her face was worked into a paroxysm of tears and relief. "Mr. Thole!" she was shouting. "Mr. Thole! They said you'd been killed at the crossing! We've been all over the city and at every police station and undertaker's looking for you!"

"Winifred!" said Mr. Thole, who was understandably startled by this declaration and a little abashed to have his servant throw her arms around him.

An older man approached them from the street, shaking his head in agitation. "They told us you'd been killed," he said quietly. He wrung his hat before him like a dishrag.

"This Broumnage Club again?" asked Sundry of Frederick Covington.

The minister nodded. "It must be. The only way to get everyone out of the house. They sent Mr. Thole out to the station with the telegram, then communicated a fatal accident on the rails to his servants."

"The Broumnage Club," said Sundry again. "I don't much think I'm going to like them."

14. Emulating the Chairman

It was noon before Ephram, Eagleton, and Thump were gathered in one place and ready to fulfill the duty they had taken upon themselves for Mister Walton. The day was so fine and they were so exhilarated by the prospect of their errand that they determined to walk to the City Hotel.

They met several people and greeted them with great feeling, and crossing Congress Street in the direction of the Exchange, they fell in with the hurly-burly of business and enterprise. Christmas, or rather the anticipation of Christmas, was with them as well: The shops were filled with delicacies and temptations; greenery and bright packages in store windows were the order of the day. Feet clattered on the walks; a bell rang as the door to a confectioner's opened; traffic in the street rang loud in the crisp air.

The Moosepathians paused at many a store window to marvel at the trinkets and treasures thus displayed. Here was a season to rival, or even surpass, the height of summer! They each had pleasant childhood memories regarding Christmas, and they carried with them certain well-used emotions about this time of year. The pleasures of the season were ready to be felt in the Moosepathian breast, and Ephram, Eagleton, and Thump were glad to oblige such obliging sensations!

When they crossed Middle Street, the tall windows of the City Hotel reflected back the buildings and the people behind them, giving no hint of life or commerce within. A doorman let them in with a pleasant word and directed them through a busy foyer to the manager's desk. The manager himself stepped from his office and said good morning.

Hats in hand, heads indicating a trio of slight bows, Ephram, Eagleton, and Thump returned his greeting and then looked at one another; when making their plans the previous evening, they had not discussed anything further than this moment and consequently were wondering which of them should tender the purpose of their mission.

The manager looked upon their hesitation as an indication of the seriousness of their purpose, and the longer the three men looked at one another, the more serious he was sure that purpose must be. It did not help matters that the expressions upon the Moosepathians' faces grew more doubtful with every passing moment, till the manager was sure that some dread fate had found him out, and finally (while Ephram, Eagleton, and Thump gradually took on the look of complete desperation) the man could think of nothing that would merit such reluctant concentration (not to mention concentrated reluctance) but the imminent visitation of death and destruction.

The stricken look upon the manager's face meanwhile did in no way reassure the members of the club.

"Good morning," said Ephram again, and the manager shouted with alarm.

All heads (including those of Ephram, Eagleton, and Thump) in the lobby turned to see what was the matter. Thinking some missile might be flying through the air (he had been reading a gripping adventure entitled *Fennell's Final Volley* just that morning), Thump threw an arm over his head. Eagleton turned about on one heel—back straight, eyes wide—and exchanged startled sounds with a large woman who was standing behind him. Ephram, who had been taking Mr. Tempest's letter from his pocket, dropped the missive and, stooping to retrieve it, bumped his head against the side of the counter.

When all grew quiet once more and nothing but confused looks punctuated the air, Ephram tried again by clearing his throat slightly.

"Yes?" said the manager, his panic having subsided a little.

Ephram nearly dropped the letter again, but then he waved it in the air and said, "Is there anyone by the name of Burnbrake staying with you, sir?"

"Burnbrake?"

"Yes, sir."

"We have an errand regarding Mr. Ezra Burnbrake," elucidated Eagleton. He looked over his shoulder and nodded to the woman behind him. The woman drew her eyebrows down into a fierce scowl, and Eagleton's eyes widened accordingly.

The manager looked now not as if he were searching his mind for the answer to this question but as if he were searching his inclination to answer at all. Once he had calmed his nerves further, he made a decision. "Yes," he drawled, in not an answer, but only an acknowledgment that he had heard. He considered his register. "Are you a friend of Mr. Noble?"

"I do not, I think, know a Mr. Noble," said Ephram. "Do you, Eagleton?"

"The name is not familiar," said Eagleton, and he submitted the question to Thump, who was equally unfamiliar with a Mr. Noble. As one the three men handed the manager their cards.

"I see," said the manager. He peered down his nose at the cards; he had not liked being startled just now and was not entirely of a mind to be helpful to these fellows.

Throughout this recent dialogue the members of the club had maintained the mildest of expressions.

"If you will wait in the sitting room," said the manager, pointing past Ephram's left shoulder, "I will discover if Mr. Burnbrake is seeing anybody just now." He lifted their cards to indicate that he would give them to the party in question, came around the counter, and moved without hurry up the stairs.

They repaired to the sitting room, which was a large space, filled with the requisite chairs and divans. A fire snapped merrily in the oversized fireplace opposite the entrance; there was the rustle of newspapers from several silent readers and a low conversation taking place between a man and a woman in the corner. Standing at one of the tall windows, the three friends looked out upon the busy winter street and remarked how pleased everyone seemed. They turned whenever someone entered the room or paused at the doorway but were not rewarded by the sight of an obvious Mr. Burnbrake, nor did any men search them out.

"The manager did appear to be out of sorts," said Eagleton after a while. He had been greatly impressed by the man's shout of alarm and hoped to avoid further exclamations.

"I think he was concerned about the woman behind us," ventured Ephram.

"She did frown," agreed Eagleton.

They wondered if the manager had disappeared altogether, without forwarding their cards, when a woman stopped in the door and scanned the room. Ephram, Eagleton, and Thump did not of course make a practice of staring at people, but there was something arresting—one might say lovely—about the woman that slowed the movement of their eyes. There was a contradiction about her, for she carried herself with an energy that lent her the appearance of youth, yet she appeared that type of humanity that is sometimes spoken of, even in its childhood, as an old soul. She was a woman in her middle years, with expressive blue eyes, broad cheekbones, and light brown hair intermingled only slightly with a strand of white here or there.

Her eye passed over the three friends while she took stock of the room, then fell upon them again, as they seemed the only occupants to be expecting someone. Her expression was solemn, even cautious as she approached them. She had the look of a person who is ready to defend herself at all costs.

Ephram, Eagleton, and Thump were so absorbed, first by her striking appearance and then by her demeanor, that they very nearly forgot to genuflect in some manner that was proper in the presence of a lady.

She had their cards in hand, and she referred to them as she approached. "Messrs. Ephram, Eagleton, and Thump?" she said in a pretty voice that yet offered no sentiment.

"We are!" said the men in concert, and their combined voices carried enough volume to startle themselves as well as to raise several heads in the sitting room.

A few months before, such a meeting would have held some terror for the Moosepathians; it was difficult to know how to proceed in the presence of a woman. Some experience, however, had come their way since the inauguration of their club, and Ephram in particular had conducted a successful conversation with a young woman by the name of Sallie Riverille during the previous October. There was also the example of their chairman to follow, and only the night before they sat in the presence of Mrs. Covington with no discernible complications. Remembering some mention of a niece to Mr. Burnbrake, Ephram proceeded by inquiring, "Mrs.?"

"*Miss* Burnbrake," informed the woman with a hint of severity.

This was the extent of Ephram's bravery at the moment, and he offered nothing else.

"You asked to see my uncle," said the woman finally, after considering each of their faces.

"We did!" said the men as one, and again heads came up in the sitting room.

The woman was puzzled. "Did my cousin send you?" she asked solemnly.

Ephram looked to Eagleton, who looked to Thump, who looked to Ephram. "Your cousin?" said Ephram, who was looking at Thump, who looked at Eagleton, who looked back at Ephram.

"We have a letter," said Eagleton, ever helpful.

"A letter?" said the woman. She held out her hand for the missive. "I suppose Roger has found some reason why he *can't* escort Uncle Ezra to Hallowell!"

"I have not been apprised of its contents," said Ephram meekly. He placed the letter in the woman's hand.

"You can tell Roger that he will not find me unguarded or alone! I shall take Uncle myself if needs be!" The woman never for a moment looked angry, but only deeply hurt. The stricken expressions of those before her, however, reminded her that this outburst was not in keeping with so public a venue, and she glanced about the room, color rising in her face.

Ephram, Eagleton, and Thump were greatly distressed; people were watching them suspiciously, as if they were persecuting this woman. One man, at least, looked ready to come over and see what was wrong.

Miss Burnbrake snapped the letter from its envelope and applied herself to it. Their mission accomplished (however unpleasantly) the members of the club wondered, in collective silence, if they should be moving on to other things, primarily *any* other things that would take them some distance from the present scene.

"I beg your pardon," said Miss Burnbrake. Her expression softened to wonder as she perused Mister Walton's pleasant hand. When she reached the bottom of the note, she considered the crabbed signature from two or three angles before looking up. "I do thoroughly beg your pardon," she said.

The three men made sounds prefatory to remarks denying any need for an apology.

"This is from Mr. Tempest?" she said.

"I believe that *is* his name," said Ephram.

"*Adam* Tempest?"

"I am embarrassed to say . . ." began Ephram when he had, by way of wide eyes and raised eyebrows, entreated his friends in vain for information on this count. "I am sorry to say that we never learned his Christian name."

"We didn't meet him, actually," explained Ephram. "It was our chairman."

"Wonderful fellow!" exclaimed Thump.

"Oh, yes, marvelous," agreed Ephram.

"Our chairman!" declared Eagleton, and it was difficult to say if he were clarifying whom they were speaking of or simply invoking the man as a sort of salute.

"It has fallen to us," explained Ephram, "by way of our chairman, to deliver a letter from Mr. Tempest to Mr. Burnbrake, who I gather is your uncle."

"Ezra Burnbrake," she said to avoid any confusion.

"Ezra Burnbrake," said the three men all at once.

"Mr. Tempest dictated the letter to Mister Walton," said Eagleton, as if this were a happy thought, "as you will see; the signature and the body of the note will not be in the same hand."

The woman read the letter again, and the three men did everything but watch her. Ephram peered at the fire across the room, Eagleton looked up at the ceiling, and Thump considered the carpet immediately below him. (There was an unusual pattern in the carpet in which Thump thought he could see a series of Indian elephants in porkpie hats.)

"I don't understand all of this," she said when she had perused the letter again.

"I beg your pardon," said Ephram.

"Please do excuse us," said Eagleton. It sounded like the statement before leaving. "Best regards from the Moosepath League."

"The Moosepath League?" she said. There was something disarming in the name itself.

"Seventeen," said Thump (he had been counting the elephants).

"An errand for our chairman," Eagleton was saying. He and Ephram waved their hats before them as they backed away; they bowed several times and all out of pace with one another. (Thump was still captivated by the chapeaued pachyderms.)

"Oh, my!" she said. "What have I done? I beg your forgiveness for my abrupt behavior."

"Good heavens!" said Ephram. "Never abrupt. Would you say, Eagleton?"

"Certainly not abrupt," said Eagleton. "Rather we were abrupt, if anyone, wouldn't you say, Thump?"

"Indian elephants *are* the ones with smallish ears, aren't they?" asked Thump, and when he realized that this was not the expected response, he added, "I beg your pardon?" A smile had brightened Miss Burnbrake's already pretty face, and Thump struggled, in its light, to recall what had been discussed in his absence.

"We were saying," said Eagleton helpfully, "that Miss Burnbrake was *never* abrupt."

"Certainly not," he insisted.

"We were perhaps abrupt in our presentation of the letter," thought Ephram aloud.

"Giving *you* no reason to be otherwise, I fear," added Eagleton.

"Not that you *were* abrupt," assured Ephram.

"Oh, dear, no!" said Eagleton.

"You are too kind," she said, for it was clear to her now that they were just that. Her smile remained soft, but its effect was profound. She indicated the letter, saying, "It is clearly out of your way and a favor for strangers all the way around."

Ephram, Eagleton, and Thump found themselves blushing.

"In fact," she continued, "if you will indulge me a little more, I would ask you to come up to our rooms and meet my uncle."

Mr. Ezra Burnbrake looked fragile and ancient when he lifted himself from his chair; but his grip was firm, and his eyes had a certain clarity when he considered each of their faces. The old man's breathing came in short, shallow intervals; his head shook slightly upon his thin neck. He was surprised that his niece had returned with these three strangers but was the gracious host and asked them to sit by the fire.

Miss Burnbrake, as it turned out, was pleased to share such congenial company with her uncle, and she insisted that the members of the club have coffee or tea with them, whereupon she called down on the apartment telephone for service.

Mr. Burnbrake read the note from Adam Tempest with little expression, and when he finished, he nodded and peered at the signature. "And you wrote this for him?" asked the old man, looking from one to the other of them.

"Our chairman, actually," informed Ephram. "Mister Walton."

"They are from the Moosepath League, Uncle," said Miss Burnbrake, who could not pronounce this without the hint of a smile.

"*Are* they?" said the elderly fellow. He had never heard of the club but seemed to think it sounded impressive. He returned to the letter in his hand, however, and said a little sadly, "It is all a little mysterious, isn't it? And *you* have done Mr. Tempest a kindness, Charlotte," he added.

"He is right in that I don't recall," said Miss Burnbrake. She sat in a chair opposite her uncle and their guests. The old man passed her the note, and she considered it again.

"I am not surprised," he said. "Those quickest to kindness are also quickest to forget when they are kind."

Their guests considered Miss Burnbrake's expression, her almost serene features, and they could believe that these words applied to her quite accurately.

"But our trip seems unnecessary now," said the niece.

"Do you think?" replied her uncle.

"I think that Mr. Tempest has backed out of his agreement," she said, stating that which appeared pretty obvious.

"I think that I should like to know why."

"Do you think Mr. Tollback will be able to tell you?"

"And what about these '*others unnamed who will take up*' Mr. Tempest's '*intended mission*'?"

"It does make one curious," she admitted.

"I shall go to see Mr. Tollback, and Roger will go with me," stated Mr. Burnbrake. "It was very kind of you to bring this to us," he said to the Moosepathians.

Ephram, Eagleton, and Thump mumbled their embarrassment in chorus.

"I'm afraid I wasn't very gracious to these gentlemen when I first met them," admitted the niece. This admission to her uncle was a renewed form of apology, and the three friends continued to look abashed.

"Please forgive Charlotte if her reception was other than congenial," said the older man. "She and I are half expecting some communication from her cousin and my nephew Roger Noble, which by its nature must have been troublesome."

Ephram, Eagleton, and Thump knew about troublesome cousins, since they had each recently read *The Misery of Millicent Babbington* by their favorite writer, Mrs. Rudolpha Limington Harold. (*"Our fathers might share parentage,"* declared Miss Babbington, *"but there is that which is unnatural about you, Dirk, like the oak limb, raised in winter and necessarily withered!"* Eagleton shuddered a little even now as he recalled this passage and the dire events that followed.)

"I have some errands in Hallowell," continued the old man, "and while Charlotte visits with friends, my nephew Roger Noble is to escort me to my appointments. I am an old man, but I could certainly make my way by myself." He said this with a meaningful glance at Charlotte. "Conscripting Roger's company was the only way with which I was able to convince my dear niece to leave off the self-imposed task of watching after her ancient uncle and to take some pleasure and leisure here, where she spent much of her childhood."

"I wish you gentlemen could talk Uncle Ezra into allowing me to take him instead."

"Nonsense!" said the old man.

"Roger's reliability is in question," she added.

The old man considered his gnarled hands, which lay folded in his lap. "Unfortunately Roger is something of a dark sheep—"

The withered limb of the oak! thought Eagleton.

"—and a trial for his cousin."

"Uncle," said Charlotte Burnbrake, who thought too much had been said already.

The three friends consulted wordlessly with one another; then Eagleton straightened in his seat before saying, "We would be greatly honored, Mr. Burnbrake, if you would allow us to join your nephew in escorting you."

"No, no, no," said the old man.

Miss Burnbrake was shaking her head. "It is marvelous of you, but we simply couldn't, Mr. Eagleton, and I'm sorry that we have burdened you with any of our problems."

The members of the club were convinced they had stumbled upon a matter of urgency and distress and were just as convinced (more convinced probably) of what Mister Walton would have done in their place.

Thump stood to his less than moderate height, said, "Ahem!" and proceeded with the following, after an awkward silence. "Miss Burnbrake," he said (and she could not know how difficult it was for him to address her so directly), "as you are concerned for your uncle's well-being, you must allow us to accompany him." Then he turned to the elderly man. "Mr. Burnbrake, as you surely want to mitigate your niece's worry, you must do the same."

It was positively *Waltonian!*

"Good heavens, Thump!" said Ephram.

"How marvelous!" declared Eagleton.

Thump had captured the essence of the chairman himself in that single inspired moment: the sharpness of mind, the forthright kindness, the insistence upon doing the right thing! Why, he even resembled the chairman at that moment! Except (as Eagleton later pointed out) for his full head of hair, his magnificent beard, and his height—not to mention the lack of spectacles. Thump was barrel-chested as well (it was conceded later on), whereas Mister Walton had the advantage of being portly.

But the very sight inspired Thump's friends.

"I can't tell you," insisted Eagleton to the old man and his niece, "how pleased we will be to visit Hallowell, where our chairman has met several people and where we might view the vicinity of some of his recent adventures."

"Of course," added Ephram, "we will make our own way, linger on the bench"—the Moosepathians had begun to pick up some baseball parlance since attending several games with Mister Walton—"and be there as needed."

"We will take the train," said Eagleton, who stood now with Thump, "and you may consider us a separate yet interested party."

Ephram stood, then, and said, "When do we leave?"

Uncle and niece looked up from their seats in astonishment. More than considering themselves or each other, the Burnbrakes could not bear to disappoint such generous intentions.

"Well," said Ezra Burnbrake with a chuckle, "it seems you have no reason to worry at all, my dear." He looked to the men apologetically. "I *was* planning to leave tomorrow," he said.

"Snow beginning by morning," said Eagleton. "Expected moderate to large accumulations. Wind in the northwest."

"High tide at twelve minutes to six," said Thump.

"It's twenty-three minutes before the hour of three," said Ephram.

"He's not to suppose that he has been relieved of his duty," said Charlotte after the members of the Moosepath League had bowed their way out. She was standing at a window with the curtain pulled aside so that she might watch them leave the hotel, and she was a little astonished, now that they were gone, that three strangers had stepped into their apartment and garnered such complete trust.

"He's not relieved of anything," answered her uncle. "The important business is to keep him well away from you." The old man felt tired, though he thought he should rise from his chair and tend the fire. "It has been a strange affair from the moment Mr. Tempest first wrote," he mumbled. "But I shall go with Roger as planned; only now there will be company along the way to make the travel pleasant and someone to call upon for a day or two if Roger proves difficult."

"I'm very glad," she said. She hadn't seen the three men leave yet but gave a start when she saw the figure of her cousin Roger Noble gazing up at her from the other side of the street. She dropped the curtain and walked away from the window without saying anything to her uncle.

15. The Reason Why

"The connection came to us in a circuitous manner," began Frederick when they had rails moving beneath them again. Counting the train they had arrived on, they had missed two departures, and the third arrived only after some delay. "It started with the simple curiosity of a student at Harvard who passed the home of the Broumnage Club five days a week on his way to his classes and one day a week on his way to church. He told a teacher last spring of a peculiar conversation he had with a member of this society. It seems he chanced to meet the man who was coming down the steps of the Broumnage Club.

"The student tipped his hat to the fellow, wished him good morning, then inquired of the man the origin of the society's unusual name.

"'It is the name of our founder,' said the man, but there was something off-put in his manner, as if he had been surprised by the question and even a little angered by it. 'And what is your name?' asked the man, as one might ask a miscreant caught at his crime."

"The question no one thought to ask our pickpockets," said Isabelle.

Frederick gave his wife a quick glance. "The student," he continued, "told the man who he was, and the fellow turned on his heel and walked off. The student tipped his hat to the man's back, said good day, and hurried off to school. When he turned a corner and glanced back, he saw the man standing some distance down the sidewalk, watching him.

"The teacher, who is a fellow seminarian of mine, would have thought little of the incident if the student hadn't been so taken by it. A day or so later he asked the young man if there was anything to add to the tale, and the student repeated his interest in the name of the club since he had been unable to find the name of Broumnage in any directory or history at the college library. He also thought that he had been followed on his way home the previous evening."

The car they occupied was less crowded than the previous one, and they had deliberately found themselves the loneliest seats. Frederick Covington spoke carefully, though it was not natural to him (he was a preacher, after all) or to his strength of nerve to speak in hushed tones.

"It was about this time that I was first disappointed and appalled at the vandalism of a possible artifact in Londonderry, New Hampshire, and during my brief investigation of the business, I happened to hear of a group of men who had been staying in a nearby inn, the Broumnage Club. I knew nothing of the student's experiences at this point and thought nothing of them, of course, besides noting their odd sobriquet.

"At Harvard, however, the teacher began to ask around the college if anyone had ever heard, or knew anything, of the Broumnage Club. The name had tickled his fancy, and it occurred to him (which suggestion he made to his student) that the name might be an anagram. The student and some friends, it seems, took this notion to heart and spent a Friday night rearranging the letters of the name, and they were able to come up with only a single sensible combination."

"Norumbega," said Sundry Moss, who had given no indication that he was doing anything other than listening.

Covington looked startled. "Mister Walton," he said, "you did not tell us that you had a prodigy in your employ."

Sundry himself seemed surprised. "Am I right?"

"I would have long since ceased to be surprised by Sundry's powers," said Mister Walton, "if he did not . . . continue to surprise me."

Sundry was embarrassed. The engine gave out a long whistle as they neared a crossing. Augusta fell behind them as they hugged the eastern shore of the Kennebec.

"Norumbega," Mister Walton was saying. "It was where Bangor is now, wasn't it?"

"That has been generally accepted," said Frederick. "But for years it was known only as the City of Gold and thought to exist somewhere in the interior of the continent. Many believed that it was connected also to the great Northwest Passage."

Even the legend of such a place is a great satisfaction to contemplate, and Mister Walton's expression was filled with pleasurable wonder.

"But there are those," explained Frederick, "who still insist that such a place as the City of Gold, the true Norumbega, existed and that it lies within the confines of some great forest or beneath the rubble of centuries."

"The Broumnage Club in particular believes this," said Isabelle, "according to the Pinkerton man who was hired." It was the first bit of information she had offered to the tale.

Sundry gave a low whistle. Mister Walton leaned forward in his seat, as if to catch the Covingtons' words more quickly.

"As you may know," said Frederick, "legend has it that the Vikings who came to this continent were among the only Europeans ever to set foot in the great city."

"But that still doesn't explain—" said Mister Walton. He stopped himself, and there was silence among them as he put together what he had been told. "Of course," he said finally. "The Broumnage Club has taken it upon itself to find evidence of Norumbega and also to destroy that evidence so that others will not find it before themselves!"

"And there you have their purpose and their method," said Frederick Covington. "Any possible Norse artifact is a possible signpost to Norumbega, the City of Gold."

"My word!" said Mister Walton. "It's disgraceful. But do the *Broumnagians* know of your destination?"

"The existence of the artifact came to *our* attention only last week," said Frederick. "Unfortunately Mr. Thole's query reached me indirectly, and I fear there have been several links by which they may have learned of it. No"—he corrected himself—"by which they surely *have* learned of it. But this is the first brazenly criminal act that I have been able to connect them with, besides the vandalism of the artifacts themselves. Perhaps by this rash conduct we can set the police on them and bring their purposes to the light of public censure."

"I have a question," said Sundry. "How did you know that Mister Walton and I were not members of this Broumnage Club?"

Frederick looked again to his wife, then said, "Mister Walton's friendship with Lawrence Seacost would have been recommendation enough. However, there is one element of the Broumnagians, as Mister Walton calls them, that we have discovered; every one of them is blond-haired and blue-eyed."

"Sons of Vikings themselves, it seems," said Isabelle, who appeared more at ease now that the story had been told.

Sons of something else entirely, thought Sundry.

"The Blond-Headed League," said Mister Walton.

"But those men who tried to pick your pocket!" said Sundry.

Frederick smiled ruefully. "You may remember that I chose our seats."

"And you sat yourself just behind them," said Sundry.

"If you're going to have an opponent, best to know where he is."

"Did I ruin your plans then, getting them kicked off the train?"

"Not at all. It is possible that they have nothing to do with the club," said the clergyman, but his wife looked as if she doubted this.

"It does encourage a person to look for men with blond hair and blue eyes," admitted Mister Walton.

"It does," agreed the minister. He was looking out the window as they approached the next station and the next settlement. It was near to three o'clock, and already the sky looked darker. "I did in fact, to begin with." He considered Mister Walton with a very likable and clear-eyed smile. "But upon reflection I decided that I would rather miss a hundred members of the Broumnage Club than cast aspersions on one innocent blond-haired, blue-eyed man. I told Isabelle long ago that I would rather lose a hundred artifacts than spend my life mistrusting people of Nordic descent or fearing the next man named Ericson."

"All Broumnagians may be blond," said Mister Walton, "but all blond men are not Broumnagians. Very right, of course."

"Ericson was the name of the Pinkerton agent," said Isabelle, and it was obvious that her reference to this organization was meant to underscore what she deemed to be the seriousness of the matter.

"Then you *did* hire a Pinkerton," said Sundry.

"I would not have myself, but some people with common cause and deeper pockets hired him, and it is from his investigations that we acquired our little knowledge of the group. With a name like Ericson, you can imagine that he took a private concern in the matter."

"Should we be making such a beeline for Skowhegan?" wondered Sundry. "They must be watching us."

"I don't know," said Frederick. "If they knew to go to Mr. Thole's home, they may know now to go to Skowhegan. They may have discovered the general vicinity of the artifact and have been looking through Mr. Thole's photographs for clues to its specific whereabouts. Certainly they are out there, and if they don't know what town the artifact is in, they can't know that we're *not* leading them on the wrong track."

Mister Walton could not help smiling.

"It is a little," began Frederick, "circuitous, is the word we used earlier?" He glanced out the window. "It will be too dark once we are settled at Skowhegan. Tonight perhaps we can visit your friend."

"*Perhaps*," said Mister Walton, "while you and your wife are dining, Sundry and *I* should visit him."

"Certainly," agreed Frederick. "They would be watching me most of all, I suspect."

16. Calling Capital Gaines

"What do you think of this business?" asked Mister Walton when Sundry pulled up in the hired sleigh before the door of the Wesserunsett Inn. Glancing at the second story, they counted the windows and sought the illuminated panes that represented the Covingtons' room, listening, in the brief silence that followed Mister Walton's query, to the stream from which the inn had adopted its name.

The horse seemed anxious to be traveling the snowy roads, and Sundry steadied the animal before giving his employer a hand up. "I think that I do not trust to the better nature of the Broumnage Club."

Mister Walton nodded; he situated his hat safely upon his head, his bald pate flashing briefly in the light that spilled from the lower windows of the Wesserunsett. "If I thought I could, I would talk the Covingtons out of this expedition. The trespass and the destruction at Mr. Thole's trouble me the more I think on it."

"Mr. Covington seemed angry but not very daunted," offered Sundry. He had only to give the reins the smallest shake to encourage the horse down the road.

"*Mrs.* Covington perhaps understands better the possible danger." Mister Walton gave his friend an odd look and said, "I hope our recent experiences with kidnappers and brigands haven't made a cynic of me."

Sundry smiled at the contradiction in Mister Walton's words. "Not to worry," he said, almost chuckling aloud.

The portly fellow was looking ahead and did not detect the humor in Sundry's voice. "I will be glad to have Capital with us, if he will come."

Traveling more or less parallel to the stream, they were not far from the center of Skowhegan when Mister Walton began to watch for a row of giant pines, beyond which appeared a lane. The old farmhouse down this road was one of the earliest built in the area; it occupied the side of a knoll out of the prevailing wind and was surrounded by great maples and oaks.

It had been a small house once, but had been much added to, so that its wings looked like the products of rambling second thoughts; it appeared cozy withal, with the glow of a fire warming the parlor windows. Silence carried the air, with hardly a breeze to bend the column of smoke rising from the main chimney. Beyond the house was a large barn, and beyond this, a moonless night over acres of field.

Sundry hitched the horse, and they clumped up some rickety steps to the side door nearest the glowing window and had barely knocked before the door was opened and a crackly voice declared, "Evening!"

"Who could it be? Who could it be?" came a high-pitched voice from within.

The man at the door turned about on his heel and said, in something lower than a shout, "You be quiet," though there was nothing very harsh in the command.

"Who could it be? Who could it be?" continued the other.

"Mr. Capital Gaines?" said Mister Walton, with obvious pleasure coloring his own voice. He doffed his hat, as if the sight of his bare head might better identify him to the man.

The man at the door leaned forward, got the breath of cold air upon his face, thrust steam into the air, and, after a brief glimpse toward Sundry, set his eyes on the bald pate and glimmering spectacles. "Come in, come in!" he said; he hadn't identified the visitors, but it was cold outside, and he couldn't think of anyone he didn't want to see. "Come in, come in!"

Mister Walton and Sundry entered the hallway; Mister Walton bent forward in a courtly bow, and when his head came up, the man at the door had a good look at that pleasant countenance and bright eyes. "Toby Walton!" declared the fellow. A small man of about sixty years, Capital Gaines had retained much of the figure of his youth *and* the animation. He had only a little hair at the top of his own head, but his beard was neat, and trim, and silver. His eyes were active and bright, and immense schemes were obvious behind them. His voice had not grown more mellifluous with years. "By gum, if it isn't!" Mister Walton let out a hearty chuckle, and they shook hands with real vigor. "Toby Walton! By gum!"

"How have you been, Mr. Gaines?"

"Toby, I've told you a hundred times, 'Call me Capital!' I'm going to begin thinking you don't like me!"

"Good heavens!"

"Toby Walton!"

"Capital"—Mister Walton tried again—"how are you?"

He was born Robert Augusta Gaines (for generations his family had named their people after the places they were born), and as a child he had often been reminded that his interior appellation was of feminine form, which was no great matter to him; as long as anyone could remember, everyone had called him Capital. There wasn't very much he hadn't done in the way of making money, for he started with very little, cutting ice down in Richmond, and ended with quite an abundance, running a lumber mill, opening a store or two, and sharing in the fortunes of several ships.

Between the little and the abundance he had indulged in some small adventures and a large one, which was the Civil War. He had reached the rank of major but hadn't particularly liked killing Confederates and didn't particularly like being remembered for it, however efficiently he had accomplished the task.

Because of the tradition concerning middle names in the Gaines family, one had only to trace their genealogy to find out where they had been. Following Capital's fathers in this manner, one backtracked to Kittery, to Portsmouth, and Falmouth, then to Montego Bay, and finally to Skye, where the tradition was first invented.

It was claimed that James Montego Bay Gaines, born in 1719, first acquired King Philip, the large colorful parrot that, in 1896, was still in the possession of James's great-great-grandson. (It was from this creature that Mister Walton and Sundry had heard the high-pitched call of "Who could it be? Who could it be?")

Several years previously Capital Gaines had grown rather sick of making money; in other words, he had already made enough to set *several* people up in more than comfort for as long as *he* could reasonably expect to live. Taking with him his companions and employees (once army subordinates) Mr. Noel and Mr. Noggin, he moved to Skowhegan, where Capital was able to indulge his great love of the outdoors and wander the neighboring forests, riverbanks, and lakeshores more or less at will. Here also he had done his best to relinquish the bachelor's life by courting a widow at a neighboring farm, though without the famous "Capital" fortune.

Some would have thought that the softening hand of a woman might have benefited the rooms through which they passed and most particularly the parlor (more properly a den), where Mr. Noel and Mr. Noggin waited to greet Mister Walton and meet Sundry. The den was a monument to every art that carries man from his hearth: Fishing rods and trophy catches hung upon the walls, and a crowd of snowshoes and a pair of skis leaned in pickets in a corner; a shotgun held the place above the mantel, and Capital had to find another corner for a pair of rifles that occupied an old over-stuffed chair; a leather harness was draped over the sofa where someone had been oiling it; and three pairs of boots stood before the fire.

At least of an age with Capital, Mr. Noel and Mr. Noggin were as confirmed-looking a brace of bachelors as Sundry had ever seen; their clothes were clean but well worn, their hair clipped to a practical length with no thought to fashion or appearance. They smelled of leather and gun grease and woodsmoke. They were shaven merely as a matter of habit.

"I remember Mr. Walton, don't you, Mr. Noggin?" said Mr. Noel.

"I do, Mr. Noel," said Mr. Noggin.

Mr. Noel was tall and angular, with a large nose and doleful brown eyes; he had great, wide hands. Mr. Noggin was more of a height with Mister Walton and either more fond of the trencher than Mr. Noel or more affected by it; he had scant blond hair, bright blue eyes, and a way of gesticulating whenever he spoke.

If they all were bachelors, they yet lacked nothing in courtesy, and chairs were quickly found for their guests. Mr. Noel hied off for the teapot and victuals despite protestations from Mister Walton and Sundry.

"It seems to me a spread is in order, Mr. Noel," said Mr. Noggin.

"I just made bread this afternoon, Mr. Noggin," said Mr. Noel.

"Open a new jar of peach preserves," called Capital after the man when he had disappeared into the kitchen. "Make them ourselves," he said proudly, and that was a sight Mister Walton and Sundry both would have paid to see.

"Mr. Noel says it will storm," said Capital Gaines.

"There was talk in the papers," said Mister Walton.

"It's my elbow," said Mr. Noel, but no further explanation of this weather-predicting joint was tendered.

"The Covingtons are adamant about finding the place tomorrow, however."

"These other fellows are that eager," said Capital.

"Eager enough to ransack Mr. Thole's home, top to bottom."

"The picture looks from a height," said Capital, holding one of Mr. Thole's photographs before him. "Look at the tops of trees beyond. The boulder itself seems to be in a clearing or above the woods."

Standing on a slope—in the image—was a large glacial boulder, on the side of which was etched a column of figures three or four wide. The rock took up the foreground of the picture, though there were some birch trees below it and more trees in the unfocused distance. Capital knew nothing of Viking runes and would not have recognized a Norse alphabet from hen scratch, but he remarked how clear were the markings on the boulder. "They chalked these markings, I'd guess."

"Mr. Thole did when he discovered them, yes," replied Mr. Walton. "He keeps some in his pack evidently, to mark his trail. It was admirably shrewd of him."

"It's very strange that I don't recognize anything. I've traveled those woods backward and forth, or so I thought."

"It isn't the old Council Hill?" wondered Mr. Noggin, his hands making the shape of a mound before him. "I've heard tell, but never seen it."

Capital considered the photograph again and let out a low noncommittal sound. "I think you are right, Mr. Noggin," he said at last. "It may be the Council Hill." Mr. Noggin beamed.

"You know where this is then?" asked Mister Walton, but Capital sat back in his chair and was in deep thought, pulling absently at his beard.

His attention surfaced briefly. "These folks—the Covingtons—insist upon coming with us?"

"Honestly," said Mister Walton. "Mr. Covington is the only one who can positively identify the writing—"

"Yes."

"And Mrs. Covington will not allow him to go without her."

"Really?" This put Capital in mind of something. "I can get them there. I don't have sufficient sleigh for us all, but the widow does—"

"The widow?"

"Do you want me to go down and ask her for it?" wondered Mr. Noel.

"What?" said Capital. "Not at all. I owe her a visit, I think. What time is it? I should hurry over tonight. You gentlemen will forgive me, we'll need a larger sleigh."

"The storm doesn't worry you?" said Mister Walton.

Capital shook his head. "There are camps we can reach, if need be." He was fired suddenly by the entire notion or perhaps simply by the opportunity to visit "the widow," and he found his boots by the fire.

"Won't she be abed?" wondered Mr. Noggin.

"Well," drawled Capital, "I don't know about that." Mister Walton was amazed at the energy with which his friend donned his boots and jacket.

"I believe she might be abed, Mr. Noel," said Mr. Noggin.

"I don't think the notion is a constraint, Mr. Noggin."

"Ahrr!" came a voice from the corner, and Mister Walton was a little startled. "Ahrr! Tide's out!" King Philip seemed agitated by Capital's haste; the parrot paced the bar on which he was perched, looking for all the world like a little ruffian with his shoulders hunched as he walked his seagoing gait. "Ahrr!" he screeched again. "Tie the line and tether the boat! Tide's out!"

"My friend Mr. Thump would find him a kindred soul," said Mister Walton with a laugh.

"Tide's out! Ahrr! Ahrr! Tide's out!"

❦ BOOK THREE ❦

December 5, 1896

17. Lovely, Dark and Deep

"There's weather coming," came Capital Gaines's high-pitched voice when he lit down from his sleigh. It was the very first thing he said, before "Hello," or "How do you do," or "It's me." "I went down to the telegraph office to see what was the latest, and there's a blizzard been crossing the White Mountains since last night, and it's just touching Portland, even as we speak. How do you do, I'm Capital Gaines." He offered his hand to Frederick Covington.

After Mister Walton had happily introduced the older man to Isabelle and Moxie, Capital looked up at the sky and repeated his assertions regarding the weather. They considered the atmosphere, which was clear for the most part and gave no sign of things to come.

"It's all the more reason to go today," said Frederick, "before we're truly delayed and our mysterious opponents have time to catch up with us." It was the first time that Mister Walton and Sundry had seen Covington without his clerical collar, and standing outside the Wesserunsett Inn, the minister looked like a rough-and-ready sportsman, with his boots laced to the knees, and his faded trousers and his old winter coat. He had a brown tweed cap and a pack at his feet like a guide.

Isabelle was decked out in slightly newer, slightly more fashionable, but no less practical clothes. Her wool skirt was layered like a quilt with petticoats, and though her boots must remain a mystery above the ankles, they looked very much like her husband's. She had a coat with a beaver collar and a fur hat that might have been amusing if she hadn't been so fetching looking out from under it. Capital said later that it was the hat that convinced him she knew what she was doing.

"You sure you are going, Mrs. Covington?" he asked only once, and she took no offense.

"I am, Mr. Gaines," she said with the sort of quickness that indicated she knew the question was coming.

"Capital," he said.

"If you wish, thank you. I am Isabelle." Her determination was somewhat contradicted, however, by an uneasiness that she could not entirely conceal. Her presence, in fact, *and* her lack of ease had been under some discussion between Mister Walton and Sundry, and they rightly considered that though she would rather none of them had ventured on this mission, she was unwilling to allow her husband to venture without her.

"Courage can only visit the fearful," Mister Walton had quoted.

"I see *the widow* allowed you the use of her sleigh," said Mister Walton with almost a wink.

"She did," said Capital, and standing before the sleigh, he quickly altered the subject by telling them his plan, which he had devised in the dark hours of the morning with Mr. Noel and Mr. Noggin. He'd been almost too excited about the whole business to sleep; he looked game, however, and none the worse for a restless night.

"I'm sorry Mr. Noel and Mr. Noggin aren't coming with us," said Sundry.

"You might see them before the day is out," said Capital. He absently stroked Moxie's head as he told them the roundabout method by which he hoped to confound their opponents, giving the affair the shine of a real adventure. "Well, sir," said the old major to no one in particular, "let's burn to it."

The entire state had been snowed upon several times since Thanksgiving, but the white drifts were deeper this far inland than they were in Portland. Roads were not generally plowed in those days (only the railroads had the power and mechanics to push snow from their course), and when the roads were groomed at all, they were rolled so that the snow was compacted into a hard surface. Sleighs were the mode of travel, and horses were bred with their ability to winter in mind.

The road from Skowhegan to Canaan therefore was not a straightforward means of travel but was filled with the hazards and difficulties consequent to the season's already heavy weather. Capital had a good horse for this sort of thing, however, and once they had their gear packed in the back of the sleigh, they were soon skimming over the snow like a coaster.

They were not long getting out of the general settlement and were heading south toward the Kennebec when Capital Gaines asked, "What do you think these runes say, Mr. Covington?"

"That's just it. They seem to be runes—their shapes match actual figures in Norse writing—but they don't seem to *say* anything. In one or two places there will be a short recognizable word, but you could lay down letters at random and do that much."

"I took note last night of a strange shape down by the bottom right," said the old man. "What could that be, do you suppose?"

"You can't see it very well in the photographs," said Frederick. "The sun was low, it seems, and in order to expose the other marks properly, he had to underexpose that one figure. It looks almost like the pictograph of an ox. Our own letter *A* developed from something like it, the two rays of an angle and an intersecting line about halfway along the rays. The head of an ox."

"What would that mean?"

"I couldn't say. I'm not familiar with pictographs in rune making. Do you have a theory, Mr. Gaines? I would be greatly appreciative of one."

Capital Gaines laughed.

"A directional marker?" wondered Mister Walton, who sat back to this conversation.

"The thought had crossed my mind," said Frederick.

"Are the runes abbreviated directions then?" asked Capital.

"I'm not sure they *are* runes."

"Ah, well," said Capital, "it's pretty out in the forest this time of year."

Twice when they reached the height of a steep slope, their driver and guide stood on his seat and surveyed the road before and behind them. For a while they followed the flow of the Kennebec. Below them the dark waters and snow-covered islands seemed void of color and motion.

It had been a long time since Mister Walton and Sundry had seen so much forest, and the dark ranks of trees that closed on their left, then on either side as they left the river heightened the mysterious nature of their mission as much as would the Gothic ramparts of a castle. Sundry thought he caught sight of a small, doglike creature skirting the edge of the trees; then the swift shape disappeared amid a stand of alders. He ruffled Moxie's downy ears and wondered what her nose was telling her.

They traveled for more than an hour, west and southwest of some prominent wooded hills. Then in a shadowy hollow, while the sky had begun to show signs of coming weather and the wind had risen, Capital drew the mare up and let out a "Hallo!"

Moxie let out a surprised bark, and the others in the sleigh were similarly startled.

"Hallo!" came an answering call from the woods.

"Get your gear," said Capital, and he nickered the horses a little closer to a stream that crossed the road just ahead of them. The water disappeared through a screen of evergreen and brush, beyond which they could barely see a little glen, as dark and tidy as a gnome hole, with glaciated boulders and ancient deadfalls surrounding it like purposeful boundary keeping. Capital rubbed his horses' noses and simply said, "Stand," to them.

A man was picking his way down the stream by way of a series of stones, and he cried out a "Hallo!" again as he peered up from the confines of the glen to see whom he was greeting. "Capital?" he called.

"It's me!" called the man, and with his own gear slung over his back, he half slid, half leaped down the snowy bank to the stream. Moxie capered alongside him, and neither of them looked more than a young man or a pup.

"Capital!" said the man, with more emphasis than volume, and they gripped hands. "What are you up to, you old scalawag?"

"Paul!" said Capital.

Sundry, who had taken his own things and Mister Walton's, was quickly down the slope and pulling up beside the two men. Paul was of an age with Capital, a tall, wiry man, his curly hair and heavy beard a mix of coal black and gray; his face was weathered, and he had bushy eyebrows that overhung a handsome, if rugged, face.

"We're off to search for buried treasure," said Capital lightly.

"You've picked a good time of year for it," said Paul, whose voice carried with it the rhythm and inflection of Acadian French.

"We thought the deeper it was buried, the more we'd find," suggested Capital.

"Then wait a day or so, and it will be buried deeper." Paul was watching as Frederick and Isabelle preceded Mister Walton down the short slope to the stream. Clearly his interest was up. "Shall I do for our tracks before I take your sleigh?"

"That would be fine. My friends, this is Paul Duvaudreuil, who has been my friend for longer than either of us would care to admit."

Mr. Duvaudreuil was pleased to meet them all, and he laughed when Moxie offered her paw. For the dog he could speak his native French, and

Moxie was as pleased to hear endearments voiced in this language as in English.

"You'll have to trust me to explain another time, Paul," said Capital. "But the quicker you have my sleigh on its way to Pittsfield, the better."

"I am on my way," said Mr. Duvaudreuil. He had a short knife out of the sheath at his belt and was cutting pine boughs.

"And we must be gone ourselves," said Capital, and without further adieu, he led his small party over the same stones that Paul Duvaudreuil had traversed. In two minutes they had passed through the cathedrallike stillness of the glen (the stream rippling was itself like an aspect of silence) to a border of juniper thicket. "I hope you won't find this difficult traveling in your skirt, Isabelle," said the old man, but he did not hesitate before leading the way over the junipers, using them much like the stepping-stones in the stream.

Sundry had heard of this way of hiding one's tracks; the junipers were thick and heavy enough to keep a normal person from making much of a track beneath it, and if one was able to step in their very center, he hardly left a trace of his passing. The native Indians could fairly dance over a stretch of juniper.

"Our tracks from the road," said Frederick, a little out of breath keeping up with their guide.

"Paul will have covered those and his own already," said Capital. "It's not as easy as it sounds, but he learned the trick from an old Indian when we were boys, simply as a means to have fun with me one winter. He's done the same with his own tracks coming in from another path."

They broke through a stand of fir then, and Capital watched as Isabelle joined them. She seemed as ready as ever, and he simply nodded his approval. They were in a small clearing, and there was another sleigh above them on a little rise. Two light Percherons stood in harness, looking sturdy and willing. The woods all about were muffled with snow, and Mister Walton marveled that it was only December.

"I've seen it like this, back in '72, in October," said Capital. "A little north of here," he amended, "but we had snow in Augusta."

Sundry and Frederick were loading the sleigh with their gear, and the clergyman lifted his wife into a seat. Mister Walton and the husband climbed after, and Sundry clambered up alongside Capital. A crow called from a nearby tree, and the older man chuckled softly. The black bird lit on a dancing pine bough and cocked an eye down at them.

"That's as good as a telegram for declaring where we are," said Capital. He put a hand to his mouth and gave out a croak that would have sounded rude in a parlor back home.

The crow turned its head and applied its other eye. Capital called again. For some distance the bird said nothing, but curious, it passed from tree to tree, following them. Moxie barked at the creature once, and Frederick hushed her and ordered her to settle between them.

The horses were like dancers in the snow, their handsome legs flashing through the drifts and their broad chests pressing forward with the illusion of small labor. They followed the western shore of the stream for perhaps three-quarters of a mile before they crossed a brook and came within sight of Oaks Pond.

"The ice is probably strong enough, cold as it's been," said Capital, "but tracks on the pond can be seen from any high bank. Better to keep ourselves a little concealed among the trees. There are some trails near the water, however, and the way will be easy till we come to the brook that leads to Lake George, where we will have to make some decisions."

Along trails that deer had broken, the horses only gained speed; they seemed born for the task, and the lake to their right flashed in and out of the trees. The broad expanse of sky above the plain of ice gave greater evidence of the coming storm—a palette of gray had conquered the atmosphere— and when this was remarked, Capital assured them that he knew of more than one hunting camp where they could see a blizzard through. "It may seem the middle of nowhere," he said, "but we're not so far out."

The accompanying crow had chased after some breeze above the lake, racing ahead of them by half a mile, but they could hear it calling, and several others of its kin answered from other corners of the otherwise silent woods.

18. John 19:27

He never discovered where the old woman was going, and he wished afterward that he had inquired. He never knew her name.

Snow was drifting from the clouded atmosphere.

Eagleton had just spoken to his landlord at the front door of the house on Chestnut Street when he first heard the altercation; he was raising his hat back to his head as he closed the door and stepped onto the stoop to follow his bags to the awaiting cab.

A second cab stood at the curb, and the driver was down from his seat and berating an elderly woman in thunderous tones and blasphemous verbiage. He had a worn hat tilted to one side, a cigar in the hatband; he was unshaven and red-nosed. The man's eyes bulged with anger, and he did everything but shake his fist at the woman.

She was a small person whose command of English, slight from the start, had evaporated with anxiety. She wore dark clothes and a broad scarf over her head and was from her accent a person of Acadian extraction. She was attempting to explain something to the driver but was thwarted by her own tears and his unwillingness to listen.

Eagleton would have been the first to admit that displays of anger and the use of profanity were, by practice, reasons to move swiftly in another direction, but the discrepancy between the cabdriver and the elderly woman was so great that he swallowed his uncertainty and, stepping past his own cab, approached the scene.

"I was never meaning to pick up one of you people!" the man was saying even as he laid a hand upon the woman's collar. "What's this here then? That trinket will cover the cost *and* my aggravation, you can bet on it!"

"No, no!" the woman was shouting. "*Mon fils, mon fils!*"

"Good heavens!" was all that Eagleton could find to say.

"Lay off!" said the man before Eagleton could get within a pace of him. "She takes my cab, then pretends amazement when she doesn't have a purse or a penny to her name!"

"I have my purse lost!" the woman pleaded.

"Is it inside?" wondered Eagleton.

"It's not inside," said the rough man, grinning most disagreeably. "She's an Egyptian." He still had her collar in one hand and with the other attempted to lift something from her neck.

"If she *were* Egyptian, it would not matter a whit!" Eagleton declared, and he was about to suggest that the woman was speaking French when the situation became intolerable and he did the unthinkable, which was to lay a hand upon the man's arm and shout, "Sir!"

The driver swung his gaze like a ship's boom into Eagleton's face, that horrible sneer still occupying the lower half of his face. "You had better have good reason to be laying hold of me, mister!" he spit. "'Cause I don't care how fine your hat is, but what I'd be glad to knock it off—and your head with it!"

Eagleton's driver had joined the scene by this time, and it was not apparent whether he was prepared to come down on one side or another or whether he was simply wanting a ringside seat.

"Sir!" said Eagleton again, followed by "If you will be so kind, I will happily defray the cost of this lady's travel."

"You'll pay her fare?" said the man.

"I will indeed!" said Eagleton, who was growing uncommonly warm.

"And if you will not cease your belligerent manner, not to say your cowardly language, I will be forced to express my displeasure to the authorities!" He had by this time produced his own wallet and put in the man's hand a sum that would have made the driver happy had he given the old woman three tours of the city.

"He never earned that!" said Eagleton's own driver; he snatched the money from the first cabbie's hand and returned it to Eagleton. "Give him a couple of coins, and if he doesn't take it, I'll knock the hat from *his* head!"

In his highly emotional state Eagleton thought that the transaction had grown complicated, but he did as his driver told him, and the unpleasant cabbie climbed back onto his seat, shouting, "She can't even speak English!"

"She seems to be speaking English *and* French," countered Eagleton's driver, "and that's two more languages than you command."

The unpleasant man spat on the sidewalk at Eagleton's feet and drove away with several sinister deprecations.

Eagleton and his driver both apologized to the elderly woman, the two of them as men and the driver as a member of his profession. Eagleton was averse to being late for his meeting with his friends and Mr. Burnbrake, but he doffed his hat and said in careful syllables, "Is there anything else I can do for you, ma'am, or any place my driver and I can take you?"

The woman took Eagleton's face in both her hands, and he thought that she was going to kiss him. "You with the beautiful hair!" she said, her English returned to her now that the moment of crisis had passed, and indeed, Eagleton's blond locks seemed like a source of light on this overcast day. "How like a good son to come to an old woman's rescue!"

"Oh, well," said a reddening Eagleton. "I am sure one of my friends would have done more."

Then the woman reached for the back of her neck and unclasped the delicate chain hanging there. "My heart, it would be broken if that man took this, but to you I give it."

"My word!" said Eagleton, with a hand raised to indicate the absolute necessity of his refusal.

But the woman took hold of the hand with a surprisingly determined grip and laid in it the chain, from which hung a tiny silver cross. "You cannot deny me," she insisted. "My son is dead—almost forty years at Bull Run—and to me this was his last gift!"

"But, ma'am!" cried an astonished Eagleton.

"You will give it to your mother," she said firmly, and when he seemed frozen in place, she took the cross and chain from him again and deftly fixed them about his neck. "I had a dream last night," she said, "and my son told me he would send another son to help me from trouble, and here you are." Her sweet wrinkled face smiled up at him. She had tears in her eyes, and the condition seemed contagious. Both Eagleton and the driver were clearing their throats and hemming and hawing and blinking as she moved away from them down the sidewalk.

"What should I do?" wondered Eagleton aloud.

"I should count it a worthy charm," said the driver.

The chain had slipped beneath Eagleton's collar, and he could feel the tiny silver cross (it was plated silver, to be sure, though the old woman had never suspected) just above his breastbone. The cross was strange, even problematic to him; Eagleton was a "good Methodist," which persuasion did not hold with wearing such symbols. But if it seemed awkward as a religious emblem, it rather warmed him as a gift from the old woman's heart and indirectly the same from her long-dead and well-remembered son.

Eagleton was a little nonplussed as well because he could not follow her directive; his own dear mother had died some years past.

"That was a good piece of work, mister," said Eagleton's driver. "You're going to the Grand Trunk then?"

"I am, thank you." Eagleton thought to express something further to the old woman, but she was gone from the sidewalk when he looked for her. "Yes," he said to the driver. "I am. Storm increasing by the hour," he informed the man. "Expected to taper off after midnight. Winds twenty to thirty knots, in the northwest."

"Consider the fare paid," said the driver as he opened the carriage door.

19. The Undisclosed Motives of Roger Noble

Charlotte Burnbrake brought her uncle's bags into their apartment's little parlor while her uncle roasted his old bones by the fire, in anticipation of the cold and the snow that he would encounter between the hotel and the train at the Grand Trunk Station.

"Is Pacifa coming soon?" asked Ezra Burnbrake.

"In an hour or so," answered his niece. She sat beside him and took his hand.

"I hate to leave you alone." He spoke quietly. Without wife or children, the old man had an appreciation for the vast power of loneliness and hardly understood that Charlotte might relish time by herself. "What will you do?" he asked.

"In the hour before she arrives or when she's here?" asked Charlotte with sympathetic amusement.

"Whenever," he said, sensing, though not hurt by, the small bit of teasing in her voice; he was simply interested in everything she did, he loved her so. His brother could have done nothing more for him than provide this niece, who had been light and song in his elder years. "I am glad you will have time with Pacifa," he said. "I like her very much."

Charlotte, to be truthful, would be a little glad to have her uncle gone for a few days and felt guilty for it—contradictory impulses. "We shall take a walk in the snow," she said, and the thought of strolling the streets of Portland with Pacifa made her happy.

Uncle Ezra began a litany of dangers to avoid upon the street but cut himself short with a laugh and finished with "I warrant you'll be safe with Pacifa." Pacifa Means, contrary to her name, could be a turbulent creature and a force to reckon with.

"I warrant *you* will be safe with the Moosepath League," she returned with a smile. She had been touched and amused by the club members, but she wondered if they would really show; their visit the day before seemed so strange now. "Give them my best," she added as a mark of faith.

The hotel manager himself came to announce that Mr. Noble had arrived, and there was a hint in his bearing that Mr. Noble had not been pleased to wait downstairs. Uncle Ezra rose from his chair, embraced his niece, and allowed the manager to escort him down the hall. A porter came soon after and retrieved his bags.

Charlotte waited at the window, where she could watch, through a crack in the curtains, the bent shape of her uncle and the straight, arrogant figure of her cousin Roger Noble entering a cab at the sidewalk. Noble paused before he disappeared into the carriage and looked up at the very window. She knew he couldn't see her, but she flinched. She held the curtain steady, however, and gave him no token of her observance. The snow had begun, just barely, to drift from the clouded sky.

Charlotte lost herself in the contemplation of these first flakes and was finally roused by the sound of Pacifa's energetic knock upon the door.

Since the first light of morning the skies over Portland Harbor had been that unvariegated gray that drains color from the water and the snow and the rock, mutes the shadows of day, and appears to draw so close that mariner and landsman alike might wonder if a ceiling had been constructed while they were sleeping. Before the first train was pulled alongside the platform of the Grand Trunk Station, lazy spirals of snow had already drifted out of that gray field, only visible as they crossed the dark shapes of buildings or perhaps not till they had lighted upon a shoulder or a glove.

"What's the wire saying?" wondered the conductor when he came into the station from his routine inspection of the train.

"They've hardly seen daylight west of York County," informed the stationmaster, in what may have been an exaggeration.

The conductor nodded. He was philosophical. Some would get where they were going, and others would not. Anywhere on the rail was his place; the train itself was as much home as his little rooms on Warren Street. From the side windows he could see that the yardmen had dollied a plow out of the roundhouse, though the snow had hardly started and there was only a freckling of white over the tracks. The flakes were fat but sparse, falling like spring fluff. The engine blew a preliminary gout of steam and the damp cloud burst from the stack into a roiling confluence of scattered snow.

"What's the wire say?" said the engineer, when he stepped into the station.

Together the stationmaster, the ticket man, and the conductor painted a picture that was as bleak or cheery as their distinctive personalities.

"I suppose that it will snow whether we keep school or not," said the engineer, who was himself philosophical. He and the conductor were more interested in the weather than they let on, however; the running of their train and the safety of their passengers were points of honor with them, though they faced these issues with bland expressions. They had returned to their train before the Grand Trunk Station's customers and other people began to arrive.

The first of these came under the heading "*other people*," it seemed, for they got off the first trolley of the day and wandered into the station with none of the purpose that radiates from the ready traveler. The three of them looked about the waiting room as if it were oddly familiar.

"I think I could sit down," said Humphrey Brink.

"Remember not to lie down, or they will exact a toll," said Aldicott Durwood.

"Do not ask for whom the bench tolls," intoned Brink, "it tolls for me," and he answered his own poetic call.

"Does anyone see Mister Walton anyplace?" wondered Roderick Waverley.

"Would it be a terrible encumbrance," wondered the ticket man, "if I were to ask why you gentlemen seem to have no homes?"

"Don't believe everything that seems," suggested Brink.

"It's an illusion," said Waverley.

"It's the result of a poorly conceived wager," explained Durwood. "Our acquaintance here," he continued, indicating Waverley, "was exhorting certain ruffians with news of our youth, wherein he described an entire week in which purportedly we never made use of our own beds. For a week."

"If we are to believe our acquaintance," said Brink, "then we made the streets and the docks and such places as this our domicile."

"For a week," said Durwood again. "When we were younger. Home wasn't safe at the time. Our fathers wanted us to work."

"*I* don't remember it," said Brink.

"That's no proof against," said Waverley.

"No doubt it was summer," said Durwood. "And we were young."

"Waverley made a wager . . ." said Brink. He spoke with his eyes closed. Perhaps they had forgotten the ticket man entirely; they might almost have been talking among themselves or even *to* themselves. ". . . that it could be done again."

"Though it is winter," said Durwood.

"I hope it was a sizable bet," said the ticket man. From his expression one could not tell if he were amused.

"Moreover," said Waverley, "it is an affair of honor." Durwood and Brink nearly came to their feet at this communication, and he assured them, "But it *was* a sizable bet."

Brink's attention was taken up by something new at this juncture. Through the glass doors of the station entrance he could see two men—one elderly, another of similar age to his friends and himself—mounting the steps slowly. The younger man was haranguing his companion in tones that could be heard well ahead of them. A door was opened, and the volume of this tirade grew respectively.

"I tell you, you have no right to keep me from speaking to her!" the man was saying, and some quality of his own voice in that place (perhaps the echo, as if some sentient creature were repeating his words) brought him up short.

Durwood, Waverley, and Brink made no pretense of uninterest but blinked at the man. "It's the amiable Roger Noble," said Brink. His voice carried through the station in the sudden quiet.

"You won't be able to rest here for long," explained the man in the ticket booth to Brink, "bet or no bet. There'll be a lot of folk through here this morning, hoping to beat the storm."

Roger Noble shot darts around the room, to Brink and his associates, then back to the elderly man, his uncle, Ezra Burnbrake. To look at, Noble, tall and blond, was all that one would ask for in a man of that name;

his were straight good looks and a clear eye. He kept his chin high, but his mouth had taken a twist, brought on no doubt by a growing propensity to frown or even to sneer. He had struggled against his boyish features and had won out only too well.

"Roger," said Durwood as the nephew and uncle advanced to the ticket booth.

"These aren't the fellows you were talking about?" wondered Noble.

"These men?" said the elderly man. He peered at Durwood, Waverley, and Brink, adjusting his spectacles as he took each of them into account. "No, these aren't them. Do you know them?" He was out of breath, but Noble did not offer to lead him to a seat, nor did he answer the question.

"I thought," said Noble accusingly, "anything like the Moosepath League sounded too suspicious to be right!" Clearly he had not listened to his uncle or had simply discounted what the man had said.

"The Moosepath League!" said Brink; Durwood and Waverley echoed him. "You couldn't have a *thing* to do with Mister Walton!" added Brink.

"*That* was the name of their chairman," said Mr. Burnbrake.

"Don't feel you have to come along," said Noble darkly.

"We won't," said Brink, who had no idea what the man was referring to.

"We simply haven't bought our tickets yet," said Waverley.

"We haven't?" said Durwood.

"We aren't part of the Moosepath League, are we?" wondered Brink of his companions.

"I don't think so," said Waverley.

"I thought perhaps Mister Walton had inducted us without our knowing."

"Then we wouldn't know, would we?" said Waverley.

"That is very true. I hadn't thought."

The doors to the station opened just then, and three men hurried inside. They were very different from one another, except that each carried a newspaper under one arm and took his hat in the opposite hand upon entering.

"I have a feeling about these gentlemen, gentlemen," said Durwood.

"Could it be?" wondered Waverley.

"Mr. Burnbrake!" called the first of these newcomers. "How good to see you again, sir."

"Ah!" said the old man. "These are the fellows!"

Ephram, Eagleton, and Thump strode up to the small assemblage, even while—from other doors, and behind them—the station began to fill with travelers and baggage. Several porters and a driver stumbled in with a great load of bags and followed the Moosepathians.

The members of the club had discussed among themselves the best way to greet Charlotte Burnbrake's "troublesome cousin," and their decision was to face such a personality with a manner that was cordial yet guarded.

"Matthew Ephram," said that worthy, and he held out his hand.

Noble took it, but sparingly, as if he had only so much greeting allotted to him, and it was Ephram's motivation that pumped their hands.

Eagleton and Thump introduced themselves, and since the *first* three men seemed to be of the party, they were drawn into the circle of introductions and handshakes. When Durwood, Waverley, and Brink offered their cognomens, however, Ephram, Eagleton, and Thump were astonished.

"Good heavens!" said Eagleton. "The Dash-It-All Boys!"

Brink's head shot up.

"We are the Moosepath League!" declared Ephram, as if he were announcing himself to a long lost relative.

"It is like dire fate!" said Waverley.

"The Moosepath League!" said Durwood. "Mister Walton!"

Thump, who was then shaking Durwood's hand, beamed to hear his chairman's name spoken in exclamatory tones. Durwood peered into the great density of Thump's beard in hopes of ascertaining what the bared teeth meant.

Ephram, Eagleton, and Thump were very eager to be shaking hands; they made the rounds of their new acquaintances more than once (and in fact found themselves shaking with one another). Durwood, Waverley, and Brink peered at their own hands, as if expecting these appendages to be somehow altered by all this agitation. Mr. Burnbrake was also greeted affably, and Eagleton insisted that the elderly fellow take a bench.

"It was very good of you to come to the aid of our chairman," Ephram said to Brink.

"Was it?" Brink couldn't recall doing any such thing and was a little shocked by the suggestion.

"He never found his hat," said Durwood.

"He didn't, thank you," said Eagleton.

"Oh, don't thank me."

"And are you coming with us?" asked Thump.

"For a bit," replied Brink. "Waverley, you were going to get our tickets."

"Was I?"

"Come," said Thump, "let us go together!" He half accompanied, half led Waverley to the ticket booth, where the seller was watching with interest. Thump thought it terrifically congenial (and even jolly) to be performing such a function with his Dashian counterpart.

Ephram and Eagleton meanwhile were astonished to hear that the Dash-It-All Boys had seen their chairman only the day before as he and Sundry left with the Covingtons. The news precipitated another round of handshakes that Thump was loath to miss, and though he had not been informed of this new turn of events, he took Waverley's hand at the ticket booth and shook it heartily.

Roger Noble stared at all this bonhomie with something like disgust.

Ezra Burnbrake looked up from his bench with a quiet smile, considered his nephew and thought it good for him.

It is curious how goodwill is irksome to some people, how sincerity of spirit and honesty of heart can rile particular tempers to the boiling point, as if every pleasing word and unmitigated smile were the bite of a gnat or the buzz of a mosquito.

Misery loves company, it is said, and so perhaps does choler. Roger Noble, who arrived at the Grand Trunk Station in an absolute fury because he had been denied an audience with his cousin Charlotte, found his indignation further prodded by the unaffected pleasantness of the Moosepathians, as well as by the somewhat wryer amiability of the Dashians.

The storm's advance guard had pushed past the environs of Portland, and the first serious regiments of snow fell upon the city even as the train pulled out from the eastern end of Commercial Street and began its peripheral march below the promenade. Back Cove disappeared behind the snowy distance on the one side of the trestle that led toward Falmouth, and the great harbor paled on the other. Noble stared at his half reflection without perceiving the storm, and the Dash-It-All Boys were involved in earnest conversation with the Moosepath League; Ezra Burnbrake felt he was able to sleep in such agreeable company, and he closed his eyes.

At first the Dash-It-All Boys were up to this new diversion, and their conversation was mightily perplexing to the members of the Moosepath League, no more so than when Eagleton announced his great desire to see the Smoking Pine of Hallowell.

"Has it been smoking long?" wondered Brink.

"Oh, yes!" said Eagleton. "For years!"

"It must be very charred by now," suggested Durwood.

"It is a wonder there's anything left to see," added Waverley.

"It isn't on fire," explained Ephram. "But there is an odd sort of effluence that hovers above it sometimes, so that it appears to be smoking."

"It is part of a grove of pines," continued Eagleton, "thought to be the reincarnated spirits of the last Wawenocks."

"How long did the Wawenocks last?" asked Durwood.

"I beg your pardon?" said Eagleton.

"I believe I would rather return as a hackmatack," observed Waverley.

"And why is that?" wondered Brink.

"I don't know, but I like saying hackmatack."

"Durwood saw a smoking oak once, didn't you, Durwood," remembered Brink.

"Did I?"

"You should know if anyone does."

"There does seem to be a fleeting recollection."

"I shouldn't wonder," said Brink. Then to Ephram, Eagleton, and Thump he added, "Nearly burnt his aunt's house to the ground."

"Not to the ground, I don't think," said Durwood in his own defense. "The third floor was a little poorly."

"Good heavens!" said Eagleton. "What started it?"

"Some of her parlor furniture, I think," said Durwood blandly.

The Moosepathians were flabbergasted.

"Three sheets to the wind," said Brink.

"I beg your pardon," chorused the Moosepathians.

"Durwood," said Brink. "Drunk as a lord, he was!"

Ephram, Eagleton, and Thump were stunned by this indictment. None of them but Mr. Burnbrake could have been alive before the Dow Law, which prohibited liquor in the state of Maine, and so Brink was suggesting unlawful behavior as well as intoxication. The two trios of men gaped at one another for some moments, and even Roger Noble turned from his contemplation of the whitened atmosphere to see what the silence meant.

Then a strange noise emanated from Thump; he appeared to be laughing, though it was hard to be sure since his facial growth so concealed his expression. Thump's friends knew him well, however, and they too began to chortle. "Good heavens!" said Eagleton again. "Good heavens!"

Ephram put his head back and laughed as he had seldom done before.

"You quite had me believing you," said Thump to Brink.

"Did I?" said Brink.

Eagleton was slapping his thigh. "Drunk as a lord!" he declared. "I must write that down. Oh, good heavens!" He found his notebook and was jotting this exchange into it when it occurred to him that he had something to tell his friends. "It occurs to me," he said, "that I had something to tell you."

"Oh?" said Ephram. Thump too leaned forward.

Eagleton was fingering something beneath his shirt, and they watched him do this with interest and curiosity. "I can't recall," he said.

"How unfortunate," said Durwood, and his fellow Dashians appeared disappointed as well.

"It will come to me," assured Eagleton. Ephram patted Eagleton's shoulder.

There was yet another thread of conversation among these fellows that would prove consequential to the Moosepathians in a later season (not to mention extraordinary interest, even debate, among historians of the society): While describing certain adventures they had experienced since forming their club, Eagleton happened to mention the remarkable Mrs. Roberto. It was on the previous Fourth of July that this lovely woman, in the performance of her celebrated parachute drop from an ascended balloon, accidentally landed upon Thump, who was attempting to regulate a boxing match between two politicians!

The tale, when it was told, fascinated the Dash-It-All Boys on several levels. "It is a new electoral process then?" wondered Brink.

"The lady actually settled upon you?" said Waverley.

Thump, who had taken very little part in the telling of it, looked red beneath his beard; he had never gotten over his brief encounter with Mrs. Roberto (he had actually danced with her the following evening at the Freeport Fourth of July Ball), and he was quick to come to her defense if anyone was rash enough to disparage her parachuting abilities.

"I met the lady once," said Durwood.

"Did you?" said his friends, as well as Ephram and Eagleton. Thump's eyes widened with sudden interest.

Durwood was perhaps remembering the famous shape of that woman, which was not small but was entirely proportionate; he had, by the mild look upon his countenance, admired her.

"I know the woman," said Roger Noble, and as this was the first instance of his joining their conversation since the train pulled from the Portland station, all eyes turned to him.

"Do you?" said Thump.

Noble smiled unpleasantly. "She is a woman of *many* talents," he said, with an insinuation that touched the Dashians, if not the Moosepathians. "She used to live down by the waterfront in Portland."

"I think you mean a different person," suggested Durwood.

"I don't think I do," said Noble.

"The waterfront?" said Thump. He didn't know that there were *any* very nice places in that section of the city.

"I think Mr. Noble is referring to a different person," said Durwood.

Noble seemed to think better of pursuing this line of thought and turned with a sneer to the window.

But Thump fell into a deep study after this portion of their discourse, which musings did not go unnoticed by the Dash-It-All Boys, who nonetheless succumbed to several nights of carousing and, one by one, put up a remarkable chorus of snores. The members of the Moosepath League continued to think upon the lovely Mrs. Roberto, but soon they too were lulled by the cadence of the rails and the continuous veil of snow outside their windows.

It was not till they changed trains in Brunswick and both clubs roused themselves (and Mr. Burnbrake) that they realized Roger Noble was gone.

Ezra Burnbrake, chiding himself for his carelessness, sent a telegram of warning to his niece, which she received too late.

20. Frantic Whispers and Pointed Dispatch

Roger Noble left the train at Yarmouth; it was a simple thing, a sudden inspiration touched with alarm. He waited more than an hour for a Portland-bound train, and all the while his heart thumped to think that he had defied his uncle (for whom he still held an unaccountable fear) but, more important, that he would soon be face-to-face with his cousin Charlotte Burnbrake.

He had not seen Charlotte for three years now, and three years ago, when he *did* see her, it was considered (by Charlotte and Uncle Ezra) an accident. He had not been allowed to speak with her alone. Before that he had spoken to her alone many times and—since they were very young—always to the same frustrating, maddening end.

It was worse than thirst to Noble; enough money and enough industry can find a bottle anywhere, but there was only the single face with which he was obsessed, and that was denied him.

Once they had been companions, and he had held Charlotte's hand and even kissed her; they had walked in his parents' garden on summer nights. She was older than he by three years, and he had watched with admiration and growing passion as she trembled from child to womanlike adolescent to woman. Since that final transformation, his life had tumbled by in an agony of waiting, which was relieved only by an absolute torment of disappointment whenever he chanced to see her again.

In his waiting and in his obsession, he managed to make good every prediction of his prodigality and profligacy. He had burned through his legacy within a year of his father's death and been forced to beg of his uncle an annual stipend, which passed through his hands like water. He was continually in debt, fearful of meeting his creditors, and more often than not behaved as if *he* were owed money. As is so common with those who lack true self-possession, he carried with him a monumental conceit for his own worth and abilities, an egotism all the more dangerous for being fragile.

His hands shook as he bought a ticket in the Yarmouth station for the trip back to Portland, and he felt a weight in his chest that labored his heart and hindered his breathing.

Believing her cousin to be out of town, Charlotte Burnbrake thought that Portland in the snow was something like paradise. Though the weather already blinded the harbor, accumulating quickly upon the sidewalks, the populace was not to be daunted; the streets were swift with carriages, and the stores lively with business. Charlotte and Pacifa Means delighted to see boxes and packages done up in Christmas wrap, and they stood to listen as a man sang carols at a street corner.

Pacifa was a small woman with a large, sometimes comical manner; her eyes were almost black and flashed alike with amusement or temper; her eyebrows were perfect arches, deft at communicating her frame of mind. Beneath her hood she wore her dark hair in a pile upon her head, lending her small features a patrician quality that she used to benign, if sly, advantage. She and Charlotte walked arm in arm, bundled to the chin in fur collars, their hands muffed, the hems of their long coats dressed with snow.

At a shop window they stopped to look at great ranks of toys, and a man standing beside them asked their opinion regarding the probable Christmas wish of an eight-year-old girl. Pacifa pointed out the doll with eyes that closed when it was laid down. Charlotte favored the miniature tea set. They left the fellow peering from one to the other of these items, and he was such a picture of indecision that Pacifa made Charlotte stop some distance down the walk to watch him.

"Just see if he doesn't scratch his head," said Pacifa, and when the man took off his hat to do so, she made Charlotte laugh, she was so gleeful.

"Pacifa!" said Charlotte, fearing they were drawing attention to themselves. "You always make me unruly!" she said, laughing. Pacifa thought the idea of an unruly Charlotte Burnbrake was itself very funny and was therefore subject to further imprecations from her friend.

Charlotte's and Pacifa's fathers had been business associates, as well as owning large shares in the same two brigs, the *Hallowell* and the *Estimate*. Charlotte, her brothers, and her sister had been raised in nearby West-brook, but the friendship with Pacifa's family occasioned many a fondly remembered outing to Portland, and the concerns in the two brigs drew them to the excitement of the waterfront whenever one or the other arrived at her home port.

It was during these years that Charlotte came to know her cousin Roger Noble and in those days to welcome his company. When Charlotte was nineteen, her parents and her sister died during a snowless winter of deadly influenza, and with her brothers at sea or out west, she was sent to Cambridge and Uncle Ezra, with whom she had lived ever since. Ezra doted upon his niece, but now, in his aged years, the relationship between them had reversed somewhat.

While Charlotte was in Cambridge, Pacifa had been married for several years, but her husband died under circumstances that were not talked about. The two friends never had so much as a cross word between them. Neither of their lives was filled with incidents now, but they found much to say as they strolled the business district and shopped from the uncostly side of the store windows, all the while reveling in the snowy crowds.

Along the streets the eye might comprehend each individual flake as it tumbled between the dark buildings; as the eye gazed over the harbor, through a vast field of snowfall against the overcast sea, all the senses were hushed by that silent and endless multitude. Ship's spars, themselves repeated into the waterfront distance, had collected a mantle of white. More than one crew had, for St. Nicholas's Day (which was tomorrow), tied boughs and mistletoe onto the highest cross member of their vessel's mainmast, unintentionally adorning the Christian symbol with the pagan but lending a Yuletide charm to even this rugged neighborhood.

The women were well exercised when they returned to the City Hotel, their cheeks red with exertion and the weather, and they brushed themselves and each other off as best they could before entering the foyer. There they found a young man who promised to have lunch sent to their rooms.

"And coffee please," said Pacifa with a shiver.

"I sent one of the boys up with a telegram about half an hour ago," said the manager, who stepped from his office.

"Oh?" Charlotte thought that her uncle might have wired her of his safe arrival at Hallowell.

"He slipped it beneath your door, ma'am."

It seems early, she thought when she passed the tall clock in the lobby. They hurried up the stairs, hoping the fire in the apartments was not out.

They were hungry from their exercises and they strode the upstairs hall with as brisk a pace as might be considered ladylike.

The first surprise, and the first inkling that all was not as it should be, came when the door to Charlotte's apartments opened before she turned the key. A terrible suspicion seemed to emanate from the knob in her hand, till it touched her heart with apprehension and near panic.

The parlor was small but elaborate in its furnishings. Three large chairs cornered the room; ornate electric lamps hung from the ceiling and stood against the walls. The fire in the grate burned merrily. Charlotte had the door more than half opened before a tall man was revealed in the near right corner of the room, and she wondered if he were hiding from all but the last possible moment of discovery.

It's just Roger, she said to herself, and then, *It is* never *just Roger*. She stepped on something and without thinking bent down to pick the telegram from the floor.

Roger Noble was smiling, not simply to indicate the pleasure of seeing her but to suggest that their meeting was mutually happy. Then that smile evaporated into something almost childlike in its need. She saw that he had been reading the letter from Adam Tempest, and he laid it down upon the table where he found it. He was the first to speak, pronouncing her name as if he had just come up for air.

"Roger," she said, unable to wash affection entirely from the address.

"Mr. Noble," said Pacifa as she appeared at her friend's shoulder.

Irritation flashed in Noble's eyes. "Mrs. Means," he said, attempting to recover his passive veneer.

"I am surprised to see you, Roger," said Charlotte quietly.

He looked like a boy expecting reprimand, and this suggestion of his youth, this flash of the child in the man, made the moments that followed the more painful for Charlotte. She realized that she was standing in the door, blocking Pacifa's entrance and dripping with melted snow. The women brought their coats to the opposite corner, so that Noble was left standing like the member of a separate party on the other side of the small room.

"You are supposed to be with Uncle," she said as both reason and anger returned to her.

"He has escort enough, it seems," said Roger. There was impatience in his eyes, and every fear that Charlotte had concerning him was very simply resubstantiated.

"And yet no family while we speak," she said.

Pacifa took a poker and made a great deal of noise shaking up the coals in the grate. Roger watched her as she made herself conspicuous; under other circumstances, it might have been comic, how severely she peered at the painting above the fireplace.

"I am like no family at all to that old man," he said, turning back to Charlotte.

"And if that *were* so, who is at fault, pray tell?"

"Charlotte, I must talk with you!"

"Nothing has changed, Roger."

He sent Pacifa another uncertain look, then pleaded with Charlotte. "You can't know that," he said, though he might have been saying, *How far must I humiliate myself?* Standing alone, he looked dangerously impotent. He had aged since she saw him last; his clothes and his hair were in the fashion of youth—too youthful really—but the pockets beneath his eyes, the pallor of his cheek declared his unhealthy existence.

There was an impasse; Charlotte was herself mortified by this scene and could say no more, and there was yet enough social restraint in Roger Noble that he *would* say no more in anything but the most private surroundings.

Pacifa's restraint at present was a manifestation of her love for Charlotte, and nothing more. She stood with her back to the fire, her exquisite eyebrows raised and her chin in the air.

But Roger Noble had not braved the wrath of his uncle, returned to Portland, and stolen into Charlotte's room by way of his talent for jimmying locks, only to turn away at the first rebuff, and Charlotte could see this. In his petulant expression there was again the young man she had known and cared for, and not for the first time did she wonder how something so short as childhood could command such respect and duty over the remainder of a person's life. There were tears in her eyes: tears of apprehension, tears from the shock of seeing him (and seeing him look so old), and tears for the beautiful little boy still discernible in his face. "Let us go into the next room," she said, and touching Pacifa's hand to stem any dispute from that quarter, she led the way to the little alcove that gave access to the bedchambers.

Charlotte nodded when Noble reached for the door. He closed it softly behind them, and she saw Pacifa step briefly into her line of sight before they were shut from each other. It was curious to her that he stood with his hand upon the door as if *he* might have reason to flee at any moment.

He looked at her, hardly able to believe that here was not simply a manifestation (a hallucination even) of his desire but the woman herself. She could not at first meet his eyes but looked down at her hands. She stood with her back to the door of her room, but the alcove felt like a place of no escape, too small for her emotions, hardly offering enough air to breathe.

After the briefest sort of eternity she asked how he had been since she last saw him, the question sounding dull and stupid.

"My God, Charlotte!" he said. "You are more beautiful than ever!"

She did look into his eyes then, and sharply; his declaration somehow left her with more self-assurance and less guilt. She still saw in him the little boy, but not for the first time she thought she could recall the deceit and dissipation of the adult in generative form within the face of the child. It gave her room to breathe, not to feel such sadness for that young man.

"Charlotte," he said, "I *do* have something to say to you."

"What is it, Roger?"

"I know, of course," he began, "that your father left you with a handsome legacy." The look on her face indicated renewed suspicion, and he raised a hand to stop her from speaking, his words coming faster. "I also know that the swift loss of my own inheritance is no secret, to my family or my friends, not to say my enemies." Charlotte looked ready to stop him at any moment, but he rushed onward, saying, "My dear, it has dawned on me and I understand how completely you must fear that any attachment with me would endanger your security. It is with that in mind that it occurs to me that I should, should have long ago, offered to suffer any legality, sign any paper to assure you that your bequest remains your own, with no danger from my imprudence, along with those assurances I repeatedly give you that such a marriage would be all I need to throw off the bad habits and low companionship that have heretofore characterized your opinion of me."

Charlotte was appalled yet knew he was grasping at straws, that his understanding of her was lost beneath a distressing tangle of emotions. "Roger, I do not love you! Or if any love remains, it is the love of one cousin for another, the love that blood demands!"

No sooner were these words spoken than he launched himself at her and pinned her against the door to her room. He did not mean to shake her, but he was vibrating with such fear and anger that it translated itself to her like a current of electricity. Her first impulse was to cry out, though she thought it weak to do so, even as she realized that it was foolish not to.

There was Pacifa to think of, however, and least of all she wanted to draw her friend into this unhappy affair. She wondered what Pacifa could hear. Their previous words had been in tones no louder than would be considered conversational, but as he pressed her, his cheek against hers and their mouths within an inch of one another's ears, what was said came in gasps and whispers, more rapid and furious and less comprehensible.

"You made a promise!" he almost sobbed, and repeated over and over, "You promised me! You made a promise!"

"We were children! Just children!"

The scent of her filled him: her hair, her skin, her breath, the pale and familiar essence of lavender. He gripped her shoulders in a rough caress and pressed his mouth to her cheek. They both wept, she more in sorrow than fear, he almost in rage. He pulled his face away, and the sight of her beautiful eyes welling with tears seemed only to increase his anger. He held her face, and she made a small, animallike cry, sure that he was going to force his mouth onto hers, when a sharp knock came upon the door behind them.

"Charlotte," came Pacifa's voice. "Charlotte, you have a visitor."

"Yes?" said Charlotte. Noble stood away from her with a startled jerk.

"There is a gentleman here to see you," said Pacifa through the door.

Charlotte was sure that Pacifa must be inventing a caller, and though Roger would be furious, he could be no more so than he was a moment before. Roger Noble meanwhile feared any man's finding them in such straits.

"Yes," said Charlotte. She had a handkerchief out and was wiping her eyes and wondering how she could put herself in order before the door was opened and realizing how improper it looked to have Roger and her step out, flushed and out of breath. She thought to ask Roger to wait in Uncle Ezra's room, but that would be counter to Pacifa's rescue of her, so she stepped past him and wrenched open the door.

A man *was* standing in the parlor, and Charlotte could hardly have been more surprised. He was a regular-looking fellow, hardly taller than she, with a pleasant face and broad mustaches. He was well tailored, and he held a crisp fedora before him. He blinked when she opened the door, and she knew that her face was blotched with emotion and that her eyes were still wet.

She stood stupidly in the door to the alcove, with Roger watching over her shoulder. "I beg your pardon," she said, and with sudden inspiration asked, "Are you here to see my uncle? I am sorry, but he left this morning."

"As it happens," said the fellow, glancing from one to the other of the three people before him. "I *was* looking for Mr. Burnbrake, if he is your uncle, though it was more in the way of finding the Moosepath League."

"I beg your pardon?" said Charlotte.

"The Moosepath League," he said again, the drawl in his voice indicating just how much he belonged in the state of Maine.

"The Moosepath League," she said, suppressing a sudden need to weep again. "The Moosepath League *is* with my uncle, sir."

"My name is Daniel Plainway," said the man. He nodded to Charlotte and Pacifa, then took in Noble.

"This is my good friend Charlotte Burnbrake," said Pacifa, and she all but swooped Charlotte away from Noble. Roger was left in plain sight, and he mechanically stepped into the parlor.

"I apologize if I came at a bad time," Daniel said as they shook hands awkwardly.

"Not at all," said Pacifa. "We were just talking about lunch. Perhaps you could stay."

Charlotte shot her friend a startled glance.

"Thank you, no," said Daniel. "I'm simply interested in where I might find the Moosepath League—specifically, I should say, a Mister Tobias Walton. It is a matter of some urgency, as I have information that I know he has been waiting on for some time." The man worked at the brim of his hat.

"I haven't met Mister Walton myself," said Charlotte, "but I can give you the address my uncle was reaching today, and from there you are sure to find Mister Walton's friends, who may be of more help." She moved across the room to a table beneath a window where there were some papers.

"Let me," said Pacifa. Charlotte didn't know how Pacifa could have any idea where her uncle would be, but her friend was across the room and scribbling something on a piece of paper before she could think of a response. "There," said Pacifa, and she handed Mr. Plainway the supposed address.

Daniel Plainway thanked the dark-haired woman and nodded to the others. He knew that he had stepped into a private complication and was thankful to have what he came for so that he could leave. "Miss Burnbrake," he said, then glanced at the piece of paper in his hand. There was no address on it at all, but only the words:

If you are at all gallant you will not leave until he is gone!

21. Beyond the Forest of Fallen Trees

"We can keep to the wooded trails," said Capital Gaines, "but from a distance the steam from these creatures might look like a train passing through. Probably the snow is hiding us."

The Percherons gave no evidence of tiring, but the vapor that rose from their backs, as they plowed the drifts, rose (when the snow and wind did not hinder it) to the height of a four-story building, well above many of the middle-aged pines and hardwoods ranking the banks of the brook that connected Oaks Pond with Lake George.

Twice Capital stopped the sleigh and, with a hammer, knocked off the snowballs that accumulated on the horses' hooves. More than once, one of these accretions flew off of its own accord and banged loudly against the dashboard of the sleigh.

Capital's passengers had only to appreciate his skill with the animals, squint through the increasing snow, and marvel at the wintry silence that occupied the woods and water. Mister Walton thought the husband and wife looked like a pleasant lithograph, snugly wrapped in their furs and blankets. He himself was a picture of wintry delight, with his bespectacled bright eyes and rosy cheeks; his hat was crammed down over his head as a precaution against losing it.

Though he had been impressed by the burglary at Mr. Thole's home, Mister Walton likened his emotions to a child playing hide-and-seek, when the fear of being found grows out of proportion to the game. It was not altogether an unpleasant sensation, but he didn't think it would remain so for very long. The hushed atmosphere, the hiss of falling snow, and the steady rush of their progress only heightened the sense of secrecy and the dread of discovery.

They reached the top of a particularly tall slope, and through the snow, as well as through a line of trees and over the heads of other pine and fir below them, they could see the frozen plain of Lake George. They had lost sight of the crow, though occasionally they could still hear a raucous call through the woods. Capital drew up the sleigh and considered their itinerary.

"There is someone on the lake," said Sundry. He was standing on his seat, hoping that his own long form was hidden by the trees before them.

"What's that?" Capital pulled a pair of binoculars from the pack at his feet and trained them toward Lake George. The falling snow between themselves and the lake made for an obscured view, but he was able to locate at least three dark figures some yards from the near shore. "They're not moving," he said after a bit. The others were straining their own necks. "Ice fishers, maybe," he suggested. He pointed to two hills in the east. "There's a small settlement at the foot of those mounds," he continued, "and there's a road along the opposite bank."

"But that's the other side of the lake," said Isabelle.

"No telling where the best fishing is," said the man.

"It's an odd day to be fishing, isn't it?" wondered Sundry, considering the rising storm and the persistent and heavy snow.

"It's an odd day to be out at all," said Capital with some humor. "They either are fishing or want us to think they are. There's probably no telling, unless we go up and ask them, so I suggest we take note and carry on."

"Do you know where we are going from here?" asked Frederick, who was feeling an increasing need for hurry. Capital had them moving, even as the clergyman spoke.

"We'll head almost directly towards Foster Hill and into a wood of fallen trees."

"Fallen trees?" said Sundry. "It's been cut?"

"Not at all, but you'll see for yourself."

The horses seemed to enjoy charging down the opposite slope, and the passengers felt as if they were almost falling. Mister Walton held his hat to his head and thought of tobogganing down the Eastern Promenade.

The "Forest of Fallen Trees" (as it has been identified in the relevant annals) was not a grove brought down by the hand of man but a curious testament to the speculative character of the natural world.

Forty years ago the country they traveled had been stripped of forest; many a house still stood and many a ship sailed that owed its physical existence, if not its soul, to the giants that once guarded these hills. But once the emptied land had been left to its own devices, the descendants of former pine and spruce, of oak and maple, and the soon-to-be-doomed elm, reoccupied the slopes deserted by lumbering armies, and the quicker growths of softwood ventured even into tracts where only bush and fern would safely grow. In peaty soil, amid stands of granite, the pines and their relatives increased their standard foot a year till the poor ground had not sufficient leverage against the wind and the weight of wood.

Throughout the year, but more commonly beneath the burden of snow and ice, the great trees crashed in the otherwise silent forest, as one by one they reached some unstable height, and though new trees continued to raise their skeletal shoots, this expanse of thin soil had become a graveyard of leaning trees, the massive networks of roots, round as wheels, lifted like the upturned feet of dead and decaying giants. Snow hung upon everything, and the dark horizontal trunks were thickly shrouded in white.

But this was not an unknown stretch of land, and hunters had cleared a way through this wreckage to the stalking grounds beyond. It was a little sobering to ride past this natural destruction, where the trail picked its way between the fallen trees, occasionally ducking beneath the raised trunk of the largest of them. Mister Walton was reminded of cities he had visited after the war in the former Confederacy, where shattered buildings and heaps of brick lay abandoned and barren.

While they crept around one of these deadfalls, Moxie bounded from the sleigh and charged through the drifts ahead of them. Sundry envied her a little, thinking it might be pleasant to stretch a leg and explore this strange place more closely. The knock from a woodpecker came from the other side of the dying wood.

As the trail avoided the largest of these obstacles, it led them away from the stream and back again several times, so that their weaving path might have been laid out by a drunkard. The brook rose with the land, and the horses heaved against the steepening slope where even the dead pines grew few and massive boulders and sharp verges of granite formed the primary crop. They came to a narrow plateau above which there rose an abrupt and craggy height, what would have been called a *tor* in the Scottish Highlands.

This eminence lay another ten or twenty yards above them and was impossible for the horses and sleigh to reach. Frederick was the first to throw off his covers and jump down; he was surprised by the depth of the snow and a little daunted to think it would be that much deeper on their return. Isabelle was peering into the sky as he handed her down, as if she might gauge the snow that had yet to fall, but at present they were blinded from the sky itself by an atmosphere filled with heavy flakes.

Moxie bounded alongside them, looking ready to play. Mister Walton had never seen a dog so at home in the snow.

Frederick took up a shovel that he had packed in the rear of the sleigh and shouldered a bag of instruments. Mister Walton and Sundry stood aside, waiting to help with anything that Capital deemed necessary to bring. The older man, however, simply threw the strap of his field glasses over his shoulder, then reached beneath a blanket at his feet and produced a rifle.

"You never know what might be in season," said Capital when he saw Mister Walton's wide-eyed expression.

Mister Walton himself had handled a similar firearm not many months before, and the memory of knocking a man down with a single shot was perhaps uppermost in his mind. Frederick and Isabelle too were a little taken aback by Capital's particular readiness.

"That's not a rabbit gun," said Sundry wryly.

"Swamping a man's house is a severe business," said Capital simply, referring to the burglary at Mr. Thole's and suggesting, at the same time, that those capable of such a deed might be capable of other things as well. "You've thought of that?" he asked, and there was every indication that he was enjoying himself.

"I appreciate your caution, Mr. Gaines," said Frederick.

"Capital!"

"I appreciate, Capital, your caution, but it seems—"

"Well?"

"I can't imagine—"

"Can't you!" Capital shrugged. "As you wish, Reverend," he said with a wink, and he slipped the rifle back beneath its blanket, then vaulted down from the sleigh like a young man. "Will your dog stay with the sleigh?"

"I think, yes," said Frederick.

"Then tell her to give a bark if anyone comes sniffing around."

Daniel's Story
(May–June 1891)

They were coming out of choir practice one Wednesday evening when Clayton Bond told Daniel Plainway about seeing "the Linnett girl and that odd brother of Asher Willum's down by Ten Mile River." Clayton was a good fellow, and the information was not offered as a piece of gossip; it was an observation, like seeing an owl by day, and he was reminded of it at that moment only by a passing reference to Nell's voice as he and Daniel were discussing the need for another alto in the choir. It was late in May, but the weather had been as warm and sultry as July; the spring had been mild and everything was early: the flowers, the leaves on the trees.

"Do you mean Jeram?" said Daniel. There were several odd Willum brothers in his estimation, but he knew the general consensus.

"I was out checking the west fence," said Clayton. He was searching his pockets for tobacco, his pipe idle in the corner of his mouth. "They were a little ways away, and I didn't know them at first. Sitting beneath one of those wild crab apples down by the river." A Linnett and a Willum in casual conversation were odd enough to merit note.

"They were probably both out walking," said Daniel, who wanted to make the least possible news out of this. "Their places are not so far apart, really."

"In one sense," said Clayton; then he added, "Jeram always seemed harmless enough."

The conversation turned elsewhere, but Clayton's last comment on the subject of Nell and Jeram held more meaning than was easily apparent. Daniel was known as a good friend to the Linnetts, and perhaps Clayton was absolving himself of his duty regarding this accidental knowledge by passing it over to his fellow tenor. Truthfully Daniel rather enjoyed the idea of a friendship between the two young people, Nell was well liked in the town and among her schoolmates but had never gotten very close to anyone her own age. Jeram, as far as he knew, had no friends at all. Then again, as he had said, they had probably simply been out walking separately and their meeting had been accidental.

The thought of Nell with Jeram Willum wasn't what disturbed Daniel; it was connecting Nell with the Willums at all, as if Jeram might carry a disease, the symptoms of which he had yet to show. That shadowy den on Trafton Pond, hidden even from the water by a crowded stand of willows, stood out in Daniel's mind like that unfortunate dog, straining at its chain—to be pitied perhaps but feared as well.

He took his own counsel, however—a good, lawyerlike decision—and put the concern from his mind. As it happened, something led his steps to the Linnett house the next afternoon, and he talked with old Ian about town affairs and the recent problems with Canada over fishing grounds. Eventually he asked after Nell, who had not met him at the front door.

"She'll be combing the fields," her grandfather said. "She does love walking the grounds after school. I don't believe this hogwash about young women staying indoors. If the sun and the fresh air are good for me and you, they will be good for her, I say."

Daniel nodded his agreement.

"It was the matter with her mother, I think. She faded from lack of enterprise, though I'd never say it to anyone else."

Daniel was pretty sure he had heard just those words from Ian Linnett before, and among other people than himself.

> If a body meets a body,
> Coming through the rye . . .

The song followed Daniel home that afternoon, and why wouldn't someone occasionally meet another body if one frequented the fields and forests? He himself had hailed another fisherman on the opposite bank of what he had considered a secluded pool and been warned of the approach of yet another by the sound of a snapping twig in a hushed autumn wood.

That Sunday, however, before dinner Nell announced that a friend was joining them, and no one was any more startled than Daniel Plainway when the knock came at the front door and Nell escorted Jeram Willum into the parlor. The dominoes of Daniel's imaginative constructions began to fall, no more so than when Ian Linnett greeted the boy with a friendly handshake and he and Dora accepted Jeram's presence with the very soul of graciousness. It appeared as if the old man and the great-aunt had known more about this friendship than Daniel could ever have supposed.

Dinner was the scene of further cordiality, and Nell beamed with pleasure, even as Jeram came some distance out of his strange shell and ventured an opinion or two about matters under conversation. He carried himself surprisingly well at the semiformal affair that was the Linnetts' Sunday dinner, primarily, Daniel suspicioned, because of Nell's careful tutoring; she did in fact watch him with both the nervousness and pride of a teacher.

Jeram was not made to feel that he must hurry after their meal, but when an appropriate amount of time had been spent in the parlor, he complimented the cook, thanked his hosts with great feeling, and took his leave. Ian himself saw the boy out.

But when they returned to the parlor, Daniel sensed a great wind let out of the old man, and Daniel's own muscles tensed with sudden apprehension. Ian and Dora, Nell and Daniel had only settled themselves again when the old man spoke up, quietly and (by the tone of his voice) kindly.

"You will not of course invite that boy again."

Nell was confused, at first, then stunned as the import of Ian's words struck home. Daniel considered his knees, hardly daring to glance at either the old man or the seventeen-year-old girl.

"Grandfather?" she said.

"My dear," said the old man, "it is very kind of you, and young Jeram seems like a nice enough lad, for a Willum. But he is a Willum, and if he does not behave like an animal, he is yet kin to those who do."

"It was not kind of me at all!" said Nell with more vexation than Daniel had ever heard in her voice. "He is my friend."

"Yes," said Ian, "and that does raise another difficulty." He raised his own eyes to hers for the first time since they returned to the parlor. "Any friendship between yourself and this boy would indicate that you have spent time together before today."

Nell straightened in her chair, not knowing what to make of Ian's tone. "We have met a time or so, walking—"

Ian's gaze did not break, nor did his expression alter a whit.

"I have been helping him with his reading," she continued. "I lent him a book or two."

"He's not the sort of boy I would have for you, Nell," said the old man.

"Because his last name is Willum?"

"Yes, and other things."

The girl was clearly angry now, and Daniel hated to glimpse such emotion in her eyes or hear it in her voice as she spoke to the old man.

"He is a very fine person," she said. She was shaking, fighting back tears. Then her control faltered, and she rose from her chair.

"You will stay with us or go to your room," said the old man flatly.

Daniel could almost hear her swallow as she paused to consider this choice. He *was shamed for her humiliation and looked down at his knees again. Then she was gone, and they heard her footsteps on the stairs.*

Dora let out an exclamation of astonishment.

"Thank you for standing by me in that, Daniel," said Ian Linnett.

"I beg your pardon?" said the lawyer.

The old man nodded to Daniel. "For adding your tacit support."

A maxim returned to Daniel: The heighth of presumption is the heighth of ignorance. *He found himself standing, as if he were in court.*

"Ian," he said, "I was quiet out of respect to both you and Nell and with the understanding that I was privy to a private concern and therefore had nothing to say. But if you ask me to take a side in this issue, some thought on the matter may not bring me down where you are standing, and if Nell thinks as you that I support your banning, out of hand, Jeram Willum from her company, then I would ask for the opportunity to disabuse her of the notion." Though he cared deeply for Ian Linnett, Daniel was yet a little daunted by the old man, and it took some nerve to pronounce these thoughts when he had hardly disagreed with the man in eighteen years.

"And you would allow a child in your care to mix with the Willums?" asked Ian.

"To befriend Jeram *Willum, not the entire clan," returned Daniel quietly. "I have known villains to rise from good families and good from bad."*

"It's true," conceded Linnett, his great white head nodding, "given some generations, there might be Willums of worth, and given the opportunity, Jeram might be the seed from which such a tree could eventually bear fruit."

"I would judge the boy on his own merits, rather than those of his ancestors or his descendants."

"I beg your pardon if my presumption has offended you," said the old man simply, now looking away himself, "and also if I don't see you out this afternoon, Daniel."

Daniel gave a short bow, then nodded to Dora, who had remained silent and troubled throughout the preceding scene. In the hall he found his hat and was almost out the front door when he glanced up the front stairs. On the top step sat Nell, in neither the parlor nor her room, and it was the first instance, he thought, that he had ever seen her disobey her grandfather.

There were tears on her face and an unreadable expression, but when Daniel turned and looked up at Nell, she gave him a frail smile and mouthed the words Thank you.

He did not know whom he had betrayed in the last few minutes. What if the whole town had taken an interest in the boy? *he wondered.* What if I had? *He tried to smile back at Nell; then with a wave he left.*

The following Saturday, when Daniel was stepping out of the post office and general store, Jeram's wild brother Asher came riding through town on a handsome brown mare he had acquired by Lord only knows what means. Daniel took note immediately that someone in dress and petticoats was riding tandem behind the rake and stood gaping for some minutes after they had trotted by and he had seen Nell Linnett bouncing behind Asher with her arms about his middle.

22. Stones in the Lake

Roger Noble's voice was cold and unwelcome after a brief silence in the parlor. "If you catch the next train," he said to Daniel Plainway, "you might find the Moosepath League by this evening."

From the moment he first saw Roger Noble, Daniel had felt a quiet dislike for the man. It was obvious that Noble had caused Miss Burnbrake distress, which was reason enough, but now his otherwise polite suggestion was couched in such ruthless tones and the use of the Moosepath League's name was pronounced so flippantly and with such disrespect (Daniel had come to like these men though he had yet to meet them) that the lawyer felt his first impression of Noble unfavorably confirmed.

Daniel contemplated the scrawled note in his hand. He looked up, his expression difficult to read, and said, "I was just thinking that I *haven't* had any lunch today."

"We'll call down," said Pacifa with a great show of pleasure.

"They serve a very nice meal in the dining car," said Noble.

"But they do not provide such lovely company," replied Daniel. Such blatant flattery was not natural to him, but he nearly pulled it off without blushing.

"We're sorry you have to leave," said Pacifa to Noble in a very offhanded manner.

"I said nothing about leaving," said Noble without taking his eyes from the other man. His enviable carriage stiffened. He was a hand and a half taller than Daniel and quite willing to wield his height in belligerent meetings with other male animals.

Daniel's expression remained mild, his own posture unmoving. Pacifa stood between them, one dark eyebrow raised. Charlotte stared at the carpet; her face was flushed with shame. Noble's glance went from Daniel's almost humorous look to the dark woman's quizzical eyebrow to Charlotte.

"Is that your coat?" asked Pacifa.

On his way across the room, Noble deliberately walked toward Daniel, who only stepped aside, and if Noble could have seen who looked foolish and who looked wise at this juncture, he might not have worn such a rigid smile when he snatched up his coat and marched to the door. "Good-bye," he said in a growl before stepping into the hall; then below his breath he said, "I *will* be back." He did not quite slam the door behind him.

Now that the imbroglio was done, Daniel looked down at his hands and said, "I beg your pardon."

"Good heavens!" said Pacifa, who had not entirely lost her humor.

"I must beg *your* pardon, Mr. Plainway," said Charlotte. "I am sorry and deeply ashamed for having relied on your gentlemanly nature."

"Quite the contrary, Miss Burnbrake," said Daniel, with the lightest bow of his head. "I am grateful if I have been of any service."

"Forgive me if I retire now," said Charlotte, and unable to look the man in the eye, she hurried through the alcove to her room.

Daniel was profoundly affected by what had transpired these past minutes (hardly five had passed since he first stepped into the parlor of the apartment), and he looked distressed when he turned back to Pacifa. "If there is anything else I can do," he said.

"You are very dear," she said sincerely. She scrambled through the papers on the table and with a sound of discovery found the address that Daniel had first requested. "I wish I could welcome you to lunch, after all, Mr. Plainway, but—" She gestured toward the inner rooms.

"Of course," he said. "Please don't let me keep you." He did stop at the door, however, and spoke without exactly looking at Pacifa. "I hope Miss Burnbrake will feel better soon."

"I shall tell her." Pacifa let the man shut the door himself, and after a moment in which to take a breath, she bustled into the alcove and rapped on Charlotte's door.

"Charlotte, dear," she said, knocking again, and at a soft note from within, she opened the chamber door. The windows were heavily curtained, and in the shadows it was difficult to tell Charlotte's clothes from the bedcovers. Pacifa thought she would find her friend crying, but when she sat at the edge of the bed, Charlotte was only lying on her side with a crumpled handkerchief in one hand.

"Why does he persecute me?" said Charlotte.

"He's gone," said Pacifa.

"And in front of a stranger—"

"Be glad Mr. Plainway came when he did."

"What did you write on that note?" asked Charlotte.

Pacifa thought that curiosity was a healthy signal.

"Oh, dear!" said Charlotte when Pacifa explained.

"He thought nothing of it," assured Pacifa.

"How could he not?"

"It is the difference between a chivalrous man and your cousin."

Charlotte sat up and began to fold her handkerchief when she realized that she had a crumpled piece of paper in her hand. It was the telegram from Uncle Ezra, warning her that her cousin had abandoned him and that she should follow her uncle to Hallowell.

"I'll have to leave immediately," said Charlotte.

"I was afraid you would say that," Pacifa's expression mitigated her disappointment with a soft smile.

"Uncle will be worried to death. Perhaps you would send him a wire that I'm coming."

"Of course. I'll help you get your things together. I can't come with you, unfortunately."

Charlotte nodded sadly. "He hasn't the smallest notion what he has done and what pleasure he has spoiled, even by the most indirect means."

"You might find the Moosepath League's company more agreeable than mine."

"I hope everything is well with them," said Charlotte when she thought of this. "That gentleman seemed to think it urgent that he find their Mister Walton."

Descending the broad stairs of the City Hotel, Daniel cast his eye about the foyer for the figure of Roger Noble. He had half expected the man to be waiting for him and was a little relieved to reach the door without a confrontation. Outside, the snow had accumulated so that traffic in the streets had slowed; the sidewalks were nearly empty.

The last few hours had been something of an odyssey for Daniel; in fact the last week had taken him to many unexpected places. The previous night he had spent pleasantly with Sheriff Piper and his family in Wiscasset, and this morning he was on the first train south. It was snowing with real intent by the time he arrived in Portland. He hired a carriage to take him to the Newspaper Exchange, where he found Editor Corbell of the *Eastern Argus*, working in his office within a smoky haze of his own making.

Sheriff Piper had shown Daniel several articles concerning the little boy that had appeared in the *Argus*, written by a competent wordsmith named Peter Mall. Editor Corbell was evasive, even cagey, when Daniel told him he would like to meet the writer. "You want to talk to Mister Walton," is what Corbell said several times during the course of their conversation, puffing furiously at his cigar, and when Daniel realized that—for whatever reason—he was not going to meet this Peter Mall, he asked where he might find Mister Walton, whose reputation had already reached an almost legendary peak by way of the praise heaped upon him by Sheriff Piper.

It was nearing noon when Daniel arrived at Spruce Street and the home of Tobias Walton. The estate's elderly retainer Mr. Baffin expressed regret that his employer was not at home but gave Daniel the address of Matthew Ephram, charter member of the Moosepath League. At this address Daniel was given the address to Christopher Eagleton's apartment, and he had almost resigned himself to visiting the home of every person ever involved with this situation when the man at Eagleton's informed him that the entire club was traveling with a Mr. Burnbrake, who had—at least till this morning—taken residence at the City Hotel.

Christopher Eagleton must have heaped some praise upon Mr. Burnbrake's niece, and the servant at Eagleton's was quick to pass on these good words. The man understood that the niece had been left behind, and Daniel hardly hoped that he was a little closer to finding where everyone had got to.

"I'm glad I left my bags at the station," he said to himself as he left the hotel. He stepped out into the storm, turning the collar of his coat against the wind that drove the snow eastward down the street. He stopped again on the sidewalk and peered up at the second-story windows. The troubled face of Charlotte Burnbrake had affected him more than he had realized.

Charlotte dreaded even opening the door to the hall, she was so terrified of finding Noble waiting for her.

"Come," said Pacifa, "it is better if we're out among people." They found a man to help them with Charlotte's bags and felt a little safer as he escorted them to the foyer, where he excused himself and went out onto the stormy sidewalk to find a cab.

The scene from their carriage window was almost purely white, and Charlotte felt the storm pressing in on her. The closer they got to the station, the more bitterly hurt she was about it all, the absolute injustice. She and Pacifa said almost nothing till they had climbed from the carriage and paid the driver.

The train was giving one of its final whistles before leaving the station. "You take care," said the cabdriver, adding, "This'll be the last train out till the plow comes through."

Pacifa walked her friend to the nearest car. Charlotte tried to apologize again, but Pacifa held a hand to her mouth. "We'll get together soon," said Pacifa, and she shushed Charlotte up the steps.

Charlotte sat by a window and looked for Pacifa, but the day was dimming, and the snow—that which was falling and that which had fallen but was now drifting—blinded her view; the station house was hardly more than a shadow. Charlotte sat back in her seat and glanced at the man on the other side of the aisle. He was reading a newspaper, and his brown hat sat in the otherwise empty seat beside him. She hadn't been looking at people when she was seating herself, and she was a little startled by him.

As for the man, his expression was as mild as ever, and he did not press her with familiarity by looking directly at her when he spoke.

"Miss Burnbrake," said Daniel Plainway.

23. Speech at Midnight

Past Brunswick conversation lagged and after announcing the time, tide, and weather at regular intervals, Ephram, Eagleton, and Thump looked to their newspapers, hoping to glean some item of interest for their new acquaintances but, most important, for Mr. Burnbrake, who was so concerned about the disappearance of his nephew and the well-being of his niece. The snow had increased so that there was very little to see beyond the windows of the train.

It was Thump who found in his chosen organ a column of some curiosity and conveyed its gist for the edification of them all, thus prompting an anecdote of decided curiosity from another party altogether. "I do recall some discussion concerning the mysteries of Christmastide at the Shipswood the other night," he said, as preamble to his reading.

"I too seem to remember," agreed Eagleton.

"What have you there, Thump?" wondered Ephram, who looked forward to some instructive thoughts from his friend.

"It says here," said Thump, "that *'deep and manifold are the secrets of the Yuletide, not the least being that deed of nativity that is the feature of our celebration in this season. But man's desire for the enigmatic and his fanciful penchant for elaborating even so extraordinary a tale have led to the fabrication of many a wild idea. This writer takes, for example, the long-declared belief that on the night of the winter solstice, the spirits of the dead are permitted to roam their former environs.'*"

"I never knew it!" said Eagleton, searching his pockets for his journal.

"The day of Doubting Thomas," said Brink helpfully.

"Is it?" said Ephram.

"'*St. Thomas gray, St. Thomas gray,*'" quoted Brink, "'*The longest night and the shortest day.*' My grandfather always brought his Christmas tree in on the twenty-first because it made the ghosts happy for some reason."

"Did it?" said Ephram.

"Oh, I am sure it did."

"Spirits can be very troublesome this time of year," said Waverley.

"Can they?" said Ephram.

"I can't tell you how often spirits have kept me up at night so that my head pounds fearfully the next morning."

"That's all year round," said Durwood.

"Oh, so it is."

This was yet more cryptic talk from the Dash-It-All Boys, and Thump was encouraged by Ephram and Eagleton to continue his reading.

"'*Strangest of all,*'" he did read, "'*and yet surely more prevalent still, is the almost universal conviction in the mystic powers of Christmas Eve itself, when at midnight the creatures of nature are said to be granted the fleeting gift of speech.*'"

"Why, that very thing was discussed at the Shipswood!" exclaimed Ephram.

"The writer here finds it ridiculous," said Thump, who, reading further, was a little disappointed with the drift of the column.

"The notion seems harmless enough," said Eagleton.

"I would have thought," said Thump. "But this fellow insists that it has a deleterious effect upon our attentions to the season."

"Good heavens!" said Ephram.

"'*Pagan superstition,*' he says."

"If he had been with me one midnight on Christmas Eve, some years back," came a new voice to the conversation, "he would think twice before dismissing the theory, I can promise you right now."

Thump turned to look at a man who sat across the aisle and behind him by one seat. Already facing in the stranger's direction, Eagleton and Ephram simply leaned a little toward the aisle. Mr. Burnbrake, who sat beside Thump, cocked an ear but did not turn around, and the membership of the Dash-It-All Boys gave various interpretations of a raised eyebrow or a puzzled frown.

He was a very trim-looking man who might have been seventy, or he might have been eighty. (He was eighty-six.) He wore a close-cropped beard and fine mustaches of white, and his pate gleamed through thinning hair. When he turned sideways in his seat, the better to address the members of the two clubs and Mr. Burnbrake, they were apprised of a pair of bright blue eyes, wrapped in crow's-feet and peering from a pair of spectacles.

"He would think twice, I promise you," the man said again. "Gentlemen," he added, in greeting. "I beg your pardon, but I couldn't help hearing the tendency of your conversation."

"Not at all," said Eagleton.

Durwood had not raised himself much above a recumbent position for several miles and did not bother himself even now, but spoke without actually seeing the other man. "Are you saying, sir, that you have heard the animals speak at midnight?"

"I am saying that I heard one animal speak at midnight," returned the man, "Christmas Eve, eighteen seventy-nine."

"You interest me greatly," said Durwood.

"The tale has some worth, I think, no matter what some pencil pusher might have you believe." The older fellow gave a nod to himself and looked ready to turn back in his seat.

"We would certainly like to hear it!" said Thump.

"Oh, it is an old story," said the man, and though he dismissed the thought with a wave of a hand, he was smiling.

"The older the better! Wouldn't you say, Eagleton?" said Thump.

"I think it is safe to say," said that worthy. "Wouldn't you say, Ephram?"

"I was about to say that very thing," said the third Moosepathian.

The old man laughed. "I shall not make a long tale of it," he said, "though it has room for a wrecked ship, a shank of sheep, and wrong-heeled boots. *And* there's a dog, several cats, a shipload of rats, and a blue jay. How far are you going?"

"We are getting off at Hallowell, sir," said Thump.

"Are you, really? Why, that's my destination, so let me tell it."

As the man commenced his tale, even the Dash-It-All Boys managed to straighten their postures so that they might have a better look at him. He looked up at the ceiling of the car and thought for a moment before speaking again. (Ephram, Eagleton, and Thump looked up with him.)

"What did I say? Eighteen seventy-nine? Yes, that was it. Eighteen seventy-nine. I was taking it a little easy by then, living down Georgetown way on a moderate height of land overlooking the ocean on the one side and Sagadahoc Bay on the other. I had bought a little place and the sheep that came with it sight unseen from a man named Musterhag who'd taken a sudden fear of water and went, the last I heard, into the Arizona Territory, where he met and fell in love with the daughter of a French count or something and eventually set up household with her in Saskatchewan."

"And that's the *last* you heard of him?" wondered Waverley.

"I had a horse," continued the storyteller without pause, "that would sit down when you told him to stand, so when I was on my way to Georgetown to take possession of my new abode and two men with shotguns accosted me and ordered *me* to stand, the horse sat down, and any retreat was summarily ended before it began. Being the philanthropic sort, the highwayman relieved me of that particular animal, and I was left on foot.

"Now this did not seem an auspicious beginning for a new endeavor, but I was philosophical and not entirely unpleased when it turned out that being on foot meant that I was able to wander in search of a distressed bird I caught wind of on the Stage Road within sight of Flying Point in Arrowsic. On the far side of a fold in the field, overlooking the Sasanoa, there was a thicket of alders, where I found a half-grown blue jay.

"I'd had a crow once, as a youngster, and a macaw too, from the West Indies, not to mention a turkey that hid beneath my bed come every Thanksgiving, and so I thought nothing of taking up the little mite and carrying him in my coat pocket. I named him Mr. Thicket.

"I hadn't a cent on me to eat by, but a fellow by the name of Carny Shalleck gave me a ride in his buckboard, the last mile or two, and when he heard my tale, he lent me some fish, which amounted to my first meal in my new home.

"It was a handsome little white two-room house with red trim, standing by itself on a bit of granite overlooking the point of land before it. Below the house was a small shack where the sheep stayed in bad weather, though most days they roamed the rocky soil in search of feed. Mr. Thicket took occupation of the windowsill above the sink when he was indoors and the peak of the house when he was without, and out or in he liked nothing better than to holler and screech every morning till I was up and scrounging something special for him to eat.

"For myself, however, a little more than mutton seemed in order before too many weeks passed, and I was fortunate enough to take on with Carny Shalleck, who lobstered for a few dollars in his pocket till August and line fished for his own pot and his own amazement when the weather permitted thereafter. First thing in the morning I would hike down to the beach and Carny would bring in his dory, and we would go out for the day, which made for a pretty good life as Carny was practiced at both silence and fine storytelling by turns; you never got too weary of either.

"Now my shoes had not been thick when I began my trip to Georgetown, and the unexpected distance I had ridden shank's mare had worn them to a considerable nothing, so that I repaired to the local bootmaker as soon as I had a few extra coins in my pocket. Feeling a little penurious, however, I accepted a pair of boots from the man with the heels on wrong.

His son had made them but wedged the heels the wrong way and simply turned them back to and nailed them, the result of which was that I made a strange print, with the toe of my boot pointing in one direction and the heel indicating the direct opposite. I kind of liked them.

"Mr. Thicket was with me when I got the boots, flying about, that is, and grazing the top of my head or landing briefly on my shoulder whenever he thought I had forgotten him. When we returned to the slopes that overlook the rocks and shore, I was startled by the sight of a four-masted schooner foundering on the wrong side of Outer Head. Two or three boats were already meeting her in case she required abandoning, which she quickly did, and I clambered down the cliffy banks to see how I could help.

"I knew the ship was doomed when a school of tiny heads appeared between her and the shore. It is a strange sight when rats abandon a ship, and I was astonished, though I had been to sea, how many of these brutes paddled their way onto the little spit of sand where I stood. It is some eerie too when a swarm of these creatures reach the shore and mow by you like a herd of tiny buffalo, but they were past me and disappeared into the cliffside and the brush above before I had much time to think about it."

This image was proof to some shivers among the old fellow's listeners, and Thump in particular looked wide-eyed and astonished to think of such an army of rats swimming to shore.

"No one was lost in the wreck, and the ship itself was recovered soon after, which is a story itself, but I went home with my wrong-heeled boots and Mr. Thicket swooping over my head and thought the day had provided something interesting.

"I had not been long in my new abode before I noticed that a small herd of cats wandered by on most mornings, at about eight o'clock, like they were going to work, and I was careful about them around the house with Mr. Thicket nearby. I thought perhaps they were finding sport among the new rats in the neighborhood. There was also another old fellow, by the name of Hughie Borkhum, who had a large dog, and I seldom actually met the man, though I did see him once or twice, from my kitchen window, as he and the dog walked the short stretch of sand below my house.

"I rarely saw them, however, as they were not such early risers, and I was an hour or two out with Carny before Hughie made his rounds with his great dog.

"It was about this time that some odd things began to happen—that is, a run of bad luck. My sheep got further afield, and once or twice I was obliged to search them out. They knocked down a side of their shack one night, and I grew conscious that the rats were inhabiting the height of land with me and my sheep and Mr. Thicket with impunity. *What were the cats doing?* I wondered.

"Now there are several creatures that follow man about the globe—the flea, the bedbug, the mosquito—but none so daunting in its craftiness, or so difficult to be rid of, as the rat that populates every wharf and ship's hold and wanders the corners of the earth as well as we do. If you have ever tried to dominate a piece of acreage or a cellar over the ambitions of a single one of these creatures, you will know that it takes some doing to catch or kill them. I was facing, then, an entire ship's company of rats *and* whatever recent offspring they were busy raising, and it became all-out war that I must eventually lose, without the aid of the neighborhood cats.

"And then my well, which was spring-fed, dried up, and I searched out the source of the water on a height above me; the bank on the opposite side had broken away, and the spring was now flowing down the further slope. I tried to redirect the water back toward my home, but my engineering skills and a shovel were not up to the task. Any headway I made was soon knocked down by the force of the stream itself or the next rain.

"That was the late fall, and it did rain pretty hard through November, and I set up a cistern. Carny didn't like the weather much, so we never got out for a month or so, and I had leave to think on the bad run of luck I was experiencing. I lived on mutton and rain till winter came.

"When the weather got bad, Carny would come up and play cards with me and we would talk about what was occurring in the neighborhood: a new set of twins, a boat lost in a storm, Hughie Borkhum, who was convinced that some sort of water troll or selkie had been frequenting the beach. He'd even gone so far as to plant a cross on the dunes above the sand, and as sign of the creature had not returned, Hughie considered the measure successful.

"Winter set in with due earnestness, and I hadn't looked toward a snowy season with so little promise since I had a farm half wrecked up in Shirley Mills—well, come to think of it, that was a Christmas Eve as well . . ."

The man scratched at his beard, thought of something, and fished through his pockets till he found a pipe and some tobacco. There was not another word heard in the car, people were so anxious to hear the rest of his tale, but the wind howled outside the car, and the snow sprayed the windows.

When he had the pipe lit and puffed a few billows of smoke, the old fellow took stock of where he had left off and said, "Yes, Christmas came apace—all *too* quickly, for my money, since I knew how slow the rest of the winter would seem. I have often thought they should move Christmas to February, at least around these parts, when a body needs real distraction.

"Some of the neighbors came around on the day before Christmas, and there was a little cheer beyond the strict tenets of law, I am sure, but everything was fat and jovial, and I met several people I had only heard of before then. Everyone was glad to visit with one another, for the winter could be a long and lonely affair, there being some distance yet between houses outside the village.

"But I was near wore out with talk and a drop here and a drop there by the time the yule log was blazing and Mr. Thicket and I were dozing before the hearth. I must have fallen right to sleep after Carny Shalleck up and left, for I don't remember much but a strange dream or two. I had a good deal on my mind in those days, for the rats had offered to join our little household and the battle had grown accordingly. I had even gotten myself a cat, along with an added nervousness for Mr. Thicket, but the great orange tom seemed disinclined to do his duty and slept beneath my chair, where he thought the rats would be least likely to bother him.

"Don't imagine that I was living with the creatures running over me at night or scampering across the floor, but they were about, skittering in the walls and gnawing at the floor timbers. My dreams that night were filled with them, and nagging me as well was the sense that something indeed had brought me ill luck: the rats, the sheep ranging too far, the broken wall in the shack, the dried-up well.

"Then came a voice, saying, 'It's your boots! It's your boots!'

"I woke with a start. I had no idea anyone was in the house with me, and I nearly tipped my chair into the fire as I leaped to my feet. The room was dark, save for the lowering fire, and I scanned about to see who had spoken.

"'It's your boots!' came the voice again, and it sang out with an odd, somehow familiar pitch.

"'What's my boots?' I asked, and lifted one foot then another to glance at them, though my feet were but shadows in the dark room. 'Who's talking?'"

"'Quick, it's midnight!' came the voice, and I located it with enough accuracy to be pretty sure that Mr. Thicket, sitting on the mantel, was speaking to me.

"You can imagine that I pinched myself pretty hard, and I did. But Mr. Thicket cocked his head, gave a wink, and said again, 'It's your boots, Ish!'

"'My boots?' I said. 'Are they bad luck then?'

"'Hughie haunts the beach with his dog, and the cats don't come,' said Mr. Thicket, and then he let out a more normal sort of screech for a blue jay and I knew that the minute of midnight was over."

The fellow's pipe had gone out. Hardly stirring himself from his languid position, Brink was able to offer the man a lighted match.

"Thank you," said the white-bearded fellow.

"Had Hughie Borkhum been seeing your footprints on the beach?" asked Mr. Burnbrake.

"He had indeed," said the man. "And he was alarmed to see something shod so waywardly as to have the toe pointing in one direction and the heel in another. It didn't help that my prints always came down off the dunes and disappeared into the water, where Carny picked me up in his dory. Of course the waves would wash away the footprints nearer the water as well as the keel sign of the boat.

"So Hughie was haunting the beach for hours at a time with his great dog, and his dog would chase after the cats when they came, so they quit coming and simply took up visiting someone's fish shack on the other side of the point. The rats were left more or less unhindered, and as their population increased, they frightened the sheep and ate their feed. The sheep of course knocked down a wall of the shack to get away from them one night and began, as is understandable, to range further for something sweet. Nothing was sweeter than the ground surrounding the head of the spring, but with the grass and plants grazed down, a good rain was all the further bank needed to wash out and redirect the water away from my well!"

The storyteller looked up to find one of his listeners scratching away into a book. The mention of the cross upon the beach had reminded Eagleton of the cross he wore beneath his shirt, and he was torn between recording the story that was presently being yarned and recounting the experience with the blasphemous cabdriver and the French lady before he lost the sense of urgency and all the details.

"I never did disabuse Hughie Borkhum of his notions regarding the sea troll, he was that pleased with driving the creature off with his cross in the dunes. I enticed the cats back with a trail of bait, and it was not long before the rats had packed their things and floated themselves out to the wrecked ship, just as she was being raised. During the winter I was able to shore up the opposite bank of the spring, and my well filled up again."

There was half a minute's silence then as the Moosepathians and the Dashians and Mr. Burnbrake digested it all.

"The bird spoke," said Thump quietly, trying to imagine such a thing.

"What happened to him?" asked Waverley.

"Mr. Thicket? He has passed on to his reward." The old man nodded, but barely, and looked into his pipe as if something interesting were there.

"And did you ever hear him speak again?" wondered Mr. Burnbrake.

"I never did. I don't know if it was considered good form to actually communicate with me, but we were good friends, and it *had* been a rough season. You can imagine, though, that I have stayed up past midnight most Christmas Eves since."

"St. Nicholas won't come by if you're awake," assured Durwood.

"That's another story," said the fellow, and he nodded softly again.

"I am sorry I didn't get that fellow's name," said Eagleton later in the day. "I know the name of the bird, but not the man." They had gotten off at Hallowell and bid the storyteller a good day, then hired a sleigh to the Worster House. The snow had not let up, and they wondered that the driver could find his way. Eagleton wished he had a name to attach with the story of the talking jay, and in his concern he once again forgot the chain around his neck and the talisman that depended from it.

24. The Tor

The way up the side of the tor was steep and treacherous, flanked by ledges that rose in a circle about the conical hill like giant steps, and bristling with low brush and scrub trees. Two or three of these ledges they used as goals in their climb, and Sundry, who took the lead, helped the others as they came up behind. They were a fit party: Capital was a common haunt in the woods, and Frederick and Isabelle were plainly used to physical exertion of this sort; even Mister Walton, despite his portly figure, proved to have strong legs and good lungs. While the others caught him up, Sundry looked below them, where Moxie sat dutifully beside the horses, and behind them in the woods, where silence and snow reigned.

At the very last bit of ledge before the top, Mister Walton caught Sundry frowning and asked what was the matter. Sundry only shook his head and turned his face to the last length of their climb, but he had lost sight of Moxie and thought she had left her post.

The head of the tor was surrounded by boulders and lengths of granite unfixed from their natural strata by the work of ancient glaciers.

"Or perhaps the labor of ancient men," proposed Frederick when they were gathered there. The peak of the tor was almost level for a diameter of thirty feet or so, and the battlementlike rocks at its perimeter did have the look of human motive the more they considered them.

"This is Council Hill," said Capital.

They looked out over the woods to the west, where long hills, faded behind a veil of snow, seemed to hover like shadows against the sky. The wind blew harder at this elevation, and they squinted into the teeth of it. The flutter of something black interpolated between white branches; snow flew as a limb danced with sudden weight and their friend the crow peered at them.

Sundry was moving with Frederick and Isabelle through the center of the little plateau toward a great head of rock overhanging the northeastern corner of the tor. Frederick let out a long breath, something between a sigh and a gasp of discovery. His sharp and educated eyes had caught sight of something that Sundry missed till he drew closer to the boulder. Isabelle stepped up with her husband, and the two made an affecting picture, handsome and handsomely dressed, she with both hands upon his arm and the snow all about them and falling upon their collars and hats.

Standing behind the Covingtons, as Frederick brushed at the granite, the others could see upon the face of the rock a column of odd striations that rose to the level of about seven feet and dropped below the mantle of snow. It was the artifact of Mr. Thole's photographs, though a good deal more impressive in the live rock. The markings were regular and regularly distanced from one another, each about nine or ten inches long with three or four in each row.

"It *must* be a human hand has made this," said Mister Walton. Indeed, the entire place had the aura of human refinement, and they could believe that this had long (and long ago) been a place of messages and meetings, of tribal decisions and intertribal conclaves.

"Is it Indian?" wondered Sundry.

"As far as I can tell, it isn't," said Frederick. "The aboriginal people had no writing as such, though there is some evidence of pictographs. This bears resemblance to none of it."

"And here is your *ox*, over to the side," remarked Sundry. He leaned nearer to the boulder and touched the design that had been scratched into the rock face a foot or so away from the other figures.

"I can't help wondering if it isn't something separate from the runes," said Frederick, "if they are runes."

Mister Walton adjusted his spectacles and peered at the form in question. The figure was very simple, merely two rays of an angle, both intersected by a single line about a third of the way from their joining. He turned his gaze back to the runes, as he had already begun to think of them. "Are they Viking?" he asked.

"If I could make them say something, they might be," said Frederick. "Let's clear the snow away, so I can examine the entire stone. Mr. Thole might have missed something." Covington was in his element now, serving out instructions like an officer. "Perhaps you wouldn't mind scouring the other rocks along the perimeter for more of these figures." He rummaged through his instrument bag for a magnifying glass, unaware that his companions had frozen in their tracks. The crow took off with a sudden startling cry.

Sundry reached down and gripped Frederick's arm meaningfully, and the clergyman looked up and beyond the others to see a stranger standing on one of the boulders at the southwestern corner of the tor. The man held a rifle, relaxed but ready and pointed in their general direction. He was well dressed for the weather and the snow formed a frosting upon his great blond beard.

"Good afternoon, sir," said Capital as if they had met on a city street.

"Stay together, where you are," said the man, his voice deep, but sounding distant through the snow and the current of wind upon the tor. He was sizing them up, frowning as if something were amiss. He threw the quickest glance behind him, then pointed his rifle into the air and fired a single shot.

Those gathered below the inclined boulder started with the report, and the echoes had hardly returned from the western hills when a flash of black and white leaped up behind the man and dragged him backward over the boulder. There was the sound of a human cry and the angry snarl of a dog even as Sundry charged across the tor. Then another shot split the air beyond the rock wall, and Sundry was scrambling over the point where the stranger had disappeared.

On the ledge below, possibly a ten-foot drop, the blond-bearded man was curled into a protective ball as Moxie struggled and snarled with his rifle arm. Sundry vaulted down to the ledge, missing the man but driving himself into the snow up to his knees.

The man with the rifle was attempting to get his free hand back beneath the trigger guard, but he had lost his glove and feared to put his unprotected flesh within reach of the dog's teeth. Sundry had seldom seen such terror, and once he had struggled out of the deep snow, he very benevolently put the blond man's fears to a temporary rest with a single sharp blow to the side of the head.

Moxie left off the limp arm, then let out another angry growl. The snow beside her erupted on the heel of a third gunshot, and Sundry saw over his shoulder a second figure on a slightly higher ledge some twenty feet away on the western side of the tor. The dog would have charged, leaping over the gulf between, but Sundry threw himself at the animal and shoved her some yards down the steep slope. He could hear another round being levered into the rifle and was using his momentum to follow Moxie down the hill when a fourth explosion came from above.

There was a shout of pain and anger, and Sundry looked up from his stomach. The men on the ledges were blocked from his view, but the head and shoulders of Capital Gaines were plain to be seen at the top of the slope.

"That was not a miss, hitting your rifle," Capital was saying in a very clear and steady voice.

Sundry lifted himself up from the snow and could see that the old man was gripping a long-barreled pistol. Other heads, most noticeably that of Mister Walton, appeared behind Capital, looking for signs of Sundry and the dog. *Get down!* Sundry wanted to say, but his voice seemed unable to respond. *There might be more of them!*

Frederick was following Sundry's path over the boulder, and Capital waved the others back.

"Sundry!" called Mister Walton. "Sundry!"

"I'm healthy, Mister Walton!" called the young man, finding his voice. Moxie had righted herself and was scrambling back up the slope, but Sundry reached out and got an arm around her middle. "Easy, girl, easy," he repeated, along with "Good girl! Good girl!" He found terrific comfort in burying his face in the fur behind her ears.

Capital was half climbing, half sliding down the path they had ascended, hardly taking his eyes or the intention of his pistol from the second man. When Sundry had clambered back up the slope, with Moxie alongside him, he could see the second stranger leaning against the rock wall above the other ledge. There was blood on his face and on his hands, and his rifle lay at his feet, its stock in splinters.

Frederick had reached the man, and it was clear that some rather unclergylike tension occupied the husband. He matter-of-factly inquired of the stranger's injuries, however, and inspected the wounds on his face and his hands (wrought by the splinters from the rifle) with a degree of gentleness that Sundry admired, even if he knew he would not have been able to summon the same. The clergyman took the opportunity, also, of assuring himself that the man carried no other weapons.

Isabelle in the meantime had retrieved the first man's rifle and expertly levered another round into the chamber before informing the fellow, who was then rousing himself from Sundry's blow, that she was not a member of the clergy and thereby not beholden to that brotherhood's charitable tenets. She emphasized this thought by prodding the man in the back with the business end of the rifle and seemed to be thinking of other means to impress the point upon him. In brief, she was livid.

"We mustn't sit on our hands," said Capital. "These gentlemen can climb down or tumble down. I don't care which." Moxie growled at the second gunman as Frederick helped him across the gap to the first ledge. "Good girl!" Capital declared. Then he grabbed the man's collar and put the pistol to his head, shouting, "I would back away if I were you!" When the others looked up, they saw the flash of someone disappear from behind the rocky battlements. "Come, come," said Capital quietly.

Isabelle escorted the first man down the hill, followed by Mister Walton and Frederick and finally by the second man in the grip of Sundry and the sights of Capital's pistol.

It was an awkward and nervous descent, and no less a wait while Mister Walton demonstrated a hitherto undisclosed talent with knots as the two blond men were bound and placed at the bottom of the sleigh. It was a crowded place when they all climbed in; Moxie jumped onto the backs of the prostrate men, where the others' feet were also resting.

Several figures, apparently armed, appeared at the top of the tor, but Sundry and Isabelle had the rifle and pistol nudging the backs of their prisoners' necks. Capital pulled his own rifle from its place at his feet and passed it to Mister Walton. "I'm not so sure," said Capital, "that they wouldn't rather lose these two than let us get very far, so don't hesitate to make them duck up there." He cracked the reins, and the horses, snorting steam, limbered their legs a little with some preliminary shuffles before pulling the sleigh around.

"I am heartily sorry for bringing you into such a dangerous situation," said Frederick. "Isabelle."

She flashed a look at him that was sharp and forgiving all at once. "I should guess, my love," she said, "that a man of the cloth without a trusting nature would be of little use to anyone."

"They've left the tor," said Mister Walton.

"They'll be following," said Capital.

The wind was rising, drifting snow into the tracks they had left.

25. Others Lost Their Hats as Well

When they arrived at Hallowell, Ephram, Eagleton, and Thump escorted Mr. Burnbrake to the Worster House. Even the Dash-It-All Boys came along, and there was some discussion among Durwood, Waverley, and Brink whether someone they knew might discover them if they took rooms there.

"It isn't cheating, I think," suggested Waverley, "unless you're caught."

"What *did* you bet?" wondered Durwood. "Perhaps it would be worth our splitting it three ways so that we can sleep in a bed tonight."

The members of the Moosepath League and Mr. Burnbrake were not privy to this discussion and were rather more concerned with the disappearance of Roger Noble. It was a relief therefore when a telegram from Pacifa Means arrived saying that Miss Burnbrake would be joining them by the next available train. Mr. Burnbrake had been on the verge of making the return trip himself, and his great concern only deepened the suspicions in which the Moosepathians held the "troublesome cousin."

The Dash-It-All Boys were never very near to the discussion regarding Mr. Noble, but the suspense surrounding his disappearance must have been too much for them, for they wandered off—out of doors! "Distracting themselves," said Thump, "with the tangible challenge of the blizzard."

"They were that distressed!" said Eagleton, shaking his head.

"It's rather grand of them," said Ephram.

As for Mr. Burnbrake, he decided to rest after his journey and retired to his room. Ephram, Eagleton, and Thump found themselves in need of diversion while lunch digested and dinner drew apace, and since the Dashian example was much admired, they decided to emulate their new acquaintances by following their footsteps—in a metaphorical sense.

Thus, with the temper of the snow and the determination of men, the die was cast. Further deeds were in the offing.

There is only the one word for it in the English language, and that is *snow*: not *sleet* or *hail* or *freezing rain*, but *snow*—white, light, and cumulative, thrall to the vagaries of sun and wind, impermanent blanket, poor man's fertilizer.

There is only the one word, in English, but snow is a phenomenon of many dispositions: There is light snow and wet snow and crusted snow and snow that is fine for skiing and snow that is fine for snowshoeing and snow that encourages one to stay indoors, but only seldom does that singular snow, that *snow of perfection*, fall, for under certain conditions, snow will form easily into a ball that fits in the human hand and cries to be flung.

There has been infinite discussion on the street corners of the world's wintry belt regarding the elements that best facilitate a good snowball (though less dialogue than one would expect in the responsible journals), but suffice it to say that a mysterious blend of granularity and temperature is necessary to bring about the proper factors and that it is a gift from on high (at several natural and theological levels) when it deigns to visit us with its superior presence.

There is no guarantee, of course, that even contiguous communities will be equally blessed in this capacity, for on a single day, during a single storm, the atmosphere of Newcastle might be deadly with white missiles, while in Damariscotta, just across the river, young men are puzzledly discussing the snow's propensity to fall apart in their hands.

It is a riddle.

Strangely (and despite one of their number's great fascination for all things weathery), this is a subject that, until December 1896, had never been discussed among the members of the Moosepath League.

All that *was* discussed when they stepped out of the Worster House that afternoon was the determination of the blizzard, which was deemed sufficient. Thump was the first out, and he turned the top of his top hat directly into the wind while Ephram and Eagleton joined him.

They stood with their haberdashery crammed over their ears and gesticulated in several directions before making the stouthearted decision to face the teeth of the storm and climb Winthrop Street. There were no gale-force winds onshore that day, but the charter members were accustomed to sitting blizzards out, and it is no wonder that they were thrilled by the challenge of the elements as they trudged the steep slope.

"Good heavens!" called Eagleton over the storm, "it reminds me of *Arabella's Winter Home* by Mrs Alvina Plesock Dentin."

"Exactly!" agreed Ephram. They all had read the book avidly. "It does remind one, don't you think, Thump?" Ephram and Eagleton stopped when they realized that their friend was not alongside them.

He was in fact standing a few paces below on the slope, holding his hat to his head and looking very stern as the wind coated his magnificent beard with snow. "'*I have turned the corner of an eye to the white wind!*'" he quoted. "'*I have felt the bite of the winter storm upon the moor, and known the heart-bruising twinkle of uncertainty when all about and every landmark is hidden behind a curtain of snow; when direction means nothing and even something so simple as up and down comes to question; when there is not a blade of grass with which to compare your perceptions!*'" This he boomed out above the sift of precipitation and the wail of the wind in the nearby trees.

"Good heavens!" cried Eagleton, for he recalled this passage.

"Marvelous!" pronounced Ephram.

"It is very like," said Thump, squinting into the storm. The hill was indeed steep, and the wind blew against them so that they had the impression of walking almost parallel to the sidewalk. "I do hope the Dash-It-All Boys have not lost themselves," said Thump, and they peered through the storm for some glimpse of Durwood, Waverley, and Brink.

As it happened, Durwood, Waverley, and Brink were not far away. They had left some twenty minutes before and had traveled partway up the slope before turning down a street, the sign of which was covered in wet snow and so not recorded in the pertinent annals. This sticking capacity of the present precipitation gave rise among the Dash-It-All Boys to fond memories of snowball fights long ago, and they reminisced in melancholy tones upon the various methods with which they had knocked other folk down and the wistful pleasures of stuffing snow under people's collars.

"There is very little like it," said Waverley. He remembered, in particular, the many gallons of snow he had, throughout the days of his youth, crammed down the neck of his sister, who unfortunately rarely talked to him anymore.

Durwood was actually weighing a snowball in his hands and saying, "You know, there is never enough of the right stuff when you're young. I don't know when I have seen such perfect snow!"

"Wouldn't it be the thing to stumble upon a good battle just now?" thought Brink. "Or perhaps start one?"

Just then the storm hesitated for the briefest moment, and as the curtain of white lifted, they were witness to a line of boys hunkered behind a snowbank. Missiles were being lobbed from some unseen source and with expert precision, for the boys were being pelted with remarkable accuracy.

Brink couldn't imagine that his desire for a battle had been so readily answered. "I've never had that happen before!" he said, taken aback. The storm reasserted itself, and the scene before them disappeared. "You don't suppose I've used up a wish or something, do you?"

"If you have," said Waverley, "you've spent it magnificently."

It did not take long for the three men to race through the sheets of snow and join the boys behind the bank, where they inquired after the fortunes of war.

"They are!" informed a small fellow, when he was asked, "Who is winning?" He and his cohorts were hardly seven or eight years old.

Durwood, Waverley, and Brink wasted no time but tipped their hats, leaped over the parapet—dodging several snowballs—and joined the eleven- and twelve-year-old boys behind the opposite bank.

This older regiment looked with mixed amazement and horror at the arrival of three grown men.

"Yes!" said Waverley. "Very good!"

"Sound the bugle!" said Durwood.

"I think we can rout them with one good charge!" asserted Brink. "Don't you?"

"Yes, sir!" said one of the older boys, and the entire regiment burst into sunny smiles as visions of seven- and eight-year-old children running in terror danced in their heads.

Ephram, Eagleton, and Thump experienced a strange sensation as they climbed Winthrop Street: the perception that the top of the hill was further away the further they traveled. It had appeared quite manageable when they began their journey and not so manageable when they had covered about a quarter of the distance. When they stopped for breath at about the halfway mark, the crest of the hill seemed leagues away.

"Perhaps we really couldn't see it from the bottom of the hill," suggested Eagleton, and that seemed reasonable.

They were standing in the wind and the snow, thinking about this paradox, when several shadows became visible down a side street. Thump saw them first, and he peered past his friends as if he were attempting to read a distant sign. Ephram and Eagleton were not very conscious of the approaching figures before the boys were upon them, and two or three nearly ran Thump down altogether, as they were more concerned with what lay behind than before them.

"Good heavens!" said Eagleton.

"My word!" said Ephram.

"What can it mean?" wondered Eagleton, and no sooner had he said this than something of a reply was forthcoming and his hat flew from his head.

The boys hesitated to run further, being out of breath and supposing that the company of three adults might constitute protection.

Eagleton was looking for his hat and Ephram was pointing to it when Ephram's hat took similar leave from its perch, and no sooner were they retrieving this piece of headgear than Thump's topper bounced from its place. As he bent over, something hit Eagleton in the end that does not wear a hat, and he straightened up with a shout. A very large portion of snow caught Ephram in the shoulder, and while he was wiping the cold stuff from beneath his collar, he saw Thump chase after his own hat, which was being encouraged by several missiles to cross the street.

While the Moosepathians drew fire, the young boys, of whom there were eight or nine, were afforded some respite from attack, and they began to return nearly as good as Ephram, Eagleton, and Thump were getting.

Eagleton was conscious of laughter through the storm but hardly had the opportunity to look in its direction as he was being pummeled with a great many snowballs. Thump, however, retrieved his hat and stalked back to his friends, despite the white missiles that shattered and scattered against his broad chest. One snowball caught him in the chin, and were it not for his magnificent beard, it might have stung rather badly.

Ephram alone, once he had his hat back on his head, seemed immune to the continuing volley. "Good heavens, Eagleton!"

"Yes, Ephram!" called Eagleton, picking up his hat for the third or fourth time.

"Thump!"

"Yes, Ephram!"

"I believe we are under attack!"

"You better stay off the street!" came a shout from behind the lacy sheets of snow.

"You better watch out, Harold Marsh!" returned one of the boys standing behind Ephram, Eagleton, and Thump. A laugh came back in reply.

"Stay off the street?" said Ephram. "Well, I never! Have you, Eagleton?"

"No, not ever! Have you, Thump?"

"Well, once, I think."

The volleys were less frequent now, and the Moosepathians were learning how to dodge them, more or less, with their hands raised above their shoulders like innocent bystanders at a robbery; to an uninformed observer they might have appeared to be dancing some eccentric Highland fling, leaping in the air, then ducking down or simply raising a foot. Even the younger lads behind them grew to like it.

"Who are those people?" inquired Ephram in the course of this joggling.

"Just some older kids from school," said one of the younger fellows.

"Well, they are difficult."

"Two or three of them are very tall," said Eagleton, who caught a glimpse of some larger figures behind the first line. The sport was too easy, it seemed, for the older boys were tiring of it and they drifted away in an organized retreat.

"We'll be back tomorrow!" shouted one of the younger boys. He shook his fist in the air.

"Oh, my!" said Eagleton.

"We are going to have to fight them tomorrow," asserted the boy. "Thank you for your help."

"Certainly, you are welcome," said Eagleton, who shook the lad's offered hand. "Anytime."

"Would you come and help us tomorrow?" The small boy's face beamed with sudden hope and inspiration.

"Tomorrow?" said Eagleton.

"It's Sunday tomorrow!" said Ephram. It seemed altogether too warlike an activity for the Sabbath.

"There will be a big one after service!" said another child.

"You could throw further than any of us!" said a third.

"They're all bigger than we are," said the first boy, "but we're not afraid." He looked doubtful despite the assertion.

Now there is something in the Moosepathian soul (a soul that despises very little) that does despise a bully. Courage, on the other hand, is greatly admired, particularly after their reading, in *Polly's Conundrum* by Elsa Wattel Berry, that *"One who knows not fear can know no courage."* The leader of the younger boys was so obviously daunted by the prospect of tomorrow's battle, yet so intent upon waging his side of it, that the three men could not think of abandoning them.

They were a sturdy lot, the boys, dressed in knee-lengths with coats barely warm enough for the weather. Some wore caps, and one, with his blond hair sticking out from beneath like straw, wore a battered bowler.

"We could never return fire ourselves," said Ephram.

"That would be inappropriate," agreed Eagleton. They did not want to be bullies in return.

"But we could—" began Ephram.

"Well, certainly, we might—" tried Eagleton.

"We shall lead them!" averred Thump. He looked very determined, with his hat cocked slightly to one side and his beard full of snow; they had all but forgotten the storm, and his friends were quite taken by the sight of Thump fleeced in white from head to foot. "We shall direct their forces!" he added.

"Bravo, Thump!" declared Ephram. "It is just the thing!" It did not occur to the Moosepathians, just then, that there was not a modicum of experience in tactics and strategy among them.

"Let us meet," said Eagleton to the boys, "before the Worster House after services. Wind significantly decreasing by midnight, clearing by morning, tomorrow clear and bright."

"High tide, adjusting for the distance from the ocean, should be about ten minutes before twelve," calculated Thump.

"It's twelve minutes past the hour of two," announced Ephram.

"The woods are filled with Indians!" pronounced Waverley when the Dash-It-All Boys returned to the Worster House and found the Moosepath League drying themselves before the parlor hearth.

"We had no idea!" said Ephram, rather astonished.

"Is there forest nearabouts?" wondered Eagleton. He threw looks to several sides, as if he might see from the Worster House parlor these Indian-filled groves. Their chairman had met a distinguished member of that race during the adventures of the previous fall, and they were accordingly much interested.

"There were only the young boys we met," said Thump seriously.

Waverley had been referring to these very lads by metaphor and was a little surprised at having been taken so literally.

"Were they good lads?" wondered Brink.

"There were some who were a little high-spirited, we thought," offered Eagleton.

"Quite honestly?" said Waverley.

"Knocked our hats off with snowballs," added Ephram.

"Good heavens!" said Durwood.

"Good heavens?" said Brink, who had never heard so polite an exclamation from Durwood's lips.

"Yes," said Durwood, looking bland. "Good heavens, I said."

"We said much the same," sympathized Ephram.

"And these young fellows assailed you with snowballs?" asked Waverley.

"There was a younger group of boys who took protection behind us."

"Ah!" said Durwood. "Very gallant of you!"

Ephram, Eagleton, and Thump were abashed. "We are going to lead them into battle tomorrow," said Thump.

"How grand!" said Waverley.

"You don't think it will be taking a gross advantage of the older boys if we direct the actions of the younger?" wondered Ephram. This ethical question had plagued them.

"Not at all!" assured Waverley.

"We won't actually participate in the hurling," added Eagleton.

"Won't you?" asked Waverley.

Ephram, Eagleton, and Thump shook their heads, saying in chorus, "No, no, no, no."

"What harm a snowball or two?" wondered Brink. "Knock one of the big fellows on his ear!"

"Oh, my," said Eagleton.

"You've dealt with criminals and pirates in your day," agreed Durwood. "These ruffians should be of little consequence to the Moosepath League."

If not actually emboldened by this praise of their society, the members of the club were at least reinvigorated with a sort of robust pride. Just the knowledge that the readiness of the Moosepath League had communicated thus far to the public at large added to their resolve to see through the challenge of the morrow.

"Perhaps you have had some experience at snowballs yourselves," said Thump, bright with sudden inspiration.

"Good heavens, no!" said Brink, who seemed to have caught Durwood's decorous turn of phrase.

"We stay well away from such conflict," said Waverley.

"Leave it to fellows like yourself," said Durwood.

"Ah, well," said Thump. "I thought you might have some thoughts on the matter."

"Oh, we do," assured Waverley, but he said nothing more, and Ephram, Eagleton, and Thump thought it was perhaps impolite to inquire further.

26. The Banks of Lake George

It was the crow that caused Capital to draw up, just the other side of the forest of fallen trees. They had almost begun to relax as they fled the woods, nearly silent and all but hidden by the snow. The black bird—perhaps thinking, after its discussion with Capital earlier in the day, that the bearded fellow was a kindred soul—lit before them on a fallen tree, where it flapped its wings and let out a terrific squawk. Capital pulled back on the reins and drew the horses to one side.

The old man stood on his seat and looked about them till he thought he saw the shadow of something moving parallel to their track. Moxie, lying on the two prostrate men, let out a low growl.

"What is—" Isabelle started to say, but Capital let out a "Heeah!" and snapped the reins above the horses' backs. The crow shot into the snowy atmosphere without a sound, and they sped by the fallen tree.

Sundry saw them to the other side as well, forming a running gauntlet beyond the veil of snow and a row of leaning pines. "Why don't you scooch down, Mister Walton," he suggested, but the portly fellow only shook his head and peered after the dark movements in the wood.

"Down!" said Capital sharply, but he was only warning them of a low-lying limb, and Sundry barely ducked his head in time.

Frederick did insist that his wife hunker down, assuring her that they could argue about it later, and as they veered about another deadfall, he used the force of the turn to leverage her below the back of the seat.

"If you please, Mrs. Covington," said Mister Walton quietly, and Frederick indicated his thanks to the man silently.

Mister Walton wondered how Capital and the horses could see far enough to keep them out of some trap of deadfalls, and indeed, they were sweeping through denser growth than they had traveled on the way in. Dark limbs and snow-streaked trunks loomed out of the blizzard like phantoms, and more than once they tottered over some long-fallen tree that lay just below the snow. Their self-appointed escorts flashed into view from behind a stand of trees or in a sudden, if temporary, decrease in the storm.

Sundry had the safety of the rifle on, but he fingered the button as he swung his head from one side to the other. He felt as if his heart were in his throat, and the silent chase and the blinding snow only made the swift minutes the more awful.

Then they broke from the acres of deadfall into an open grove, and emerging from the woods mere seconds after were a pair of sleighs on each side. There were two or three men in each sleigh, drawn by a single horse, and they only looked onward, with not a glimpse in the direction of their quarry. There was something eerie about this and Sundry felt like taking a shot at one of them just to gain their direct attention.

Capital shouted to the horses, and they picked up speed where the land opened up. He gave a fierce and frightful haw upon the reins, and the Percherons plunged to their left, crossing the path of the oncoming sleighs. A collision with their pursuers seemed imminent, the more so since the drivers had their heads thrust forward, but in the last instance the pilot of the first sleigh hawed as well and collided instead with the second sleigh. Snow and runners and limbs spun in a tangle, and only the horses kept their feet, dragging the remains of the vehicles in a path perpendicular to the sleigh in flight.

Sundry thought he would leap out of his seat, and he let out a whoop of sheer delight. In this new direction they were that much farther from the pursuers who remained, and they were feeling a surge of triumph when a shot rang out and the snow erupted just ahead of the left-hand horse.

Sundry had the safety off from the rifle in an instant, and as the others very willingly ducked, he threw himself against the back seat and sighted over the barrel at the closest sleigh. "They're shooting at the horses!" shouted Capital, and he actually veered the sleigh and its occupants between their pursuers and the Percherons. The sudden lurch nearly spilled Sundry from his seat, and before he had the opportunity to realign his sights, they were dipping over a steep bank.

"Hang on!" shouted Capital.

Past sheets of snow, Lake George lay like a plain below them, and Sundry was horrified to see the dark shapes of several sleighs waiting for them on the ice. "What are you doing?" he called out as Capital drove the horses in a direct line toward the sleighs before them.

"Get down!" shouted Capital, but with the two blond men piled at their feet and the rest of them hunkered down as best they could, there was little place for Sundry to go. Another shot rang out from behind, and the corner of the sleigh splintered over Frederick's back. There were several shouts, one from Isabelle for her husband and another from Mister Walton for Sundry.

The sleighs before them were surrounded by people, many of whom had rifles leveled at the slope, and Sundry thought he was letting out his last gasp at the sight of fire and smoke erupting from that line of barrels.

"Take that, you—" Capital's rough colloquialism was lost as the roar of those guns reached them. "Beg your pardon, ma'am. Mr. Covington," he added, but he was grinning ear to ear and nearly laughing.

An unmotivated glimpse back told Sundry that the sleighs behind them had pulled up. Then he looked ahead. They were almost falling down the last stretch of bank, the Percherons seemingly tireless as they thundered onto the lake.

Capital snapped the reins, which was a signal for the horses both to carry on and to ease their pace. Sundry's trepidation of that row of rifles turned to confusion and then happiness as he recognized Paul Duvaudreuil, who had exchanged sleighs with them that morning, and Mr. Noel and Mr. Noggin, whom he and Mister Walton had met the night before.

The remainder of that armed band, some of whom were women, were relatives of Paul's, and there was a concert of Canadian French amid the cheers and shots that greeted them. Capital pulled the sleigh around and lit onto the lake, where he was immediately attended by Mr. Noel and Mr. Noggin. Others were instructed as to the care of the two blond men, and several tended the horses, breaking them from harness, throwing blankets over the animals' backs, and walking them down. Snow hissed on the Percherons' backs.

"We didn't really think to shoot till we saw them hit the sleigh, did we, Mr. Noggin?" said Mr. Noel.

"Certainly we didn't, Mr. Noel," said Mr. Noggin.

There was much praise in the air for Capital's handling of the sleigh, and when his passengers looked back at the slope they had traveled to the lake, they wondered that they hadn't all rolled down the bank, sleigh over horse.

"That's why I asked Capital along," said Mister Walton to Sundry, "but I didn't know it at the time."

"It's a wonder they were able to turn around on that slope," said Sundry. "They must have had to get out before the horses were able to pull those rigs back up."

"I wasn't watching," admitted Mister Walton. "Are you all right?"

"Not a singe."

"Gentlemen, I can't tell you," began Frederick as he and his wife approached them. "I can't tell you how very fortunate I feel that you came with us and how very sorry I am as well."

"We are only glad," informed Mister Walton.

"If Moxie ever has any pups," said Sundry.

"It is the very least we owe you," said Isabelle. "Not to say Mr. Gaines and these other magnificent folk." She spoke to one of the women nearby, and her French was very pretty.

"If they are that fearful of what we might know, Mr. Gaines," said Frederick quietly, while his wife was otherwise engaged, "*I* fear what they might attempt still. And if they've guessed that I haven't been able to translate the figures," he surmised, "they'll realize they have only to stop me and get the photographs to keep anyone else from doing so."

"I believe," said Sundry, who had stepped up to this conversation, "that I have an idea how to make your knowledge in the matter a moot point."

"I have always been amused by that word, Mr. Noggin," said Mr. Noel. The two men had joined Capital and Frederick and Sundry. "Moot."

"I am not familiar with it, I don't think, Mr. Noel," said Mr. Noggin.

Someone was lighting a lantern. Mister Walton looked into the mill of snow. "It's getting dark," he said to Sundry.

Daniel's Story
(July–November 1891)

"It's a shame we hadn't known all along Nell was that kind of girl."

Joel Parson couldn't have realized that Daniel was nearing the porch of the general store, or he wouldn't have said it; some of the other boys facing Daniel were a little uncertain, in fact, when the statement fell from the young man's lips, and Joel himself looked as if he had been caught poaching by the sheriff himself. Joel Parson was a nice young man, really, though like most young men (and most people, to be fair), he spoke from time to time without thinking.

Daniel had dreaded hearing something like it, ever since it had become common knowledge that Nell Linnett was spending every available hour with Asher Willum, and now that the thought was in the air, he simply mounted the steps to the store and confronted the boys. Joel Parson was the ultimate focus of his attention, and there was silence for a moment.

Daniel said, "I have never had the inclination to strike a person, Joel, but I might have just now if I wasn't so sure that you are a better man than your words would indicate."

Joel looked almost sick as he stared down at his feet. Daniel knew that Joel would carry this blunder with him the rest of his life and that it would raise its head at unexpected moments to trouble him time and again; Daniel knew this because he had blundered enough himself.

"I don't think one of you boys," said Daniel to the rest of the crowd there, "have ever had so much as an unkind word from that girl."

There was the sound of shuffling feet and the sight of several nodding heads, which irritated Daniel vaguely, so without another word he went about his business. Gemma Clyde didn't say much to Daniel when he made his purchases, and he knew that she had heard him; it wasn't only the young folk who had something to say about the fall of Ian Linnett, which was how recent events were perceived by some in town.

There were others, however, who were simply concerned about the safety of Nell Linnett, and no one saw anything but tragedy rising out of any association with Asher Willum. Asher himself would walk the porch with more than his usual measure of conceit and smile at people as if he had discovered something indecent about them all.

Word had gotten round that Asher and Nell had been seen dallying in the tall grass by Trafton Pond, and the heartbreak of it to Daniel Plainway was the pure sweetness of the image by itself: a young man and a young woman, handsome and beautiful, lingering in the warm July sun beside a calm water, amid the sounds of bees and warblers. How absolutely sweet might Nell think Asher Willum's attentions, and how absolutely undeserving Asher was.

Word also floated about that Asher was still keeping time with at least two other girls in Brownfield, and there were days when Nell was seen without him, looking lonely. She said very little the few times that she and Daniel saw each other, and Daniel could not bring himself to speak to her about anything more profound than the weather.

It amazed everyone that Ian Linnett had not thrown his granddaughter out *of the house, but when Daniel visited one Saturday, he found the place silent and sad. Aunt Dora had left to stay with relatives in Rockport, and the old man himself looked like a man furious, who yet is unable to vent that fury. Daniel had never seen such bitterness. There was very little said between them, and Daniel did not stay long.*

Summer came to an end, and Asher Willum disappeared from public view. For days Nell was sighted along the paths and roads, wandering listlessly on her own. Daniel himself saw her walk past his house, on the outskirts of town, with Jeram. Some wondered, not silently, if something "had happened" to Asher, which euphemism was pointed toward old man Linnett himself, but Asher was spotted some towns away by a drummer who knew the parties in question, and it was conjectured that he had tired of Nell and cast her aside.

The leaves began to turn, and weeks went by; Asher seemed to have quit the area entirely. Daniel began to hope that some lessons had been learned and that if Nell were to visit relatives herself, she might start over. When he found her at home one evening, and while her grandfather occupied the other end of the house in granitic silence, she cried the entire time Daniel talked with her, otherwise revealing nothing of herself, of her relationship with Asher Willum, or her plans.

A week later, during the early days of a cold November, Nell left home, and Daniel heard that she was living at the Willums' place. A few days later he barged into the old man's presence to ask if it were true that Nell had married Jeram Willum and that Ian himself had signed the papers of consent.

"I beg your pardon," said the old man, without looking at Daniel, "if I have offended you with my presumption."

27. The Span Between Trains

Daniel Plainway was not sure what he should do, once Charlotte Burnbrake inadvertently seated herself across the aisle from him. While he suspected, after what had happened at the City Hotel barely an hour before, that his presence might be a source of embarrassment to her, it seemed that by removing himself to another car, he would appear to suggest she had reason to be ashamed.

Charlotte was not unaware of his quandary and true to human convolution felt a sympathetic discomfort for him on top of her own. They were doing their best to appear interested in whatever was before them, Daniel scanning (without reading) the sentences in a copy of *Silas Marner*, Charlotte considering a piece of paper (consisting of a list of errands she had written for herself several months ago) that she had taken from her purse.

It did seem that this might be the last train out of Portland before the end of the storm, and there were few people on it; as if persecuted by the Imp of Perverse, Daniel and Charlotte found themselves nearly alone in the car as they pulled out of the station. The car shivered with a sudden gust of wind; the station and the surrounding yard disappeared behind a white blind, but Charlotte was so concerned about the awkward circumstances that she had hardly room in her mind to worry about the inclemency without.

She felt deadened by the events of the past two hours and by her inability to rise to the present challenge; then it occurred to her to consider what Pacifa Means would do. She looked out her window at the white squall, took some deep breaths, and, before she knew what she was about, said, "It was agreed between Pacifa and myself that we were fortunate in your arrival this afternoon." She said this loud enough but said it while still looking out the window. After a moment she turned and gave Mr. Plainway as bland and as brave an expression as she could muster.

"You are kind to say so," he replied, still staring at his book, "but another person would have been of more assistance than I." Quite by accident he mimicked her movement by taking off his half spectacles, once he had said this, and looking at her.

Charlotte was struck by something that had not occurred to her till that moment, her voice revealing the process of her thought. "I am not sure that is true, Mr. Plainway. You understood, I think, however instinctively, that a steady presence was required *rather* than active assistance. Another less circumspect man would have said more and made matters worse."

Every ounce of compliment, stated or implied in these words, had its effect on Daniel, and he was moved to blush. He realized then that she was smiling and (not for the first time) that she was beautiful.

She in turn surprised herself by experiencing an almost puckish delight in making him redden.

The conductor came through the car, punching tickets. "There is a chance that the rails will be closed between here and Hallowell," he said when he saw their destination. They simply nodded in reply, and he looked from one to the other of them, clearly wondering what they were doing on opposite sides of the aisle. When he was gone, Daniel tried to think of what to say next.

Again Charlotte found her voice. "Do you believe, Mr. Plainway," she said, "that some people are, by nature and their very being, unhappy?"

"I have known folk who have suffered terrible misfortune," he ventured to say, after some thought, "who yet knew some measure of content, who were perhaps grateful for small blessings, and others who might be embarrassed by their riches, worldly and otherwise, and who rarely smiled."

"My cousin, then, is one of these," she said, meaning the latter.

"Mr. Noble?"

She nodded.

"A stone thrown in the lake."

"I beg your pardon?"

"It is an Indian proverb. 'Each is a stone thrown in the lake.' The lake is life, and everything we do or say causes a ripple. The Abenaki would say that a person might cause good ripples or bad. I represented an Indian in a land dispute, and it was his own brother that brought his interests down. No one was entirely happy with the outcome of the case, but my client was philosophical. When I remarked on the damage his brother had done, he only said, 'A stone in the lake.' It was not meant, I think, as a direct criticism but only as a general statement about us all."

"It was perhaps a warning," said Charlotte, who liked the ambiguous nature of the proverb, "a reminder to himself."

"That is it exactly, I think."

"Roger and I were very close when we were children," said the woman. She looked down at the aisle between them now, as if she were speaking to herself. "He is three years younger than I, but he always carried himself like an older child and was precocious in his understanding . . . of certain things. There was something foolish and romantic in me that was flattered by his attention, and I was only seventeen when he cajoled from me a promise of faithfulness to him. I thought it was all simply a chapter in one of the books I read with such passion. Cousins often fall in love in books."

It would have taken more time than their trip allowed to explain all that had happened between Roger Noble and her, to explain the physical beauty of his youth, the rugged athleticism matched with his curly blond hair and almost girlish handsomeness. He *had* been precocious, and she had allowed him to kiss her behind his father's garden wall at the house in Cape Elizabeth—first chastely, then with more passion, till finally he had wrested from her such an indiscreet promise.

She had hardly thought of him when her family was not visiting his or when she was not reading one of his barely restrained letters, and in retrospect she felt a terrible guilt for this. To her it had been a game played with a cousin seen three or four times in a year.

One night, as she neared her eighteenth birthday, she walked again (and as it happened, for the last time) in her uncle's garden with Roger. The game had begun to pale for her by then; she was more aware and even a little fearful of his single-minded passion; she was more sensible to his temper, his petulance to everyone but herself, and her pleasure in his company had withered slightly as she considered how they had deceived their families. Yet as they strolled beside the moonlit roses and as he held her hand, a culpable excitement reawakened within her.

In a shadowed nook of the garden they stopped, and she had willingly lifted her face to his. The warm night, the scent of roses, the salt breeze from off the cape were like rhymes in a soft sonnet. She put her hands in his curly hair; she felt the weight of him press her shoulders against the brick of the garden wall. She could still remember every sensation, the thrill and the absolute fear, all these years later.

Roger had not been content with promises and stolen kisses behind their parents' backs but had pressed on to other familiarities, and here her better judgment had risen up, and she had pushed him away.

A gust of wind drove snow with the sound of scattered sand against the side of the train. The entire affair, from childish sweetness to mature reflection, had traveled and occupied her thoughts for the span of about ten seconds.

Daniel only surmised the details of her story but felt as awkward as he would have had she told him everything. During this minor lapse in the conversation he wished he could think of something to say. It seemed incredible that her cousin could have been persecuting her for all these years, yet he considered her beauty and what he thought he understood of her nature and remembered what he knew of men like Roger Noble. He decided that it was time to change the subject.

"Your uncle has business in Hallowell?" he asked, not realizing that this was as close to *not* changing the subject as he could have gotten.

She looked almost startled, for it had been her bachelor uncle, Ezra Burnbrake, who had been sitting in the darkened garden, not ten yards away, and Uncle Ezra who had come running when Charlotte found herself struggling with Roger, and Uncle Ezra in his prime who had raised his walking stick and thrashed his fifteen-year-old nephew to within an inch of his life.

"It was the last time we ever came to Cape Elizabeth," she said aloud. Then she said, "I am sorry."

"Not at all."

"What do you do, Mr. Plainway?" she asked, falling back upon a lifetime of polite conversation.

"I'm a lawyer," he said simply. "I live in Hiram."

"And do you have family there?"

"A sister. The town is like family, you know." He had been so absorbed by this lovely woman and her melancholy state that he had, for the first time in several days, momentarily forgotten the sad tale of the Linnetts and the plight of the little boy named Bird. Mentioning family brought them back again.

Charlotte caught the flash of this remembrance in his eyes and said, "I hope there isn't bad news for the Moosepath League," and she could not help smiling when she pronounced the name of the club. "In the short time I knew them I liked them very much. And they have high regard for their chairman, it seems," she added with continued good humor.

"I've never met the man, but he certainly leaves an impression wherever he goes," said Daniel. "No, I hope I have *good* news for them, Miss Burnbrake."

There was a reservation in his words that caused her a moment of sympathetic apprehension. "I hope so then," she said.

Some alliance of spent emotion and the rhythmic shiver of the train conquered Charlotte Burnbrake, and she drifted to sleep, quite unintentionally, while they talked about weather and travel and anything that did not directly touch upon whatever truly concerned them.

Daniel returned to his book and was able to concentrate, after some effort, upon the sorrows and joys of the old miser. He occasionally looked across the aisle at her, taking advantage of her sleeping to view her pretty features and feeling a little dubious about it.

The first and only warning of something wrong was when, three or four miles out of Richmond, there came a sudden blast of steam and the squeal of braking wheels upon the rails. The initial tug toward the front of the train frightened Charlotte awake. Daniel gripped the back of his own seat with one arm and poised himself as best he could against the inertial force while readying himself to catch Miss Burnbrake if the car should lurch in another direction.

Someone at the other end of the car let out a frightened cry. Past Charlotte, through the windows, Daniel had the glimpse of a man with a red lantern hurrying away from the tracks. The brakes had taken on a scream of their own. The train was slowing. Daniel held his breath, his eyes wide, his heart pounding. They seemed to be crawling, but the great mass of the engine and its several cars continued to push them, and when they were hardly moving at all, there was a sudden jolt.

For an awful moment, the car (and presumably the rest of the train) leaned, as if it were going to tip over altogether. Charlotte reached across the aisle and took hold of Daniel's hand; they froze in apprehension.

With a shudder the train settled back onto the tracks, and they were stopped. Great gouts of steam sped past their windows, roiling the falling snow in hectic spirals. Shouts came from outside, and someone shouted out a prayerful thank-you.

"Are you all right?" asked Daniel.

"A little shaken," Charlotte admitted, and realizing that she still had hold of his hand, she let him go.

This contact had a profound effect on Daniel, but he only said, "I'll go see what has happened," and hurried down the aisle.

The conductor appeared at the end of the car, all unhurried business, and inquired if everyone was safe.

"Yes, thank you," said Charlotte, for herself.

"What is it?" asked Daniel, who stood at the door.

"The train ahead of us is off the track."

"We didn't hit anything?" offered Daniel.

"No, but the other train kicked the rails out when the caboose tipped over, and our engine was almost stopped when it wheeled off the break. The other train knocked down the lines between here and Richmond, so a wire wasn't able to get through."

"Could it have been the train my uncle was on?" wondered Charlotte before considering the time elapsed since Ezra Burnbrake and his party left Portland.

"I think there have been several trains since this morning," assured Daniel. He was half out the door by now, and he pulled his collar about his neck as he clomped down the steps. He had not thought to take his hat or coat, and the driving snow stung his face. Up ahead there were lights and the shadows of men in the snow. A man with a lantern stopped by the next car to crane his head and answer a question from an opened window. With the storm, evening came early, and the lamp of day turned down with almost visible speed; even as he watched, the lanterns up ahead burned more fiercely, and a grove of trees nearby was lost against the approach of night.

"Mr. Plainway," said Charlotte. He was surprised to find her standing beside him, holding out his hat and coat. She herself was well bundled, and there was the look of excitement in her face, as if a train derailment had been the very thing to take her mind from her unfortunate day.

He thanked her as he took the hat and then the coat, shivering beneath them as he realized how cold he had been.

"Shall we go and see?" she asked. They might have been friends all their lives there was such a note of cheer in her voice.

Daniel's only concern was that the train was settled firmly. He looked up and down the line of cars but could tell nothing in the gathering dark. "Yes," he said, "we might as well find out what's expected of us."

Quite naturally she took his arm, and they plodded through the drifts to the fore of the train. For her part Charlotte felt at ease with this man. He was indeed *steady* (as she had characterized him); she (as a rule) was serene in herself, and it would be difficult to explain why the one was so different from the other.

Others were coming off the train, and someone shouted questions from a window as they went by. A small man in engineer's garb approached them, his face wet with steam and dark with coal dust, and he hoped aloud that they were unharmed after the incident.

The further they walked, the more flurried the activity around them. They came into the light of a dozen lanterns when they reached the broken tracks. The engine of the one train and the caboose of the other were not thirty feet apart.

A railroad man tipped his hat to Charlotte, then said to Daniel, "They've already roused some folk at Iceboro, back down the way a mile or so. There's a road, just on the ridge above us, and most of the passengers from the other train have been taken to lodgings already. The sleighs will be back soon, and we can get you folks off in half an hour, I'm sure."

They stood back and watched as the engineer directed some safety measures. Loose rails were pulled from the bed and chocked against the wheels of the train. The engine still listed, and the conductor decided that everyone should wait outside for further transportation. Another man shoveled a bucket of glowing coals from the firebox, and a fire was started with some brush and a broken rail between the two trains.

"We just need a pond and some skates," said Daniel.

The engineer passed them again, tipping his hat to Charlotte. "I do believe he thinks I am your wife," said Charlotte with that same impishness that had taken pleasure in Daniel's blush earlier.

"Does he?" Daniel was befuddled by this statement and wondered if she wanted him to correct this misapprehension. "Perhaps I should explain—" he began, and even took a step in that direction.

She kept hold of his arm, however, and laughed aloud. "I don't think it will matter to him," she said. There was the sound of relief in her voice, as if she had feared she had lost laughter altogether that afternoon. It was a deep, heartfelt sound, and Daniel was not offended to find himself its object, there was such comradery in the way it was shared. The woman, in her fur-collared coat, and her voice in the snow reached the level of beauty that only the unexpected can attain, and there was at the same time something so natural about her presence there that he could take a truly long look at her while she smiled in reply.

"No, I don't suppose it will," said Daniel.

28. More Sense of a Letter

"Capital?" said Sven Henslaw, when he answered the door and found the silver-bearded man at his back stoop. "What is it?" Sven peered past the old man at the small crowd gathered around several sleighs outside his house. The tail end of the storm drifted into the realm of a nearby street-lamp, and in that halo they looked like a calendar lithograph, bundled in furs and wrapped about with scarves and blankets.

"We've come to ask you a great favor, Sven," said Capital. "Could we come in?"

"Not all of you?" wondered Sven, wide-eyed.

"No, no. Three or four of us, perhaps."

"I don't know, Capital. Mina likes to know ahead of time if company is coming."

"Well, maybe two or three more than that," added Capital, who wasn't really listening to the man. "You don't mind if we talk to the sheriff in your kitchen, do you, Sven, while you do us a favor?"

"Good Lord, Capital! What's happened?"

"We'll explain the whole thing while you print some pictures for us."

"Print some pictures? Can't that wait till tomorrow? We were just sitting down to dinner, Mina and I."

Capital's eyes shone with both humor and apology. "Well, Sven," he said, "I wish I could say we won't take up much of your evening."

A small commotion had started out on the sidewalk, and a large, rugged-looking man pushed his way through the crowd toward Sven's door. "What's going on here, Capital?" said the fellow with the air of someone who has the right, perhaps the duty to know.

"Good Lord!" said Sven. "It *is* the sheriff!"

A dog was barking. Mr. Noggin and Mr. Noel, along with Paul Duvaudreuil and some other brawny fellows, were escorting a pair of men, none too gently, up the walk to the kitchen door, and Sven realized, after a look or two, that these two men had their hands bound behind them. The sheriff was quick to see this as well and didn't seem too pleased about it.

"I'm surprised to find *you* at the head of a mob, Capital," he said.

"Mob? We're orderly enough."

"Well, I want those men untied immediately."

"Soon as we get them in the kitchen, Sheriff."

"The kitchen? Capital, have you gone foolish? I thought there was trouble here at Sven's!"

"No trouble here, Sheriff!" declared Mr. Henslaw. "And I want none. Mina and I were just sitting down to dinner." Mrs. Henslaw at this point chose to appear behind her husband, and she demanded to know what was happening.

"Bernie," said Capital to the sheriff, "have I ever given you reason to think I'd go off half cocked?" While the sheriff frowned and thought about this, Capital added, "Well, all right then. Let's get them in Sven's kitchen. We'll get Sven working on a little favor for us and explain the whole thing all to once."

Throughout this conversation the two blond men never altered their expressions, which were respectively bland and uninterested.

Sheriff Bernard Darwin gave the two bound men a curt look, then let out a large, heartfelt sigh and nodded to Sven. "Better let us in, I guess," he said, and led the way through to the Henslaws' kitchen. "You be easy with those fellows!"

Sven and Mina Henslaw lived near the northern end of Skowhegan's main street, and not in the largest house, though it was very spruce, and the kitchen smelled nicely of the Henslaws' dinner, which was simmering upon a cheerily humping stove. There was some confusion as Capital waved several people into the kitchen: Mrs. Henslaw stood across the room and continued to query anyone who would listen.

"Now, just hold on, Mina," the sheriff said. "I don't know myself. Get those men untied," he demanded of Paul and some of his kin, who had lumbered after the Covingtons, Mister Walton, and Sundry Moss. "Are all these people necessary?" wondered the sheriff.

"You have the picture?" Capital asked Sundry.

The young man waved a photograph in the air. "Mr. Henslaw," he said, "if we could take advantage of your talent with a camera as well as your good nature . . ." He sounded rather like Mister Walton, and Sven appeared slightly mollified as he led Sundry toward the back of his house, where he kept his studio.

As the two blond men came free of their bonds, Capital made sure they were securely fixed in seats behind the Henslaws' kitchen table.

"Now, really, Capital," said the sheriff, "for the last time, what is this all about?"

Capital Gaines was not to be hurried, however, and he conveyed introductions between the sheriff, Mrs. Henslaw, the Covingtons, and Mister Walton. "You know Paul and his family," he finished.

The sheriff nodded to the Duvaudreuil clan, members of which continued to fill the kitchen. "Shut that door!" demanded the sheriff. "And who are these fellows?" he asked, nodding to the two seated men.

"They are simply the men who shot at us, out beyond Round Pond," informed Capital.

"Round Pond? Today? What were you doing out in the woods in this blizzard?"

"Reverend Covington here was searching for a particular artifact that he believes might be of Viking origin."

"Come again?"

"And these ne'er-do-wells," continued Capital, who wasn't ready to begin repeating himself just yet, "found it in their hearts to threaten us with guns—they and their accomplices—and even to shoot at us on three occasions." Capital looked almost happy to say it.

"I am sorry for such a commotion in your house," said Isabelle to Mrs. Henslaw, but their hostess had realized she was to have some excitement tonight with none of the attendant trouble once everyone was gone; it would be story enough to keep them the rest of the winter.

"Good heavens, Mrs. Covington!" said Mina Henslaw. "They shot at you?"

"And what's *your* name?" demanded the sheriff of the beardless blond man.

The man replied as if he were in danger of going to sleep, "I don't believe I am obliged to say anything under the circumstances."

"I am pretty sure," said the sheriff, "that it would behoove you to be on a first-name basis with me."

The man gave Darwin a look of impeccable boredom. "Arthur," he said simply. "This is Edgar."

The sheriff was not to be irritated by any such fatuous methods, and he turned to Edgar. "Can you speak?"

"Yes," said the bearded man with as much enthusiasm as his companion.

"And what do *you* have to say about this?" inquired the sheriff.

The bearded man raised his chin, barely cleared his throat, and took in the remainder of the room with hooded eyes. "I came upon these people trespassing," he began in a firm and untroubled tone, "and was simply wanting to know what they were about when I was attacked by their dog."

"Trespassing?" said Frederick Covington, but the sheriff raised his hand.

"My friend here," continued the man, with a nod to the other blond man, "did shoot once, hoping to drive the dog and the young man who just left with Mr. Henslaw away from me. The young man knocked me in the side of the head, and I was briefly unconscious. My friend was held at gunpoint. We were tied up like so much game, thrown into a sleigh, and carried off. Realizing that we had been kidnapped by these people, other friends came after us and did give warning shots in the pursuit."

"Warning shots!" shouted Capital. "That's a pretty story!"

"Trespassing?" said Frederick again.

The blond man actually smiled, the dubious light of which fell rather blatantly upon Isabelle, who offered no expression in return.

Capital shook his fist at the bearded man. "I'll give *you* a shot that's more than warning!"

Darwin demanded order, threatening to clear the room. Then the sheriff's attention fell upon Mister Walton, who remained as calm as ever. Anyone else would have taken this as a signal to say what was on his mind, but the portly fellow simply said, "I beg your pardon?" as if the sheriff had said something he hadn't heard.

"Please, speak up," said the sheriff, who was only too glad to see a thoughtful expression among them.

"There is, you will easily believe," said Mister Walton, "some history behind this, which can be explained easily enough. However, Mr. —the gentleman calling himself Edgar has used the term *trespassing*, which would indicate that he and his fellows either own or are the agents of those who own the land where the unfortunate events took place. Otherwise they have no reason, or right, to be pointing guns at anyone."

"It's not customary to point guns at all in these parts," said the sheriff. He turned to Arthur and Edgar.

"We *are* the owners of that land," stated Edgar flatly.

Frederick was incensed with the declaration. "How can that be when you didn't even know of its existence until today? When we ourselves probably led you there?"

Edgar never took his eyes from the sheriff. "You have only to go to the Registry of Deeds, where you will find the land in question to be under the ownership of the Broumnage Club."

"The Norumbega Club, you mean," said Frederick quietly.

Edgar managed to alter a small look of surprise into one of puzzlement as he turned to the clergyman.

"Broumnage Club?" the sheriff was saying. "I've never heard of it."

"It's a sporting association," explained Edgar.

"A league of vandals!" spouted Frederick.

The sheriff shook his head and sighed again. "I need someone to rouse up the town clerk," he said, "and go with him to the Registry of Deeds." And when, with proper instructions from Capital, Mr. Noel and Mr. Noggin (who seemed everywhere together) were after this errand, the sheriff asked for a chair and a careful accounting of the day's adventures.

The notion of photographing a positive photograph was a new one to Sven Henslaw; but as a professional he was interested in the challenge, and Sundry kept the man happy by explaining why he was missing his dinner and also why his kitchen was filled with people.

"You mean it!" Sven said several times while Sundry explained the possible origins of the artifact in the photograph, and "Good night!" another several times as the young man related the events of the day. Sven was adept at his craft and quickly formed a negative from the photograph, which they dried in the darkroom amid the acrid chemical fumes.

"The runes are the important thing," said Sundry as they waited for the first print to come to life, but what he focused on, as it appeared, was the pictograph (an *ox*, Mr. Covington had thought) carved apart from the main column of figures. "We just need as many copies as we can make," he said.

"Ah!" said Mr. Henslaw as he pulled the photograph from its bath. Shadow reigned over more of the scene than in the original, but they could make out the runes upon the boulder.

Sundry, who had never seen this process before, was enthralled, but in a little while he left Mr. Henslaw and returned to the kitchen to report their success. Mr. Noggin and Mr. Noel had returned, and the two blond men did not seem as complacent as before; Arthur was arguing with the sheriff about the state of deeds at the town registry, while Edgar simply stared at the table before him, appearing angry and astonished. "I am telling you that it is simply an oversight!" Arthur was shouting.

Sundry looked to Mister Walton, who stepped up and said in a small tone, "The deed to the parcel of land that contains the Council Hill was *not* in the name of the Broumnage Club, as these two clearly expected."

"How could they have expected such a thing if they only learned about the location of the runes today?"

"They must have known their general whereabouts and needed Frederick to lead them to it directly. To cover eventualities, they meant to have the land under ownership."

"But they don't."

"It seems not." Mister Walton took Sundry by the elbow and moved him toward the pantry, where he could speak without being overheard. "Mr. Tempest's letter, as it happens," he said, "has had its effect."

"Mr. Tempest?"

"Indeed."

"The man on the ship? The one whose letter you wrote and delivered?"

"Or rather the Moosepath League delivered. The deed to the land where we encountered these fellows is in the name of Ezra Burnbrake." Mister Walton chuckled at the look on Sundry's face. "I had no more notion than yourself. But the letter that Mr. Tempest dictated makes more sense to me now. Mr. Tempest himself was to have been the agent by which the Broumnage Club meant to obtain the land, but he had a change of heart, it seems, and in rather oblique terms he called off the deal and warned Mr. Burnbrake from making a similar one with anyone else."

"But where does this place Mr. Tempest?"

"As a member of the Broumnage Club himself perhaps."

"And traveling on the same ship with the Covingtons was a way to watch them," said Sundry.

"I have not mentioned the business to anyone else, fearing that Mr. Tempest's decision may have put him in some danger with his fellows."

"But if he was a member of the club?"

"He had tired of the people he represented and said as much. And he also, now that I think of it, said something about dying."

"Was he being prophetic regarding his friends' reaction?"

"I wonder."

"Gentlemen," said the sheriff. He entered the pantry and was obviously interested in what they were speaking about.

"It is a peripheral business," said Mister Walton, "which I would rather not speak of in . . . mixed company." He indicated the blond men with a glance.

The sheriff nodded. "Arthur, Edgar," he said to the blond men, who had not offered their surnames, "you will allow me to be your host tonight at the county jail."

"You have no right to lock us up!" spat Arthur, his fair complexion turning ruddy with anger. Edgar sat straight in his straight-backed chair and glared at the sheriff.

"It was all one word against another, as far as I could tell," explained the sheriff, "but you stuck it out a little too far with this claim of owning the land. Something isn't square here, and perhaps the light of day will have a beneficial effect on my ability to understand the problem."

"They kidnapped us!" pronounced Edgar.

"And brought you straight to the sheriff," said Darwin. "Would that all kidnappers followed the same scheme. I know it's Sunday tomorrow," he said to the remainder of the room, "but I think we had better rectify things in the morning."

"Thank you, Sheriff," said Frederick.

"Bernard," said Capital.

With the assistance of some of the other men, the sheriff ushered the two blond men to the door.

"If you will pardon me, gentlemen," said Sundry, "I have something for you." He advanced upon Arthur and Edgar, and though he wore the most amiable of expressions, they shied a little at his approach. The sheriff watched Sundry closely. "This is what you were looking for, I think," said Sundry, "at Mr. Thole's house in Augusta." And he held out the photograph of the boulder on Council Hill.

Edgar and Arthur considered the offered photograph with suspicion.

"Don't thank me," said Sundry. "We're giving them to everyone in town and will be sending more to the papers in the morning."

There was the flash of something dangerous in the expressions of the two men at the door, but Sundry only cocked his head to one side and thrust the picture toward them again.

"I am not finished with you," said Edgar, whose cheek was still bruised from Sundry's fist.

"If that's a threat—" began the sheriff.

"Only of legal action," said the man, but Sundry was looking into the man's eyes and sensed the threat of something else entirely.

"You haven't translated it, have you?" said Arthur to Frederick with something like a sneer, before they were prodded out the door.

"Don't concern yourself," assured Mister Walton, with a hand on Frederick Covington's arm; "neither have they."

29. Number Two in a Series of Three

There were bells on the harness of the horse that pulled their sleigh, and Daniel almost laughed, it so completed the cozy picture as they skimmed the white street beneath the lamp that bobbed on a pole behind them. There were two other people riding with them, and Charlotte sat in the seat opposite from Daniel but kept the accidental intimacy between them alive with happy conversation, making it difficult for him to be sorry about the train's derailing.

They were not long arriving in Iceboro, the community named for the ice-cutting industry that was at its height in those days along that portion of the Kennebec River. The settlement itself was impressive for its huge warehouses and ice plants and the great boardinghouses that slept and fed the workers who cut the ice in winter and loaded ships with their precious harvest throughout the warmer months. "I take it we will not have to bunk with the ice cutters," said Charlotte wryly to the driver.

"Mother Rose will take you in," said the man around a long-stemmed pipe.

"Mother Rose?"

"She runs the hotel hereabouts."

Mother Rose's was more properly an old tavern, now making the most of its trade as an inn, and that rather briskly tonight. The ancient sign at the tavern door was adorned with a briar rose, lit by the lamp in an upper window, and swinging in a spiral of snow.

Daniel took up Charlotte's bag as well as his own and followed her into the inn. The floor of the long tavern room was wet with snow from the boots of previous arrivals, and coats hung upon the near wall. The driver stomped in behind them, mumbling something about a warming draft; he leaned his head into a doorway to their left and hooted after help for his passengers, accepted a generous coin from Daniel, and left with a tip of his hat.

A young woman came in by the left-hand door and greeted them pleasantly. "You'll be wanting a room for two then?" she asked, before Daniel could, with some awkwardness, explain that he and Miss Burnbrake were simply fellow travelers. The young woman begged their pardon, and perused her register accordingly. She was a smart young lady, with a pretty smile, and when Daniel asked after Mother Rose, it was his turn to beg her pardon since he was speaking to the very individual. "It's what the ice cutters in town call me," she said with a laugh, and hurried up the stairs to prepare, first, a room for Miss Burnbrake.

"She's not what I had expected of a Mother Rose," said Daniel to Charlotte. He didn't know why he should be in constant embarrassment around this woman.

Charlotte didn't know why she should be in such constant amusement; neither did she know why it felt so easy to speak with humor and frankness to this man. "I suspect she is a happy surprise to many a weary traveler," she said.

They heard a door slam shut, and a man's voice called after Rose, who stood at the head of the broad front stairs.

"Yes, sir?" she said.

"My bed has been slept in," came the voice.

"Yes, it's an inn, you know," she said, managing the answer without sounding altogether flippant.

"But the sheets are old," said the man with irritation rankling his voice.

"They are not new bought, if that is what you mean," returned the young woman, "but they are clean, I assure you."

"Get me the manager!" demanded the man.

"You are speaking to her," said the woman.

"There must be someone else—"

"You can consult with my father if you care to brave the churchyard tonight," she returned. By now another man came out of his room and added his own stare at the unseen malcontent.

Daniel couldn't say why that irate voice vexed him so until he glanced back at Charlotte and saw that she had lost all color in her face. Then Daniel stepped around the register desk to get a look at the man before he disappeared back into his room; but there was the sound of a door slamming, and Charlotte caught his sleeve, saying, "Please, it's him!"

"Could it be?"

"He must have been on the train ahead of us. I must go somewhere else. I can't face him again after today, Mr. Plainway."

"The driver was certain that everyone else was full up," reminded Daniel. "Perhaps I had better speak with him. He might do the decent thing and find lodgings elsewhere."

"He will not, I assure you."

Rose had returned to her desk, and she watched the conversation for only a moment before she realized that the newcomer's agitation had something to do with the man in the room above. The door of the man's room sounded again, and with marvelous prescience, Rose hurried back up the stairs to stop Roger Noble from coming down. They could hear her placating him with promises of new sheets, and while she kept him busy, Charlotte and Daniel snatched up their bags and hurried onto the porch of the inn.

The storm had weakened considerably, and there was that soft hissing calm that accompanies the finale of such a snow. A horse and rider trotted past the inn and down the main street of the settlement. Lights blazed from a sprawling boardinghouse on the ridge above them.

"What would you have me do?" asked Daniel plainly, putting himself completely at Charlotte's beck.

"If you could just find a sleigh and driver who would take me to the next town."

"Perhaps there *is* a room somewhere else."

She shook her head. "I couldn't sleep, wondering if I'm to see him on the street tomorrow. I would have stayed in Portland if I had known he was coming this way!"

Daniel was only now understanding the depth of Miss Burnbrake's fear, and the more he understood, the less he liked Roger Noble, and the more his peaceful nature was nettled by a desire to punch the man in the nose. "You understand," he said quietly, "that I can't simply put you on a sleigh and send you into the night, and this storm could pick up again."

There were tears in Charlotte's eyes. "I've put you to such trouble already."

"Not at all. It's only that you'll have to put up with my company for a while longer if you want to sled out of here."

She put a hand on his arm, and her relief appeared to weaken her. "Could we, please, without delay!" She sent a look of apprehension in the direction of the inn's door.

"Yes," he said, "let's go quickly." When they were some distance up the street, they heard a door slam, and looking over his shoulder, Daniel thought he could see a figure standing on the porch of Mother Rose's, smoking a cigarette.

Roger Noble heard the jingling of a harness somewhere up the street and he walked around the corner of the hotel porch out of idle curiosity and the need to move about. A sleigh was barely visible as a shadow flashing under the streetlamps in the direction of Gardiner. The lamps themselves had the appearance of producing the snow within the circle of their light.

He could not have put himself in worse straits: He had dared his uncle's ire, distanced himself further from Charlotte, and now he was trapped in a country burg without diversion to while the hours and placate his fears and conscience. It occurred to him that he could hire a sleigh up the street, but the emotions that rankled him conversely sapped him of his will to take action against them. He looked up the hill to the boardinghouse for the ice cutters and wondered if there was anything as lowly as a card game or a bottle of beer to be had there.

A man stood below the porch steps watching Noble, and Roger was a little startled to think it might be a member of the Moosepath League. They had seemed fools to him, but they were connected to his uncle and he was uneasy about them.

"Good evening," said the man as he mounted the steps. He took his hat from his blond head and smiled with the self-assurance that Noble spent most of his energies feigning.

Noble put his cigarette to his lips and drew on it while he watched as the man brushed the snow from his hat. *How long was he standing there?* wondered Roger. He simply nodded to the man.

"Bit of an unfortunate accident," said the man, and when Noble frowned, he added, "The train."

Roger didn't consider this statement worthy of a reply. He wondered about the man, who seemed too well dressed to be a drummer.

"A rough day altogether," continued the man, and there was something so pointed about the statement and so knowing about the manner in which it was delivered that Noble narrowed his eyes at the man and spoke for the first time.

"Do I know you?"

"No, Mr. Noble, I don't believe you do."

I must owe him money! thought Roger, and his stomach lurched. He wanted a drink. He began to bring the cigarette up to his lips again, but his hand was shaking. *But how could I owe him money if I don't know him?* He lowered his hand and took on an air of irritation. Then it hit him that the man was a debt enforcer and he wondered if he could make a run for it.

"No, you don't owe any money to anyone *I* know or represent," said the man, as if Roger had voiced his thoughts. Then with continued and unwarranted bonhomie, the man added, "But my colleagues and I may have the power to resolve some of your debts."

"At two hundred percent and the risk of broken thumbs, no thank you," said Roger, regaining some of his irritable mien now that his fears were momentarily placated.

"Not at all." The man still had his hat in his hand, and he pointed at his head and said, "You have a calling card that allows you the opportunity to join my colleagues and myself in an enterprise that will enrich all involved."

Noble narrowed his eyes again with renewed suspicion.

"We have been watching you, Mr. Noble," said the man, "ever since we first instigated business with your uncle; and I am pretty sure that we can help to put you in an enviable position with Ezra Burnbrake as well as with your lovely cousin Charlotte. You see," continued the man cryptically, "we've been caught short, you might say, as two of our colleagues north of here have just found out. And as *you* will find out, our society does not take kindly to embarrassment."

Daniel thought afterward that the driver they hired at the nearby livery hid his drink well. He was a young man, and if there was anything odd about his behavior, it went unnoticed; Daniel blamed himself for not, at least, smelling it on the fellow's breath until it was too late.

The manager of the stable was not on duty, so the driver had no one to answer to but himself, and he readily agreed to take them to Gardiner, where there would be lodgings. Daniel helped him harness a horse to a small sleigh. Though the snow had slowed considerably, the way was not short for a clouded night, and Daniel insisted on some additional throws for Miss Burnbrake and found an extra lantern in the livery office.

They put Iceboro behind them faster than Daniel would have credited. Charlotte glanced back more than once, as if she expected to see her cousin, riding like the devil himself behind them. Daniel resisted looking back.

Night and distance swallowed them; they sensed the hills and trees to the west without seeing them, and the Kennebec along the eastern bank of the road harbored the wind so that the shifting air whined over the ice and these gusts blew over them at every point of exposure to the river. The horse kept a steady pace, undaunted by the dark and the snow; but a mile or so outside Iceboro, with four or five miles to go before they reached Gardiner, the driver got himself crossed up at a fork and put the horse and sleigh off the road.

Daniel had closed his eyes and had no idea they were in trouble until the sleigh took a lurch; he clutched the side of the seat and watched as the horse foundered in a drift. Still, it didn't seem a terrible problem, and he was about to jump down and help lead the animal back to the road when a sudden snap and another lurch told him that they had broken a runner.

Charlotte fell against Daniel, and he helped her out of the sleigh. They struggled through the drift and away from the horse and vehicle. The lantern jiggled at the end of its pole, then leaped from its perch into the drift. The horse struggled in the ensuing dark, almost panicking, in the traces, and the driver managed to get himself knocked down before Daniel could pull him away from the animal.

It was then that Daniel realized the man was drunk, and astonished at himself and furious with the driver, he began to read the riot act.

"I ain't drunk!" asserted the fellow, and Daniel saw there was no talking to him. Obliging enough till now, the driver grew surly when accused of that particular sin and called on his grandmother, who had passed from this vale, to bear him out. Daniel didn't see how the boy's grandmother, in whatever state, was going to be of service, and when the boy declared that he would get help, the older man tried to talk him from taking the horse, fearing he would break his neck or die of exposure if he fell.

The young man was adamant, promising that he would retrieve another sleigh, and as the driver took off in the dark with the halter in one hand and the extra lantern in the other, Daniel wondered what else could crash before the night was over. (Things, he later decided, often came in threes.)

"Now I've gotten us into a scrape," said Charlotte , who had said little during the last few minutes. The snow had increased again, and the wind off the river was sharp.

"You didn't stop the train," said Daniel, "and you didn't ditch the sleigh." He relit the first lamp, and while she held this, he tipped the sleigh on its side; they used the cushions to sit upon and the blankets to wrap about them, with the sleigh itself a screen against the wind. Nevertheless, it seemed none too warm, and they kept the lantern as close as they dared to get what heat they could from it.

"Will your business with the Moosepath League suffer if you don't reach them tomorrow?" asked Charlotte, who continued to worry herself over the deleterious effect she was having upon Mr. Plainway's affairs.

"Not at all," he replied. "It is only news of a sort that I have for them, and it has waited for some time now, so it can wait a little longer."

"I'm glad," she said.

"Two or three months ago," he explained, "the Moosepath League was involved in rescuing a little boy from a gang of thieves, and the only clue they have to the child's identity is the portrait of a woman with whom he shared, according to the account that I read, an unmistakable resemblance."

"Do you know who he is then?"

"I know who the woman in the portrait was and that her son has been missing these past three years or more."

Charlotte put a hand to her breast, as if she suddenly found it difficult to breathe. "The poor woman! She must be mad with grief! But you *must* hurry!"

"She is dead," said Daniel. Even these years after, the thought shocked him a little, and he glanced away from the light of the lantern.

"I'm so sorry," was all she said for some time, but finally she asked, "His family?"

"All gone. On his mother's side, they're gone. As for his father's side, I'm not sure that they are any better than the thieves he was rescued from."

"Will he remember them?"

"His people? I don't think so. He's only four or five now."

Charlotte shivered, and Daniel tried to give her one of his throws. "No, no," she insisted. "It wasn't really the cold."

"I'm sorry," he said. "My choice of news could have been happier."

"No," she returned, "it's just that there are so many people in the world willing to drive tragedy."

"There are as many," said Daniel, "*more*, really, who are willing to help put things right."

She did not respond to this at first and looked as if she doubted the sentiment. Finally, however, she said, "There was the Moosepath League, of course, rescuing the little boy. And they were very kind about Uncle Ezra."

"There's this Mister Walton," added Daniel, "whom I have yet to meet, but from the tales I have been told, he is a veritable engine of good works."

"Well," she said, smiling softly into the night, "there are other people too."

When another shiver ran through her, he began to think they should look for other shelter. More than three-quarters of an hour had passed, and he thought it time enough for someone to have gotten back to them.

He may have broken his neck after all, Daniel thought but said nothing.

"Do you suppose he's forgotten us?" wondered Charlotte. That of course was the other possibility.

"I think we've waited long enough," said Daniel. "Let's find the nearest house while there are still lights on to guide us."

"Oh, yes," she said. "I hadn't thought."

Daniel helped Charlotte wrap a blanket about her like a cloak, then took up one for himself. They had noticed several lights in the distance and with the lantern to guide them back to the road, they made steps northward, toward Gardiner, and toward the lights they deemed the closest.

"Where is he now?" asked Charlotte while they walked. "The little boy."

"I am told he is with a family up in Veazie."

"You were a friend to his people?" she said.

"I was their lawyer first, but yes, they were my friends."

"Has he a bequest then?"

"Would you believe, if there *is* a bequest, it's been hidden somewhere, and the boy may be the only one who can find it?"

"I don't understand," said Charlotte, intrigued. "How can a four-year-old find it if no one else can?"

"I don't know myself," admitted Daniel. "It was something his grandfather said to me once. Then again, I may have misunderstood him. But it is certainly the reason he was kidnapped in the first place."

Staying on the road was more difficult than they would have guessed; everything was so white, and the snow had drifted. The lights they were following disappeared for a while behind a rising bank, then appeared a good deal closer than they had expected. There was a house, but any driveway was invisible and they scrambled up a bank, deep with snow, to a wide front porch.

The house was a massive thing, couched in its bed of snow and surrounded by extraordinary trees; the house rose so loftily, with tall wings on either side, and the tree trunks were so wide, themselves like walls, that the house and the wooden giants seemed like one edifice, whether natural or man-made.

"If your story didn't sound like something from a book," said Charlotte, "we have certainly walked into one."

There were lights in the lower windows on the right-hand side of the house and a dim glow through the panes on either side of the front door. The drifts on the porch were nearly as deep as in the road, and Daniel had to kick snow out of the way to open a heavy storm door. Beyond this was a proper Gothic portal, and he knocked at it three times.

He sensed Charlotte shivering beside him and thought how pleasant it would be had he the license, the privilege, to put an arm about her. It was perhaps not just the cold that made her shake; there was something a little eerie about standing on this strange porch with the great house looming over them. The night was dark, and they were distant from the general warmth of humanity. They would know no one.

No one came to the door at first, and Daniel knocked again. Then he started, for someone appeared and peeked from below the glass in the door, pulling the lace curtain aside to reveal a single eye. He heard a sound of surprise from Charlotte, even as he realized that the person was not a sneak but by nature short or stooped. It was a bright wide eye though marked by age. He raised the lantern so as to illuminate Charlotte, thinking that the face of a woman was bound to cause less apprehension on the other side of the door.

A second eye joined the first, every bit as wide and bright, and Daniel thought he caught the note of a voice. Another figure moved like a shadow behind the first, and soon two pairs of eyes were considering them. There was a definite discussion then and finally the sound of a key in the lock. The door was tugged at several times, and Daniel kept himself from giving it a good shove. *Let them let us in*, he thought.

"Haloo?" came a reedy voice from within when there was a crack in the door. "Is someone there?"

"Yes, ma'am," said Daniel. "We've been stranded. Our sleigh foundered, and we need a place to sit and warm ourselves."

"Oh, dear! Louella, help me here! I must rescue these persons!"

This time Daniel *did* lend a little weight to the struggle with the door and he stepped aside so that Charlotte could enter first. Relative warmth and the comfort and smells that accompany oiled floors, oriental carpets, and rooms crammed with furnishings greeted them like an overwhelming act of generosity. The two elderly women did their best to wrestle the door closed behind their unexpected guests, and Daniel offered his assistance.

"Allow me," he said, his hat in hand, and having pulled shut the storm door, he closed the front door as well.

"Oh, my!" said the first woman. "How strong! Curier could never do that!"

"Curier shuts the door all the time, Lavona," said Louella.

"Yes, I suppose he does! But in such a storm! Oh, my! How strong!" Lavona turned a sweet face to Daniel. "I was just saying how very strong you are!" Everything she said was at a pitch somewhat louder than normal and therefore had the sound of an exclamation.

"Lavona is always pleased with strong men," explained Louella.

"Oh, well," said Daniel, a little abashed, "I'm afraid I won't please her *very* much."

Louella's face wrinkled into a beautiful smile, and she waved a hand at him. If Daniel hadn't seen her face, he would have thought the laugh coming from her was a sob. He realized, then, that a third elderly woman was standing at the head of the broad stairs before them. She was saying something he couldn't hear, but the first two women knew the problem. "She's just gone upstairs!" said Lavona.

"Dear," said Louella, "you're shouting."

"What's that, dear?"

"You're shouting!"

"I'm shouting?!"

"You are!!"

Lavona laid a hand on Daniel's arm and shouted apologetically. "I do shout, I know!"

"Please, I didn't notice."

"Oh, dear, you're cold," said Louella to Charlotte. Charlotte had taken off her gloves, and her hands did look a little blue. Louella took one of Charlotte's hands and rubbed it. "Dear, dear."

"Bring them in!" said Lavona.

The third woman was halfway down the stairs, and Daniel gave her a smile and a nod as he and Charlotte were led into a brightly lit parlor, where they were made to stand before the fire. Two more elderly women sat near the hearth, and they were introduced to the unexpected guests.

"This is our sister, Larinda," Louella was saying.

"Oh, my, what a terrible night," Larinda intoned.

"And this is Lavilda."

"Have you had supper?" wondered this person.

"And here is our baby, Alvaid," finished Louella when the woman from the stairs entered the room. "We are the Pettengills."

"You're all sisters?" wondered Charlotte. There were smiles all around for an answer, and Charlotte declared, "How marvelous!"

The pronouncement pleased the old ladies and even made them laugh a bit. "That's Father and Mother," said Louella, pointing to two intrepid-looking individuals caught in oil above the mantel.

"They're magnificent!" said Charlotte, quite sincerely, and Daniel thought three or four years fell off the Pettengill sisters right then, they were so proud.

The marvel of it was there couldn't have been a one of them less than eighty years old, and though they were of different stature (and Alvaid was not as thin as her older sisters), they were like distinct creations of the same hand, perhaps images of the same subject in different moods or light. They were fine, delicate-looking creatures, every one of them exquisite in the absolute honesty of her age.

"I think there's pie in the kitchen," said Larinda, the way a person might tease a child with sweets.

Daniel knew the way to these ladies' hearts, and he went straight to it without compunction. "I will be honest with you, ladies, and tell you that we have survived a wrecked train and a ditched sleigh and as yet have had no supper tonight."

Oh, the cries that went up! Every one of the women must rise from her seat or wring her hands in horror at such news, and as one they hurried—in a shuffling manner—toward the hall and stopped only occasionally to draw Daniel and Charlotte along with them to the kitchen.

"I can see you are a hand with the ladies," said Charlotte with the sort of puckishness she had exhibited earlier.

Daniel, who had not expected such an immense response to his tactics, chuckled.

"I shall watch myself in future," said Charlotte.

30. Advice Did Not Come Cheap

When Miss Burnbrake did not arrive at the Worster House by nightfall, her uncle began to fret, and when word *did* arrive that two trains had been stopped by a derailment south of Hallowell, the old man was beside himself and hired a sleigh that would take him to the scene of the accident. Before he was able to leave, however, a sequel to the story was broadcast over the wire, stating that no one had been injured in the accident and that the passengers from both trains had found quarters in nearby inns and private homes. With these assurances, Mr. Burnbrake was prevailed upon to stay at the Worster House and wait upon his niece's arrival on the morrow. A practical man, having assuaged his fears, he went upstairs to take a nap before dinner.

He rose an hour later, dressed, and joined the Moosepath League and the Dash-It-All Boys in the dining room; it made for a jolly table, and Roderick Waverley himself stood from his seat with a glass of cider raised and declared, "Though we part, members of our separate societies—the Moosepath League and the Dash-It-All Boys—let us tonight think of ourselves as the *Moose-Dashians!*"

Ephram, Eagleton, and Thump were so moved that they rose as one and cried out, "Moxie!" This was completely inexplicable to the Dash-It-All Boys but did not discourage them from taking part. Durwood, in particular, derived some pleasure from declaring, "Moxie," at odd intervals throughout the meal.

Neither Moxie nor young cider, however, interested the Dash-It-All Boys very much, though Brink did find some medicinal tonic in a pocket, and the addition of this to the mugs of the Dashians greatly elevated their level of energy. Ephram, Eagleton, and Thump admired Durwood, Waverley, and Brink's animation; Mr. Burnbrake was pretty sure they were tight.

After dinner the Dash-It-All Boys bade good evening and wandered into the lobby in search of their hats and coats. It was here that Durwood found on the manager's desk a short stack of card stock that was meant to be used for messages and addresses. "How is your hand?" he asked of a young housemaid who walked past him at that moment.

"I beg your pardon," she said.

Waverley and Brink took interest in the question and gathered around him. Durwood waggled his hand in the air, as if he were writing something. "Do you have a nice hand?" he said.

"It looks very nice to me," expressed Waverley.

"Go away," suggested Durwood.

"Both of them, in fact," added Brink.

"It is nice enough, I suppose," said the young woman.

Durwood snatched up one of the blank cards and laid it beside the register pen. "Would you do me the favor of demonstrating?" he inquired.

Though the request was unusual, the young woman was accustomed to obliging the hotel's patrons; she stepped up to the desk and dipped the pen.

"Would you please write 'Mrs. Dorothea Roberto'?" asked Durwood.

A pair of eyebrows lifted, one each on the faces of Waverley and Brink. They joined Durwood in leaning close to the work as it was accomplished. The young woman had a very nice, formal hand, and feminine; the requested name was expressed in many fine loops and curls, and one might have thought that something of the actual Mrs. Roberto had been discovered in those letters.

"Marvelous!" said Durwood, and he answered the young woman's obliging nature with a generous gratuity. She looked back as she continued on her errand but soon forgot the business. Durwood fanned the card in the air till the ink was dry.

"And what is that toward?" wondered Brink.

"Oh, I don't know," said Durwood. "The woman was on my mind, and I thought I would like to have some remembrance of her." This seemed logical enough (for the time being), and Waverley and Brink led the way from the lobby. "And she never lived on the waterfront," said Durwood with great finality.

So they left the Worster house for some unnamed establishment, though the storm had not abated, and they did not return till well after their Moosepathian counterparts had retired.

Whiling the remainder of their evening in the parlors of the Worster House with Ezra Burnbrake, Ephram, Eagleton, and Thump began to wonder if they were prepared to lead forces into battle.

The shank of night passed in swift fashion; the dinner had been excellent, and there had been enough of it, Mr. Burnbrake was amiable, if quiet, company, and the sitting rooms at the hotel were handsomely accoutred and filled with many interesting people. Between pronouncements concerning the weather, time, and tide, however, the subject of discourse eventually did turn upon the appointed snowball fight, and it was Thump in fact (or rather the obvious depth of his musing after dinner) who raised to light the concern so universal among them.

"You appear very thoughtful, Thump," said Ephram.

"I am mindful of tomorrow's contest," said Thump, after the moment it took to rise from his reverie.

"Ah!" returned Ephram, and his relief was plain, for it was clear to him now that Thump had been applying his significant aptitude to the stratagems and tactics necessary to their martial responsibilities. But they waited in vain for some pronouncement or plan from their bearded associate: Thump only blinked back at them as if confused by the sudden attention.

"The snowball fight," said Eagleton finally.

"Was there?" wondered Mr. Burnbrake, and he was wide-eyed and amused as they explained the details of their conscription.

"Good heavens," said the old man, "I used to join in some awful campaigns when I was a lad."

"Did you really?" said Eagleton, who couldn't imagine such a thing.

"Oh, certainly," said the old man. "I was hiding behind the stoop at my home in Concord one day—I couldn't have been more than eight or nine—waiting for my best friend, Harmon Oldgate, to walk past. I saw a shadow preceding someone up the sidewalk and let fly with as tightly packed a snowball as I ever threw. Hit a constable." The memory made Mr. Burnbrake laugh, but the members of the club were stunned to think of it.

"My word," said Eagleton, who searched in his pockets for his journal and pen.

"Did the constable know?" wondered Ephram.

"I should say he did!"

"But what did you do?"

"Ran like fire!" And Mr. Burnbrake laughed some more—from retrospective relief, Thump guessed.

"We must watch for constables," suggested Ephram solemnly. Mr. Burnbrake's tale awakened them to the true and chancy nature of battle.

"Perhaps you could give us some advice regarding tactics," said Eagleton.

"That's a very good idea, Eagleton."

"Thank you, Ephram."

"Load quickly and fire at will!" declared Mr. Burnbrake with another laugh. "Perhaps you should ask old Colonel Barkoddel. He's fought the real thing."

"Colonel Barkoddel?" said Eagleton. He glanced around the room.

"There. By the fire," said Mr. Burnbrake. He indicated with a nod of the head a man sitting at the other end of the room, who was more elderly than himself.

"Do you think?" wondered Thump.

Mr. Burnbrake reminded them of their chairman then, his laughter had such a Waltonian quality about it; there was both humor and kindness in his voice. "The poor colonel hasn't been with himself as of late, I'm afraid. His mind is on those other battlefields."

And the conversation was allowed to drift to other matters till Mr.

Burnbrake retired. As soon as the older man was gone, however, having assured them that he was quite able to climb the stairs on his own, Ephram, Eagleton, and Thump began to wonder if approaching Colonel Barkoddel with questions regarding the expected dispute might encourage some advice from the elderly fellow.

Having discussed this at some circuitous length, the Moosepathians moved in concert to the hearth, which glowed with great cheer and vigor. Colonel Barkoddel, as it happened, was nodding in the warmth of the fire, and they stood for several minutes looking at him before considering it beyond the gravity of the situation to wake him.

They had just settled upon this last point when the old man's eyes snapped open, and he cast his rheumy sight upon the three friends. "Have you their position?" he demanded in a rather sharp tone.

"I beg your pardon?" said Ephram, to whom, in the absence of their chairman, the capacity of spokesman often fell.

"They'll show soon enough, I daresay," growled the man. "Though I'd rather know from what quarter, and I wonder that you hazard to return without anything but a 'beg your pardon.'"

"There's to be a contest tomorrow," ventured Eagleton.

"I'll say there'll be a contest!" declared the fellow, the volume and the emphatic nature of his words drawing attention from several other people in the parlor. "I daresay some of you won't see the end of it!" he added, in what seemed a dire prediction. The Moosepathians were attempting to take a graceful and courteous leave, but the old man followed their every movement with a glaring eye. "What is it then?" he said. "You didn't come here to ask me what you already know!"

"We would like to know the best way to lead our boys," spoke up Thump, much to the surprise and admiration of his friends.

"What?" said the colonel.

Thump had read some books on military affairs, and apparently the terms therein had adhered to his mind more completely than he had realized. "Whether to take advantage of the terrain," he added, "and make the sneak attack or to press forward with a bold charge."

"Load quickly and fire at will, I say!" said Colonel Barkoddel. "What? Up to it again, are they?" he continued, seemingly in another conversation altogether. His eyes took on a new light. "The devil!"

"Oh, my!" said Ephram. He knew that military men had the reputation for startling oaths and was sorry to have occasioned this one by their discourse. The three friends looked to one another with profound misgivings. "Seven past eight," declared Ephram, and he checked a second watch to be sure of this.

"High tide at about fifty minutes past eleven," offered Thump.

Eagleton smiled at certain onlookers and bowed politely. "Clearing tomorrow; wind to fall off after midnight." Then to the elderly fellow before the fire, he said, "It has been a great pleasure, Colonel."

"The devil!" shouted Colonel Barkoddel again.

The three men jumped, reached for hats that weren't on their heads, bowed, bumped noggins, wobbled away from the fireplace, nodded to several of the people who watched them with either curiosity or annoyance, and hurried upstairs in the wake of Mr. Burnbrake. They could hear the colonel shouting something as they hurried down the upstairs hall.

31. The Ox at Plow

"You said yourself that Norumbega was simply ancient Bangor," said Sundry to Mister Walton when they were calling the exhausting day done in neighboring rooms at the house of Capital Gaines. They had met in the upstairs hall, both on their way to say good-night to their host.

"Did I?" Mister Walton said.

"Well, you indicated that it was more or less common knowledge."

Thinking back on the conversation of the day before, the bespectacled fellow laughed softly. "Perhaps I was trying to impress Mr. Covington," he offered. "It is more a common *belief* than a knowledge, I think."

Sundry knew better than to concede to his employer's self-criticism. "But it is a pretty well accepted belief, for all that."

Mister Walton nodded. They were paused at the top of the stairs. Mr. Noel and Mr. Noggin came in from a walk around the immediate property and hailed the guests on their way to the kitchen.

"If there is an ancient crumbling city within a hundred miles of where we stand," said Mister Walton, by way of answering Sundry's implicit question, "it would be a strange thing that no one has stumbled upon it by this time."

"Still," said Sundry, "these fellows are putting a great deal of effort into searching such a place out."

"People will attach themselves to all manner of curious tenets," said Mister Walton. He recommended his journey down the stairs. "What might be viewed from the outside as the boundaries of logic might seem from within simply boundaries to be got over."

"And yet, as you said, it would be a strange thing if such a place existed."

"But I would like to know what is written on that stone," admitted Mister Walton.

Sundry nodded his agreement.

"Have you gentlemen sorted it all out then?" asked Capital Gaines when they entered the kitchen.

"I am so weary," said Mister Walton, though he looked bright enough, "that I will be lucky to sort out the bedclothes and get between them."

"Mr. Noggin is warming some bread and apple butter," said their host, "if you've a mind before you retire. That and a cup of hot milk will do wonders for a night's sleep."

This sounded a pleasant way to finish their labors, and the five men sat about and did for two loaves of bread before they were finished. In the midst of their repast, however, Mister Walton raised the mysterious business again by stating, "I say that I have no theories regarding the runes at Council Hill and the attendant business, but I wonder if Sundry hasn't been lending his keen mind to the problem." It was clear, from his earlier questions, that Sundry was pondering the situation, and Mister Walton was curious what direction his friend's thoughts were taking.

"Bust her feeding," said Sundry.

Mister Walton expressed his "beg your pardon" with wide eyes.

"It's something my father always says whenever he sees a team of oxen at the plow. 'She'll bust her feeding.'"

"Does he?"

"Well, he does." Sundry was considering this deeply and looked unlikely to offer more on the subject.

"It seems an unusual expression," suggested Mr. Noggin.

"Doesn't it?"

"I've never heard anything like it," announced Mr. Noel.

"She'll bust her feeding?" asked Mister Walton, wondering if he had heard aright.

"To begin with, it was just 'bust her feeding,' but now *he* always says, 'She'll bust her feeding,' whenever he sees an ox at the plow."

"But an ox is not a *she*, is it?"

"That's what makes it odd."

"Part of it, at any rate."

"What do you make of it, Capital?" asked Mister Walton.

"This is a farm, to be sure," said their host, "but it's Mr. Noel and Mr. Noggin keep it running. I'm a woodsman by inclination. It's an odd locution, though, no doubt."

"Dad knows he's saying it wrong," admitted Sundry.

"He does?"

"It's some word, really, he's using: Greek or Latin. His own father used it, and *he* learned it from old Parson Leach, an itinerant preacher who used to come through years ago."

"Bust her feeding," said Mister Walton to himself.

"Bust her feeding."

Capital and Mr. Noggin and Mr. Noel each tried their hands (or rather their tongues) at the odd phrase but could make nothing out of it.

"Does this have anything to do with that figure on the rock?" wondered Mister Walton. "The one that Frederick thought might depict an ox?"

"The pictograph?" said Capital

"I was just thinking," said Sundry, "that it might be a plow rather than an ox."

"Were you?" Mister Walton wondered that this element of their recent experiences had caught his friend's attention so.

"Yes," replied Sundry. He cut himself another piece of bread and proceeded to lose sight of it beneath a slab of butter. "But I'm also thinking," he said, raising the bread to his mouth, "that it might be the same thing—ox or plow—one way or another."

32. The Third Crash

"Do you know?" announced Lavona, more to her sisters than their guests. "We haven't had married people under this roof for years!"

"We've had Mr. Petty," said Larinda.

"*And* Mr. Bungle," added Alvaid.

"But not their wives!"

"Oh, Lavona!" exclaimed Louella with something like a laugh.

"Nor Mrs. Sharpsteen's husband," agreed Lavilda. "Good heavens! Do you suppose we haven't had a married couple beneath this roof since Mother and Father died?"

"Posh!" said Louella, but she was thinking on this very heavily.

The kitchen was spacious, with two stoves, numerous cupboards, and doors to pantries and cellars. The long simple table that ran half the length of the room had once accommodated servants at their meals and their tasks. Daniel and Charlotte were very nearly pushed into their seats with orders to do absolutely nothing toward their own comfort, while the sisters tended to their guests and discussed the dearth of married people beneath their roof.

Daniel was blushing by this time, and Charlotte smiling. The lawyer cleared his throat. "I beg your pardon," he said, "but Miss Burnbrake and I are not married."

All heads came about. Lavona turned from the warming oven, where she was retrieving the pie: Larinda hesitated in the doorway to the cold pantry, where other victuals and milk were kept; Louella paused in her getting of an extra chair (there were only six at the table, and she had refused Daniel's help); Lavilda stood with the silverware in her hand, and Alvaid with the table linen.

"Not married," said one of the sisters, and the elderly women glanced from Daniel's discomfort to Charlotte's smile.

"Saints and stars!" declared Lavona. "They're eloping!"

Now the cry that rose was that of five schoolgirls who have just been informed of some gloriously romantic notion. Larinda sat down, she was so out of breath with it, and Lavilda dropped the silverware.

"In the snow!" declared Alvaid. "In the storm!"

"Are there many after you?" asked Larinda.

"Oh, my!" said Lavona. "They'll be pursued! Just like Mother and Father!"

Daniel was attempting to get a word in edgewise but was not assisted by his own astonishment, or by Charlotte, who was fit to be tied with laughter, her hand over her mouth. It was the sight of Daniel laughing that finally stopped the ladies, though not before they had constructed a scenario that would have done the rashest, most fire-headed melodramatist proud. Charlotte let out a single peep of laughter when the room quieted, and apologized by saying, "Oh, dear, I am tired!" She wiped a tear away and told the sisters, "We've met only this morning."

But the Pettengill sisters had been so convinced by the cry of elopement that this announcement produced a stunned silence.

"My, that's quick," said Larinda finally.

Louella swatted the air and clicked her tongue. "What she is saying is that they are not eloping."

"That's too bad," said Larinda.

"But Mr. Plainway has done a valiant service in rescuing me nonetheless," added Charlotte, who couldn't bear to leave the sisters with nothing after the ecstatic peak of their previous misconstruction.

The elderly women cast glowing eyes in Daniel's direction, and the man realized that he was outnumbered with no hope of reinforcement.

"I was truly and physically threatened this morning, when Mr. Plainway arrived, and since then he has been nothing but benefit to me and I nothing but trouble to him."

"Nonsense," he said, but it was so under his breath that it was hardly heard. He cleared his throat again and said a little louder, "Nonsense."

"I have much to thank him for," she finished, and it was perhaps less awkward for her to say her thanks in such a public manner than to wait for a private moment.

"There's hope for them yet," whispered Lavilda to Alvaid.

"We certainly do beg your pardon," pronounced Louella. "Mother and Father eloped, you know, and we have always just loved the tale."

"They *didn't* elope in the end," said Alvaid.

"Well, it is all the same as if they had."

"Oh, my!" said Lavona with a dreamy smile. There were tears in her eyes. "Mother was so beautiful, and Father so very handsome!"

"You always say that," countered Larinda, "but they were no more than plain good-looking people."

"Didn't you think they were very beautiful and very handsome?" asked Lavona of Daniel.

Daniel thought back on the portraits in the parlor and, glancing from one sister to the other, gave the impression of a Solomon-like reflection. "Paintings of course do not always do their subjects justice, but what I was most impressed with was that they appeared to be very *fine* people."

One of Charlotte's very fine eyebrows lifted a quarter of an inch.

"*That's* not a big enough piece of pie for you, Mr. Plainway!" said Lavona, though it was herself serving it. She whisked the plate from under the man's nose and returned to the warming oven to find a piece large enough for a man of such perspicacity.

Larinda brought a plate of ham and a bottle of milk from the cold pantry and set it on the table. "We don't always give our guests the *cold shoulder*," she said as she uncovered the meat, and her sisters laughed.

"You must forgive us," said Louella. "We have guests too infrequently these days, though there was a time when this house was filled with people."

"Summer on the back lawn or down at the riverbank," said Larinda with a sigh.

"The oak swing," said Alvaid.

"The oak swing," said Lavilda. "I haven't thought of it for years."

"How do you get along?" wondered Charlotte, for the situation of these ladies had begun to concern her.

"Oh, we have friends, you know," said Louella. "Curier is by every day. No doubt you'll see him in the morning."

"Whose rooms shall we put them in?" wondered Lavona in her usual shout.

"Oh, please," said Charlotte. "Don't go to any trouble. Certainly not this late at night."

"I can fit on a couch in the parlor," said Daniel. "Or even the floor by the fire."

The sisters would hear none of it and discussed among them whose rooms would be used.

"Please," insisted Charlotte, "we couldn't turn anyone out of her room."

"No, no, dear," said Louella. "You misunderstand." She patted Charlotte's shoulder softly. "When Father passed on, he left the house to all of us, but certain rooms very specifically."

"He left individual rooms to particular people?" wondered Daniel.

"Yes," said Larinda. "He divided it up quite fairly."

"And expressly left the halls and entryways for the use of us all," said Alvaid.

"We've just never been very sure if that means we actually own the halls and entryways!" added Lavona.

"He was a very peace-loving man," breathed Lavilda.

"But he was death on curiosity!" exclaimed Lavona.

Larinda let out a heartfelt sigh. "Though we never suspected it while he was alive, bless his soul," she said.

"No?" Daniel knew enough of human nature to sense a story here.

"Oh, my!" said Lavona. "The inquisitive wouldn't survive long in *this* house! There's the locked room, you know, in the west wing!"

"Lavona!" said Louella.

"Am I shouting again?"

"No . . . well, yes, you are, but more important, you are telling tales."

"Howsoever, it is true! We've never seen the other side of that door!"

"I think, when we were young, it wasn't locked," said Lavilda.

"You always say that!" shouted Lavona.

"Well, I always think it!"

Larinda leaned close between Daniel and Charlotte, encouraging the guests themselves to lean forward. "We're not even sure that we should be talking of it," she said in something of a stage whisper.

"It used to smell very nice outside the room!" shouted Lavona.

Daniel had taken it upon himself to cut some portions from the shoulder of ham, and Charlotte was only now realizing (as she warmed up) how hungry she was, but this last statement lifted their eyes from the table, and they exchanged perplexed glances before Daniel spoke. "And what harm is there in talking of it?" Daniel wondered.

"If we ever saw the inside of that room, we'd lose everything!" asserted Lavona.

"What?" said Daniel.

"If any *one* of us saw it!" said Lavilda, shouting like her sister.

"Good heavens!" said Daniel. He looked to Louella.

Louella nodded, saying quietly, "It's what we've been told."

"Has it?" Daniel couldn't imagine such an article in a will and didn't know if it was binding if it existed.

"Mr. Edward has been very definite on that subject," agreed Lavilda. "No one is to go into the west wing room save for himself."

"Mr. Edward?"

"Yes."

"And he is your lawyer?"

"He is. He was Father's lawyer before Father died."

Alvaid added her own note, saying, "Mr. Edward is the one with a key."

Daniel returned to the ham and laid some slices on Charlotte's plate.

Lavona had doled out some herculean portions of pie, and Louella placed glasses on the table. The sisters were pleased as could be to have the two "young people" eating heartily at the table. Appetite did indeed overtake curiosity as Daniel and Charlotte made a late dinner, but when the edge was gone from his hunger, Daniel found his mind considering the mysterious west wing room and this Mr. Edward, who kept its secret hidden.

"Never heard of such a thing," he said to himself as he looked across the table at Charlotte, who was listening very intently to a genealogy of the Pettengill family. His curiosity was again whisked aside, but by something else entirely, as he watched her.

"Mother and Father might never have been married if not for an old Finn who lived in Hallowell in those days," said Larinda.

"Old Kalf," added Lavilda.

"And did he help them elope?" asked Daniel.

"He helped them *not* to elope, in a manner of speaking," said Larinda.

"He was a magician," said another of the sisters.

"A wizard, I think," said still another. "I think the Finns have wizards."

Charlotte sat back in a large wing-backed chair, a quilt over her knees, as she soaked up the warmth from the hearth and grew spellbound by the flames. Standing with his back to the fire in the parlor, Daniel lost track of who was speaking as the words came thick and fast.

"A wizard *is* a magician."

"I'm sure I don't know, but I've seen a magician when I was a girl, but I've never seen a wizard."

"There was a magician who came to the fair."

"I think there *may* be a difference."

"The difference is that a magician has tricks."

"Well, the story! Old Kalf had his tricks, to be sure!"

"Mother and Father believed it! Grandmother believed it!"

"They all saw it!"

"They saw something, certainly, but—"

"It is very impolite to be carrying on like this when Mr. Plainway and Miss Burnbrake haven't the slightest idea what we are talking about."

This last was from Louella, and they quietly accepted her chastisement, falling silent while the burden of the story found its speaker. Daniel glanced over his shoulder at the portraits above the mantel; they *were* fine-looking people, he mostly bald with large mustaches and a square jaw, she with dark hair in a bun and her own chin lifted a little defiantly perhaps. They had thoughtful eyes, however, and Daniel could believe that they were both kind.

"Father's family had been greatly dashed by the Revolution," said Larinda. "Their political aspirations *and* their fortunes suffered, for they were Tories, you see." Glances sped from sister to sister as this admission was made. "But as unwanted as they were in Boston, they found themselves without welcome in New Brunswick, where so many of their persuasion fled after the surrender at Yorktown. Despised by the colonists, they were condescended to by the English, and Grandfather took his family, which had yet to include Father, to the coast of Maine, where the ownership of land was much in dispute and where a person might settle without reference to his past.

"Father was born in 1784 and grew up in the tavern that his parents built and managed downriver from here at Bowdoinham. It was a rough-hewn affair at the outset, but Grandfather made improvements over the years so that there was hardly a finer inn or finer food to eat along the river than at the Kennebec House."

Daniel thought that a man telling this story must have a pipe or a mug of something before him, but Larinda told her tale with a sweet, sad smile and her hands knitting without needles before her. Her head leaned to one side, so that she had the wistful air of one who listens carefully for something she wishes, but doesn't expect, to hear.

"As Father and his siblings grew, they became part of the tavern, and as his older siblings came to maturity, they went off to sea, or married perhaps and helped settle some nearby town, till there were only Father and a sister left to help.

"One day the stage came up, as it did several times a week, and a man, his wife, and their daughter took rooms at the Kennebec House. Father was sent out to get their things, and he was pulling their bags from the top of the carriage when he first set eyes upon Mother."

A general sigh went up among the sisters. "It was a love match from the first," informed Lavilda.

"That is what they always said," said Larinda. "Mother was a frightened young woman. Her family, as it happened, was running as well, but from matters of less credit, I fear. The story was never fully told, but Mother's father was fortunate, it was whispered, to leave Kennebunk in one piece. He had purchased land in Richmond and planned to set himself up in business.

"But Mother's family's stopping at the Kennebec House was, as they say, fate without hiding its face. They stayed three days, and on the first, Father said, he spoke to Mother as a servant, on the second he spoke to her as a peer, and on the third he spoke to her as a suitor. He was twenty, and she was only eighteen, neither yet people of their own in the eyes of the law. She was frightened of him, really, but did not forget him when she and her family continued on to Richmond, and Father contrived somehow to see her now and again, though without her parents' knowledge.

"One day he went to Mother's father and announced his intentions, whereupon he was called a rapscallion and his father a traitor, for the old man had heard rumors of their Tory background. Well, it was worse than the pot calling the kettle black—"

"The kettle calling the porcelain black, is what Mother called it!" said Lavona.

"Mother's father had all but been convicted of criminal doings," continued Larinda, who seemed oblivious of the interruption, "and here he was cursing a man because his father honestly stuck to his beliefs. But Father was a canny one, you see, and let the old man believe he'd been subdued by the tongue thrashing. He conspired to see Mother again, in Richmond village, whereupon he proposed the elopement.

"Father was not one to leave anything to chance, so he traveled the roads to Augusta like a scout and arranged the wedding and considered every possible pitfall. Then, by chance, he heard of Old Kalf while tarrying at a tavern in Hallowell; the Finn was something of a legend in the town, and it was said he had the power to talk with animals and affect the weather.

"I am told Old Kalf's house even now stands upon the bank, overlooking the river, and that there are shadows still upon the ridge, not entirely the manufacture of the oaks and maples there." Larinda's eyes glistened with the mystery of her words, and she appeared to have much in common with some younger variant of herself. "Old Kalf's house was on the way home for Father that day, and the ancient fellow himself was sitting on his stoop looking out over the river when Father passed by.

"'A fast bit of work cut out for you, aye, boy?' the old fellow said when Father pulled his horse up below the wizard's house.

"Father never blinked. 'I wished the next time I pass here,' he said to the old man, 'I had leave to be as untroubled as now.'

"'Ah, well,' said Old Kalf, 'there's things might get between you and those behind.'

"'Do you have something?' asked Father, as bold as can be.

"'I have some weather in this bag,' said Kalf, 'which is doing me no good and is fit to spoil.' He held up a cloth sack, pulled tight with a drawstring. 'It was a big wind when I put it in there,' said the old man, 'but it'll be nothing more than a little rain and a sunny day thereafter if it isn't used very soon.'

"'If you have no use for it,' ventured Father, 'I might find something to do with it.'

"Whereupon Old Kalf offered the bag up to Father, saying, 'Point it where you will, but remember that the wind will do nothing for you that your own goodwill won't do better.' And the Finn, his beard down to his waist and his eyes mostly blind, turned about and disappeared into his strange house.

"Now Father didn't exactly believe in wizards, and he didn't believe at all that you could catch a wind in a bag, even if, as he said when Mother wasn't nearby, his prospective father-in-law was something of a bag of wind." Larinda laughed, and one of her sisters gave a "tut-tut."

"But the bag itself had a peculiar way about it, bobbing in the air like a kite where he tied it to the pommel of his saddle, or like an empty barrel in the water, and when he put his ear to it, he thought he could hear the sound of a wind, but far away, as if there were a storm in the next county.

"And he brought it home, and he hid it, and he made his plans, and the next time that Mother was to meet him, he came with an extra horse."

"You should understand, Mr. Plainway," said Louella, "Miss Burnbrake, that Mother was more than fond of Father by now. He was a gallant sort of young man, she told us, tall and with a straightforward way of looking a person in the eye."

"He had hair then too!" shouted Lavona.

"Of course he had hair," said Louella.

"Father had bought a new cape for Mother," continued Larinda, this time more conscious of the interruption but willing to overlook it. "A new cape as a wedding present and as a means to disguise her, he hoped. It was broad daylight, however, and some word was quickly broadcast that Mother had left with a strange young man. Mother's father was furious and charged after with several pillars from the village community.

"Father was an excellent rider, but Mother had little experience on horseback, and their progress was necessarily slow. By the time they were crossing the line into Hallowell, they had glimpses of pursuit from the tops of hills. It was early May as well, and the roads were still wet enough so that their tracks were plain to see, and turning off would do them no good.

"Finally, at the top of a rise, Father turned about and saw their pursuers cresting the hill behind them. He and Mother came to a small bridge that crossed a stream, a tributary to the Kennebec, and here he told Mother to ride on. Taking Kalf's bag from its place at his saddle, he laid it in the road, pointed it toward the bridge, and pulled it open.

"He felt as if the ground were shivering beneath him, and the sounds coming from the bag were like the sounds of a gale when you are safely indoors. He did not stay to hear or see any more but jumped on his horse and rode after Mother. The sound behind them only increased as they hurried toward Hallowell. But as they came up beside Old Kalf's house, Father reined in, for the wizard was sitting on his stoop again, looking down at them.

"The roar of the wind behind them had grown almost deafening, and Father called up to Kalf, 'What have you given me?'

"'What have you taken?' asked the old man in return.

"Father heard other sounds—the crash of water and the cries of men—and he wheeled his horse about and charged back to the bridge, which was gone in a sudden wind-rushed torrent. Several riders were steadying their mounts on the opposite side, but Mother's father was not among them, and the men were shouting and pointing. Father saw a horse scrambling up the bank of the swollen stream and also the figure of a man struggling in the water.

"Without thinking twice, Father leaped from his horse and dived in after the man who had cursed him and his family. Mother arrived on the scene in time to see the two of them carried by the torrent to the Kennebec and thought then she had lost both father and lover.

"But down the stream Father caught hold of the old man's collar with the one hand and a length of exposed root with the other. It was the root of an oak tree, and the oaks around this house were grown from acorns found beneath it. Father filled his pockets with them before he left that place."

"So he saved your grandfather," said Charlotte when there was a lengthy silence. Daniel thought she had gone asleep and had been watching her a little more intently than decorum allowed. Now he was startled, thinking that she might have been watching him in return from partly closed eyes.

"He did indeed," said Larinda. "And it is difficult to bear ill will against a man who has risked his life to save your own. They were never overly fond of one another, Father and Mother's father, but the old man gave permission for his daughter to be married as soon as she was twenty."

"And what happened to the bag?" wondered Charlotte dreamily; the heat of the fire seemed to slow even her speech.

Larinda was astonished by the question, and she referred to her sisters, each in turn, and met the mirror image of her expression in them all. "My word!" she said when she turned back to Charlotte. "We never asked!"

The fire in the parlor hearth was banked, and the lamps were dimmed. Louella and Lavona led a procession up the stairs, and they paused at the landing to listen to the hiss of snow and the wail of the wind. The sisters embraced one another gently, and those sisters not accompanying one of the guests bussed Charlotte and Daniel as well; then they wished one another "Happy St. Nicholas's Eve" and parted.

The hall above the kitchen, where Larinda and Lavilda had inherited their rooms (and a room or two besides), was deemed by the sisters to be the warmest and Charlotte and Daniel were led to chambers on opposite ends and opposite sides of this wing.

"I think one of Father's nightshirts would fit you just fine," said Larinda, who stopped before one door and, from her own candle, lit the candle that sat upon the stand outside the room. "I'll get you one."

"Please," said Daniel, "I will be fine without it."

"If you are sure?"

He nodded. His eye was caught by a large, ornately carved door across the hall. Charlotte, who was being led by Lavilda, stopped to consider the portal.

"That is the locked door," said Lavilda when she realized that Charlotte had not kept up with her.

"Don't say a thing," said Larinda, in a hush that could be heard the length of the hall. "Lavona is convinced we'll fly up in flames if we so much as blink at it."

"It's very impressive," said Charlotte.

"It's the locked door," said Lavilda again, nodding softly. She waved a negligent hand. "I hardly see it anymore."

Daniel wanted to approach the door, to touch its heavy carvings, to peer through the keyhole, which, he suspected, must have a hinged guard on the inside.

"Thank you, Mr. Plainway," said Charlotte. She was in fact glad for the company of the two sisters at this point.

The two sisters, contrarily, wondered if they should scramble out of sight and stood uncertainly, even awkwardly in the midst of the hall, blinking at one another.

"It has been a memorable day, Miss Burnbrake," returned Daniel, "and a pleasant one." Her smile, as she turned away, was reward enough.

"Leave your boots outside the door, Mr. Plainway," said Larinda, with a shake of her finger, after she had pecked him on the cheek.

"Oh? Do you have a bootblack, or are you afraid I'll run off in the night?"

"No, silly," she replied. "It's St. Nicholas's Eve. You must leave your boots outside your door so that he can leave you sweets."

He made no answer but a silent O and nodded his understanding. Down the hall Lavilda was showing Charlotte her room.

"Good night, Mr. Plainway."

"Good night, miss," he intoned to Larinda.

His candle seemed of little value in the lofty room beyond the door. In the far corner was the dark form of a curtained bed, and he considered the spectral shapes of draped furnishings as he made his way across the carpeted floor. The shadows upon the ceiling as he moved were dim and shapeless, and a chair by the bed looked like an animal, crouched and watching.

He pulled off his boots and wondered how he could be so tired and not have noticed it till this very moment. The distance between the chair and door seemed like a mile to him, but he dutifully picked up his boots and carried them back. The hinges of his door whined; leaning from the room, he laid his boots on the hall runner.

Across from him was the locked door, and he considered this for a brief moment. Then he looked down the hall toward Miss Burnbrake's room and saw her dropping her own boots outside her door.

Charlotte gave him a conspiratorial smile, and he thought she even laughed softly to see him set his boots out for St. Nicholas. Daniel chuckled all the way to the bed; it had a deep feather mattress that he sank into, feeling the warmth of his own body reflected back upon him almost immediately.

There was a sudden crack and a crash as the bed broke beneath him. Daniel was startled almost into shouting but found himself laughing quietly instead. He climbed from the embrace of the feather bed, disentangled himself from the covers, and considered what was to be done. Had anyone heard? Would they come knocking in a moment to see what was the matter?

He waited, but no one knocked, and the room was so dark he couldn't see well enough to think about putting the bed back together—and he was weary. He shook the mattresses all the way to the floor and climbed back in beneath the covers, the ghost of his former warmth still glowing there.

He lay for some time, thinking of his day, and finally realized that the crashes had indeed come in threes. He thought Charlotte would be amused. *She missed this one, however,* he thought, which was unintentionally suggestive, and he blushed in the darkness.

❧ BOOK FOUR ☙

December 6, 1896

33. Gifts

The sound of the ax struck Lydia's nerves; it hadn't the rhythm one came to expect, and of course she knew, as a parent would know, the effort and pain that went into every stroke. It was not the first time she begrudged Sean for preceding her into the next world; such burdens, such pain and effort, bear better on two pairs of shoulders.

It had been more than a week since Wyck began to work with the ax, and his mother wasn't sure that he had done anything but harm to himself. He had pushed too hard that first morning, and the second morning he had not lasted long, shaming himself. On the third day he worked a little more slowly and on the fourth day he worked a little longer again. Each day he returned looking pale and used up, and each day Lydia felt a little used up as well.

Mollie Peer was the name of the young woman who had given Wyck the ax, along with the tale of her own father who had brought a shattered knee to life by riding a bicycle, and it was Mollie Peer's name that sometimes rang in Lydia's head with every ax stroke. Wyckford had plainly fallen for the young woman, and Lydia knew that her son's feelings—unacknowledged, if not entirely unrequited—hurt worse than the near mortal wound.

Bird too had a strong attachment to Mollie Peer, which was more difficult to explain; Mollie's had been the deed that set all else in motion, but she was also the person most perplexed by his admiration. She had revealed an awkward affection for him the time she had come to the O'Hearn farm by bringing him a toy, the same day she had given Wyck the ax and left with a self-conscious handshake.

The ax blow came again, more the impression of a sound than the sound itself, but loud enough to Lydia's ears and always out of rhythm. Wyck would swing the ax, then wait for the pain to subside so that he could swing it again; sometimes the pain was greater, and sometimes he got angry and didn't wait for the pain to die, and sometimes the ax slipped from his hand. The days had grown more difficult, Wyck's intentions further hampered by several snowstorms, not the least of which had been dying this morning when Lydia rose from bed (having dressed herself under the sheets).

The house was quiet, save for the thunk of the ax. She wished Ephias were home to keep an eye on Wyck from the barn, but Ephias and Emmy had made the trek into church by sleigh and hadn't yet returned. Lydia's fat dog, Skinny, lay at her feet, asleep.

Bird stood on the porch, looking cold. Wyckford wouldn't let the boy near him when he was chopping wood, certainly for safety's sake, but also so that the little boy would not see him in such pain. Bird had lost interest in helping Ephias with the chores the last few mornings, and Lydia thought Ephias missed him. But Bird wanted only to stand on the porch and wait for Wyckford, to know as soon as the big man returned around the corner of the barn that he was all right. There might be other reasons, less obvious for this, and Lydia had been thinking on them.

She was a practical, God-fearing farm wife who had little use for superstition. Her kitchen had no herbal charms (only remedies), no upturned horseshoe or rabbit's foot; if she spilled salt, she scraped it off the table and put it back in the bowl, with none wasted over her shoulder.

But she lived in a world of superstition: words to ward off evil influences and prescriptions to avoid hats upon the table or empty shoes beneath it. Even Ephias, who eschewed such beliefs, would stop a chair from rocking when someone got up from it, and few would open an umbrella in the house or whistle past a graveyard. Lydia believed in cleanly scoured surfaces and simple prayer. Ghosts and the remnant intentions of the dead did not enter her philosophy.

Yet she had heard these past few nights some strange sounds that were difficult to pass off as the voice of an owl or the wind in the limb of a tree, and she began to wonder what Bird had brought with him or, rather, what had followed him here.

Or was it simply her own sense of motherly love and sadness? She had lost two children herself and could well imagine that had she gone first, some part of her might have hung about to see that her babies were well cared for. She had little use for superstition, but somehow she was utterly convinced that Bird's mother was dead and half convinced that some aspect of her, like a sleeping memory, was searching for him but had not yet quite found him.

Lydia could see the little fellow from the parlor where she was knitting, this being Sunday and a certain amount of reflective activity on the Sabbath being part of her upbringing. She was just considering if she should call him in when she saw Bird turn about on the porch and step inside.

At first she was startled, sure that something had happened to Wyck, but then the ax blow came again, and she was simply puzzled. Bird appeared at the parlor door, and she told him to come in with a warm note in her voice. He looked out the parlor windows as he passed them, still watching for Wyck.

"When the snow goes," she said, "we are making more effort to get to church." She fell to counting stitches and only caught the boy's quiet reaction to her announcement by the corner of her eye.

He stood in the middle of the parlor floor for some time before speaking. "Are you Wyck's mother?" he asked.

This made her look up. "Yes, of course," she said. "You know that."

The reply was not a reprimand, but Bird sat on the edge of a chair and looked down, an unconscious sort of expression she had seen in her own children when they feared another's displeasure.

"Bird," she said, "there's no fault in asking questions." The retreat inward, so clear upon his face, had struck her fiercely.

"Are you *my* mother?" he asked.

Now she felt the wind had been rushed from her. There was the space for two or three long breaths. He was looking down at his knees, his feet dangling a few inches from the floor. "Oh, dear," she said under that third breath. "Do you know Mister Walton sent you something a few days ago?" she asked. "I've only been waiting for the right moment to give it to you."

He looked interested, but vaguely, as if he could not offer more until he knew more, and here was an indication to his character or what had been formed of his character by living in cellar holes with madmen and criminals.

She didn't know why she hadn't shown him the picture when it had arrived—*more* than a few days ago, to be truthful. The portrait had existed with him in Eustace Pembleton's strange den beneath Fort Edgecomb, and she suspected that it was a sign of that furtive life, which must have been of equal portions dullness and fear. Partly she worried that it was an object of morbid interest; partly (she must admit to herself) she was somewhat jealous, even of this image that might steal his thoughts from herself and her son.

"You stay here and watch for Wyck," she said, and she set her knitting aside and went to the front hall closet. The picture was wrapped in brown paper, but she could see Bird's interest increase severalfold when she returned with it. It was not the original portrait; Mister Walton had that in his own keeping, as he was the person coordinating the search for the woman it represented. The picture Lydia unwrapped was a photograph of the portrait, which Mister Walton had gone so far as to have tinted after the original.

The woman's face came to the dim light of the parlor, and Bird left his chair to gaze at it closely, his features almost without expression.

Her hair was darker than Bird's, but they shared the large brown eyes and the full lower lip, which was curved in the portrait into a gentle smile. She looked a little downward and to one side, her hands resting in her lap. The pale green of her dress seemed to melt into the atmosphere of the picture. There was more than the cast of a cheek or the color of an eye, however, that joined Bird with this lovely woman; there was a quality of sweet introspection in both their faces, a natural disposition to smile, however mildly.

"Is she my mother?" asked Bird very plainly.

"We do think so," said Lydia. She turned her head to one side as she studied him. "Do you?"

He thought about this, then said, "She's very pretty."

"Yes, she is," Lydia agreed, and surprisingly, she had the sudden wish to have the young woman in the room with them.

"Do you know where she is?" asked Bird. In some ways this was more conversation than she had ever had with him.

"We don't. I'm sorry. But wherever she is, here or in heaven, she loves you, I know." Lydia considered the portrait again; its very existence seemed to indicate some gentility in its subject, yet how did the boy, who bore such a strong resemblance to this woman of class, arrive in the grimy hands of Eustace Pembleton, living a furtive life along the wharves of Portland?

Bird fairly drank in the lovely face.

"Would you like me to put it on the wall, so that you can look at it when you want?" she asked. She barely registered his nod. "I'll do that," she said, then noticed that Wyck stood in the parlor door.

They had not heard when he ceased chopping or when he entered the house. Usually, after his sessions with the ax, he retired to his room, hiding his sweating gray pallor. This morning he came into the room and sat in a chair opposite the picture. He leaned his forearms upon his knees, as if catching his breath, his red hair wet.

"You brought it out," he said, and sounded, by his tone, as if he thought it should have been brought out sooner.

Lydia said nothing; she was a little angry with him suddenly. She was almost angry at Bird, though he couldn't be held responsible for the extra burden on her heart.

"Come here," said Wyck, and the little boy climbed into the big man's lap. Together they considered the woman in the picture, and quite surprisingly Bird fell asleep.

"Didn't he sleep?" asked Lydia.

Bird shared a room with Wyck, and Wyck, Lydia knew, did *not* sleep well, so that he would know the state of Bird's night. "He snored half the night," said the man.

"There's a lot to tire him out, I suppose, poor little fellow."

"I heard Emmy's owl last night. At least I thought it was an owl."

"I heard it too," said the mother. "I woke up thinking someone had spoken to me, but it was something outside."

"That was it," said Wyck. "I thought it was in the room at first. It sort of startled me. Then I realized that it was too far away."

Lydia thought that Wyck's color was looking better. Bird looked as if he could hardly be comfortable (and Wyck with him) the way he was sprawled in the big man's lap; but his face was devoid of worry, and his mouth gaped with the trusting sleep of childhood. It made Lydia glad to see him sleep so completely, so completely trusting. She returned to her needles, her pique gone as quickly as it had come.

34. Advanced Uses for a Hat

Doc Brine had been in an alcohol-deprived stupor for three days. He couldn't have guessed himself what brought on this sudden determination to resist drink since he had given Lincoln N. Washington the sole coin in his pocket. He had felt remarkably strong until Friday night, and then the shakes and the cold sweats and the horrors had visited him. Last night, St. Nicholas's Eve, had been the worst. He reeled in his bed, while at the same time he could see the water- and body-logged gully at Fredericksburg. The last part of the night he spent talking to the old saint himself, arguing with him, actually, about the snakes that had crawled into his room and praising the usefulness of St. Patrick in their eradication. St. Nick refused to be offended by the comparison, however, and Doc realized, when the first glimmers of dawn were casting shadows in his room, that he was talking to himself.

Then, as now, he considered his recently acquired hat, which hung neatly on the wall beside the door of his single room. He was lying on his bed with the clothes pulled over him. He wondered what day it was.

I should have looked in on that bay at the livery by now, he thought. It occurred to him that the horse might be dead from his inattention, and he sat up on the edge of the bed. The room was cold. The fire in the grate was almost down, and he wondered why it wasn't out altogether till he remembered his landlady coming in and stoking it, presumably with her own coal.

Doc reached for the hat on the wall, which was several feet away, and would have cracked his head on the floor if his arm hadn't been outstretched. The door to his room opened soon after, and Mrs. Plaint, his landlady, and the old salt (Doc couldn't recall his name) who lived below him hurried in and helped him to the edge of the bed.

Doc took some deep breaths, saying, "I'm fine, I'm fine." He thought his head was clearing, and he *knew* it was clearing when the irony of a mind's *thinking* it was clear occurred to him. *Does a mind need to be clear to think it is clear?* he wondered. *Or is a mind fuddled that considers the issue at all?* "Thank you," said Doc. "I must have been walking in my sleep."

They both knew better—they *all* knew better—but nothing was said to contradict him.

"I have to see to that bay at Sporrin's Livery," he said, more to himself.

"Don't you think you should be lying down?" wondered the old mariner.

"I've been lying down for three days now." Doc flashed a smile. "I think I'm rested up. Hand me that hat, would you, please?"

He didn't even know which of them passed him the required article, but when he placed the homburg on his head, he was sure that he could move now and attend to business. He thanked them both again and retrieved his coat. He surprised himself with his vigor as he clomped down the stairs. The old salt and Mrs. Plaint stood in the well above him and watched with concern.

He had just reached the downstairs hall when he was conscious of a child's sob coming from the room to his left. He knew the young woman who lived there with her little boy, but barely. Her husband was at sea these past two and half years and hadn't even met his son; her old apartment had burned a month or so ago, and she was left with hardly more than what she wore on her back. Of course finding work with a two-year-old child to care for was difficult, and she had been beholden to the kindness of strangers for their occasional meals and to the landlady for the better part of her rent.

The sobs of the child on the other side of the door seemed to paralyze his legs, and he stood for a minute or so staring at the apartment. There was a voice added to the tears, and he understood that the mother was doing her best to sing to her child. Then, as if his presence had been sensed (or perhaps the young woman had heard him coming down the stairs), the door opened, and she stepped into the cold hall with her child in her arms.

"Doctor Brine," she said, an unreasonable sort of relief visible on her face, "could you look at Jeremy for me? His mouth is terribly sore, and he has bruises where he hasn't even hit himself."

"Ma'am, I daren't take a guess what is wrong with him. I'm but a horse doctor, you know."

"Just to take a look," she said, and he could see that she was nearly mad with worry.

The former chief surgeon—Brevet Major Alexander Brine—of the Second Maine Regiment stepped into the woman's room feeling the need of a long drink. The young woman laid her son down on an ancient divan, where he gazed up listlessly as Doc Brine settled himself on the edge of the seat. The boy's eyes had the glassy look of malnutrition and pain, but he gave a small grin to the old man with the handsome hat. The smile revealed bleeding gums, and Doc Brine knew the little fellow's teeth would be loose. He hardly needed to roll the child's sleeves up to know what shape his bruises would take.

"Doctor," said the mother.

"Yes, yes," said the old man. He heaved a single sigh, turned on the edge of the divan, and realized that the old sailor and the landlady had followed them into the room. He glanced from face to face, finally settling upon the little boy, who had stopped his crying. "You wait," he said to the child with a wink. Then he allowed something like a smile to give the mother hope. "You wait. I'll be right back."

Standing on the street-side steps of the old tenement house, Doc wrapped his coat about him. He needed a piece of rope now that most of his buttons were gone. "The child has scurvy!" he said to himself. He was a little astonished and (at whom he didn't know) a little angry.

The day had turned bright and sunny, but the corner he reached looked lonely and cold. The streets were nearly abandoned, and snowdrifts had piled up against the southern and eastern walls. The snow was deep, and he found walking difficult till he fell in behind a small crowd of boys who were pelting the occasional carriage with snowballs. They did not harass him, however, since he had garnered respect among these rascals long ago for saving the life of an old mongrel that belonged to one of them. The boys even escorted him across the street, where he entered a grocery store and was thankful for the sudden warmth.

"Morning, Doc," said Henry Hamblin, the proprietor.

"Well, good morning," said the old man. He stepped up to the counter and considered the displays there before venturing forth. "Lemons, or limes, or oranges."

Hamblin looked a little tentative. "Oranges, just come in on the *Grace Bradley* last week."

"Didn't she have a rough coming in?" said Doc. "They're not all bruised, are they?"

"No, no. They were in crates, not bags."

Doc nodded, and after a moment's silence, he said, "What sort of credit have I got, Henry?"

"For oranges?" Henry frowned. "They're not cheap this time of year. I don't know, Doc, that last bill took you six months to make good on."

It was the answer the old man had expected, and he gave a fatalistic shrug of the shoulders. "I know, Henry." He considered pleading the little boy's case, but then thought, *This is my problem. Henry hasn't taken the kid on.* He looked up at the ceiling as if for inspiration and caught sight of the brim of the homburg.

He was embarrassed at first that he hadn't taken it off when he came inside, but then a thought came to him. With the hat in his hand, he said, "Henry, this hat is all but new. I acquired it last Thursday, to be exact, and it is a handsome one, as you can see."

Gemma Pool, Jeremy's mother, was waiting at the door with her son in her arms when Doc Brine knocked. The old man thought she would pull him off his feet she tugged on the door so hard.

"Oranges?" she said when he placed the bag of a dozen bright balls on her little table.

"Now you give him one of these a day. Chop them up if you have to. He might have some trouble chewing them at first. And his gums might sting a bit. See if you can't get two into him before tonight. I bet in three days you'll see him better." Doc was feeling more in control of himself than he had in years. "Open your mouth, in fact," he told the young woman, and she obeyed him without thinking. "Share a piece or two with him yourself," he said with a nod.

"Thank you," she said in a choked whisper, and he continued to nod as he left the room.

His head felt cold. "I'll look in," was all he said.

Henry Hamblin considered his newly acquired hat. It was just a tad small for him, but he didn't like a hat that rode his ears, and there was something particularly well made and handsome about this homburg. He thought his girl would find it bound to shine!

He hadn't really needed a new topper, and under the circumstances *half* a dozen oranges would have sufficed to pay the price for a hat you hadn't requested. But he knew Doc, and he knew those oranges had been for somebody else, and when—several days later—word got around why the old fellow had wanted the fruit, Henry sent several cans of lime juice down to Gemma Pool's.

And when he went to his girl's that night, he left his old brown derby at the store and proudly strolled the snowy sidewalks with his new hat.

Daniel's Story
(November 1891–April 1892)

There were other concerns in Daniel Plainway's life besides the Linnetts: The events of town and church occupied much of his time, as well as his practice; his sister came to live with him after the death of her husband. But the Linnetts had been like family to him here in Hiram, and when news of Nell's marriage to Jeram Willum startled its way through town, he knew that he had to see the girl herself to accept it.

When Daniel braved the Willums' place again, however, Nell only appeared at their front door, with one of the little Willum girls standing in front of her like a shield. He didn't really know what to say or how to ask the questions he wished to have answered, most especially with Willums glowering from every window, and Parley himself standing in the very place where the dog had been chained (Daniel wondered what had become of the poor creature); Parley Willum spat tobacco juice as a punctuation to his silent pleasure in Daniel's discomfort.

It amazed Daniel how much Nell looked like the people about her—he had never seen her hair in disarray; her clothes were her own but not recently washed— and yet she was still Eleanor Linnett, and he remembered his first impression of Elizabeth Willum (who even now hovered near) as a comely woman trapped (and won over) by harsh circumstances.

"How are you, Nell?" was all he could say at first.

"Uncle Daniel," she said, looking stricken, "I am so sorry."

"Sorry!" came Elizabeth Willum's sharp voice. "If you're so sorry, you can find some other place to take up space!"

"No, no," Nell was saying. "Oh, please, Mrs. Willum!" The young woman looked desperate to speak with Daniel alone but couldn't seem to let go of the child who stood in front of her and whose shoulders she held in a grip. "I'll be fine, Uncle Daniel. Jeram's looking after me. He's gone to town for things."

Daniel was rooted where he stood, an awkward distance from the door, so that he almost had to shout to be heard. "You can come and stay with Martha and me anytime," he said. "There's a room for you there now."

"Thank you," she said, though he had to read her lips to catch it.

"Jeram may come too," he said, after a pause, but there was no response save for a renewed tongue-lashing from Elizabeth Willum.

"You see, you're not needed or wanted here," said Parley Willum, "and the next time I see you on this path, I'll count it a sign of trespass."

Daniel was going to ask Nell if that was it, or if she was sure, or something— anything—that would give him reason to linger and her more time to think, but he could see, though she might want to go with him, there was nothing in his power to make her do so; asking again would only make the moment more painful. "Good- bye," he said, and he made the long, heartbreaking journey back to the road.

It was in April, toward the end of a long and siegelike winter, that Daniel saw Nell again for the last time. He had continued to come by the Linnett house, though for all intents and purposes it was already barren of life.

Old Ian was a hulking shell, living in the parlor where a single fireplace barely drove away the chill. He seemed impervious to cold or hunger, and only occasion- ally was Daniel able to rouse him out of a hibernationlike stupor. Daniel could not interest the old man in coming to Thanksgiving dinner with him and Martha. He visited Ian at Christmas but never mentioned the day.

But with warmer weather bound to come soon, Daniel hoped the old man might regenerate and come to life. Nell was not dead, after all, and it isn't simply a hollow cliché to say, "'Where there's life there's hope."

But one April day at home Daniel looked out the study window from his desk and saw, coming through the cold rain, the herald who would dash hope. Jeram hadn't the opportunity to knock before Daniel whipped open the front door and nearly pulled the boy inside. The lawyer had a hundred questions and demands for the young man but hardly got the first of them out before Jeram announced that Nell had just given birth.

"Lord have mercy," said Daniel. Then he took stock of Jeram's pale face and realized there was more.

"Dr. Bolster says she's dying."

"Dr. Bolster! Why wasn't I told?"

"He's been with her all night. I only dared come now myself."

"Let's go then," said Daniel, and he grabbed his coat without a hat and hurried out the door.

Jeram called after him, "You had better get the sheriff. My father said he'll shoot you if I bring you back."

"I don't want to take the time, Jeram."

"Mr. Plainway, I'm really frightened if you go down there alone."

"I am too, Jeram." Daniel paused long enough to turn and consider the boy's pale blue eyes, his too finely chiseled features, his slender build. "But you braved your father to come here, didn't you?"

The young man's nod was almost imperceptible. With no choice in the matter, Jeram had learned to be brave.

"Then I take courage standing with you. Let's go."

Never had Daniel taken such a long journey, the fear of Parley Willum all but scattered by the storm of his fears for Nell.

"Is that all it was?" he said aloud as he drove them along. "Why didn't she come home with me?"

"It's a boy," said Jeram. The statement was a sad afterthought since neither he nor Daniel was really concerned about the child just then.

Daniel was reconsidering what he knew about Nell and Jeram and thinking about her reckless summer with Asher Willum. Suddenly he understood why Asher had left town, why Jeram had married Nell, and why old Ian had signed the paper allowing it. "You're a bit of a knight, Jeram," he said simply.

"I'm not anything I need to be, Mr. Plainway," said the young man.

"I would be proud to have a son like you, young man."

The path from the road to the Willum place was a challenge just to walk, but Daniel took the horse and carriage down it, not willing to waste time on foot and hoping that such an appearance would daunt Parley Willum just a little. He had only just pulled up before the house when Parley stepped up from behind an outbuilding with a shotgun raised to his shoulder and pulled the hammer back.

"I guess your memory isn't very long, Mr. Plainway," said the man.

"I guess you don't know that I have been sent for," said Daniel, hoping to throw the need of defense back in Willum's lap. "Detain me, and I will have you up on charges of negligent homicide. Murder, Mr. Willum."

"Murder?" Parley looked at his son. "What nonsense have you been—"

"If that girl dies because of your neglect," said Daniel, "I will have you behind bars so fast you won't have time to blink." Daniel was letting his anger carry the conviction of his otherwise empty words.

"Get in there then!" growled the man. "And the devil with you! And you," he said to his son. "You can go with him when he leaves, you and that rich man's daughter and her brat!"

They hardly heard him as they hurried up the steps; they burst into the house without a knock or permission. In a corner by the fire, where Dr. Bolster had insisted on carrying her, Nell lay among dirty, dark-stained sheets, gazing with such lifelessness that Daniel feared they were too late. The doctor, however, nodded when Daniel sent him a frightened look.

"Nell." Daniel hardly realized he had spoken.

The young woman's lips moved, as in a dream, but no sound left them. He felt a little life in her hand when he held it, and she gave him the quietest, weakest squeeze.

"I've had twelve of them in that very bed," said Elizabeth Willum from a doorway at the back of the room. "I don't know what her fuss is with that measly thing."

Daniel ignored her, taking note for the first time of the wee creature at Nell's breast. Her lips moved again, and he put his ear to her mouth.

"Bertram," she said. "After Daddy."

"Bertram," said Daniel.

"He's a sweet child," she breathed.

The sight of tears in Nell's eyes hit Daniel like a kick in the chest.

"How will I know if he's taken care of?" she asked.

"Nell," he said, his voice choking, "of course he'll be—"

"You'll let me know," she whispered. Tears poured down both her cheeks, and he wondered that she had the energy left in her to weep so. "You'll let me know," she said.

"Mr. Plainway," said Jeram, "I think I should get her grandfather."

"I don't think that is a good idea, Jeram," said Daniel.

"She would want him here, I know—just as she wanted you. And he'd want to be here. I know he would."

"I don't know, Jeram—"

"He was awfully nice to me the day I came for dinner."

"Yes, he was." Daniel felt as if something weighty had been laid upon his chest, and he had trouble breathing. "I'll go."

"No. You have to stay here. You're like a second father to her, Mr. Plainway. You stay here. I'll go."

Daniel considered this. "Let me write you a note," he said. "Get me something to write with."

Dr. Bolster produced a pen and Jeram handed Daniel a copybook. Flipping through it in search of a blank page, he could see where Jeram had been practicing his writing, his spelling, and his grammar. He scribbled quickly:

Your granddaughter has just given birth, and I fear she will not linger as long as her mother. If you do not come, and quickly, this will be the last communication you will ever have from me.

Perhaps, *he hoped*, this will rouse him, *and he signed the note.*
"Take the carriage," he said, and Jeram scrambled out the door.

Then Daniel felt another squeeze from Nell's hand. He leaned close to her lips once again, and they brushed the side of his face like a kiss. "Every day," she said below a whisper, "I thank God for you."

When her grandfather appeared, she still had enough life in her to know him and that he had received the baby from her like a gift. Daniel left them, hearing and seeing nothing of what passed there.

The doctor came over to tell him she was gone and advised that the child be gotten from the Willum household as quickly as possible. "We need to find a wet nurse. Mrs. Cutler over by the mountain has a baby three or four months old now, and a little extra money would help out over there."

Daniel hardly heard any of it but registered the man's words on a peculiar level of consciousness he had rarely experienced before. Ian Linnett was standing before him with the baby in his arms.

"Where is Jeram?" asked Daniel, something like ice touching his spine.

"The boy?" said Linnett. "I never saw him."

Two days later Jeram Willum's body was found among the reeds of Clemons Pond. Daniel's note was not to be found upon him.

35. The Last of the Wawenocks

I'll never understand why she did it, thought Daniel. He had been dreaming.

The day dawned bright behind the heavy drapes of the room, so that knives of light pierced even the dark confines of his broken curtained bed. His breath was plain before him when he turned onto his back. He was not a young man to be adventuring over the countryside, and the rigors of the day before spoke in his muscles and bones so that he lingered for a while before braving the cold chamber.

He stumbled into his clothes, wishing he had taken his bag from the sleigh when they walked off. Had anybody come after them? He doubted it, or they would have found their tracks or at least called upon nearby houses looking for them.

The room where he had spent the night was of a completely different character now, though only slivers of day found their way around the perimeters of the dark hangings. The room itself was cleaner than Daniel would have credited, if there were only the five elderly sisters to tend to household duties: no dust, or cobwebs, or kittens beneath the rocker by the curtained window.

But everything was nearly ancient and faded with age: the wallpaper (particularly where daylight leaked from behind the hangings), the carpet, which was once (no doubt) a deep red behind an oriental design of vines and flowers and switchbacks, the prints upon the wall, and the painting of a moonlit river above the bricked-up fireplace. Daniel suspected that nothing had changed since Father had died and perhaps since long *before* the man's demise.

He gazed around the room in search of his boots, then remembered leaving them outside the door. With a yawn he leaned into the hall for them and thought to search each boot with a hand before putting them on, smiling to find several wrapped sweets tucked into the toes. He peeked into the hall again—first at the heavily carved door across from his, then down the hall to Miss Burnbrake's door. Her boots were gone, meaning, at least, that she was up and possibly that she was waiting for him downstairs. He heard the sound of plateware clinking below and realized that he was famished.

By daylight he was able to raise the bed back up on its slats, and though there was a broken one, he thought the new configuration might hold a body. He would warn the sisters of it. He was not long getting downstairs, where he found a cheery fire in the parlor, and followed voices to the back of the house and the kitchen.

"Good morning!" he offered as he entered the room, and the Pettengill sisters chorused a cheery greeting in return. They sprang from their chairs and bustled about, though everything was nearly done in the way of making breakfast. They had it all laid out before he temporarily declined in hopes of breakfasting with Miss Burnbrake.

"Of course!" shouted Lavona. "What could we be thinking?"

"And here she is!" announced Larinda. "Oh, dear, you look lovely!"

Charlotte Burnbrake looked no different from last night, unless she looked a little better rested, which was to say she looked lovely indeed. Daniel stood as she entered, and they greeted one another with a sense of awkwardness. The unexpected comradery of the day before seemed strange, even a little silly, in the morning kitchen with straightforward daylight streaming through the windows. Daniel was sorry not to sense the intimacy that had enveloped them so easily when the train was stopped, when they fled Mother Rose's, and when the sleigh was overturned.

"How are you this morning, Mr. Plainway?" asked Charlotte, and he thought there was not nearly the warmth in the address that there had been when she said good night some hours before.

"Pretty well, I guess, Miss Burnbrake," he returned, feeling formal. "I trust you slept well."

"Thank you, yes," she said.

There were glances exchanged among the sisters, and Alvaid even pulled a sigh, as if some beloved verity had come into question.

"What you need is breakfast," said Lavilda, as if there really *were* some problem besides the practical light of day, and a good meal could solve most anything.

Daniel was almost mollified by the presence of so *much* good food when he was so hungry, and Miss Burnbrake herself looked ready to make a proper meal of it: toast and jam, rashers and pan-fried potato, eggs and biscuits and gravy and milk and coffee gathered like a week's reserve. The sisters helped dish out the servings and never allowed their guests to touch a ladle or a serving fork. Daniel felt his courage rise with every ounce gained by his plate, and his wits gathered as well.

He looked up at his fellow guest with a twinkle in his eye and said, "Was St. Nicholas good to you, Miss Burnbrake?"

Perhaps he purposely caught her with her mouth full—she was very hungry—for she was first surprised and then amused at his question, but it took her a moment to answer, during which time the twinkle in his eye seemed to cast a like reflection in hers. "Yes," she said, "he was very kind. I ate a chocolate in bed before I came down."

The thought made Daniel smile, and she raised one of her pretty eyebrows in either amusement or warning. "I should have done that," he said quite sincerely.

"I rather thought I was a child again," she said, considering herself wise for having done it herself.

The sisters were hugely amused by all this, not the least because they had played St. Nicholas at three in the morning (and giggled a great deal too, so it was amazing they hadn't wakened their guests).

But Daniel had looked absolutely sincere in his humor and goodwill, and had so cleverly refused the pragmatic light of day with his whimsical question, that Charlotte had been encouraged (however unconsciously) to lower the self-conscious bastion she had constructed.

"I was in a third crash last night," said Daniel.

"Were you?" she said, a little bemused.

"Yes," he replied. "My bed fell," whereupon he laughed at the cries of horror from the sisters. "It was a small thing after our previous adventures, I assure you," he said.

"And where are you going today?" asked Louella when he had explained what happened and the sisters had calmed down.

"We each have people to meet in Hallowell," said Daniel.

"Hallowell!" said Lavona. "You didn't say so when we were going on about Mother and Father's elopement!"

"It was quite a storm they blew up there," said Charlotte.

"Not as big a storm as they blew up later!" declared Lavona.

"Oh? Did they?"

"You would have thought so if you had seen the five of us running about the house!" declared Larinda, and her sisters joined in with laughter, and "Land sakes!" and "My, we were bad!"

"But it was only the *second* storm in Hallowell's history that bears speaking of," said Louella.

"Was it?" Daniel had so liked the tale of their parents that he hoped for another one like it.

"What storm?" wondered Lavilda.

"The storm that ended the Wawenocks, dear," said Louella, and Lavilda remembered this with a reverse nod.

"My word, yes," said Larinda, "the Smoking Pine and all that."

"Smoking Pine?" said Daniel.

"Oh, yes, Mr. Plainway," said Louella, "and it does smoke, I assure you, Father used to say."

"I've seen it myself," said Charlotte, "though I doubted what others told me when they brought me there. 'It doesn't *always* smoke,' they said to me, and this sounded like a good hedge against the certainty that it wouldn't. But that day a storm was on its way—which is said to be favorable for sightings of the pine's smoke—and a sort of vaporous column did seem to be rising from the topmost branches. It was very strange, and I don't believe I have ever heard a proper account of it."

"Oh, my," said Louella. "It's a sad story, really. It is a strange phenomenon, Mr. Plainway, and difficult to perceive for some people. The eye, you know, often wants to make still things move and to make other things to exist where they aren't at all. Father used to say that a person might convince himself of what he saw simply by straining his eyes long enough, but Father was sure that he had seen it—trusted his own eyes, in fact, because he hadn't been looking for it in the first place."

"And it is simply a vapor rising from the tree?" asked Daniel.

"It is a disturbance in the air, a fluctuation. Have you ever seen the shadows the air itself can make against a building on a hot day? It is like that perhaps, though you might see it tomorrow, if you look, with snow on the ground and the north wind blowing. And it rides above a towering pine among a great grove, as many pines as people who lived on that spot before that other awful storm.

"They were the Wawenocks, a tribe decimated by their own warlike nature, driven out of Pemaquid, and hunted like animals by the surrounding clans—the Passamoquoddies and the Penobscots and the Tarratines. But the Wawenocks came, in their ramblings, to Hallowell (known then as Keedumcook) and the banks of the Bombahook, which empties into the Kennebec. The great river teemed with salmon and bass, the Bombahook itself was a legendary trout stream, and the surrounding forests were filled with game.

"The Europeans who had settled in those parts were alarmed to have this tribe of warlike reputation camping so close to their homes; but Assinomo, the chief of the Wawenocks, met with the elders of the local settlement and asked for land and protection, and though the Wawenocks had ended many another life with their slaughter, they swore never again to raise their clubs or notch their arrows, except in defense of the small against the large or the weak against the strong. 'Even as water flows in the Bombahook,' said the chief, 'we shall surely smoke the pipe of peace,' which words would prove prophetic.

"And the elders of Hallowell granted the Wawenocks land to pitch their tents on the southern banks of the Bombahook."

"It may have been the very same stream from which Father saved his future in-law," suggested Lavilda.

"It may. It may," said Louella. "But the Wawenocks were granted the land, *and* they were granted the protection of the town, and there were scarce a hundred of their tribe remaining.

"But if the neighboring tribes could not attack the Wawenocks outright without making war also upon the town of Hallowell, there were other ways to avenge their dead, and one muggy August night a terrible storm was conjured up—a storm that could be heard at the center of the European settlement itself, though it never so much as turned a weathercock there—and the Bombahook rose up in flood and swept every last Wawenock into the Kennebec, and since the days of the Judges there never was a tribe so completely abolished from the face of the earth in one terrible blow.

"It was not many summers later before nature had reclaimed the washed-out banks of the Bombahook, and near its uppermost reaches, where hard wood would expect to take hold, there grew up a long rank of pines. One of the elders, who had been present at that first meeting with the Wawenocks, went out and walked one day among the young trees, and when he came back in the evening he claimed to have counted them to the exact number of people who were lost in that terrible flood. And that elder was the first to see the unearthly smoke rising from the tallest of the pines, so that they were reminded of what Assinomo had said. 'Even as water flows in the Bombahook, we shall surely smoke the pipe of peace.'"

Daniel and Charlotte were quite charmed by the story, and Louella might have been telling it to a roomful of children, her sweet, aged voice was so animated and her eyes were filled with such daydream and illusion.

"Those trees did grow with unnatural speed"—she ended her tale—"and people let them be, for they began to think that the trees were the Indians themselves, come back to fulfill their vow."

36. The Battle of the Smoking Pine

As Eagleton had predicted, the day was bright and clear, so that folk squinted against the glare of the snow and the south-facing eaves began to drip. Snowbirds flitted and called in the bushes.

As the hour before noon approached, Ephram, Eagleton, and Thump were more secure about the approaching contest, having attended services at their respective denominations. Had they compared the messages they received that morning, however, they could not have been blamed if they derived some measure of ambiguity from their collective lessons. Ephram, for example, had heard from the Baptist preacher sentiments regarding the Golden Rule, while Eagleton had listened attentively as the Methodist minister fixed a hard eye upon his congregation and proclaimed the wisdom of God's vengeance. Thump's guidance had been the strangest, since the Episcopalian service had been upon Job, 39:25—"He smelleth the battle afar off. . . ."

But men will find comfort where they may, and the Moosepathians considered themselves properly encouraged for the task ahead. The younger boys met them upon the appointed ground, before the hotel, arriving in three or four distinct groups. There were nigh onto fourteen of the little chaps, for tidings of their newly acquired leadership had encouraged enlistments and their ranks had grown accordingly.

The Dash-It-All Boys had not been sighted that morning, and it was supposed by the Moosepathians that their counterparts had gone further afield in quest of worship.

"They did seem a little troubled about the snowball fight," said Thump, who hoped that Durwood, Waverley, and Brink had slept well despite this concern.

"Where is this encounter to take place?" wondered Eagleton.

"They'll be coming to the field at the corner of Winthrop and Pleasant," said one of the boys—Brian by name. He was a game little fellow, with the look of hazard in his eye.

"Let me go!" came a voice from the steps of the hotel. "Let me go, I tell you! How am I to look to the troops if you've hold of my arm like an old nanny?" The members of the club were startled to see Colonel Barkoddel struggling through the front door of the hotel and tussling with the manager.

"But, Colonel," the manager was saying, "the steps are slippery, and the road is far from clear."

"The devil!" declared the old man, and he waved a stick about him, so that the manager must suffer harm or put some distance between them, of which choice he split the difference by contracting two or three blows before retreating. "Come up here and get me!" shouted the fellow to Ephram, Eagleton, and Thump, and they managed three or four steps before Eagleton slipped into Ephram, who fell against Thump, and they finished where they began, though in less order. "The devil!" shouted the colonel, and they were surprised to find him standing with them at the bottom of the steps when they regained their feet.

A horse and sleigh pulled up before them, and Colonel Barkoddel took occupation of this, his stick waving erratically above him as he let the throws be tucked over his knees. Ephram, Eagleton, and Thump wondered if they were supposed to join him till he used his stick to keep them at bay, shouting, "To the field! Onward!" And though he kept the driver to a slow pace, the men and their troop of seven- and eight-year-old boys were hardly able to keep up with him. "We must be there to choose the ground!" the old man called back at them. "No dallying now!"

The day was glorious, and the Moosepathians were sorry to be so out of breath when they met folk coming home from church; they raised their hats but were able to express their greetings only with the simplest of grunts. The boys, on the other hand, seemed to gather energy with every yard, shouting and whooping with excitement, not the least because the colonel exhorted them to do so. They were laughing uproariously by the time they reached the chosen field, but their laughter died at the sight of several older fellows manning the snowy ramparts of a fort that had been constructed halfway across the meadow.

"Look!" shouted one of the older boys from the fort wall. "It's a bunch of old men!"

Colonel Barkoddel couldn't be expected to hear the details of this taunt, but he caught the tenor of it and shook his stick at the opposing ranks.

Those ranks were gaining force at every moment; figures hurried from the neighboring woods or the adjacent streets to fill the garrison, and one of these boys stood in plain sight, like Hector upon the wall of Troy.

"We are outnumbered as well as outweighed," observed the colonel.

The Moosepathians were aware of this discrepancy and a little concerned about it.

"Should we leave our hats?" wondered Eagleton, who well remembered yesterday's imperiled headgear.

"The devil, you say, sir!" roared the colonel. "Wear your hats and draw fire, I say!"

Ephram, Eagleton, and Thump flinched at the old man's colorful locutions.

"Colonel," suggested Ephram, "with the young fellows about—"

"What!"

Ephram looked to his friends for help.

"What Ephram is trying to say, Colonel," attempted Eagleton, "is that a certain intemperance of speech—"

Thump stepped forward and cleared his throat. "If you wouldn't swear in front of the boys, Colonel," he said quietly.

"Very good, Thump," whispered Eagleton.

"Bravo, my friend," said Ephram quietly.

"What?" shouted the colonel. He glanced about with a wild eye but was somewhat abashed as he took in the boys. "Yes, of course!" he added. "Where is my glass?" He glared at the men and boys, then realized that he had possession of the requested item and produced from the folds of the throws about him a telescope that he put to one eye and applied to the snowbank beyond.

They watched as Colonel Barkoddel took in the terrain, and they could hear him grumble and growl to himself. The sun gave a blinding glint from the end of the spyglass as he veered it from one side to the other, and when he lowered the piece, he seemed satisfied.

"Ah!" he vocalized. "There's the fatal mistake, I tell you. They have the high ground, but I warrant there isn't much to stand on atop that bank, and a well-placed hit or two will likely knock some of those defenders from their place." He looked down at his small army, which had grown by two or three boys since they arrived. "What are you doing?" he declared. "Arm yourselves, gentlemen! The hour is at hand! Fill every pocket, and occupy every crook and elbow!"

At this command the younger troop fell into a flurry of action, and ammunition was gathered and packed accordingly. The edge of the field took on the pockmarked look of a bombarded course, and the small figures in their dark winter coats shouted encouragement to one another or called the discovery of a particularly fine patch of damp snow.

A clamor of taunts came from the snowbank, and one of the taller boys, impatient for battle, let fly with a missile that nearly covered the distance between the forces.

"Let them wear themselves out," said the colonel, with a gleeful laugh.

Ephram, Eagleton, and Thump watched the proceedings, feeling very much the fifth, six, and seventh wheels. "How are we to dispose of ourselves?" wondered Eagleton aloud.

"You're each to take a column across," said the old man, and he explained to them the plan that he had devised.

"What are they doing now?" wondered Waverley.

Harold, the unofficial leader of the older boys, stood at the rampart and considered the smaller troop on either side of the field's southern angle. "They're getting ready for something," he said, shielding his eyes against the glare. It had been an even choice, it seemed now; they occupied the high ground, it was true, but they also faced the sun.

"*Something* is good," said Durwood. "I believe *something* indicates that things will be commencing forthwith."

Brink took off his hat and peered over the bank. "They *are* gathering, and in good order, by the way. And there, I am pleased to inform you, are the members of the Muskrat Lodge."

"Badgertail Club," corrected Durwood.

"Beaverwood Society," suggested Waverley.

"At any rate, our friends are taking the field," said Brink. "Unarmed, I might add, if appearances are to be believed."

Waverley was encouraged by this report to look for himself. He took his hat off and peered over the wall. "How are we for ammunition?" he asked.

Harold indicated the several pyramids of snowballs that lined the tops of the ramparts. The older boys had not revealed the extent of their numbers or the presence of the three men, but there were at least twenty of them lying in wait, and a great deal of snickering rose from behind the fort walls. The boys were amused as well.

"Who is the codger with the stick?" wondered Brink.

"Some local hero of the late war, I shouldn't wonder," suggested Waverley. "He is a little magnificent, don't you think?"

"I'm just glad he's not coming with them," said Durwood.

"Or even by himself," said Brink. "He reminds me of my grandfather, who would like to catch up with me someday."

There was then a cry rising from the opposite field, and all heads behind the rampart lifted in anticipation.

"'Once more unto the breach, dear friends, once more,'" quoted Waverley.

"It's *our* breach," contended Brink.

"It is, isn't it."

The huzzahs and roars from the oncoming horde grew louder.

"They are coming on swiftly, for little fellows," said Durwood.

Ephram, Eagleton, and Thump had learned quite a lot about cheering the home team while observing Portland's baseball team on the Eastern Promenade with Mister Walton, but exhortations to "knock him down at first" and "kill the umpire" had never seemed very sporting (and certainly had never fallen from the lips of their chairman) and besides seemed not entirely relevant to the present circumstance. Unenlightened as to the proper words for the present occasion, they met the challenge with irregular outbursts that sounded rather like the shouts of men who are being pinched from behind.

They each led a column of about five boys—Eagleton along the left flank, Thump along the right, and Ephram up the middle, with seconds-in-command being a Peter, a John, and an Alvin respectively. The young boy named Brian, who himself had some fame as a pitcher, jogged along the middle column and was to be held aside as something of a sharpshooter. (A headhunter, the colonel had dubbed him.)

The attacking army was not halfway across the field of play before missiles began to land among them, and as these were not the softest snowballs that had ever been thrown, there were shouts of dismay; but the younger boys had their commands, and they did not attempt to return fire from a position that would certainly not honor their weaker arms. They could hear the colonel and his driver shouting from the street.

Thump lost his hat almost immediately but did not venture back for it. "Forward!" he cried, and slowing his pace only slightly as he gave out this call, he was nearly run over by his own boys.

The snowballs came thick and heavy, and Eagleton was astonished, when he looked up (just before losing his own hat), to see a small horde of older boys manning the walls. A second projectile burst upon his head and dazed him somewhat. He did not stumble, however, but plowed along through the deep snow to their intended confrontation.

Ephram was holding his hat to his head and felt three or four hat-hating snowballs thunk upon his worsening headgear; at one instance half a dozen of these projectiles collided with his chest and his jaw, and he performed a backward somersault that was much admired by his troops as they rushed by. Shaking his dazed head, he clambered to his feet and found himself bringing up the rear of his column. He had longer strides than his boys, but they had youthful energy on their side and besides did not sink so far into the snow; the result was that he found it difficult to regain his position in the van. Alvin took one look back at his leader, waved him on, then was nearly knocked onto his back by a rain of snowballs.

Thump and Eagleton meanwhile had reached the point where the next course of their plan came into play. Their columns formed up in the face of a blistering fusillade, and with the fire of battle hot in their veins, the small boys poured forth a return volley that did everything the colonel had predicted: A good three-quarters of the rampart's defenders were knocked loose of their moorings and disappeared behind the snowbank.

Brian was the first in fact to mark a casualty, by picking Harold Marsh from his position.

A few leaps brought Thump and Eagleton to the foot of the ramparts, where they handed their boys onto the walls (Thump accidentally threw the first one completely over the side), and here the third part of the colonel's plan took effect.

The older boys—not to mention Durwood, Waverley, and Brink—could not have imagined that they had been stocking ammunition for the employ of their enemies, but that is how it fell out, for the younger boys began to make good use of the admittedly depleted pyramids of snowballs that awaited them upon the walls of the fort, and with so many of the larger fellows on their backs or just recovering their feet in the precincts of the snowy garrison, it was not unlike shooting the proverbial fish in the barrel. (The younger boy who had been thrown over the side managed somehow to use the force of his trajectory to roll himself out of harm's immediate way.)

Durwood, Waverley, and Brink were shocked at this turn of fortune, and it was no doubt their own fresh arms that kept it from turning altogether. Several of the younger boys were knocked from the walls, and Eagleton, Thump, and Ephram (who had caught up with them) ran about catching the fellows with extraordinary precision.

In the confusion the attacking force hardly noticed how tall were the three boys who led a foray out and around the palisade. Suddenly the younger boys and their leaders were forced to retreat—not south toward the street, but northwest, in the direction of a line of trees. Ephram, Eagleton, and Thump had never lifted their feet so quickly or so high. Snow-balls—quickly formed and less compacted—sped past their ears and burst upon their backs, and there was a great roar from the older boys.

"To the pines!" shouted one of the younger fellows, and the retreat lost some of its haphazard quality as it formed toward a single goal.

Durwood, Waverley, and Brink exhorted their troops forward at first but then cautioned them to slow their pursuit long enough to rearm them-selves. The older boys quickly had their arms and pockets loaded with white spheres, and they pressed doggedly on, following the tracks of the younger boys.

The sound of a stream became apparent as they reached the edge of a pine wood. Their quarry fled among the trees. "No surrender!" cried the older boys. "No quarter!"

Ephram thought his lungs would burst, and he was the first to stumble to a halt; Eagleton and Thump quickly backtracked to their friend.

"Eagleton?" said Ephram between breaths.

"Yes, my friend?" said Eagleton.

"Thump?"

"I am here," said Thump.

"I believe that I will stand this ground and do my best to slow the pur-suit so that our boys can make it safely home."

"Good heavens, Ephram!" declared Eagleton.

Thump could hardly speak, he was so moved. He cleared his throat and did manage to mumble, "Where you stand, there stand I as well."

"And I!" agreed Eagleton.

They realized then that Brian and John and several others of the younger troop had backtracked themselves to see what was up, but when the plan was explained, Brian first and then the others refused to budge and were willing to take their lumps rather than leave their leaders behind. The truth was, they were exhilarated with their temporary victory and had faith that the Moosepath League would lead them forth successfully.

Alternatives were growing fewer; the older regiment was sighted stalk-ing through the pinewood. The snow among the trees was not so easily compacted, since the shadows there had kept at bay the direct light of the sun, but the younger boys used their breaths and the warmth of their hands to form a few snowballs before the hounds were upon them.

A general sort of chuckling rose out of the woods as the pursuers closed in, moving from tree to tree and informing their quarry with an ever-deepening dread.

The younger boys arranged themselves about Ephram, Eagleton, and Thump; Custer himself might have wished to have such brave company, and they did in fact look something like the popular image of that general and his beleaguered regiment. The larger boys fanned out on either side and paused only when they formed a line of about thirty yards. Three of the tallest of these boys—and tall indeed they were!—half hid themselves, with scarves about their faces, beneath the largest of the pines in sight.

Eagleton, ever the weather watcher, had an eye on the robin's-egg blue that was visible in patches between the pointed heads of the lofty pines, and above the tallest of these trees (behind which crouched the three tall boys) he caught sight of a peculiar disturbance in the air. Eagleton forgot the immediate danger and peered with his much-praised sight at what seemed to be a vapor or a waft of smoke rising from the topmost branches of the noble pine.

"Good heavens!" he said. "I do believe it is the Smoking Pine!" Quite unconsciously, he fingered the little cross beneath his shirt.

"Really?" said Brink from behind his scarf. He and his fellows peered up the trunk of the tree.

There was a peculiar stillness in the air.

And there was a great roar as the Smoking Pine and its immediate brethren chose that exact moment to let loose the great wet burden they had been carrying since the blizzard of the day before, and the entire line of older boys—and most completely the three tall "boys" beneath the Smoking Pine itself—disappeared beneath an avalanche of wet snow.

37. Curier and Therefore

"Haloo!" came a voice from the front of the house, a male voice, which seemed to Daniel out of place, where he had only heard the voices of women. "Haloo!"

"That's Curier," said Larinda.

"In the kitchen, Curier!" called Lavona.

The door swung open, and two men were revealed. The first was a man as elderly as their hostesses; a large, raw-boned fellow with huge hands and feet, he had a nose and ears to match and great, sad eyes. He arrived with unmistakable familiarity, with both the surroundings and the Pettengills. He wore overalls and a long coat that looked warm enough for brisk fall rather than the morning after a winter's blizzard, and Daniel wondered how warm the day had grown.

The second man was of middle age, a little taller than Daniel, with whisk-broom mustaches and matching eyebrows that furrowed down over his nose to complete a serious mien. He was coated and furred more in keeping with the season, and when he lumbered his broad shoulders into the kitchen his bulk seemed to soak up as much room as all five sisters. He looked less certain as he followed the first man. Both of them tracked melting snow behind them.

"Morning, morning," said the elderly man, who was Curier. He bobbed his head at everyone, betraying obvious interest in Daniel and *more* than obvious interest in Charlotte. "Morning, morning."

"How are you this morning, folks?" said the second man, his stentorian tones shivering the woodwork. He cast his eye about the room and stopped at Daniel. "Morning, sir."

"Looks to be less weather than yesterday," said Daniel.

"It is," said the man. "I'm Ergo Define." Daniel's eyes widened slightly, but the man was ready for this. He nodded, adding, "Folks call me Therefore."

"Do they?" said Daniel, whose expression, for a brief moment, was perhaps more amazed than polite. He recovered himself quickly, however, and offered his hand, saying, "Daniel Plainway, Mr. Define."

"Please, Therefore."

"Therefore," said Daniel, dipping his head.

Curier hooked a thumb at Mr. Define. "Met him coming in," he said to one of the sisters, who were watching everything with great interest.

"I trust you are the people who were left in the sleigh last night," said Define.

"We are," replied Daniel, his expression unreadable.

"I am certainly happy to find you and also that you found shelter. I am profoundly shamed and angry that a man in my employ would leave you in such a predicament." Mr. Define turned to Charlotte and made a curt bow. "I am profoundly sorry, Mrs. Plainway."

"This is Charlotte Burnbrake," said Daniel.

"Oh? I beg your pardon."

"We are traveling companions by accident," explained Daniel. "Well," he amended, "by several accidents, actually."

"I only found out about the sleigh turning over this morning," said Mr. Define. "Didn't even realize a sleigh was gone, and when I finally found the scoundrel, he admitted to leaving a man and his wife out in the snow."

"Did you spend the night?" said Curier to Daniel.

"Of course he spent the night!" said Lavona. "Do you think we left them on the porch?"

"Didn't think that, really," said Curier.

"The driver is well, I take it," said Charlotte.

"He is without employ at the moment, ma'am," declared Therefore Define.

"He didn't break his neck at least," said Daniel.

"It is a wonder, drunk as he was," said the livery manager. "Beg your pardon, ladies," he added, sorry to have raised such an unrefined subject.

"Whether with our pardon or not, Mr. Define," said Charlotte, "he was quite drunk, as it happened."

"Therefore, Miss Burnbrake."

"Yes?"

"Therefore."

"Oh, of course. Thank you, Therefore."

The man squared his large shoulders and said, "I have come to put myself and my best team and sleigh at your disposal," said the man.

"That's very good of you," said Daniel. "We were hoping to get a start this morning. Perhaps you could take us as far as the next station toward Hallowell."

"I will take you to Hallowell, sir."

"It's not necessary, I assure you."

"For myself I beg to differ."

Daniel thought about the offer. It would be colder in a sleigh than on the train, though he was pretty sure that Mr. Define (he could hardly get used to calling the man Therefore) would have geared the vehicle with more than enough blankets and throws; on the other hand, the prospect of an extended ride with Charlotte was not unpleasant. He exchanged glances with her.

"It looks like a lovely day," she said quietly.

"It is settled then," said the liveryman.

"I suppose it is. Thank you . . . Therefore," said Daniel.

"St. Nicholas's Day," said Curier in his same prosaic manner.

"We know that, Curier," said Louella.

The man made a small sound to indicate he heard.

"If you'd left a pair of boots in the hall yesterday," Larinda scolded Curier, "you would have gotten sweets this morning."

"Would have been cold walking home without my boots," he said. "You ladies are sweet enough for me." He was smiling now, and he winked at Daniel as he turned away from the sisters. There was a great deal of clucked tongues and exasperated gasps from the elderly women. "Probably would have married one of them," said Curier, in a tone only Daniel could have caught, "but couldn't decide which one."

"What was that?" said a suspicious Larinda.

"What did he say?" said Louella.

"My land, Curier!" declared Alvaid, though it was not clear what she was expressing.

"I have the things you left in the sleigh," said Therefore Define.

"Thank you!" said Charlotte. "Could I beg you to bring my bags in?"

"Ma'am," said Therefore. He followed Curier out into the hall with Daniel close behind.

Curier seemed to be explaining to Therefore how close he came to marrying one of the Pettengills. "It would have caused a row, I can tell you. They were all pretty fond of me, you know."

"Curier?" said Daniel, and the old man stopped in the hall while Therefore went on to retrieve Charlotte's things. "It *is* Curier?" said Daniel, his hand out. He hadn't understood yet whether Curier was the man's first name or last.

"It is," said the man, which clarified nothing.

"You help to take care of things here, do you?"

"Oh, yes," said Curier. He nodded his heavy features, standing over Daniel like some big, awkward bird. "The ladies wouldn't get on without me."

"I can believe it." Daniel stood with his hands behind him, unconsciously slipping into his lawyerlike deportment.

"Took a liking to Lavona for a bit, but she shouted even then," said Curier. "I think she was the prettiest of them, though, was Lavona. Nice girls. And that Alvaid, you know." Curier gave a low whistle.

"They get on pretty well then?" asked Daniel.

"They do fine, most of the time," said the man.

Charlotte came out of the kitchen with two or three of the sisters in close tow. "I'll shovel the porch," said Curier matter-of-factly.

"Thank you, Curier," said Lavilda.

Therefore came through the front door with Charlotte's things, but she stopped suddenly and wondered aloud if the elderly fellow should be shoveling.

"Curier?" said Larinda. "He's been shoveling all his life."

"That may be as good a reason as any to stop," thought Charlotte, though her voice hardly carried beyond Daniel.

"I'll go out and see if I can give him a hand," said Daniel.

The sisters tried to put a stop to this plan of action, declaring that Curier fended for himself very well and it wasn't like their household to allow a guest to apply himself to chores; but Daniel was good at countering these claims with his own, and the upshot of it was that he *and* Therefore followed Curier onto the porch, where Daniel found the opportunity to question the man further about the Pettengills, their late father, and *Mr. Edward*, whose instructions regarding the locked room had been so assiduously obeyed.

"Do you know the Pettengills very well?" asked Daniel of Therefore Define before they were very long on the road to Hallowell.

"I don't know them at all," said the driver without looking back. "In fact I've only seen them rarely, though I certainly know *about* them, or what common wisdom knows."

"And that is?" asked Charlotte.

"Common wisdom? They're a curious lot, but well-liked for all that. Mr. Pettengill was a curious man, they say, but tended business and was generous when the hat was passed around at Christmas. Their mother was a sociable lady and less peculiar than the rest of them."

"And were there no sons?" wondered Daniel.

"All girls."

"Do you know a Mr. Edward?"

The driver thought on this. "Doesn't sound familiar."

"He's a lawyer, I guess," said Daniel, "in Gardiner."

"Edward," said Therefore. He seemed stumped. Then he brightened up, saying, "Not Edward Grimb?"

"They called him *Mr.* Edward. Curier did too."

"Well, they might." Mr. Define chuckled. "Who knows? I don't know a *Mr.* Edward."

"If I weren't afraid of losing the Moosepath League again," said Daniel to Charlotte, "I'd take the time to look for Mr. Edward and inquire after this locked-room business."

"As their lawyer he wouldn't have to tell you a thing, would he?" wondered Charlotte.

"He wouldn't, of course. But I'd see the cut of the fellow's coat. I've never heard of such a stipulation in a will and can't imagine it would hold up under any sort of scrutiny."

"Do you think the lawyer is keeping something from them?"

"He has the key, we're told."

"It is a little strange."

"It is."

Charlotte's eyes were bright with the day, and her cheeks red with the wind of their movement. "You are a bit of a knight, Mr. Plainway," she said.

Daniel waved this away, but her insistent expression, which was equal parts earnestness and humor, would not brook complete disagreement. "Don Quixote perhaps," he said finally. It let him out of everything but a blush.

She looked away then, for his sake.

"They are a curious lot," said the liveryman again, as if he had not heard any of their talk.

They passed over the road to Gardiner and soon found themselves within the outer limits of that town. Church spires rose up from behind the advancing hills, and the scattered farmhouses grew smaller in their yardage, the homes of businessmen or store owners more frequent as the center of town drew close.

"Will your uncle be in Hallowell long?" wondered Daniel. It was the first mention of her plans between them, and as common and even polite as the question sounded, there was also about it a hint of intimacy.

"A few days perhaps," she answered, precipitating a nod from Daniel. "It has been an odd affair," she offered. "A man communicated with us just last week about some land Uncle Ezra has owned for years. The man—Mr. Tempest, his name is—*said* he was in the process of buying the equipment from a lumber mill that was closing up north and that he hoped to relocate it nearer Augusta, where there is much building expected. He was in a prodigious hurry to settle on a piece of land, and Uncle Ezra's acreage fitted his needs perfectly."

"He *said*."

"Yes, exactly."

"But that was not the case?"

"We received a letter the day before yesterday—the Moosepath League delivered it, in fact—a strange sort of communication, calling off the deal and warning us of others who would try to make the same deal in his place."

"This *is* singular."

"We thought so."

"But your uncle went to Hallowell anyway?"

"To see his lawyer. He wanted to discuss the whole business and learn if Mr. Tollback knew any more than we did."

"Mr. Tollback being your lawyer."

Charlotte nodded.

"I guess I'm not the only one with peculiar events motivating me," said Daniel, "though it seems your story has ended before it began. I have yet to lay eyes on the principal players in my tale, or recent eyes in the case of the boy."

"Will you go to meet him then?" wondered Charlotte. Since hearing of his search, she had wondered a great deal about the orphaned child.

"I do hope to meet him," he said.

There was enough of the romantic in Charlotte to wonder what the boy's mother had meant to Daniel Plainway. "What was she like, his mother?"

"Nell? She was a sweet girl. I never knew a gentler soul, I think, than Eleanor Linnett."

Charlotte thought that this was meaningful praise from such a gentle soul as Daniel Plainway. Though he watched a small settlement outside the main village of Gardiner go past, she guessed he was seeing something else entirely.

"The Linnetts were an important pillar in Hiram, and it was their great fault to be a little proud of it, and their great tragedy that one of their number would mix with the least of Hiram's folk."

"The prince and the milkmaid," said Charlotte.

"More like the princess and the poacher," said Daniel, then thought better of it. "No, because Robin Hood was a poacher, I suppose. The Willums were—are, I should say—the lowest and the meanest, though they have been able to produce the *figure* of an upstanding man, if not the soul of one." Daniel considered this then and corrected himself again. "That's not altogether so either, for they *did* produce one good soul— besides the boy, of course—though none of us took much notice of Jeram at the time."

"None of this sounds very happy," said Charlotte.

"Ah," he said, as if tossing the memory away.

"So," said Charlotte, "it was not the good soul with whom the boy's mother mixed?"

"Yes," Daniel said, "and no." He smiled at her confounded expression.

She looked away then, afraid that she had been too inquisitive; she hadn't known this man any longer than the day before, after all.

For Daniel's part, this was one day—perhaps the first day in recent memory—that he might have left the tale behind, the day before him was so bright and the woman beside him so pleasant and beautiful. But after a moment, in which he feared she was going to apologize for her curiosity, he said, "I should like to tell it to you, but I may have only the one rendition left in me." He was a little startled when she reached her hand over and touched his briefly.

"Perhaps when you tell Mister Walton," she said.

38. -Athians and -Ashians in Flux

"Good heavens!" said Ephram.

"I concur, my friend," asserted Eagleton. "Thump?"

"They are my thoughts as well," said that worthy.

"Good heavens!" said Ephram again; it was remarkable how often they were in concert.

Their young company had flown beyond the forest of pines and across the field of battle like the shadows of crows and felt themselves victorious simply by dint of escaping the vengeance of the older boys. Campaigns have turned on smaller events.

Ephram, Eagleton, and Thump lingered to be sure that no one had been injured by the startling avalanche, and the older boys rose from the unexpected heaps of snow, laughing and calling out to one another; never were ambushed soldiers so happy in their circumstances. The boughs of the pines above them waved in the breeze, as if glad to be rid of their burden. Eagleton gazed up to the top of the tallest tree, hoping to see again that odd disturbance in the air.

The portion of an hour struck from a steeple in the village, and Ephram consulted one of his three or four watches. "Half past twelve," he announced. He was beginning to feel hungry.

Eagleton, still craning his neck, considered the immaculate blue between the pine caps and said, "Continued fair and seasonable. Winds in the west."

"High tide at—*the Dash-It-All Boys!*" declared Thump, a declaration that Ephram and Eagleton found difficult to interpret. Ephram thought his friend had experienced a sort of linguistic hiccup (he had suffered them himself from time to time) and inquired after Thump's well-being with an "Are you—*the Dash-It-All Boys!*"

"Good heavens!" declared Eagleton, not because he had sighted the men but because he had been so startled by Ephram's shout. But upon actually seeing Durwood, Waverley, and Brink, he said instead, "Dash-It-All Boys?"

Durwood, Waverley, and Brink rose from the largest heap of snow. Durwood had entangled himself in his scarf, and it was wrapped about his forehead. All three of the Dashians had become separated from their hats, and snow had been driven down their necks and up their backs.

"That was not to be expected," suggested Waverley.

"I didn't, in fact," said Brink.

"Good heavens, gentlemen!" said Ephram. "How did you get beneath that pile?"

"I was standing there," said Waverley.

"I was standing beside him," said Brink.

Durwood was more dazed than his fellows (it was ascertained afterward that part of a branch had struck him on the head), and he was a little cross-eyed.

"Bad luck," said Waverley.

"In the wrong place at the wrong time," said Brink.

"Bad luck," said Waverley again.

"What a shame that you happened to come by just then," said Thump concernedly.

"It was," agreed Waverley.

"War will inevitably strike the innocent," said Eagleton.

"That's very good, Eagleton," said Ephram.

"Thank you, Ephram."

The Moosepathians were apologetic, though they had not been responsible for what the trees had shed. They marveled at the coincidence.

"Circumstances are peculiar," agreed Durwood.

39. Several Parties Not Necessarily Looking for One Another

PORTLAND TELEGRAPH COMPANY
Grand Trunk

DECEMBER 6 AM 10 :25
C/O SOMERSET COUNTY SHERIFF
MR. TOBIAS WALTON

MR. A. TEMPEST NOT ON CALEB BROWN THOUGH KIT REMAINS.
CAPT MATTHEWS PERPLEXED. FURTHERS?
DEPUTY CHIEF FRITH

"This news makes me sensible of Mr. Burnbrake's situation," said Mister Walton when he received the telegram from the Portland constabulary.

"I hope *he* doesn't find himself snarled in this business," said Frederick.

"Surely they have found what they wanted," said Isabelle, "and will be gone, now that Arthur and Edgar are out on bail."

It was true that the members of the mysterious Broumnage Club had found *something* on Council Hill. Earlier that morning Capital Gaines and Paul Duvaudreuil had led Frederick Covington and a small expedition of Paul's cousins back to the tor, where upon further investigation the remains of a second set of runes was discovered on the underside of a large flat rock opposite the first. Someone else had found these new runes before them, however, and had disfigured them till they were unreadable.

Frederick had fallen back upon the first runes (the copies of it already circulating throughout the town had saved it perhaps), and studying them more closely, he was the more frustrated by their cryptic nature. Arthur's final words of the night before rankled him.

You haven't translated it, have you?

The sheriff had been wakened early that morning by a letter from a judge in town, who demanded that Arthur and Edgar be released. Darwin had stuck to form, however, and waited till bail was set and someone had physically put the money in his hands before he let them go.

The state of things did not seem simpler when the telegram arrived, and it was decided that Mister Walton and Sundry should return to Portland and find Mr. Burnbrake.

"He deserves to know what this is all about, at any rate," said Isabelle.

Moxie, still basking in the glow of her heroic behavior at the tor, was without opinion on the matter. Sundry made much of the dog at the station, ruffling the long fur behind her ears; he laughed when she licked his chin.

The tracks were still closed between Iceboro and Richmond, so they had decided to stop at Hallowell, where Mister Walton could look in on Phileda McCannon's house as he had promised. They hoped the line would be opened again by afternoon. "We will wire you if Mr. Burnbrake is still in Portland," said Mister Walton.

"Let me know if Mr. Tempest is found," said Frederick.

"Let us know if you translate those runes," said Sundry.

"I think we will stay in touch," commented Isabelle with a smile.

And so they waved to one another as Mister Walton and Sundry Moss found their seats and the train took its first lurch from the station. "Another adventure done, Sundry," said Mister Walton. "What do you think?"

"I think it isn't over till we understand what happened," said Sundry.

Mister Walton laughed, but a moment later he was peering out the window and he sighed, saying, "I wish I'd gone to church this morning."

Hinkley, Shawmut, Fairfield, Waterville, Sidney, Augusta: These places fell past Mister Walton and Sundry, offering the sights of their villages and settlements and, between, the undisturbed intervals of snowy fields and treeless hills. Mister Walton saw little of it. He was thinking of Phileda McCannon and rather wished he could pass by Hallowell while she was not at home; looking in on her home, knowing she wasn't there, seemed a melancholy thing to do.

Sundry was deep in thought himself, though his mind was taken up by other things, most notably the pictograph on the rock at the Council Hill. He had no expertise in runic language, or languages at all outside his native one, yet he felt as if the meaning of that single figure—be it an ox or a plow—were on the tip of his tongue, like a half-remembered melody. He thought of his father plowing, then mused upon a neighbor, who plowed with oxen.

One passenger did beguile a few miles for them; it was the man whose duck had been stolen and whom they had met on their trip to Skowhegan.

"That man was a German, I think," said the man with the duck. The bird sat in the bag beneath his feet and ate peanuts that the man shelled for it.

"I beg your pardon," said Mister Walton.

"The man who stole my duck," said the fellow, as if the conversation of two days before had never stopped. "He was a German, I think."

"Are Germans prone to stealing ducks?" wondered Sundry aloud.

"I don't know that they are," said the man, "but there are Germans in Woolwich, I think."

"I'm German," said a man who sat behind Mister Walton and Sundry. He did not look up from his newspaper. "*I've* never stolen a duck."

"I beg your pardon," said the man, but he picked up the duck and set the bird on his lap. Nothing more on the subject of ducks or Germans was offered, but Sundry thought it was a fortunate business for it made Mister Walton laugh softly to himself.

The sun was past the meridian when they stepped onto the platform at Hallowell. The shadow of the hill behind them was conquering the town, though the slopes on the opposing bank of the Kennebec were brilliant to the eye. The wind rallied the surface of the river into whitecaps, and sleighs rather than carriages were the order of the day among the streets and avenues; there were several such vehicles out, filled with bundled folk who braved the nippy air.

The man with the duck joined them on the platform, though he had in-

dicated that he was going as far as Gardiner. The German fellow had unnerved him.

"Perhaps we should get something to eat at the Worster House," said
Mister Walton, "and then I can take a stroll up to Phileda's."

They left their baggage with the stationmaster and soon hired a sleigh
to take them to the hotel, where they had spent some days the previous
fall. The man with the duck seemed to think he had been invited to accompany them and climbed into the sleigh as well. Mister Walton and
Sundry graciously accepted his company.

Their first sight, upon approaching the Worster House, was that of a
bundle of blankets in a sleigh below the hotel steps. The sound of snoring
that arose from the blankets was so loud that Sundry wondered it didn't
startle the horses.

"I don't have the heart to wake him," said the other sleigh driver, who
stood alongside, lighting a pipe.

Mister Walton and Sundry peered into the sleigh but could see only the
red nose of some elderly person peeking from between the heap of throws
and a red stocking cap. "It's Colonel Barkoddel," said the driver. "He's had
a vigorous morning."

"Has he?" said Mister Walton.

The duck in the bag gave out a honk, which puzzled the driver. He returned to his train of thought, however, and explained, "He dispatched
troops after a superior force and was uncommonly successful."

"Was he?"

"One of the finest set-tos I ever witnessed."

"Good heavens!" said Mister Walton.

"What? What?" came a voice from the blankets. There were two or
three grunts, related somehow to the previous snores.

"Are you awake, Colonel?" said the driver.

"Of course I'm awake! Where are the men?"

"They have been victorious and retired the field," explained the driver.
"They sent us ahead of them," he explained to Mister Walton and Sundry.
"Finest scrap I ever saw, I promise you. Here they come now."

Mister Walton and Sundry were interested in the arrival of the colonel's troops and further interested to see a company of young boys and
several grown men descending Winthrop Street. Three of the men conjured particular memories for the portly fellow and his young friend, and
Mister Walton was ready to say that they reminded him of their fellows of
the Moosepath League when he realized that they *were* their fellows of the
Moosepath League!

"My word!" said Mister Walton, and that well-loved voice reached up the street and tugged at the ears of Ephram, Eagleton, and Thump. These three worthies were strolling with uncharacteristic confidence alongside the boys and three other men, and that self-possession was raised to the level of the ecstatic at the sight of their chairman.

"Good heavens, Thump!" said Eagleton.

"Good heavens, yes!" agreed Thump.

"Ephram!"

"Yes, Eagleton! I am in concurrence."

To Mister Walton and Sundry the three members did have about them the look of successful contestants: Their faces beamed, their cheeks appeared red with happy exertions, their clothes were stained with dampness, and their hats were the worse for some physical aggravation. Their strides lengthened and became brisker.

"Mister Walton," said Sundry, for he was looking past the Moosepath League at three other men.

"My word!" said Mister Walton again.

"Truth to tell, Mister Walton!"

Bringing up the rear of the column were the Dash-It-All Boys, looking less like success and more like philosophy and sodden to the skin.

"Mister Walton!" declared Ephram. "Mr. Moss! How remarkable to see you! How very gratifying!"

The nearer they got, the worse for wear they *all* looked, but Ephram, Eagleton, and Thump approached Colonel Barkoddel's sleigh with pleasure writ large upon their faces.

"We have participated in the most amusing melee, gentlemen!" asserted Eagleton.

"Melee?" said Mister Walton; it sounded entirely too warlike, coming from the peaceable members of the Moosepath League. Several people, including the colonel and his driver, began to discuss the battle. The younger boys gathered about, still excited.

"Wasn't it wonderful, Thump?" said Eagleton.

"I will remember it fondly," said that man. His eyes glowed with delight. He let out a startled shout, however, when the duck in the bag made itself known again. "Great cats! What was that?" he wondered, and the duck squawked even louder when Sundry attempted to explain.

"It's a *what?*" asked Eagleton.

"Duck!" called Sundry over the general hubbub, and the Moosepathians immediately crouched with their hands over their hats. Durwood, Waverley, and Brink did not shrink but looked about for incoming snowballs.

Mister Walton's already large eyes were like saucers behind his glittering spectacles, and he looked as delighted as his friends before he even realized what had occurred. The Dash-It-All Boys tipped what remained of their hats to Mister Walton and Sundry.

"Our fates are entwined," said Brink.

"That's rather poetic," said Durwood.

"Was it? I didn't intend."

"Caught in the crossfire," said Durwood, by way of explanation.

"The *downfall*, actually," corrected Brink.

"A hot bath," said Waverley like a toast. He raised his hat again as he passed the crowd at the bottom of the hotel steps.

"Me too," said Durwood as he followed his fellow inside.

"I hope there's more than one tub or it will be crowded," said Brink.

Another sleigh was pulling up before the hotel, and Mister Walton hardly had a moment to bid good day to the Dashians before a new commotion was begun.

"It's Miss Burnbrake," said Eagleton as a lovely woman stepped from the third sleigh. The duck was giving out a terrific roster of quacks.

"It is a duck!" said Thump. He had only raised his head again when the name of Miss Burnbrake was pronounced.

He and Ephram and Eagleton were all three telling their versions of recent events while shaking hands vigorously with Mister Walton, Sundry, and their driver, who thought he had much to tell his wife when he went home for dinner.

"Charlotte!" came a new voice from the top of the steps, and Ezra Burnbrake stood there, waving to his niece. He was puzzled to see a strange man handing her down from the sleigh with an air of familiarity.

"It's my uncle," she said to Daniel Plainway. "And, my goodness, the Moosepath League!"

"The Moosepath League?" he returned.

"Someone get me down from here!" shouted the colonel. He was struggling in the tangle of throws. The duck got itself out of its bag with a couple of flaps and landed beside the old soldier. "What?" he shouted. "Highly irregular!"

"Miss Burnbrake!" said Ephram, followed closely by similar assertions from his fellow members. All eyes turned, if not all voices stilled, for the woman as she reached them.

"How good to see you gentlemen again," she said.

Mister Walton and Sundry had doffed their hats, and the Moosepathians quickly (and proudly) introduced these two to Miss Burnbrake.

The duck was stalking the back of Colonel Barkoddel's sleigh like a sentry. "Does he think he's a pigeon?" asked the old man. The man who owned the duck was attempting to retrieve the bird.

"Mister Walton?" said Daniel Plainway when this name was pronounced. "Mister *Tobias* Walton?"

"Why, yes," said the portly fellow. He reached his hand out.

"Mr. Daniel Plainway," said Charlotte as the lawyer approached them, and there was something remarkable about the moment and about the two men as they shook hands. Even Sundry would say, years later, that here was a man to rival Mister Walton in several happy instances of character.

Here, thought Daniel, *is the man in possession of Nell's portrait.*

"Mister Walton," he said, "I have come far and long to meet you, and I believe, for the sake of people you have never met, I have much to thank you for."

Daniel's Story
(April 1892–April 1893)

If not for his suspicions regarding the death of Jeram Willum, Daniel might have had some hope for Ian Linnett when the baby came to his house. The old man appeared sensible of his responsibility and was acquiescent and even interested when Mrs. Cutler arrived to help with her own child in arm.

Linnett expressed his wish that Nell be laid to rest in the tomb that had been built for himself, but he did not attend the funeral. Aunt Dora, dark and stern, returned for the service, though she stayed in town; she said that the old man was watching the graveside service from the woods above the cemetery, but Daniel did not look back. It was a windy day in April with the sun waking to the earth between running clouds. Leaves of the previous fall moved among the tombstones.

"That's not her," Daniel told himself as the casket was carried in among the dark stones.

The day after the funeral the sheriff came to ask Ian Linnett what he knew about Jeram Willum. The young man had drowned after suffering a blow to the head, but the coroner could not be sure that Jeram hadn't fallen down a bank. Daniel's horse and carriage were found wandering half a mile or so up the road from the Linnett drive.

Ian was not helpful. He had not seen the boy. How did he come to the Willum place that day? He'd had a bad feeling about Nell and simply came. The sheriff tried to trick Ian by asking him what he had done with the note Daniel had written, but the old man only looked at him indignantly. He'd had a bad feeling.

"It seems to me," said the sheriff to Daniel, "that he would have had plenty of bad feelings before that particular day."

No one discounted in the meantime the possibility that Jeram's father had made good with a long series of threats and followed his boy to the Linnetts'. Daniel didn't know which was the worst scenario. Two days had gone by before the body was found, however, and rain had washed the fields of sign. The sheriff came to Linnett twice with no more result. Jeram's death was officially stated an accident. Mrs. Willum, looking hard and unrepentant, and some of Jeram's younger brothers and sisters came to the service. Daniel stood by himself on the other side of the grave with his hat in his hands; the day was unseasonably warm, like May. At one point during the interment, something caught Daniel's eye, and he looked up to see a robin hopping among the rows.

The next day the lawyer had a visit from Parley Willum, who claimed a legal attachment to the baby. The man's motives were clear enough, as he was willing to state them.

"That brat's in for some money," growled the man, "and as his grandfather I'm entitled to my handful!"

Daniel had difficulty remaining still behind his desk. "Inheritance doesn't generally work in that direction," he replied.

"Then I want the brat," stated the man flatly.

"I will warn you now, Mr. Willum," said Daniel, "that if you had custody of that child, the judge would surely stipulate regular visits from the law."

The thought took Willum aback; his face pinched up as if he had smelled something bad, though he was the worst-smelling object in the room. "No one's visiting regularly up that place, I expect!" he declared, meaning the Linnett estate. "And that crazy old coot there, who murdered my kin!" Parley stormed around Daniel's office before leaving, shouting, "I'll get what's coming, soon or late, you can trust! Parley Willum isn't one to come up short, no, he's not!"

From his desk window Daniel watched the man storm down the walk to his buckboard and drive off. At least I know where trouble may come, he thought, which foresight, like so much else in life, proved unhelpful.

Daniel first met Edward Penfen in July. Ian Linnett had been calling Daniel to some unusual duties in those weeks, liquidating his assets (which were rich in railroad stock, among other things) into physical wealth. Daniel had in fact sold off thousands of dollars' worth of Linnett's investments in the past months and, per instruction, bought the most precious gems he was able to lay hands upon in Portland and Boston. The lawyer had argued with his client about this strange business and would have quit it himself had he not worried that a less scrupulous agent might be hired in his place.

He had no idea where the old man kept his growing hoard. Neither, as it happened, did Edward Penfen.

Daniel hardly bothered to knock at the front door when he came to the Linnett house. The old man rarely answered, and it seemed a lot of trouble to bother Mrs. Cutler when he could easily let himself in.

On this particular day in July, however, the door opened before he had reached it, and he had his first glimpse of Penfen.

He was a narrow, wild-eyed fellow, even dressed in his best suit, which appeared well worn, if tidy enough. His hair was wanting an appointment with the shears, clean but disordered. If Asher Willum was a wolf, here was a fox, with no telling which was the more dangerous. Daniel mistrusted the man the moment he set eyes upon him.

"Mr. Plainway, I presume," said Penfen with a flash of teeth.

"You have the better of me, sir," said Daniel.

"Edward Penfen," said the man. "Mr. Linnett is expecting you."

The tale was that Penfen had been hired to look after the baby, Bertram, and that the man was qualified to be the child's instructor when the time came. Ian Linnett fell silent on the matter after the first explanation, though he made sure that Penfen was out of the room before he resumed the business between himself and Daniel.

As always, Daniel stopped by the nursery, where Mrs. Cutler would be rocking Bertram or her son, or feeding them, or singing nursery songs. She was a large woman who kept to herself and the children, venturing no opinion concerning Mr. Linnett or Edward Penfen. Daniel found the babies mysterious, if pleasant, and stayed awhile to talk to Bertram. The baby watched him with a mild, serious expression; when Bertram smiled Daniel thought he saw a flash of his mother in the child's face.

Penfen, as far as Daniel could see during his subsequent visits, did nothing, though he was sure to answer the door, a means to see who was calling upon his employer. The tutor, as he came to be known, made occasional appearances in town and failed to ingratiate himself there. Daniel said nothing about the man to anyone but waited his moment.

That moment seemed to arrive one October day when Penfen didn't greet him at the door and as the man was supposed to be "tending to personal business" in another town, Daniel thought it was a good time to bring up the security of Linnett's growing cache. The old man was standing in the front room, across from the parlor, looking at a portrait of Nell that had been painted when she was yet sixteen. Daniel had been a little put off by the picture when it was commissioned, since it had made her look older than her years, but now it seemed to fit his memory of her.

"They're safe put away," said Linnett when Daniel brought up the subject of the gems.

"Safe from Penfen?" asked Daniel bluntly.

"You're not to worry about Penfen," said the old man.

"Ian," said Daniel, "as much as I dislike to bring it up, your investments are nearly gone, and there is only enough left—by your own plan—to eke out a bare existence for yourself and your household. What if something were to happen to you? How would Bertram be provided for? How are we to know where you've hidden this cache of jewels?"

A smile, barely discernible, touched Linnett's face then, and not happily. "If he's as big a man as I am—" he said, "the boy, that is—he will see where it's been put, in his mother's eyes."

Daniel peered after the man at the portrait of Nell, exasperated, wondering if he had done something as simple and foolish as hide the gems in the wall behind the portrait. Then he saw, reflected in the glass before the portrait, the shadow of a man standing in the doorway to the hall.

"Mr. Penfen," said Daniel, "I was told you were away on business."

"How are you today, Mr. Plainway?" was Penfen's indirect reply.

Daniel had hoped that Ian Linnett was opening up to him, but the old man lost all sign of vitality upon sight of his employee. The lawyer did discover one thing, however: Linnett knew Penfen for what he was, for the old man behaved as if a leering stranger had entered Nell's very presence. "You are allowed in the remainder of the house, Mr. Penfen," said Linnett, "but you will kindly avoid this room in the future."

Penfen bowed obsequiously and backed into the hall. Linnett then turned to Daniel, and not without an expression of regard. "If you would shut the door when you leave, Daniel," he said, but he stopped the lawyer at the door by adding, "I heard her again last night."

Daniel waited.

"I hear her every once in a while," said the old man, "singing in her room."

Daniel could have wept to hear him.

Linnett looked over his shoulder at Daniel. "It's Nell, you know. I went to the door once, when I was over being frightened, but she stopped, so I stay down here now and listen." Then Linnett fell to contemplating the portrait once again.

The lawyer collected his hat and was reaching for the front door when someone spoke softly to him from the other end of the hall. Penfen stood there, beckoning Daniel like a fellow conspirator. When Daniel advanced upon the man, one would have thought them in close confidence, Penfen seemed so pleased to speak with him.

"I think Mr. Linnett is not himself," said the man, and Daniel only frowned, meaning that Penfen had better be both specific and cautious. Penfen appeared to take pains to make his next utterance as delicate as was possible. "I don't believe the dear fellow is in his right mind," he said.

"I daresay he is not," said Daniel quietly, "upon which state your presence has not an ameliorative effect."

"Mr. Plainway, we are both men of the world who can come to an agreement. It is plain to me that we are seeking the same things."

"Never in my life," said Daniel, "have I struck another man, but perhaps you would care to help me break that habit."

"Not at all, Mr. Plainway, not at all." Penfen did take a step back but continued his sly tack. "I was only thinking we might benefit from one another."

"I have but to understand the hold you have on Mr. Linnett," said Daniel, "and you are gone."

"That is devils' knowledge, Mr. Plainway, that may do more harm than good." There was a wild smile on Penfen's face, and Daniel decided that here was the one not in his right mind. The thought almost divided the lawyer from his anger.

It was at about this time that Daniel caught wind of a story regarding a discussion between Penfen and Parley Willum, held in the middle of the street, in front of the Post Office and General Store, that turned into an altercation of shouted threats and shaking fists.

In November Mrs. Cutler left the Linnett house, saying that the "dampening atmosphere" was not healthy for her boy. Daniel thought he knew where the dampness lay, and the darkness. He tried to get Linnett to hire a new woman to care for Bertram, but the old man, more lost in regret than ever, refused, and Daniel had to admit that Penfen was administering to the child's physical welfare rather ably.

"Oh, I am a man of many talents, Mr. Plainway," said Penfen. He had the child drinking from a cup. "We'll be working on his catechism before you know it, won't we, Bertram?"

At least, thought Daniel, he's earning his keep. He didn't let the man's presence drive him from the nursery, and when he sat down to spend a moment with the little boy, Bertram smiled at him. Ah, thought Daniel, there's your mother.

Penfen went to work as winter progressed, keeping the stoves and the fireplaces stoked, tending to the laundry and the meals. Ian Linnett grew thinner and more haggard. He neglected his clothes, his hair, and his beard, all of which took on the ragged measurements of a scarecrow. He rarely left the parlor and then only to consider the portrait of his granddaughter in the front room. Once, in February, Daniel came in on an argument between the old man and Penfen, and the lawyer suggested in front of the wild-eyed man that Linnett kick the repellent individual from the house. Penfen listened to the ensuing conversation with an unchanging smile.

The winter was mild and open until February, and then what they had missed began to tumble out of the western mountains and fill the skies and fields with snow. An involved business in contract law kept Daniel very busy through March, and he went to the Linnett house only twice.

In April he knew that the old man was not long for the world, and he pressed again for the location of the hidden jewels.

"His mother's eyes," was all the old man would say.

Penfen hovered over the old man like a vulture.

Bertram was walking. He recognized Daniel when he came to the nursery, and the lawyer felt guilty for having lingered away.

It snowed again. On the first anniversary of Eleanor Linnett's death, Daniel took a sleigh up to the estate. He was surprised to see another vehicle's tracks in the new snow before him. But he was a little lost in his thoughts, remembering his first trip among these oaks, more than twenty years before: the summer sound of the brook over which the carriage drive ran on its way to the house.

He was climbing from the sleigh when he noticed the footprints coming from the side of the house and descending toward the pond. Something unnamed caught him like ice at the pit of his stomach. It did not seem like Penfen to go strolling through deep snow, and as he neared the tracks, he realized that they were made by someone who moved feebly and in confusion: the footprints wandered and wavered.

Struggling through the snow, Daniel had barely crested the hill when he saw the body of the old man sprawled, facedown upon the white slope. He knew that Ian Linnett was beyond saving, was in fact hours dead, before he reached the body. But where had he been going? His stiffened arm was stretched out in the direction of Clemons Pond.

Daniel had wrestled the body part of the way back to the house when he thought of the baby. This time he was gripped by real fear, and he left Ian Linnett's remains where they lay.

"Penfen!" he called as he hurried down the front hall of the estate. "Bertram!" From the front door he ran to the back of the house, calling both for the fox and the child.

40. Two Hearts

"They were gone, of course," said Daniel Plainway. "The house was cold, the fires long dead. How many hours, or even days, Ian had been out there, the Lord only knows, *and* whether Penfen took the boy before Ian died or after. Some people assumed that Ian was going for help, but I think he was beyond even that simple office. I believe that there was little more than guilt left in him and that he was struggling toward the place where Jeram died. Looking back, I was a fool for not having watched them more closely."

Sundry Moss silently considered the floor before him. Charlotte Burn-brake, who was seated near to Daniel, watched the lawyer with no emotion telling upon her face. There were tears in her eyes.

Standing by the window of his hotel apartment, Mister Walton remembered what had been told him when he was a boy. "'What we know, we must first have learned,'" quoted the portly fellow, his hands folded behind him. "It is a *human* dilemma—and not yours alone, Mr. Plainway—that we have hindsight rather than foreknowledge, and it seems to me that you have done more for these sad people than others would have or could have."

"But I did make a promise to Nell," said Daniel, "and failed even that."

"You haven't failed at all," said Charlotte, the first words from her lips since Daniel started his tale.

"My prayers have not failed, at any rate," he said, lifting his head. "But I have never understood why she did it."

"Nor did she, I promise you," said Mister Walton sadly.

"She was greatly disappointed in her grandfather," ventured Sundry.

"But in the end," said Daniel, "her instincts were true, for she felt more shame for the old man than she did for Jeram."

Mister Walton took his spectacles from his nose and rubbed at them with a handkerchief. "I fear," he said, "we ask too much of our young people when we shelter them from life, then expect them to behave sensibly when life comes knocking." Placing his spectacles back on his nose, he let out a sigh. "We guessed it would be an unhappy tale, Sundry," he added, "but when we first laid eyes upon that little boy in the dory off Fort Edgecomb, we couldn't know that we would be so entangled with his fate."

It did seem a great deal of story for so small a person. Bird had rubbed shoulders with them in Edgecomb and Boothbay, Portland and several points in between; he had affected many, including Mollie Peer, the young woman who saved him from drowning in the Sheepscott River, and Wyckford O'Hearn, who had been shot and his career perhaps ruined in the boy's defense. Even the Moosepath League had followed many circuitous wanderings (without Mister Walton's leadership!) in its attempt to keep the boy from harm.

"And you had no further trouble from Jeram's family?" asked Sundry.

"There was a story going around town," said Daniel, "a month or so after Ian died—something of a joke among the locals, actually—that Parley took his clan to the house one night to rob the place, but they were frightened off."

"Was someone waiting for them?" asked Mister Walton.

"Only the Linnetts, if anyone. Perhaps Ian's grim visage greeted them at the door." Daniel pronounced this without levity, and it was followed by silence, till he spoke again. "The problem of the house of course takes a new turn, now that there is a surviving heir. It doesn't seem in the boy's best interests to let his legacy remain in an empty house."

"And yet," said Mister Walton, "there is 'more than coin to an estate.'"

"Exactly. A man doesn't leave his watch so that his son can pawn it."

"And the gems," said Charlotte.

"If I could find them, there would be no trouble. I could manage the upkeep on the place and have a healthy bequest waiting for Bertram when he came of age. But without them, or the wealth they represent—well, let's just say a country lawyer might get paid in apples or a side of ham, or he might get paid in two or three years." Daniel was not moaning but only stating a natural fact, and he could do it with something of a smile on his face.

Mister Walton made a low sound, and his brow furrowed with thought. Daniel said, "I should like to meet the boy."

Mister Walton's head came up from his musing. "Of course," he said. "He must know where he comes from. And he should know you, Mr. Plainway."

"Is he too young, do you think, to hear some of it?" wondered Daniel.

"He will be pleased that the woman in the portrait is his mother, I think, and certainly glad that she didn't abandon him. I wonder, however, if he should wait to see his family home when he is old enough to ask."

"I should like to burn it down," said Daniel, "or see it lighted once again and filled with people. If I could just know that Nell and her grandfather are not wandering there: Ian in his guilt, Nell waiting to hear from her child." He was conscious that Charlotte had reached across the small space between them and taken his hand. He hardly dared breathe, as if some exquisite bird had lit upon him.

Mister Walton looked out the window again. Sundry, who understood that these people had met each other only the day before, raised a surprised eyebrow, then looked after Mister Walton.

"I fear, sir, that for yourself," said Mister Walton, "they *do* still walk those rooms. Perhaps the place will *need* to be lit and filled with people once again before you can let them go. I know that my own family's house, once I was alone in it, was vastly haunted till my friends brought new voices inside its walls." Without fear of appearing sentimental, Mister Walton gripped Sundry's shoulder.

"Any of you are invited whenever you like," said Daniel, but he directed this thought to Charlotte, who drew her hand away. Daniel took a deep, regretful breath.

"I should see how my uncle is," she said.

Daniel got up and nearly knocked his chair over.

"Miss Burnbrake," said Mister Walton. He stepped up to her, purposely navigating his portly self in a manner that would most likely draw attention from the lawyer's obvious discomfort. "I look forward to seeing you and your uncle in the morning."

Charlotte offered her hand to Sundry Moss and Mister Walton; it was not as awkward then for her to do the same to Daniel Plainway, where her touch lingered as she thanked him for his escort.

Daniel nodded, his chest feeling heavy and constricted. "It was my pleasure," he said finally, and he could not have spoken more truthfully. When she was gone, he was at a loss for words; he stood before his chair, finding it difficult to stay in the moment when it was suddenly without her elegant presence.

"I like her," said Sundry bluntly.

"She is a very fine person, I think," said Mister Walton.

The lawyer was adrift with emotion. He had never told the Linnetts' story before, from beginning to end, and though it had exhausted him to do so, it had also purged him of some of its sadness. "I think I too must retire," he said.

"You have had some adventures the last day or so," said Mister Walton.

"And I am not so used to them as you," said Daniel with a smile.

"You'll build up to it," said Sundry wryly.

When Daniel was gone, Mister Walton gave out a sigh.

"What do you think?" wondered Sundry.

"I think that two pair of shoulders would bear such burdens better."

Sundry chuckled softly. It was remarkable how obvious people could be in their affection for one another, most especially when they were reticent about displaying it. It was remarkable, too, how very accurately Mister Walton's observation might have been applied to himself.

"But I do think," continued Mister Walton, "that I may have a solution to his problem regarding Bird's estate."

"Do you?"

"Or should we call him Bertram now? At any rate, I must confer with the Moosepath League. My goodness! There is a good deal to think about!"

"I should say," pronounced Sundry, who was reclining once more in his chair, his feet stretched out before him, his hands folded behind his head. "The portrait identified, new people to be considered, the O'Hearns to be informed."

"I have yet to digest the events at Council Hill," said Mister Walton. "Your ability to take quick action, by the way, continues to amaze me, and I believe we are all in your debt for it."

Sundry insisted, as ever, that it was Moxie who had saved them and no one else.

"I wonder if our friends have risen from their naps," said Mister Walton. He was clearly in need of an errand. Ephram, Eagleton, and Thump would have been invited to hear Daniel's tale if they hadn't fallen asleep after dinner, exhausted by their exploits; perhaps they had renewed themselves by now.

"They are probably up and reliving the day's battle," said Sundry. "They made great friends with the fellow with the duck." He thought he might go down to the hotel parlor and hear the details of the Battle of the Smoking Pine (as he later dubbed it). First, however, he must send Mister Walton off to where he knew the bespectacled fellow's thoughts were roaming. With this in mind, Sundry said, "And speaking of things—and people—to think about, there is always Phileda McCannon."

Mister Walton chuckled. Miss McCannon had in truth been crowding his mental facilities somewhat. "There is no harm, I suppose, in being easily read by a good friend," he said. "I only wish she were at home."

"But in her absence," said Sundry, "you should stroll by her place and see that all is as it should be." He understood only too well the romantic inclination of a heart like Mister Walton's.

"I did promise to look in," said the bespectacled fellow with a smile.

"I will report to Miss McCannon that you have been as good as your word."

41. Two More

Phileda McCannon was a compact sort of person, in body and in the manner in which she conducted her affairs. She was a brisk walker and direct in her speech and her meaning. Her father had thought she had an excess of wit, but it was always to the point and never cruel—wry, even ironic at times, but never scornful. She was a busy person and as alert as a bird. She was by no means without sadness in her life, yet she kept sadness at bay, for the most part, by outstripping it. Just the day before, she had seen to the final services over her aunt, who had died of a lingering illness. She had taken the train to Hallowell only this evening, outstripping sadness, but with the persistent understanding that it would catch her up once she had returned to the home where she was the sole occupant.

She was never sure if it was by accident that she met Charleston Thistlecoat outside the Hallowell station, but she wasn't entirely sorry to see him; she quite naturally accepted his offer to carry her bags and allowed him to drive her in his sleigh to her home.

It *wasn't* an accident that the lights in her house were blazing when they drew up to the rambling granite steps that led up the bank, past the great red maple and the stone cherubs. She had sent a telegram to her friend Mrs. Miriam Nowell but was gratified (not to mention a little relieved, with Mr. Thistlecoat at her side) to find that the Nowells were waiting for her with lamps lit and a fire crackling at the parlor hearth. She quite naturally allowed Charleston to carry her things in for her.

"Welcome home," said Miriam when Phileda stepped inside. "We were so sorry to hear of your aunt."

"Thank you," said Phileda, and the requisite expressions were exchanged between them. Phileda took her hat off; her hair was in rather a pleasing disarray, her spectacles a little fogged by the change in temperature. "You can't know how good it is to see you!" she declared. "Stuart, how are you," she said as Miriam's husband entered the hall.

"Mr. Thistlecoat, how are *you*," said Miriam as that man entered by way of the front door, Phileda's bags in hand.

Charleston Thistlecoat indicated that he was well.

"We met outside the station," said Phileda. She flashed a raised eyebrow at Miriam, but her friend appeared genuinely surprised to see the man.

Phileda had first met Charleston Thistlecoat on the night of the Hallowell Harvest Ball, the previous October, and though Mister Tobias Walton had been her escort, Thistlecoat managed to occupy a substantial bit of both Phileda's evening and her dance card. He was a man who had been denied very little and accustomed to deny himself less. He was a tall, slender man, with silver hair, black, expressive eyebrows, and a large, not altogether unattractive nose. He had a sense of humor when it did not apply to himself and more than a passing interest in Phileda McCannon that had manifested itself in unannounced visits and numerous invitations.

Phileda had successfully put off his visits on the strength of her being a woman alone; his invitations had been more difficult to treat, and she had managed some of them—those of a less intimate nature—by accepting. She did not dislike the man, though he was never as entertaining as he thought he was; but her thoughts were generally with Toby (as she thought of Mister Walton), and she was beginning to think that a firm word, not to say a fair word, on this matter was quickly becoming a necessity.

"Come in, Charleston," she said as she did her best to tame her hair. "You must warm yourself before you leave." She shed her coat as she entered the parlor, which was cozy. She smelled something simmering in the kitchen. "Ah!" she said, and rubbed her hands before the hearth. "Do I smell soup on the stove?" Charleston stood a few feet away, hands behind his back.

Phileda was in her middle age, perhaps forty-one or -two, but had kept—or perhaps attained—the slim figure of a girl by constant movement, and had adorned a nearly plain countenance with smile lines and bright blue eyes behind round spectacles. Her chestnut hair glowed in the firelight, which did not pick out the few strands of gray but tinged them with its auburn warmth. She was radiant without an ounce of realization. Charleston could at least lay claim to true discernment, for he was not unmoved.

The Nowells filled the air of the parlor with news of the town and a funny story about Miriam's dog, Nasturtium, that had an unfortunate tête-à-tête with a sleepy skunk.

Charleston did his best to look amused by the chatter; but he clearly had other things on his mind, and Phileda thought that this was one evening she was not prepared to discover them. *I must write Toby in the morning*, she thought, and wondered if he had gotten her letter of several days ago. She felt tired of a sudden and let out a sigh, which was not like her. The heat of the fire was warming her but sapping her will to move much further.

"I have been away myself recently," said Charleston.

"Were you?" said Miriam, affecting great interest but somehow demonstrating, by her near astonishment, how *very* much she hadn't realized he was gone.

"Difficulties with the line," he explained, meaning a particular railroad line of which he purportedly owned controlling stock. "But we have put them to rest."

"The difficulties?" said Miriam.

Charleston was not quite sharp enough to know if Mrs. Nowell was having fun with him, and he answered her with a long, drawled yes.

The stealthy badinage reminded Phileda of another day, when Toby had crossed swords, successfully, if not too happily, with Charleston Thistlecoat at an afternoon tea. The affair had been a little strained and, in retrospect, as it was the last time she had seen Mister Walton, more than a little melancholy. Thinking on it, she wondered that she wasn't angry with the tall man before her.

"I beg your pardon?" she said. Charleston had been speaking to her.

"Mrs. Nowell was telling me about your aunt, Miss McCannon," he said. "May I express my deepest sympathies." He bowed, rather like an eighteenth-century courtier.

"Thank you, Charleston."

He straightened to his considerable height. "I should perhaps leave you to your study then," he said. It was an old phrase, and not unpleasing, as he was able to carry it off.

"Good night," she said. "I shall see you out." He allowed her to do this, and Phileda shot a look of some apprehension to Miriam, who rounded her husband up with a crook of the arm and followed them.

"If there is anything I can do for you, Miss McCannon," Charleston was saying, "in these difficult hours, please do not hesitate to let me know."

"You are very kind," she said, and as he was opening the door while offering his services, she reflexively offered him her hand, which he leaned over briefly. She was startled, thinking for a moment that he was going to kiss it. He did not, quite. She stood in the well-lit doorway and waved to him as he descended the steps; Miriam and Stuart Nowell formed a friendly chorus behind her.

Then she hesitated in the doorway, thinking that she saw someone moving swiftly up the hill on the other side of the street. She leaned from the door, her heart taking the smallest sort of jump; she had had the impression that Toby was passing by. But she laughed to herself for the fancy, turned inside, and shut the door.

Standing above Phileda McCannon's house on the opposite side of the street, Mister Walton turned his face away as Charleston Thistlecoat sleighed past. The bespectacled man felt foolish, hiding himself in this fashion, even ashamed. He had been so surprised to see lights burning at Phileda's home that he had waited for some minutes, feeling almost disoriented and wondering if he had the right house or even the right street.

But there were the stone cherubs and the two switchback flights of steps; the great crown of the red maple, which he had last seen in its autumnal glory, was a thicket of narrow fingers, tangled with the stars. The door to the house opened unexpectedly, and Phileda appeared there with a man. It was Charleston Thistlecoat, whose attentions toward Phileda had been obvious during Mister Walton's last sojourn in Hallowell the previous October.

He was startled to see the man, and more startled when Phileda appeared to give Thistlecoat her hand so that he might kiss it. Mister Walton was terrified that he would be seen before he could hurry across the street and up the hill, and in one backward glance he was almost sure that Phileda *had* seen him. There didn't seem any way that she could tell who he was, standing in a well-lit doorway and looking out into the night, but he kept his face turned away and again looked off when Thistlecoat drove by.

"Good heavens!" he said to himself. He felt as if he'd run a mile and hardly knew how he would make it back home. "Oh, dear!" he said. He had rather flattered himself that Phileda harbored some interest in him beyond friendship and was shattered by what he thought he had seen.

He turned down the hill again, hardly sensing his own movement through the cold air. It had been such a beautiful starlit night, and now his thoughts were cluttered with the Linnetts of Hiram. *I had no shoes and complained*, he mused, *until I met a man with no feet*.

He stopped himself in the middle of the hill and thought about Nell Linnett's dark tomb, on some lonely hillside. She was with God, it was true, but this did not eradicate the sadness of her lost young life and for the child she had missed and who would miss her.

He considered other dark monuments: the cold face of carved stone upon Council Hill, dreaming as it had for a thousand years perhaps since those runes had been placed there; the long, gaunt face of Adam Tempest, waiting to die from who knew what (the vengeance of the Broumnage Club?) in his berth on the *Caleb Brown*.

Mister Walton tried to think of everything but his own sudden sorrow, and his mind fell again upon little Bird and upon Wyckford O'Hearn and—"Phileda's aunt!" he said aloud. He turned back to the house; he had walked further than he had realized. Either her aunt has recovered—

The cold had made his eyes water; he dabbed at them with a handkerchief. Nervously, he ascended the hill once more. The steps leading to the house, past the stone cherubs and the red maple, had been carefully cleaned, but the granite felt slick with snowmelt and ice.

He felt his chest tighten with the thought of Phileda and Charleston Thistlecoat; but Mister Walton was her friend, and that must come first. He took another deep breath before knocking on the door and waited. There was the shadow of someone passing by a window, and then the door was flung open and Stuart Nowell greeted him with a look of surprise.

"Come in, come in," Stuart said quietly.

"Who is it?" came a voice from the kitchen, and Phileda appeared at the other end of the hall. Her hand went to her mouth, her head tilted slightly, and Mister Walton thought she looked as if tears would spring from her eyes. "Toby!" she said, but still there was enough of her face covered by her hand that he could not tell if she was happy or upset to see him.

"I happened—" he began, faltered, then began again. "I happened to be coming by—"

When she dropped her hand, he could see that she was crying and that her mouth, contrarily, was turned up in a soft, grateful smile. Then she astonished him by hurrying down the hall and throwing her arms about his neck.

❧ BOOK FIVE ❧

December 7, 1896

42. Between Tales

"Sundry," said Mister Walton, "last night I very nearly committed one of the gravest errors of my life."

"I can't imagine it," said Sundry.

"The heighth of presumption," said Mister Walton.

"Really?"

"I promise you," assured the portly fellow. They were standing atop the front steps of the Worster House, glorying in the day, which was clear and brilliant. Sundry's eyes, in particular, were hardly more than slits as he squinted over the dazzling white of the snow; he looked to his friend for further explanation about this near disaster, but as none seemed pending, he laughed.

Mister Walton appeared more content than Sundry had seen him for some days, weeks perhaps. The portly fellow smiled, so lost in his own thoughts that he did not understand his friend's humor. "Oh, well, it has something to do with Phileda," he said.

"I thought it might."

Mister Walton told Sundry of how he had seen Charleston Thistlecoat taking his leave of Miss McCannon and how Mister Walton had very nearly allowed that to keep him away. "But then I realized there must have been some change in her aunt's situation before she would come back home."

"She must have been very glad to see you," said Sundry, thinking (but not knowing just how much) he practiced an understatement.

"She did seem," said Mister Walton.

Phileda's hug had surprised him greatly and perhaps herself as well. "Your aunt?" was all he had found to say, and she had explained that her aunt had died and that services had been only the day before.

She had taken his arm possessively and tugged him into the parlor, where she and he and the Nowells could exchange news. He was made bold, in the course of things, to wonder aloud if they might contrive to spend some part of the Christmas season together.

"That was a good idea," said Sundry when Mister Walton mentioned this.

"Won't you come with me?" said the bespectacled fellow. "Phileda will be disappointed not to see you."

Sundry liked Miss McCannon very much, but he couldn't imagine she would be dismayed if he didn't join her and Mister Walton on their appointed walk. "I think I will go see if Mr. Tolly is still at his cousin's," said Sundry.

"Very good," said Mister Walton. With his face beaming, he touched his hat and proceeded down the steps. They parted company on the sidewalk, Mister Walton hiking up the hill and Sundry turning downhill toward the water.

As the temperature had dropped considerably the night before, and as the day dawned bright and frosty, it seemed safe for Ephram, Eagleton, and Thump to venture onto the streets of Hallowell. Firstly, the cold had stiffened the surface snow into a hard crust, so that the hour of the snowball was expired for now, and secondly, all the young boys in town would be in school. The Moosepathians had been greatly exhilarated by the events of the day before, but it did not seem wise to push a good thing too far, so it wasn't till midmorning that they discussed an excursion into the brisk winter air.

They were readying themselves for this very thing when they were briefly joined by Durwood, Waverley, and Brink. "What, ho!" said Waverley amiably, and as the Moosepathians were not sure of a response, he added, "Read it in a book, I think."

"What, ho!" said Eagleton. He rather liked it.

"Can't tell you what it means."

"It is an agricultural query," suggested Brink.

"Will you walk with us?" invited Ephram.

"I think not," said Durwood. "We are returning to the Land of Ports."

"Do tell!" said Ephram.

"Are you?" Thump hadn't heard of the place.

"The Hallowell atmosphere is a little rough for our constitutions," admitted Waverley. "Avalanches falling out of the sky, gentlemen such as yourselves filling the air with missiles."

The Moosepathians were a little concerned to have encouraged the Dash-It-All Boys' early departure.

"We never brought any clothes," said Brink.

"It has been a great pleasure," said Eagleton. He offered his hand to Waverley. With his other hand he was fiddling with something beneath his collar, a gesture that his friends had noted several times in the last day or so. Eagleton had grown quite used to the little silver cross and the delicate chain from which it hung; he hadn't meant to be secretive about the gift and the incident that led to it; he had simply not thought to tell the tale when there was time to tell it, and when he *had* thought to tell it, paradoxically, the opportunity did not avail itself.

"If you ever come back to Portland from the Land of Ports," said Ephram as he took Brink's hand, "we would be delighted to have you join us any Thursday night at the Shipswood."

Thump cleared his throat, but said little as he took Durwood's hand. In the press between the two clubs, it went unnoticed that Durwood slipped something into Thump's coat pocket, even as they bade each other farewell. The round of handshakes took up some minutes, and before they were done, even the manager came within the Moosepathians' goodwill and hearty thanks, though they were not officially leaving the hotel till afternoon. The manager, somewhat confused, was concerned about the bill.

Ephram, Eagleton, and Thump removed to the dining room, however; the flurry of handshaking had worked them into an appetite, and they were in hopes of prevailing upon an early lunch.

Fearing that her cousin Roger Noble might appear on the scene at any moment, Charlotte Burnbrake accompanied her uncle to the lawyer's, where the old man hoped to garner some explanation regarding the failed land deal with Mr. Tempest. It was a curious business, but Mr. Tollback, the lawyer, had had several communications with the prospective buyer and may have in the process formed some impression of the man.

Charlotte was invited into Mr. Tollback's office, and while the two men exchanged pleasantries and recent news, she looked out the window and considered the snowy scene. She had not been at this long before the figure of Daniel Plainway, looking distracted and perplexed, appeared across the main street. He had promised her the night before that he would not leave without saying good-bye, and it occurred to her that he was simply marking time till he had that opportunity. She watched as he considered first one direction, then the next; a fondness, coupled with a confusion, both of that fondness and of a melancholy to think that he would soon be gone, welled up within her.

It had been a short adventure, but in the course of it she had felt the beginnings of a deep friendship for Daniel Plainway. Some compound of their informal situation, her own sympathetic nature, and his plain and honorable manner had enriched the growth of understanding between them. She had surprised herself by teasing him, however quietly; he had proved to have a sense of humor as well as scruples and had read less into her teasing than might have other men, though *more* might have been fairly made of it.

She wished she could excuse herself and go out to him, as much for herself as for the possibility that she might somehow relieve his distracted state. She was pleased when Mr. Moss appeared, walking down Winthrop Street, and seemed to talk Mr. Plainway into accompanying him.

Phileda McCannon had a simple way of dressing that went as far as the coat she wore, which was without braid or embroidery save at the button frogs. Her hat was austere in comparison with those of the women they met, though it did not appear so on her. Her dark eyebrows curved handsomely over the rims of her spectacles, and her hair was done up behind in chestnut plaits. She could never be deemed willowy—she appeared too strong for that—and the directness of her apparel offered every compliment. She moved with athletic energy, but being an accomplished walker himself, Mister Walton was able to keep her pace without difficulty.

They had only just started out on their walk when she asked him, "Did you think that Charleston was paying me court?" She slipped her arm in his and pulled him along the snowy sidewalk with her brisk movement and the wry look that invariably made him laugh.

The one thing that Mister Walton had kept from Miss McCannon the night before was the fact that he had seen Thistlecoat leave her house and by extension the confusion of feelings he had experienced. "I am found out," he said ruefully through a deep chuckle.

"It is simply that I had the mark of you when I noticed someone walking by," she said. "Thinking back on it, I couldn't imagine that I was so prescient as to know of your arrival before you came."

"I have no privilege to think of Mr. Thistlecoat and yourself in any context," he said, attempting a reply to her question.

"Don't you?"

"Do I?" he said, a little unnerved.

She laughed. "Toby!"

He laughed as well, but more from nervous reaction than real humor. "I suppose," he said, after scrambling for a thought, "a friend might have an opinion."

"A friend might," she said without the slightest shade of meaning.

"Well . . . he seems a decent enough fellow."

"Does he?"

Mister Walton had felt such a jealousy toward the man that he feared it would color his words if he said too much; consequently he said nothing.

"He *has* been paying me court, to be truthful," she admitted.

"Oh."

"But he's a decent enough fellow."

"Yes," said Mister Walton, though weakly. If he was able to keep pace with Phileda's walk, Mister Walton had more trouble keeping up with the pace of her conversation, and he felt that he had missed some salient opportunity when she directed the discourse to other matters.

What was she trying to tell me? he wondered, when he considered the news that Charleston Thistlecoat *had* been paying her court, and *Good heavens!* when those green feelings began to rise in him again. He fought them back, refusing to let the tall, handsome, somewhat younger man haunt his time with Phileda McCannon.

"I hope he's here," said Sundry. He knocked on the door.

Daniel glanced back at the riverbank, wishing he hadn't gotten so far afield, worrying that he might miss even a single extra moment with Miss Burnbrake. They were out on a boardwalk that reached from the shore to a small house, the pilings of which half waded in the river at high tide.

Sundry knocked again, and the door opened before the third rap touched the door. "Mr. Tolly!" he said to the white-bearded fellow who stood before them.

"Why, Mr. Moss!" said the old man, his face lighting with recognition. He and Sundry had struck up a friendship the previous fall, and Sundry had been much impressed with Isherwood Tolly's adventurous life, his knowledge of people and things, and his ability to spin verbal yarn. "Come in, come in!" Mr. Tolly was saying as he ushered Sundry and Daniel before him into a dark hallway and a further room lit by windows over the water and a cheery fire. "What a very fine surprise!" he said several times. "I only got in the other day myself. My cousin is asleep," he said. They could hear snores coming from another room.

Mr. Tolly was a small man with handsome white hair and a well-trimmed beard. He had done many things in his life, and most of them proved fodder for at least a story or two; but wild as those tales might be, Sundry had come to respect the man's knowledge and his opinions. "Have you ever heard of a place called Council Hill?" asked the young man when the conversation turned to recent events.

"I've known of several Council Hills," said Mr. Tolly. "There was one down by Parsonfield, as I recall, and another below Sabbath Day Pond over in one of the townships."

"Did you ever know of a Council Hill in Skowhegan?" pressed Sundry.

"Now that you mention it, I may have."

"But no particular tales?"

"Is that the one with the strange writing on the big rock?"

Sundry nearly came out of his seat. "Yes!" he said with more emphasis than volume. "You know it?"

"I don't think I've ever been there, but I've heard tell, to be sure. John Neptune's the man you want to talk to."

"I wish I could," said Sundry.

"No sooner said," replied Mr. Tolly. "Get on your coats, and we'll trek up the hill."

"John Neptune's here in Hallowell?"

"He's at his cousin's at Manchester, but just up Winthrop Street and within a couple hours' walk, I should say."

"I'll hire a sleigh," said Sundry. "Mr. Plainway? Will you join us?"

Daniel considered this but answered without certainty. "I'll see what's happening when we get back to the hotel."

43. Uncle Francis Neptune

From a height of land on the border of Hallowell and Manchester they caught a glimpse of Cobboseecontee Lake, "the Place of Many Sturgeon," and they were indeed entering one of the many lake countries that constitute the inland reaches of the state of Maine. Larger lakes might abide in other corners of the nation, but few tracts are more beautifully situated than that between Cobboseecontee, Messalonskee, Maranacook, and Annabessacook. By the 1890s the towns that shared these waters were drawing rusticators and sportsmen; even in winter their icy surfaces were dotted with shacks and fishing holes.

There are several Maines, and Sundry was entering one of them for the first time. The day was glorious and could not have boasted the land's attractions with more confidence. They descended some steep grades, and Mr. Tolly directed the sleigh down a side road to the west that entered the domain of three evenly spaced hills. Not far down this trail they pulled up to a small log-built house and several outbuildings; the trees and bushes in and around the yard and the structures themselves were stark and black against the snowy slopes. A single chimney rising from the house breathed thin smoke into the bright air. Two or three crows carried on a rough dialogue from an elm tree behind the barn, and Sundry was reminded of the crow that had conversed with Capital Gaines.

Mr. Tolly jumped down, as spry as a teenager. Sundry was soon after him, then Daniel Plainway; Miss Burnbrake had not returned to the hotel, and Daniel had decided that he needed distraction.

A dog was barking, and they had not reached the door of the house when a man's voice called out to them. Sundry was delighted to see John Neptune standing at the door of a small barn. "I'm graining the animals," he called, and they trudged along the path that had been beaten through the deep snow from the house to the barn.

The low-ceilinged barn was warm with the breath and heat and manure of the animals stanchioned there. It was a tidy stable, with hay strewn beneath the feet and a beautiful roan horse in one corner. Two oxen shared the general quarters with a cow and a year-old bull.

John Neptune hardly looked his years, which Sundry had estimated in the seventies, perhaps even older than Mr. Tolly; the Indian's hair was without a strand of gray, and though his face was well lined, his dark eyes shone with the peculiar interest that one expects, however mistakenly, of a young man. His back was straight, and his bearing seemed without the accoutrements of age.

They leaned on the stable gates and considered the animals; Sundry, who was farm-bred himself, recognized some fine creatures. John Neptune smiled to see the young man.

"She'll bust her feeding," said Sundry, looking over the stables. He didn't know why the strange phrase should haunt him so lately, though it was natural, he supposed, that it would come to him when he saw an ox.

"What's that?" asked Daniel Plainway.

"It's something my father always says about oxen, usually when they're at the plow. 'She'll bust her feeding.' Haven't the foggiest notion what it means."

Daniel repeated the phrase under his breath. It tickled his memory, and he searched his own farming background for a clue to the phrase's meaning.

"I've seen Eugene two or three times over by the Abadagasset," said John Neptune, referring to the juvenile raccoon that had once been in his keeping. "He seems to like it there."

"Give him my best," said Sundry.

"I will," said the Indian without drollery. The raccoon was the family totem to John Neptune, and it would not be unusual for him to hold a conversation with the creature.

"John," said Mr. Tolly, "you know that old Council Hill up Skowhegan way."

"I believe so," said the old Indian. "Up by Lake George."

"That's it."

John Neptune nodded quietly. "The blond men have been there," he stated softly.

"How did you know that?" asked Sundry, a good deal astonished. "That only happened the day before yesterday!"

"I don't know about the day before yesterday, but they were there many years ago."

"They were? Do you remember them there?"

"No, *many* years ago, long before my grandfather's grandfather, long before your people came."

Sundry grasped the import of what John Neptune was telling him. "The blond men," he said. "You mean, hundreds of years ago."

The old man nodded. "They wrote something on a rock there."

Sundry was almost gasping with incredulity. "How could you know that?"

John Neptune only laughed softly. "How could I not? My people have been here for some time now, and we have good memories."

"And you remember the Vikings coming here?" said Sundry.

"I think that's what they call them now."

"Why haven't you told anyone about this?"

"Oh, I have. I spoke to a man after the war, who was a professor somewhere, but he didn't seem very interested."

"Do you know what the writing on the rock says?" wondered Sundry.

"I think I remember, more or less. But you want to hear it from my uncle, who lives here. He will know it better than I, and perhaps it is a good thing for me to hear it again myself. It is a story I've always liked."

They followed John Neptune back to the house and kicked the snow from their feet at the door stoop. They came to a small hall filled with boots and coats; the murmurings of voices and movement and the crackling of a fire could be heard further on.

John Neptune ushered them into a cozy kitchen and sitting room. A cat sat by a stove, the firebox of which was open as a middle-aged woman stoked it with several pieces of wood. She looked up only when she was done with the chore, whereupon she turned around and greeted the visitors mildly. A man of European descent sat at the kitchen table, repairing the bindings on a snowshoe, and further into the room sat an ancient Indian, who had to be John Neptune's uncle.

Sundry had been a little surprised to hear that an uncle to John was still around to tell a tale, but here was a figure to fit the description. Uncle Francis Neptune was perhaps not as young as he looked (he looked about ninety); his hair was a beautiful charcoal gray, and his face was a web of wrinkles and lines. He had been a tall man, and he maintained, like his nephew, some remnant of youthful posture. He sat straight in his chair at the other end of the room and watched the appearance of John Neptune's friends and Daniel Plainway with interest.

The woman, whose name was Attean, was the daughter of John Neptune's cousin, and the man at the table was her husband, Hardy Millwright. Hardy was a quiet man, and after learning the purposes of his visitors, he welcomed them amiably enough and returned to his work. Mrs. Millwright put on coffee and found chairs so that they could attend Uncle Francis Neptune.

"How are you, Uncle Francis?" said Mr. Tolly.

The ancient man said something that Sundry and Daniel did not understand, and they were attempting to make a word of English from it when John Neptune said, "He says he is taking food," which was as much as to say that Uncle Francis was still functioning. He shook Sundry's and Daniel's hands and nodded while his nephew explained, in the Penobscot tongue, Sundry's interest in the runes on Council Hill.

"Sun-haired, we called them," said John Neptune when the old man spoke again. Sundry sensed that the nephew was translating pretty literally and that Uncle Francis was speaking as if he had been there himself. The old man continued to speak, and John Neptune, himself an old man, picked up the thread of those words and spun them into English. "We had never seen anything like them, unless it was a white deer, which we stalked but never killed."

"Does he know what those runes say?" wondered Sundry.

It was not necessary for John Neptune to speak to Uncle Francis Neptune in his ancient tongue; though he chose not to speak in English or found it unwieldy, he understood most of what was said in that language.

He nodded when Sundry spoke, then said something with great weight and method.

"It is a story to be told from beginning to end," said John Neptune.

Sundry wondered what the time was, knowing that Daniel Plainway had other fish to fry. But he raised an eyebrow toward the lawyer, and Daniel, who was himself fascinated by the old man as well as by the tale he might tell, said, "Let us hear it."

Sundry said to John Neptune, "Would he be so good as to tell us from beginning to end?"

John Neptune did repeat these words in the Penobscot. Ancient Uncle Francis seemed pleased to be asked, and he looked with his remarkable eyes past his nephew, past Sundry and Daniel, past the kitchen and the kitchen wall. He said something very slowly and spoke for some moments without a word of translation from John Neptune. Sundry wondered if he was to hear the entire story in a language he didn't understand when John Neptune said, "He is asking our ancestors to help him recall the time when the sun-haired people first came to the Council Hill. He is asking that everything he says be true or as close to the truth as his ancestors can re-member, since it was a long time ago and they have probably been think-ing of other things.

"But the story has been told at many fires," added John Neptune as com-mentator rather than translator, "and he will remember it, I know."

Then the ancient Indian's voice changed its tone and rhythm, and Sun-dry knew that the tale had begun. In a moment John Neptune picked up the thread once again, and they were each drifted by a timeless wind to an-other place, among the men of another generation. Sometimes the ancient man spoke of what "Grandfather says," as if he himself were merely trans-lating what he heard.

After a while Sundry and Daniel forgot that John Neptune was speak-ing at all, and it seemed as if they were listening directly to Uncle Francis Neptune's words or perhaps to the words of some tale-teller long before and long departed.

44. The Rune and the Worm

We called them the Sun-Hairs (said Uncle Francis Neptune), and we had rumor of them long before we saw them. These tall, pale warriors had landed near the winter grounds of the Wabenaki, and it was there that by peaceful means and otherwise, the tale was spread from tribe to tribe of how the Sun-Hairs were warred upon by the Delaware and Shinecock. They came in great canoes, we heard, with blankets to catch the wind, and they wore hair upon their faces and carried axes and long blades. We of the Penobscot listened with great interest, though we considered the tales of these pale men to be like the tales of Michabou, who first planted the corn and spoke with the creatures of the forest.

We were the Penobscot, who knew the forest and the seashore and the mighty Kennebec, which flowed from the one into the other like a great path, for it was an ancient legend that Michabou asked the first of our chiefs what gift he would like and the first chief said that he was greatly torn between his love of the shore and his love of the woods and Michabou cut a path that is the Kennebec so that the chief and his people might therefore travel from one to the other with ease.

We were the Penobscot and in those days the pines still lived that had been planted in the era of giants and they came in ranks to the shore like guardians, and yet it was the sight of those mighty trees that first enticed the Sun-Hairs to sail into the Kennebec.

Some boys fishing saw them first and ran to the summer camp of our clan to tell us that a great canoe was coming up the coast. We watched them for two days from the forest and were not seen, and the ship followed the shape of the shore till it came to the great river mouth, and there it entered and found a beach and was drawn up by the Sun-Hairs as we would have drawn a canoe, but with many men to pull her above the tide line.

They made a camp among a grove of birch, and we thought they were happier among the white trees then among the dark trunks of the pines. We watched them for another day, and listened to their strange chatter, and were moved that they knew to sing and laugh.

We were the Penobscot and not as quick to make war as the Iroquois and the Mohawk. We were planters and hunters and knew how to defend our homes, but Michabou had gone to the peak of Katahdin and spoken with the Great Spirit, and we learned from him that we were to make a brother of a stranger. It was my own ancestor, whom I shall call Grandfather, who stepped from the dark pines into the grove of white birch and offered up his empty hands.

There was no knowing how the Sun-Hairs would respond to the appearance of one of the Etchemin—that is, one of the "people"—and Grandfather's heart was racing. They were strange to look at with their yellow hair and their faces covered with hair. Grandfather wondered if they were indeed demons of the fire regions, as some of his clan declared.

The Sun-Hairs were startled, and Grandfather was both anxious and relieved to see that they would know fear as he did. Some of the pale men did reach for their long blades or their axes, but the tallest among them stood between his people and Grandfather and spoke firmly to those behind him as he held his hands out, empty as Grandfather's.

It was a day as brilliant as this, but the end of summer. Grandfather says the river was noisy behind the Sun-Hairs and the wind spoke in the birches. The grass was as thick as a bed around their feet. Birds called from the wood. He remembers each of these things in that moment when the pale man and he offered each other their empty hands.

They were strange to us, not only because of their yellow hair and their pale skins, their clothes and their weapons, their great canoe and their separate tongue, but because they had come at all. Some of us wondered if their ship was their country, like an island that moved from shore to shore, but they were stranger still than that.

On the following day several of us came into their camp and we exchanged gifts. There was a man among them named Erling, who drew pictures of the land on the back of birch bark and communicated in this manner that they came from another place across the great water and that they were traveling almost as a matter of curiosity. We spent a number of days learning something of each other's tongues, and as we came to understand each other, there were those among our people who told them of the great city of Norumbega, and the Sun-Hairs were very interested.

One of Grandfather's family had a piece of gold beaten into a flat disk, and some of the Sun-Hairs were excited to see it; without thinking much of the gift, he gave the gold piece to one of the pale men.

It is an easy thing to tell men what they care to hear, and some of our people blew into the tales of Norumbega more wind than the city itself could have contained. The Sun-Hairs were loath to leave for their homes without first seeing Norumbega, and there was much discussion among them.

Their chief was not ready to winter in these lands, but the power of the group was greater than his will, and he accepted their decision. They joined our clan in preparing for the snow: hunting and fishing, fashioning the tools and furnishings that would be needed. In preparation for winter travel, we tended to our snowshoes, and they used their blades to carve long, flat shapes from the ash tree, which, they told us, they would strap to their feet so they could glide over the snow like the wind over ice.

It was during these preparations that one of the men went to the rock face of a low cliff and carved strange marks there with a hard piece of stone. We watched him at his work, not understanding; we will make images of an animal or a thought to mark a moment or point the way, but these lines and scratchings were nothing we could recognize. Erling said to me, "This is our tongue, made into marks that other men might hear with their eyes."

And when the man was done, he told us what he had made there, and it was a memory of our meeting, the Etchemin and the Sun-Hairs, and the names of several of us. We were deeply moved that they could pierce their words into something so permanent as stone; but Grandfather wondered if false words could be carved as well as true, and he asked Erling this while they were speaking by the dyeing pot.

Erling found a flattened piece of birch bark and a small stick. He chewed the end of the stick until it was frayed, then dipped the frayed end into the dyeing pot, and with the dye he drew marks and lines upon the bark. When this was done, he passed the piece of bark to Grandfather with a smile that made Grandfather smile, though he did not know what amused Erling.

"What does it say?" Grandfather asked.

"'A word is not true just because it is carved in stone,'" said Erling.

Grandfather was delighted with the words, both the honesty with which Erling admitted them and the cleverness with which they had been set down. He asked Erling if he could have the words, and Erling said they were a gift. Grandfather kept them all his life, and he was buried with them.

But the next day Grandfather showed the words to another of the Sun-Hairs, and he could make nothing of them. Grandfather went to Erling, a little angry, thinking that he had been laughing at him and that the words were not true at all. Erling explained that not all his people could make the words speak and that besides, he had written them in such a way that some people would make nothing of them unless they knew his manner of putting them down. This seemed a contradictory practice at first, but as Grandfather considered it, he realized that not all words are meant for all ears—or all eyes. Erling found something to draw with and made the sign of an animal to one side of the markings. He said that his chief would be able to read them now.

Grandfather took the words to the Sun-Hairs' chief, and the chief smiled when he read them. "These must be Erling's words," he said.

Speech between the clan and the Sun-Hairs was a mixture of our language, their language, and hand signs, but we had grown to understand one another so that deeper things might be discussed.

In the fall our clan went with the Sun-Hairs on their great canoe up the Kennebec, and we were amazed that one canoe could carry us all in two trips. Not far from Council Hill they put their canoe onto an island, and here, in the midst of the Kennebec, our clan and theirs made winter camp.

The Sun-Hairs marveled at the glories of the fall, and it was clear that they already loved the land. Several of our clan men and half the party of Sun-Hairs were chosen to make the trip to Norumbega, where they would meet the many tribes and clans of the Wabenaki and the Penobscot. Grandfather and his friend Erling were among them. Snow fell, and the Penobscots took up their gear and their snowshoes and the Sun-Hairs their gear and their flat sticks that they would tie to their feet. Their chief had chosen a leader for the excursion, a dour man named Thorkal, and this man promised to leave words on rocks behind them so that the chief could follow them if they did not return in two moons.

Grandfather remembers that there was good cheer when they crossed the river from the island to the eastern shore of the Kennebec. There were shouts of laughter and encouragement from those who were left behind, and the party for Norumbega disappeared into the forest. Among them went a Penobscot shaman known as Assimiwando, and he and Thorkal spoke much together, both before their journey and during it.

The party first came to Council Hill, and here Thorkal and Assimiwando conferred about how they would proceed. Though it was not far from the Kennebec, the party spent the night upon Council Hill, and our men told the pale men about the pitfalls and dangers nearabouts and that to go west was to walk into the jaws of the bear, for the Mohawks made winter camp at a place only two rivers away and from there they harried and struck at our people.

In the morning Erling asked Thorkal about the words he was supposed to leave behind for their chief, and Thorkal said he had made them the night before and hidden them in a manner discussed between the chief and himself.

They broke camp from Council Hill, where many a decision had been made among the Etchemin, and their party headed eastward. Assimiwando was the last to leave the hill, and they waited for him at the bottom of the eastern slope. Grandfather could hear the shaman chanting above them and wondered what the man was conjuring.

When Assimiwando came down the hill, Grandfather said, "Were you calling something?" for he knew something of the shaman's songs.

"You've never seen the worm, have you?" said Assimiwando, and though Grandfather didn't understand what was meant by this, it sounded to him like a warning to ask no more, and so he put it out of his mind.

Grandfather and Erling traveled side by side, and Grandfather taught Erling much of what he knew about the woods and its creatures. On the next day Erling raised doubts about Thorkal and his intentions.

"Bad men are often madmen," said Erling. He and Grandfather had drifted away from the others when they stopped to eat in the middle of the day. Grandfather nodded but said nothing, not knowing what was meant by this; people around him were beginning to speak in riddles. "I think," said Erling, "that Thorkal and these others plan some violence when they reach Norumbega."

Grandfather was astonished. "They would be greatly outnumbered at Norumbega. The women alone would bear them down."

"They have some plan, I am sure of it, and I fear that they have left false words upon the hidden rock at Council Hill."

"Can they be so treacherous to their own people? From Council Hill, few paths are safe save to the east. The Mohawks will have parties flying like flocks of crows through the forest, and they will only avoid the roads to Norumbega itself."

"That's as I fear," said Erling. "Then they have left words that will direct the others to the Mohawks or some such danger. If you will go with me, I will return to the chief and your clan and warn them."

"Won't Thorkal stop you?"

"I will leave by night if you will go with me."

Grandfather was troubled that these men they had befriended could plan such treachery. He declined to speak to Assimiwando, but the shaman took him aside and said, "Our own chief at Norumbega is weak in the face of the Mohawk raids and in the dealings of the Etchemin, and with my magic and the sharp weapons of the Sun-Hairs, we will gain the head of the nation and prove ourselves the greater power."

"Well," said Grandfather to himself, "bad men are often madmen. And termites can visit the bark of a pine as well as the bark of a birch." "This is a good plan," he said to Assimiwando, and he wondered how many of his clansmen were part of this double-dealing.

Grandfather went back to Erling and said, "I will take you to Council Hill, and from there you will find your way to the island. Then I must hurry to warn our people at Norumbega, for I fear they will be the first to fall."

Nothing more was said, but they lay down at the next camp and slept in two watches. When Erling woke Grandfather, Grandfather was roused from a dream of meaning. In the dream he had seen Assimiwando in a hollow tree that looked like a strange animal with horns, and Assimiwando had said to him, "Turn back and you will meet the worm."

In the dream Grandfather answered, "Worms are not to be feared but by the dead and the roots of trees."

"There are worms," said Assimiwando, "and there are worms."

"It is winter," said Grandfather. He made so bold, in his dream, to move closer to the hollow tree, and now he wasn't sure if Assimiwando spoke or the tree itself did. "It is winter," said Grandfather, "and the worms are asleep with the frogs and the newts."

"Each worm turns in its own season," said Assimiwando or the tree, when Grandfather was wakened.

"I was warned about a worm," said Grandfather, and when he could make Erling understand this, the Sun-Hair was very solemn. It was the night when the sun begins its journey back to summer, which is the longest and sometimes the blackest night of all. Even by the light of the stars and part of a moon, Grandfather could see that Erling was paler than was natural to him. Grandfather could understand no terror for a worm, particularly in winter, when all low creatures sleep, but the warning meant something to Erling, and he told Grandfather that they must tread with care. *Perhaps*, thought Grandfather, *the shaman has cast some magic on any who turn back.*

He was concerned to defy Assimiwando, particularly on the night of the solstice, when certain doors from the spirit world are more widely open; but they left the camp in the middle of the night, and the moon guided their first miles. Grandfather on his snowshoes and Erling upon his skis swept through the woods like birds, and often Erling left Grandfather behind as he slid down the slopes and Grandfather caught up as they clambered up the next hill.

Dawn found them skirting the lake that lay within sight of Council Hill, and they caught glimpses of the height from a rise of land or a break in the trees. Erling thought it time they took stock of their situation and stopped them. "Did your dream say where you would meet the worm?" he asked.

"It only said that anyone who turned back would meet the worm," explained Grandfather.

"Well," said Erling, "certainly we have turned back. Perhaps it was meant to signify something else."

They followed the recently broken trail back toward the hill, and Grandfather led them toward a steeper ascent that was yet quicker if they didn't mind a climb. Erling took off his skis and strapped them to his back. He loosened the long blade at his side, They ascended the slope through the pines, only stopping to consider a bank of snow that circled the top of the hill like a collar.

"If we don't see your worm by the time we reach the top, I believe we will be safe," said Erling. He clambered over the bank of snow and was stepping from it when a look of bewilderment and horror touched his face. Grandfather had just reached up for Erling's offered hand when Erling thrust his hand into the bank instead and let out what must have been a curse in his own tongue.

Grandfather looked at Erling's hand and saw that it was not buried in snow, but in a long white fur.

A great face reared up over the Council Hill: something like the face of an elk, with horns, and like the face of a human with eyes that understand, and like neither of these things. The face itself was longer than two tall men, and from its great chin hung a white beard. Its pelt was white and beautiful. Erling was standing, not upon a bank of snow, but upon a coil of the worm.

Silently, but for its hot breath, the worm thrust its gaping mouth at them, and Erling threw himself at Grandfather so that both men were carried down the slope. They could hear the great length of the monster uncoiling from the hill, and trees snapped as the head of the worm pushed its way toward them. Grandfather leaped to a tall boulder, nocked an arrow, and let it fly. He knew his shot was accurate, but the arrow spun away.

Erling was charging through the trees with his long blade raised, charging behind the gaze of the creature so that he might strike it. The monster moved like a snake in the snow, its beard hissing beneath its great head, and Grandfather nocked a second arrow, which veered away like the first.

"It is bewitched!" he shouted over the noise of the monster's movement.

Erling raised his blade and drove it into the snow worm's side. The creature gave a shudder that threw Erling into a tree, then turned upon him. The worm had no protection against the Sun-Hairs' metal, and Grandfather shouted with triumph to think that they had the means to kill it.

Then the great maw of the worm shot out, and Erling, stunned, was snatched up and gobbled down by the beast, blade and all.

The worm shook itself and turned to Grandfather. A look of amused patience filled its great black eyes. Its monstrous head hovered among the trees, as it picked its way like a basket weave among the dark trunks.

Though without hope, Grandfather nocked his third arrow and pointed it toward one of the broad eyes. He felt the worm's hot breath. He sensed the breeze of its movement.

The worm stopped. It closed its eyes and threw its head to the heights of the trees. Its immense snakelike form stood briefly like a tall white birch. From the place where Erling had struck, Grandfather could see blood flow; but then blood shot from a second wound from within, and the point of Erling's blade rose out of the worm's side.

A great branch snapped in the path of the worm's convulsive movements, and Grandfather was thrown down by it. He felt dizzy and confounded. The clamor of the worm crashing among the trees filled the forest. Grandfather stumbled to his feet and tried to move away from its spasms, but he was knocked down again.

He thought he was not conscious, but a vision pressed upon him like a dream, and he saw a large crow settle before his face. "The worm's fur is a great totem, and powerful," the crow said, "but if you give it to my brothers, we will find the Sun-Hair."

"Yes," said Grandfather without hesitation, "find the Sun-Hair."

"He may be dead already," said the crow.

"Then he should not be buried in that creature," said Grandfather, and when he woke, the great carcass of the worm was black with crows. Already the ribs of the animal were exposed, and before long the birds flew aside to reveal the arm of a man.

Grandfather pulled Erling from the gullet of the worm, and it was clear that from that place he had smote the monster's heart, even as Michabou smote the heart of the great sturgeon that swallowed him. The crows let out a deafening chorus of approval and called down from the limbs of trees and great boulders and from the sides of the worm.

But Erling was greatly crushed, and he was dying. Grandfather carried him to the top of Council Hill and built a fire.

"Is it slain?" asked Erling.

"You have killed it," said Grandfather.

Strangely, Erling said, "I hope this is a good thing," and with his last breath he uttered, "Warn my chief."

From his place upon Council Hill, Grandfather could see the bones of the worm and the remains of the man who had slain it. He feared what might happen at Norumbega if he took the time to go back to the island in the Kennebec and warn the chief of the Sun-Hairs, but he felt a debt to his dead friend. If only he knew where Thorkal had hidden his message, he could scratch it out.

The crows flocked around the hill. They sat about the limbs of trees. They watched him with bright eyes.

Grandfather remembered the marks and scratchings that Erling had made upon the piece of birch bark, and he recalled that the chief had been able to read them. He took up Erling's blade and went to a tall, flat rock that leaned over one corner of the hilltop, and with the words on the bark before him, he copied them as best he could in great digs upon the stone face. He remembered to draw the picture of the animal's head to one side. Erling had said that it was like a fat buck. When he was done, he stepped away and compared the carvings on the rock with those on the piece of bark and thought them good.

A word is not true just because it is carved in stone.

Then he put Erling's remains in a high branch with his long blade beside him, where it could be seen from the hill. The crows did not offer to disturb the body but sat about it as guardians. Grandfather took up his snowshoes and his bow and raced off for Norumbega.

45. Between Grandfathers

It was the voice of the Grandfather, the voice of Uncle Francis Neptune, the voice of John Neptune. Sundry and Daniel and Mr. Tolly came out of the old Indian's tale as men stepping into the light of a separate day.

I wonder what the time is, thought Sundry. Daniel was concerned on this account as well, though he was not sorry to have heard this tale from John Neptune's lips, from Uncle Francis Neptune's mind, from some ancient grandsire's memory. He considered his watch and was surprised how little of the day had passed.

"Did Thorkal and Assimiwando reach Norumbega?" asked Sundry. "Did the chief of the Vikings understand your grandfather's message?"

The brilliant light of late morning fell crosshatched through the panes of the kitchen windows upon the floor and the table where Mr. Millwright had ceased to work, the weavings of the snowshoe in his lap splayed in the air like untied laces.

Uncle Francis Neptune was saying something in his ancient tongue.

"Those are other tales, with other meanings," said John Neptune. "This is to tell you what the rock upon Council Hill says to the man who can hear the marks and scratchings of my grandfather."

Rousing themselves, as from a lotus dream, the listeners found the great worm at Council Hill a persuasive memory. Sundry thought the worst of it was that he had no power to convey the tale properly to Mister Walton. *He must come and hear it before the man is taken from us*, he thought.

Uncle Francis Neptune was asleep, and they were not able to thank him, save through John Neptune, who would tell his uncle when he woke. When they stepped out into the day, Daniel Plainway said, "It's a very tidy explanation, somehow, for why the runes cannot be read." The sun hardly appeared to have moved since they entered the Millwrights' home.

"What do you suppose was written on the other rock?" wondered Sundry aloud when they were back in the light of day. "The rock Thorkal wrote upon from Assimiwando's instruction?"

"I would not want to follow those instructions, even now," said John Neptune. "Assimiwando laid a curse in those runes, even if Thorkal wrote

them down, and to follow them would be to follow a curse, I am sure of it."
They stood in the yard for a while, assimilating this wisdom. "Give my
best to Mister Walton," said the old Indian finally.

"He would want me to extend his, I know," said Sundry, and shook the
man's hand with great affection.

"It has been a great pleasure," said Daniel Plainway, "*and* a privilege."

"Come again," said John Neptune as Mr. Tolly shook the reins and the
horses tugged the sleigh from the Millwrights' yard.

"Even without the *worm*, you might find an explanation in his story,"
said Sundry as they were crossing into Hallowell again. He glanced back
at the long slope and the corner of Cobboseecontee Lake. "They were
carved not only in some sort of cipher but by an untrained hand." He
glanced toward Mr. Tolly to see how he was taking this. "Of course there
is the business about the worm," said Sundry.

Mr. Tolly did not seem troubled by the worm. He nodded with the
movement of the sleigh.

"What was it that you said in the barn?" asked Daniel Plainway.

Sundry raised an eyebrow but offered no reply.

"About the ox," explained the lawyer. "Something your father says."

"Oh. 'She'll bust her feeding.'"

"That was it."

"Do you know what it means?"

"Do you?"

"It's a word or a phrase," said Sundry, "from Latin or Greek that my
grandfather got from an itinerant preacher. Dad has no idea what it means,
and he is woefully mispronouncing it, I am sure. But he likes the sound
of it."

"You know, I think I've heard something like it myself," said Mr. Tolly.

"Have you?" Sundry was keen to know more about the phrase.

"Couldn't tell you a thing about it, though." The old fellow chucked
the reins as they neared the peak of a long hill.

Daniel looked as if he were struggling to capture a tune that had gotten
loose in his mind, and he remembered the man in the prison cell at the
Wiscasset jailhouse. What had he said? *I can hum anything that I have heard
once, but I have a great talent for not remembering the name of a tune.* "She'll
bust her feeding," said Daniel Plainway to himself several times. "Bust her
feeding."

"Tell me if you get it," said Sundry when they topped the hill on Winthrop Street and could see the roof of the Worster House below them.

46. Unfinished Knitting

The kitchen at the Worster House was exceedingly indulgent with the Moosepathian appetite, and the founding members had made a mighty lunch of it by the time Mister Walton and Phileda arrived in the dining room. But here was company that Ephram, Eagleton, and Thump did not care to miss, and as the formal meal, served at one, was nearly prepared, they decided to stay on and do their best. In something of a heroic frame of mind—indeed, without even pausing for a deep breath—they approached the organized lunch with as much enthusiasm as they had the informal one.

It was not long before Mr. Burnbrake and Charlotte joined them, and the old man prompted an inventory of the people they were missing. "Mr. Plainway is not with us," he said. "He hasn't left, has he?"

This query was directed toward his niece, who looked unhappy with the thought. "I'm sure I don't know," she said. "I did see him with Mr. Moss this morning."

"Where *is* Sundry?" wondered Phileda. "You haven't been telling him terrible things about me, have you?" she asked of Mister Walton.

Mister Walton laughed softly. "I don't know any terrible things about you," he said.

"But you would certainly warn him if you did," she countered.

There was just the slightest prickliness to Phileda's badinage since their brief words concerning Charleston Thistlecoat that morning, but Mister Walton was more alarmed than hurt by it. "Sundry *is* a good friend," he said, with more ease than he felt.

Ephram, Eagleton, and Thump were nonplussed at the merest mention of anything terrible connected with Miss McCannon, and it took a smile from Mister Walton, who noted their concerned expressions, to inform them that a light jest was being made.

"Good heavens!" said Eagleton, and he laughed.

Thump and Ephram joined their fellow as understanding struck them. "Dear me!" said Ephram.

"I was sorry to be without our corresponding fellows of the Dash-It-All Boys," said Eagleton, even as his humor subsided.

"Have they returned to Portland then?" wondered Mister Walton.

"To the Land of Ports, actually," said Eagleton. "I believe the denouement of the snowball contest was troubling to them."

"They were fine sports about it, however," said Ephram.

"*Sports* is perhaps the proper word in their context," said Mr. Burnbrake, who considered the Dash-It-All Boys suspicious, but turning to other things, he added, "I see the management has dressed the room up."

The Yuletide was gaining command of the Worster House, and today the guests discovered the ceiling of the dining room draped from chandelier to four corners in garlands and greenery, and the table itself spread with a gay cloth in keeping with the season.

"No mistletoe yet," observed Mr. Burnbrake, producing, he thought, rather a lack of response.

"It's too early for mistletoe, Uncle," said Charlotte quietly.

"I wouldn't have thought so when I was a chip!" he returned.

Mister Walton glanced toward Phileda, as he might during any general conversation, but the ramifications of mistletoe unexpectedly embarrassed him, and as he blushed, he was startled to think that Phileda might think he was thinking of her in connection with this suggestive shrub. He looked away again, hoping that Ephram, who sat to his other side, might be of help.

Not only Ephram, however, but Eagleton and Thump as well were looking about, as if mistletoe might appear at any moment and demand satisfaction. *Good heavens!* thought Mister Walton. *I am a member of the club, aren't I!* He returned his attention to his own place, smiling.

Ezra Burnbrake was not finished with his subject, however, or perhaps he felt the need to make the entire table blush, for even as Daniel Plainway was hurrying into the dining room, he began to sing in a wavery, if not unpleasant, voice:

> *The silver bowls and garlands gold*
> *Bring warmth to Yuletide hearts!*
> *But give me the bliss of the right to kiss*
> *That the mistletoe imparts!*
>
> *You're welcome to take the poppy-seed cake;*
> *Plum-duff and popcorn go!*
> *Just leave me the treat of the loveliest sweet*
> *Beneath the mistletoe!*

"Uncle!" said Charlotte under her breath; but she was looking at Daniel as he neared the table, and her smile was enough in itself to bring the color to the lawyer's face. Ezra Burnbrake looked from one blushing, bright-eyed countenance to the other and chuckled quietly. There were no seats close to the Burnbrakes, and Daniel drew himself up beside Eagleton.

"And here he is!" said Mister Walton. Sundry caught an odd look that Miss McCannon cast after Mister Walton as the bespectacled fellow rose from the tale to greet him. "Did you see your friend?" asked Mister Walton.

"Yes," said Sundry, "*and* I saw John Neptune." He was interested in what had been happening while he was away, however, and did not elaborate. He was not unaware of *something* between Miss Burnbrake and Mr. Plainway and said, "Mr. Plainway went with me, and I'm afraid I kept him longer than he expected."

"No, no," said Daniel, yet he wished he could let Charlotte know that he *hadn't* wanted to be late seeing her again.

"John Neptune!" said Mister Walton, looking wide-eyed through his spectacles.

Sundry looked from Mister Walton to Miss McCannon. Mr. Burnbrake looked from Daniel Plainway to Charlotte. Ephram, Eagleton, and Thump looked at one another. A chicken gumbo with oysters was served, and this gave them something to concentrate upon. Mr. Burnbrake hummed a bar or two of his song again, and Charlotte cleared her throat softly and gave him a pointed glance. At the table there was the sound, almost exclusively, of spoons in soup dishes.

Ephram wondered if some item from the paper he had read that morning might be of interest to the table, and he searched his memory for something appropriate. The uppermost headline did not seem to be conducive to table talk: A body had been discovered in Portland Harbor, and the authorities were still attempting, when the paper was printed, to identify it. The rest of the front page had been taken up with political matters, and since the papers of the day were unashamedly partisan, it seemed judicious to stay away from these subjects. "I came upon a piece in the newspaper this morning," he said suddenly, "that put me in mind of our friend Mr. Brink."

"Did you?" said Eagleton, who was desperately glad for a subject to converse upon and not entirely certain why.

"Yes, I did," said Ephram. He looked down at his gumbo. It was really quite tasty! He had taken two or three more spoonfuls of the dish when it occurred to him that they might wish to hear more about the item in the *Eastern Argus*. He looked up to find the entire table waiting on him. "What was I saying?" he asked.

"The paper," said Thump.

"Mr. Brink?" queried Eagleton.

"You were reminded of him," helped Sundry.

"Ah, yes, thank you." Ephram looked over the heads of the people opposite him (Eagleton and Thump looked as well), and when the item had returned to him, he said, "The author seemed to think that the night of the winter solstice was much the most favorable night of the year for the visitations of ghosts."

"I should have thought Halloween," said Sundry.

"That thought occurred to me," admitted Ephram.

"It is the length of the night," said Ezra Burnbrake.

Thump was still looking over the people opposite, wondering what his friend had seen that had taken his interest.

"Is it?" said Eagleton.

"It is the longest night of the year," said the old man. "My grandmother used to tell me that the spirits of the dead could come back one night a year, and as the winter solstice offered the longest span between dusk and dawn, they would invariably return on that night."

"Extraordinary!" said Eagleton.

"I don't see it," said Thump. He was still looking.

"I can see her now, her needles clacking as she spoke." Old Ezra Burnbrake took in his niece at a glance. Charlotte had never heard the story, and interest was clear in her expression. "'What do they do when they come back?' I asked her," continued Ezra.

"'Oh, they finish things left undone,' she told me. 'They visit folk they miss. Or they come back to see what's happened to their people.' She was knitting a sweater at the time, a great long fishing sweater for my uncle Harding, who was her son. He was the tallest man in the town—this was in Stockton Springs, before it was even incorporated—and she'd been complaining good-naturedly about the amount of yarn going into that sweater. 'Don't think I won't come back and finish this up if I die before it's done,' she said, and she laughed, though I thought at the time she was half serious."

In the dining room of the Worster House, the sound of spoons in soup dishes had quieted by now, and the talk at a table or two nearby had even dulled as Ezra went on.

"It wasn't two weeks after that she passed on—rather unexpectedly, for she was a lively old girl—and I recall standing in the parlor after the funeral and peering into the cloth bag she kept by her rocker. There were her needles, still tied up with Uncle Harding's unfinished sweater. A couple of days later Mother put the bag and the yarn and needles up in Grandmother's room, and little more was thought about it till the following December."

Mr. Burnbrake appeared to be enjoying the effect of his story, and he was so bold as to take a sip from the dish before him. "My, that's good," he said.

"Mr. Burnbrake," said Phileda, "you are being very bad."

The old man chuckled delightedly. "We thought little about it," he said. "But in December, on the night of the twenty-first, Uncle Harding woke to a series of brief sharp sounds, as if someone were tapping at the window or idly banging one stick upon another. Mother said she heard it too but decided not to wake Father, who was snoring beside her; in between Father's snores, when there was silence otherwise, she could hear it, and she was sure it came from downstairs. She fell asleep listening to it and thought in the morning that she must have been dreaming.

"Uncle Harding was a little distracted, though, when we all were down for breakfast, and I learned years later that when Father had gone to the wharf and I had gone to school, Uncle Harding told Mother that he had gone downstairs the night before and seen their mother knitting in the parlor rocker.

"It was a little confounding, of course, but they weren't afraid of their mother, in any case, and as they heard nothing in the nights that followed, they didn't speak of it again even if they didn't altogether forget about it.

"But the next December, on the twenty-first, Mother woke again and heard the clicking sound from downstairs. She met Uncle Harding in the hall, and she said, 'You get back to bed. I'll go see.'

"Mother went downstairs quietly but not secretively. The treads creaked a little. She could hear the wind in the eaves. And the sound of clicking grew louder as she reached the foot of the stairs and turned in to the parlor.

"There sat my grandmother, the only object in the room that was visible in the dark; one would have thought a light was shining somewhere for her alone, and who's to say it wasn't? There she was, rocking and knitting, as pleasant as a Sunday in June, and when she looked up and smiled, Mother felt a sort of rough thrill down her back. Of course it was nice to see her old mother again, but it troubled her that Grandmother was busying herself with something so domestic when better things must be waiting for her elsewhere.

"She came back the next year as well, diligent as you please on the twenty-first of December, and it was after *this* visit that Mother realized what to do and wondered why she hadn't thought of it before. That third time Mother sat for some minutes in the parlor and watched Grandmother knitting away. Sometimes that spirit would look up and smile, and Mother thought she was looking younger.

"Sometime the next fall Mother took the unfinished sweater down to her aunt's in Cape Jellison, since her aunt would know the stitches that Grandmother had been using. Her aunt knitted up that sweater in a week or two but Mother didn't bring it back to the house till the twenty-first of

December. That night, before she went to bed, she laid the sweater, folded up, in the rocker in the parlor. It was a little sad for Mother, you know; it was like saying good-bye all over again, but it seemed the right thing. And that night she had a dream that Grandmother was standing by her bed, looking younger than ever, and saying, 'Thank you, dear. I've been some provoked with that piece of knitting. You tell Harding to keep warm with it.'

"And when Uncle Harding woke the next morning, that sweater was folded up at the foot of his bed."

"And they never saw her again?" said Sundry. "Your grandmother?"

"They did, actually," said Mr. Burnbrake. "Or, rather, Uncle Harding did. Mother had told him how the sweater came to be knitted, and he thought it was something so filled with magic and grace that he wouldn't wear it, though he'd take it out to look at now and again.

"Come next December twenty-first, Uncle Harding had a dream, just like Mother's, and Grandmother was standing at his bedside, saying, 'You listen to me, Harding! We didn't go to all that trouble so you could hide that sweater in a cedar box. You wear it, and wear it out, do you hear?'

"So he did wear it, though he never wore it out. It stood up like iron, that sweater, and he asked to be buried in it, which he was."

There were several exclamations, most particularly from the members of the club. Eagleton had produced his ever-present journal and was scribbling the basic points of the tale.

A message boy from the local telegraph office had entered the room, and he was holding a piece of paper in his hand as he looked about him. "Mister Walton?" called the boy. He raised the telegram in his hand.

"I've never heard that story!" Charlotte was saying.

"I am here, thank you, young man," said Mister Walton. He was reaching into his pocket for a tip.

"You haven't?" said Uncle Ezra to his niece. "You mark my word," he said to the rest of the table, "if they are coming back for anything, it'll be solstice night, and no mistake."

The messenger gave Mister Walton the wire and thanked him for the tip. Mister Walton was distracted by the discussion that followed Mr. Burnbrake's story, and he held the telegram without reading it.

Daniel had said nothing throughout the account and even now was looking down at his plate, as if digesting something besides his gumbo. Charlotte made a small noise that only her uncle and Thump could hear, something between a sigh and a gasp as she realized the effect of the old man's story upon the lawyer. Leaving behind an unfinished sweater was all very well, but Daniel was thinking of people who had left behind far more and whose eternal peace might be in question.

"Good news, I hope, Mister Walton," her uncle was saying.

"Oh, dear!" said Mister Walton. He adjusted his spectacles and peered at the telegram more closely.

"Toby?" said Phileda.

"It's Mr. Tempest."

"What does he say?" wondered Sundry.

"Nothing at all, I'm afraid. The police believe they've found his body in the harbor." He passed the telegram to Mr. Burnbrake, who sat to one side of him. Charlotte looked past her uncle to read the wire.

PORTLAND TELEGRAPH COMPANY
Grand Trunk

DECEMBER 7 PM 5:17

C/O SOMERSET COUNTY SHERIFF

MR TOBIAS WALTON

BELIEVE MR TEMPEST BODY FOUND IN PORT. HARBOR THIS MORN-
ING. CALEB BROWN SAILED. PLEASE COME ASSIST IDENTIFICATION.
DEPUTY CHIEF FRITH

It seemed so very little to have of the man, a card with a name and address that fitted in the palm of her hand. Had it been very forward to ask for it? Charlotte wondered.

They waved to the foreshortened image of a face and a hand as the train pulled from the station. The platform was uncommonly empty, it seemed to Phileda McCannon and Charlotte Burnbrake, without Daniel Plainway and Mister Walton, Sundry, and the rest of the Moosepath League.

Phileda let out an unconscious sigh. "Well," she said, "I don't need to see the back end of a train."

Charlotte was struck by a sudden loneliness, yet she was aware that Phileda had been visited with some disappointment; they understood each other's emotion, though their faces were half hidden in the hoods of their cloaks and their hands were wrapped in fur muffs. They strolled together around the station, picking their way along a crudely shoveled path that led to the sidewalk and Middle Street. "He is a lovely man . . . Mister Walton," said Charlotte.

"Yes," agreed Phileda, but almost grudgingly. Then she shook herself out of her gloom and said a little more brightly, "Toby is a fine man. I can't tell you how happy I was to see him at my door last night." Just saying this, she knew a cozy moment of well-being, not altogether kindled by her wool cloak and the brilliant afternoon sun. A cold breeze did rise up from the Kennebec, past the buildings on the slope below them, to nip their cheeks.

"He seemed very pleased with *your* company," Charlotte ventured. She hardly knew Miss McCannon but felt at ease with her—perhaps because Phileda reminded her so much of her good friend Pacifa Means.

"Did he?" replied Phileda, and there was something both gratified and ironic in those two words that made Charlotte smile. "He does hurry from it."

"Certainly a request from the police was not to be ignored."

Phileda smiled and shook her head, as if this were not the point. "It is difficult to guess," she said, "whether a man is *simply* pleased with a person's company or whether he fears that pressing his suit would be indelicate."

A noisy troop of schoolboys passed them, with books tied and slung over their shoulders and mischief in their eyes. Phileda knew two or three of them and exchanged hellos; as a young girl she had often wished, not to be a boy, but to partake in their rough games and laughter. She wondered what Toby had been like as a lad.

"Do you know, my mother proposed to my father?" said Charlotte.

"Did she really?"

"It was a scandal among all the aunts." Charlotte laughed softly to remember the story as her mother had told it—so many years ago now.

"Was it leap year?" wondered Phileda wryly.

"I don't know." Charlotte considered her mathematics. "I don't think it was. No, it must have been 1847 when she proposed."

"It's leap year now," said Phileda, almost to herself; proposing to Toby did seem immoderate, however. "Could *you*, do you think?" she asked.

"I have my father's gumption, you see, which is to say, not my mother's. Some thought it presumption rather than gumption, but she considered it common sense. They were both dear people."

Phileda thought they must have been, for Charlotte herself was someone she would like to know. "She may have been right, in any case," said Phileda, "as it would probably be better to discover he *is* simply pleased with a person's company and have done with it rather than walk about in a cloud wondering when he will be so uncouth as to seek further encouragement."

Charlotte laughed aloud, saying, "Oh, Phileda! Perhaps when we have the vote." Charlotte had in fact read some fairly drastic tracts upon the subject of feminine rights but would have felt a hypocrite to prescribe a bold approach since she felt so unfit to undertake one herself.

They paused at the juncture of Middle and Winthrop streets, Phileda feeling at least the pluck that derives from native scenes and familiar faces. She spoke to an elderly gentleman as they passed him on the sidewalk. Charlotte had not that added foundation of intimacy with her present surroundings and felt as if she must return home and gather in the tether before she could right herself again.

"Do you suppose," conjectured Phileda, "that one of the great secrets of our society might be that women have been striking the initiative more often than we are led to believe?"

"It won't be me, I fear," admitted Charlotte ruefully, "though initiative, come to think of it, might be no more than a new dress or a carefully placed hat."

BOOK SIX

December 9–18, 1896

47. Several Attempts at Tying Up Loose Ends

FROM MISTER TOBIAS WALTON
PORTLAND, DECEMBER 9, 1896

Dear Phileda,

It seems, as I told you at the station, that our friendship is foreordained to interruption, and though I would not presume that this is of great moment to yourself, I will admit that I am vexed to be taken from your pleasant company once more.

The situation regarding Mr. Tempest grows stranger by the day. On the morning of the seventh the local police were apprised that a body had been hauled onto the Portland, Bangor & Machias Company Wharf, and upon investigation they were fairly certain that the unfortunate man was Mr. Tempest, who had gone missing from the *Caleb Brown*. The ship herself had left the harbor unexpectedly—that is, Captain Matthews had given the police every reason to believe that he was leaving later in the week—and the authorities couldn't help putting a suspicious blush upon this turn of events.

Yesterday, before I was able to meet with Deputy Chief Frith, a nephew and niece of Mr. Tempest's arrived by train to identify and claim the body. They came from Cambridge and Deputy Chief Frith said they must have been waiting at the Cambridge station with tickets in hand when word of their uncle arrived. I asked for a description of these people, and they were as blond as our Mr. Eagleton.

I would have turned heel-about and come back to Hallowell immediately, but in explaining my brief connection to Mr. Tempest to the deputy chief, I told him about our adventures in Skowhegan and of the Broumnage Club, and he has asked me to stay on at Portland for a few days in case there are further developments in the case.

It does seem that my path has crossed with some culprits as of late, and the local constabulary is looking upon me as some sort of adventurer, which Sundry likes very much. He says he never knew there were so many criminals in the world till he met me!

In the meantime I propose to use the time shopping for presents and discussing with the Moosepath League the possibilities of a small trust fund that would clear the taxes and upkeep on Bird's family estate in Hiram. (Or should I be calling him Bertram now, or Bert, now that we know his real name?)

We discussed, only the once, the possibility of seeing one another near the holiday, and I hope that this plan will bloom and come to fruition. If you are not too busy, perhaps I might come up to the Worster House for a day or so. Hope all is well. If you see the Covingtons, who are coming to Hallowell to meet the Burnbrakes (the Burnbrakes are understandably interested in the artifacts on their land), please give them my best. Sundry says, please pat Moxie for him.

Please take care.

Fondly,
Toby

Mister Walton sat back and considered the letter. It seemed pale and ineffective in light of the awkward scene between Phileda and himself at the Hallowell station two days ago. Seven or eight scraps of paper in the waste basket by his desk attested to the work he had put into the dispatch, however. Each successive draft was less interesting and more impersonal than the last, till he was left with this skeleton, which, not surprisingly, said little about the writer's thoughts or temper.

One of the early drafts actually began with the words "I fear that I have been a dunderhead," which was true, but the words hinted at too strong a feeling, when applied to their circumstances.

Aside from the letters that they had exchanged, he and Phileda knew one another only from three all too brief visits, and yet she occupied the bright and anxious precincts of his heart, filling him with a kind of giddy apprehension—joy and fear. Still, he could not presume that she felt anything like it for him, though he imagined—on certain days or even at certain moments—that she might.

He remembered her laughter as they walked together, her arm in his. He sighed to think of the moment before the Hallowell Harvest Ball when she had reached up to adjust his collar for him. He thought back on the previous July, when he first saw her bright eyes shining behind her round spectacles as she stepped onto the porch of the Weymouth House. Her hands were lovely, strong, and graceful. *Well*, he thought, *this describes her entirely.*

He was standing and didn't remember getting up from his desk. He held his hands behind him and paced the floor. What he wanted to say he could not put in a letter. What he wanted to say he could not seem to say to her face. He valued her friendship so highly that he feared to dismantle it by professing anything else. He left the room but turned around in the hall and returned to the study and his desk.

He folded the letter and put it into an envelope, then addressed the envelope. He laid these aside and took up another sheaf of paper. He had other letters to write: first to Mr. Plainway to tell him of the Moosepath League's plans to help in defraying the costs of the Linnett house till Bertram came of age or the hidden hoard of gems was discovered, the second to the O'Hearns to let them know that the mystery of Bird's identity had been solved.

FROM CHARLESTON A. THISTLECOAT
EN ROUTE TO BANGOR, DECEMBER 9, 1896

Dear Miss McCannon,

I must apologize for leaving Hallowell without saying good-bye, but an unexpected business arose regarding the railroad at Bangor that I must attend straightaway. The journey is tedious, however, and as I have time on my hands, I thought it practical to pen my intentions, that you might consider a proposal till I return.

I believe, at this mature time in our lives, neither of us would benefit from a protracted courtship. I find you very suitable as a companion and appreciate that you are a person of intelligence and positive philosophy. I have had the impression that I am not disagreeable to you and thought the time we have spent together (admittedly short) was spent pleasantly. You have expressed a desire to travel and an alliance with myself would benefit this inclination, as I travel a good deal in the name of both business and pleasure.

It goes without saying that my pecuniary outlook is more than favorable and that you would do without nothing that you either needed or wanted. I am quite prepared to be generous, even extravagant with a person who so collaborates with me, and I believe that what I do have would give me more pleasure for having someone with whom to share it.

As is obvious, this is a union that would please me, and I flatter myself in imagining that it might do so you as well. Certainly it would benefit you. I hope you will consider this proposal in a friendly and thoughtful light. I shall return to Hallowell in about a week, when I shall forward this offer in person and hope for your answer.

With all due regard,
Charleston A. Thistlecoat

FROM ISABELLE COVINGTON
HALLOWELL, DECEMBER 9, 1896

Dear Mister Walton,

Frederick and I wanted to take the first opportunity to thank you and Mr. Moss for your gallant assistance in the recent business on Council Hill and for your sage advice and prudent wisdom. We have also yourself to thank for introducing us to Mr. Gaines, who continues to delight and who enveloped us in a protective shell of his friends and the relatives of his friends while we stayed in Skowhegan.

At the same time, Frederick and I want to express our regrets for having involved you in such a dangerous affair, as it turned out to be. It is extraordinary the entire business, and all the more so when coupled with the tale of the little boy and Mr. Plainway's connection to it. We have had more diversion than we should connecting everyone in these affairs, and you and your fellow club members seem at the center of it all. Indeed, if we had not met you and asked you to take dictation from poor Mr. Tempest, and if your friends had not delivered the same, Miss Burnbrake and Mr. Plainway would not have met—a circumstance, I promise you, for which she was very grateful.

We have enjoyed the Burnbrakes very much, Frederick and Moxie and I, and will be traveling back to Portland with them in the next few days, when we hope to see you and Mr. Moss and the members of the Moosepath League once again.

With fond regards,
Isabelle Covington

Dear Mr. Millplate,

I was not able to find out the name of the man with the piano stools in his dining room, but the fellow at the grocery store on Exchange Street thinks he might know the man I was speaking of by sight. It is of course irksome that I am not able to be of more assistance in this matter, since it was I who raised the subject.

The weather continues bright and sunny, though cold, here in Portland, but the wind is expected to shift tonight and flurries to begin by morning. My friends Ephram and Thump came by yesterday and we took a walk to Mister Walton's, whom you met upon the train to Hallowell. Thump is reading a new novel by Mrs. Elbitha Philomena Grandoine, entitled *Riches Never Rescued*, that he says it is difficult to quit. I read Mrs. Grandoine's last novel, *Be That Ever So*, and thought it gripping, though I was a little startled by the brief episode with the dancing women. Ephram said he read the passage four or five times over, just to be sure he was understanding it, and was just as surprised the fifth time as the first! Thump hasn't returned the book yet, so I don't suppose he has read it.

It was very good to meet you the other day, and we certainly are interested in your duck. Mr. Moss says he knew a man who kept a goose in his pantry, so I wouldn't be troubled by what the fellow with the missing button said. Did the duck have a name? And I can't recall what you said your cat's name is. At any rate, all my best, and I am sorry about the man with the piano stools. If you and your duck are ever in Portland, please let us know.

I am respectfully yours,
Christopher Eagleton

48. But Some Were Double-Knotted

FROM DANIEL PLAINWAY
HIRAM, DECEMBER 13, 1896

Dear Mister Walton,

Your letter of the ninth was very gratefully received, the more so since you have offered a solution to the problem regarding the Linnett estate. I of course would like to be a partner in forming such a fund, and will begin the legal work immediately. I plan to bring everything to Portland when we are ready to put signature to paper. The terms you have suggested are perhaps overgenerous, however, and I have been working on another plan that would take care of everything for the boy and not so pluck your pockets.

I have been drafting a letter to the O'Hearns in Veazie, introducing myself and assuring them of my intentions for Bertram. If they are half as good as you have made them out to be, they are far better guardians for the little fellow than myself. I hope to meet him, however, before very long. I have been back to the Linnett house since returning to Hiram, and more than ever I am filled with the desire to put this sad tale to rest.

You will not think me mad, I know, if I tell you that I can almost believe that a part of Nell is still there, waiting to know about her boy before she wholly quits this "vale." And I still have the odd notion to light the place up once more, whether to drive away phantoms, real or imagined.

My regards to the good members of the Moosepath League and to Mr. Moss. You might also tell Mr. Moss that I have been referring to my old Greek grammar and have found the word that so troubled him. By repeating the phrase "She'll bust her feeding" his father is pronouncing the original more closely than he suspects. The word is boustrophedan, and it indeed means "as the ox plows"—that is, back and forth, left to right, right to left. I shall never look at an ox from now on without saying to myself, "She'll bust her feeding!"

I do not know how much Mr. Moss told you about our visit to Mr. Francis Neptune, but he may make something of this knowledge in the light of the tale we were told.

Mister Walton, I wish words sufficed to express my gratitude for your courage and that of your friends and also for your compassion for a little boy whose family was unknown to you but greatly loved by myself. Your good works are like a stone thrown in a lake, the ripples of which will have happy effects that we cannot guess at.

With respect,
Daniel Plainway

FROM PHILEDA MCCANNON
HALLOWELL, DECEMBER 14, 1896

Dear Toby,

It does seem as if we are to learn more about one another by post than we ever will speaking in the same room. I was sorry to have you leave but understand that it was necessary. I am also sorry to read about Mr. Tempest; he did sound an interesting man, from your description. Did you have such adventures before you came home to Maine?

I too wish we might see one another near the holiday but have recently heard from a cousin who was unable to attend my aunt's funeral but who has offered to help me close the house in Orland. She is arriving sometime this week, and I cannot tell how long it will take us or when I will be back. . . .

Phileda found herself fixated on the last words she had written. She wasn't sure why it seemed so important to turn Toby down in this manner. A house can be closed up anytime, of course; Christmas comes but once a year, and how assuredly she was aware that her Christmases were dwindling, growing more precious with every advancing year.

She did not feel old—not most days—but she knew that she was of middle age, and having met Tobias Walton now had given her a renewed sense of vigor and purpose as well as filled her with apprehension.

The first time that he had hied off, when the Underwoods' daughter was kidnapped up in Millinocket, she had been terrifically disappointed, if understanding; he had behaved as Phileda would have guessed—that is, nobly.

The second time, when he had hurried away from her to come to the aid of his fellow club members, she had nothing to hold against him, unless it was his loyalty to so many people. She was not a selfish person, but it was then that she felt the first twinge of resentment and the first inkling that he had better make up for lost ground when he returned.

He didn't. Tobias Walton was nothing if not circumspect about his place in other people's hearts and minds, and the very lack of assumption that made him so fine a person was the one aspect of his personality that made her indignant. "If you're going to gain my heart so quickly and so easily," she wanted to shout at him, "the least you could do is take note!"

The third time, though he had been called away by the Portland police, she was on the verge of tears. It was in fact the first time that she had the opportunity to say good-bye to him properly—the first time!—and she had bitten her lip to keep from showing how disappointed she was. If he had only said, "Come with me."

Ah, but Sundry had noticed; he had looked a little grimly from Toby to Phileda, and she had simply shaken her head once.

She was a woman of some initiative, it is true, but a woman of her times, and there was only so much she was willing to make obvious before he did the same; yet his very reticence might be the signal that he did not *feel* toward her as she to him. She was not such a catch, was she, after all?—with her spectacles and her hair done up without much thought and her plain, wiry body. She had no real notion that as her male peers matured, they had come to notice the eyes behind those spectacles and the grace of movement beneath her modest clothes. Some of the finest works of art, the deepest and the most meaningful, take more thought to appreciate.

Phileda glanced over Toby's letter of the ninth, searching for a hint of something beyond the intents of friendship. Then she turned to Charleston's letter of the same day, which she had received a day before Toby's. She read: "I believe, at this mature time in our lives, neither of us would benefit from a protracted courtship."

Here at least was a man who sensed the urgency of their years.

She thought: *I promised myself to grow old more gracefully than this!*

She looked out over her desk. A bird flickered in the limbs of the red maple, and she leaned forward to see if it were a chickadee or a nuthatch. She looked out over her glasses. The bird hopped and flew off before she had identified it.

She looked back at her desk and at the letter she was writing. Three or four earlier drafts lay in the basket beside her. She couldn't say why she was so exasperated with the man, except that she was so very fond of him.

When she returned to her letter, she wrote:

. . . and it would not be fair to ask you to keep your plans in the air till the last moment.

Of course, I would be glad to hear from you while I am away and to hear how you and your friends spent the holiday. Perhaps sometime in the new year we will have the opportunity to walk and talk again.

She paused, her pen hovering over the sheet of paper. Finally she wrote:

My best to Sundry. And please have a lovely Christmas.

Phileda

49. And We Were So Sure
That Was the Answer

TELEGRAMS
DECEMBER 15, 1896

PORTLAND TELEGRAPH COMPANY
Office : Federal Street

DECEMBER 15 AM 11:25
WORSTER HOUSE
MR & MRS FREDERICK COVINGTON

BOUSTROPHEDAN. EXCLAMATION MARK.
SUNDRY MOSS

"Just the three words?" said the man in the telegraph office. His gray hair might have been combed that morning, but he had a tendency to run his hands through it, unsettling his hat and disarranging his mop at the same time.

"Just those, yes," said Sundry.

The fellow behind the counter squinted one eye and directed the one remaining at the piece of paper. "B - O – U – S – T –" he said.

"Boustrophedan," agreed Sundry.

"Hmm!" said the fellow. "I've sent everything over the wires, I thought." He made some marks on the paper. "As the ox plows," he said.

"I beg your pardon?" said Sundry.

"It's Greek," said the fellow.

"Yes," said Sundry, "I guess it is."

"Boustrophedan."

"Yes."

"Just the three words then?"

"Just those."

"Hmm!" said the man again. He ran his hand through his hair, and his hat was pushed to the back of his head. "What's this?" he asked, pointing at the paper again.

"That's my name," said Sundry.

EASTERN TELEGRAPH COMPANY
Hallowell
DECEMBER 15 PM 12:10
SPRUCE STREET
SUNDRY MOSS

CONTINUED AMAZEMENT WITH YOUR PERCEPTIVENESS. UNFORTU-
NATELY TRIED READING RUNES BOUSTROPHEDAN THOUGH NOT IN
CONNECTION WITH OX PICTOGRAPH. NOTHING. SEEING YOU IN DAY
OR SO. EXCLAMATION MARKS ALL AROUND.
FREDERICK COVINGTON

PORTLAND POLICE OFFICE
Congress Street
DECEMBER 15 PM 1:05
WORSTER HOUSE
MR AND MRS FREDERICK COVINGTON

MR WALTON INFORMS YOU WILL BE RETURNING TO PORTLAND.
PLEASE CALL WHEN YOU ARRIVE. QUESTIONS REGARDING ADAM
TEMPEST.
DEPUTY CHIEF FRITH

PORTLAND TELEGRAPH COMPANY
Office : Federal Street
DECEMBER 15 PM 3:00
HIGH STREET
MR DANIEL PLAINWAY

BOUSTROPHEDAN NOT SOLUTION. THANKS THOUGH FOR PUTTING
TO REST A FAMILY RIDDLE. DAD WILL BE PLEASED. MR WALTON
WANTING TO COME TO HIRAM TO SIGN PAPERS. ALSO MOOSEPATH
LEAGUE. ARRANGE ROOM AND BOARD?
SUNDRY MOSS

50. Mutual Concerns

FROM DANIEL PLAINWAY
HIRAM, DECEMBER 15, 1896

Dear Messrs. Walton and Moss,

It pleases me no end that you and the members of the Moosepath League are thinking of coming to Hiram. I have the sense that Bertram's story will come full circle and that his legacy will once again rise above the surface of worldly ills. It seems right that those who were so consequential in his rescue should see whence he came, and I can imagine that this represents at least a portion of your motive.

Perhaps, since you so kindly offer to come to me, you will indulge me further and answer a particular whim, and that is to come to the Linnett house itself—to light its lamps and fire its hearths. I will hire help to ready the place for the five of you and myself. It will take a few days, but by the beginning of next week we should have the house cleaned and habitable again.

I have had a very nice letter from Mrs. O'Hearn, and I must thank you for whatever good report you have given of me. She has very graciously invited me to spend Christmas Eve with her family, when I can meet Bertram (again). I hope that I can find something a four-year-old boy would like from St. Nicholas.

To Mr. Moss, regarding "boustrophedan": I am sorry that the word did not provide an answer to the runes, but I wonder if you or Mr. Covington have ever seen an ox at the plow. My uncle had oxen, and he had a system of plowing that I understand is very old in some places in the world. Not everyone is adept at turning oxen hard, and some farmers will plow along the field, turning down only every other furrow—the odd furrows, if you will. Then they plow back down the field, turning up the unplowed rows—the even furrows. Some old folk in fact would plant the odd furrows when the moon was waxing and the even ones when the moon was on the wane.

Some might argue that this is the true meaning of boustrophedan—that is, every other furrow, back and forth. But perhaps you have thought of this.

I wonder if you have seen Miss Burnbrake. Has she returned to Portland? Did her cousin ever reappear? These of course were not your concerns, but he proved some trouble for her and her uncle. Messrs. Ephram, Eagleton, and Thump were very good to escort Mr. Burnbrake in the absence of his nephew. And Miss Burnbrake is a very fine person. I also can't help wonder what happened with the man the police thought drowned. There do seem to be a lot of tendrils to those affairs that met at the Worster House.

Thank you again for all that you have done, and all that you will do. I wait to hear confirmation on your plans.

With regard,
Daniel Plainway

Daniel looked from his desk over the white lawn. "I am going to suggest to Mister Walton," he said to his sister, Martha, who stood at the door to the study, "and the other men that they stay at the Linnett place when they come."

"I wondered if you would think of that," she said. She was wiping her hands on her apron. "It is too bad, though," she added, "that you won't be going to Portland."

"Oh, I can go to Portland if I want to," he said.

"I just thought you might want to look in on this Miss Burnbrake whom you spoke of."

Daniel tried to make a face that indicated perplexity. He wondered how she could know so much from what little he had told her.

"You know, I'm quite able to take care of myself, Daniel," she said.

"Now, what does that mean?" he asked.

"Only that you're not to worry about me if you had a thought to be married."

"Good Lord!" he said.

"Daniel!"

"Who's to say we wouldn't all stay right here if I were to?"

"Two women in the kitchen . . ." she said.

"Ridiculous. It's the furthest thing from my mind. And it's ridiculous anyhow. Two women in the kitchen! As likely say two men in the boat! I don't suppose you women are any more warlike than we are, and I've worked alongside some difficult fellows, I want to tell you."

She was laughing softly. "I only thought that you were a little taken with this Miss Burnbrake."

"And if I were, anything else would presuppose that she was taken with me." He turned back to his desk and wondered briefly if he had made too much of Miss Burnbrake in his letter to Mister Walton and Mr. Moss.

"She might be, for all you know."

"I think she might call me friend," was his reply.

"Edward was my friend, certainly," she said a little wistfully.

Daniel looked up again, his expression mild and sympathetic. His sister was keen proof that love transcended death. "And how did Edward first know that you were taken with him?" he asked.

"He said to me, 'How very nice to see you, Miss Plainway,' and I said, 'I will be Martha, Mr. Bailey, if you will be Edward.'"

"It was that simple," said Daniel.

"It was that simple," she replied, and again there was a wistful note in her voice. "At least it seems that simple now." She let go of her apron and brushed an imaginary wrinkle from it. "You should look in on Miss Burnbrake, I think."

"She may not be back in Portland yet, or if she has returned, she may not be there very long. She and her uncle live in New Hampshire. Besides, I have mentioned her in my letter to Mister Walton and Mr. Moss, and they are very apt to drop by themselves to see that everything is well. Is this Timothy with another wire?"

PORTLAND TELEGRAPH COMPANY
City Hotel Desk

DECEMBER 15 PM 5:47
HIGH STREET
MR DANIEL PLAINWAY

HOPE YOU ARE WELL. PLEASE BE AWARE THAT ROGER NOBLE MAY BE IN HIRAM. LETTER TO FOLLOW WITH PARTICULARS. THANK YOU FOR EVERY CONSIDERATION AGAIN. AS EVER.
CHARLOTTE BURNBRAKE

FROM CHARLOTTE BURNBRAKE
DECEMBER 15, 1896

Dear Mr. Plainway,

I hope this letter finds you and your sister well and that the efforts of Mister Walton and his friends have, in combination with your own magnanimous deeds, given you some measure of peace after the tragedies of the Linnett family. You must have realized how very moved I was by their tale, and even now it keeps a certain melancholy hold upon me.

Your own behavior in those sad circumstances was easily imagined, even though you spoke with undue modesty, for I have had firsthand experience of your kindness and gallantry.

It is of your generosity to me that I write, for I fear it may have purchased you more trouble than worth in the end. By the time that Uncle Ezra and I arrived in Portland yesterday, we were very troubled over the disappearance of my cousin Roger. It is true that he is no better than he ought to be and that he has contributed more complication to my life than happiness, but it is difficult to wipe the heart clean of regard when one has been fond in childhood of a playmate who helped while away so many hours.

Uncle Ezra himself is not without some feeling for Roger, and so when he did not return to Hallowell and did not communicate where he had gone to, Uncle went to Roger's apartment and prevailed upon the landlord to let him in.

Sherlock Holmes could not have done better than Uncle Ezra, for he hunted every surface of the apartment for clues to Roger's whereabouts, and it was during this investigation that he discovered a letter, carelessly left upon the dresser, from a Mr. Hawking, who expressed a very peculiar and definite interest in Roger's going to Hiram.

You may be as surprised as Uncle and I were at this intelligence, and perhaps you know a Mr. Hawking or can guess what coincidence would send my cousin to the town where you live. Please do not hesitate to involve the authorities if Roger proves any trouble to you! Please write and let me know that you are well. My uncle and I will be staying in Portland for the holidays. And please have a fine Christmas, knowing that little Bertram will be having a wonderful holiday himself for the first time.

I am your friend,
Charlotte Burnbrake

51. Persistence

TELEGRAM
DECEMBER 18, 1896

PORTLAND TELEGRAPH COMPANY
Office : Federal Street

DECEMBER 18 AM 10 :07
WORSTER HOUSE
MR & MRS FREDERICK COVINGTON

MR PLAINWAY SAYS THAT OXEN OFTEN SKIP FURROWS WHEN PLOW-
ING THEN PLOW THE FURROWS MISSED ON THE WAY BACK.
SUNDRY MOSS

The man at the telegraph office was counting the words and he only glanced once at Sundry when he was done.

"Boustrophedan," said Sundry.

"It's news to me," said the fellow.

The Covingtons had picked up their bags and were getting ready to leave Hallowell, after a short stay with Captain Gaines, Mr. Noel, and Mr. Noggin at Skowhegan. It was only by chance that the boy from the telegraph office caught them in the lobby of the hotel.

"Mr. Moss again," said Frederick as he frowned at the telegram. His wife found a coin in her purse and tipped the boy, who tipped his hat. "Every *other* furrow, huh?" said the husband under his breath.

"What is that, dear?"

"Mr. Moss again."

"I heard that."

Frederick was lost in thought. "There are seven rows of runes, four down, skipping every other one, and three up, catching the ones that remain." He turned around in the lobby and fished through his pockets for the photograph of the runes on Council Hill. "Let me try it," he said.

"Dear," said Isabelle, "we're going to miss the train."

"Oh, yes," he said, turning about-face. "This will wait, I suppose." Moxie fell in with them at the top of the steps.

The dog was making friends with the man in the baggage car, and the Covingtons were not long settled in the train when Frederick pulled a notebook from his pocket. He wrote some things down, copying the runes from the photograph in an entirely different order. Isabelle sat opposite from her husband but attempted to see over his work.

He smiled, even chuckled to himself, then fell back to his study, frowning, and finally he looked up again.

"Does it say something?" said Isabelle.

He chuckled again, maddening her a little. He passed her the notebook and leaned back in his seat, looking out at the outskirts of Hallowell as they fell past. "The next stop I must wire Mr. Moss," he said.

Isabelle read what he had written there. "Good heavens, really!" she said.

EASTERN TELEGRAPH COMPANY
Farmingdale

DECEMBER 18 AM 11:35
SPRUCE STREET
SUNDRY MOSS

EXCLAMATION MARK. A WORD IS NOT TRUE JUST BECAUSE IT'S
CARVED IN STONE. EXCLAMATION MARK.
FREDERICK COVINGTON

Frederick, who was not yet privy to the tale of Uncle Francis Neptune's ancient grandfather, laughed when he returned from the station.

"What are you laughing about?" asked Isabelle, who knew very well that her husband was delighted beyond words, even if he was amazed and perplexed by the translation.

"We'll see what Mr. Moss makes of *that* telegram," said Frederick.

When Sundry came with the telegram into the parlor, he was able to suppress his excitement long enough to take note of Mister Walton's preoccupied manner.

"A telegram?" said the bespectacled fellow. He seemed strangely motionless in his chair by the fire.

"You look as if you've had bad news," said Sundry concernedly.

It was then that Mister Walton lifted the letter in his hand, though he shook his head dismissively. "Miss McCannon won't be home during Christmas."

"She's not coming to Portland?"

"No, no," said Mister Walton. "She'll be in Orland with a cousin"—he looked about the old familiar room and thought that he would like to be away somewhere, but hardly had the energy to move—"closing her aunt's house," he finished.

"Oh?"

"There was a telegram?"

"From the Covingtons. Mr. Plainway's notion of ox plowing seems to be the key."

"Good heavens!" A certain animation revived the portly fellow's limbs. "What does it say?"

"Well, look."

"Good heavens!" said Mister Walton again. "Just as John Neptune's uncle told you!"

"I'm wondering what else in his story was true," said Sundry.

"Good heavens!"

"I should say."

Mister Walton fell silent again, shaking his head and making low noises of amazement.

"Perhaps you could see Miss McCannon on the New Year," said Sundry.

"She says perhaps after New Year's," answered Mister Walton. He gave an uncharacteristic sigh.

"Perhaps we should be going to Hiram, then, in the next few days," said Sundry.

"Do you think?" Mister Walton looked interested.

"Mr. Plainway seemed very anxious to have us come. *Nearly* as anxious as he was about Miss Burnbrake."

This raised a sympathetic chuckle from Mister Walton. "I am curious, I must confess."

Sundry roamed across the room to the desk, where a small calendar stood. He considered what was left of the month. "Let's go on the twenty-first," he suggested.

"Oh? What day is that?"

"Monday. It's the winter solstice."

"Yes?"

"Mr. Burnbrake assured us that it is the favorite night for ghosts to appear."

"Are you anxious to see a ghost?"

"There's one that's been wandering my family's house for years, and I've *never* seen it."

Mister Walton chuckled. "The twenty-first," he said.

"Who knows?" said Sundry. "Someone might have the opportunity to tell Eleanor Linnett that her boy is fine. I'll send Mr. Plainway a telegram." *But not*, he thought, *before I write a letter or two.*

PORTLAND TELEGRAPH COMPANY
Office : Federal Street

DECEMBER 18 PM 1:26
HIGH STREET
MR DANIEL PLAINWAY

COMING TO HIRAM ON 21ST. EXPECTING TO STAY AT LINNETT ESTATE IF STILL WANTED.
THE MOOSEPATH LEAGUE

BOOK SEVEN

December 21–22, 1896

Daniel's Story
(Mid-December 1896)

He had purposely stayed away, though he had a story to tell the old house, but it seemed a small consideration just to come by and view the handiwork of Mrs. Cutler, who, with her daughters, had been cleaning the place for a week.

When he arrived, the atmosphere was gray with motionless clouds, and the light of day cast listless shadows upon the snow. The Linnett house seemed a large, ungainly thing, and he wondered that he could harbor sentiment for an empty hulk of wood and stone; its upper-story windows looked blind, barely reflecting the featureless sky.

He hoped that simply having another living presence in the house would make some difference to him, but when he came through the front door, the voices of the womenfolk in the kitchen echoed down the hall, as if from far away. He shut the door softly and stood at the foot of the broad stairs, adjusting himself to a separate level of loneliness.

There was the smell of wax and the absence of dust; the furnishings were unveiled, and a fire burned somewhere, but the house was cold. The further end of the hall darkened with Mrs. Cutler's presence. "Mr. Plainway," she said, "I didn't hear you come in."

"I'm sorry if I startled you," he said.

"Startle me? It isn't easy to startle me anymore. Not with seven young ones."

Daniel smiled. "I don't suppose."

She was a large, presentable woman of about thirty-five years, with straw-colored hair and a ruddy workaday complexion. She had nursed little Bertram in his first year of life and was the person Daniel thought of when he knew the house needed a rough but caring hand. Two of her daughters peered out from behind her, and Daniel spoke to them. Her oldest son had brought in wood and was stacking it in the hearths so that fires could be lit when the guests arrived. Daniel heard the lad in one of the rooms above.

The place glowed with the attentions of the Cutlers, and Daniel was more than satisfied. "The house looks wonderful, Mrs. Cutler."

"There's a broken window in the pantry. My boy blocked it up."

"I'll see to it," said Daniel.

"I think someone's been in here," said the woman.

"Oh?"

"And did you know there was a secret passage?"

"I don't know that I did."

"It goes from the attic down past the pantry to the cellar."

"I know, Mrs. Cutler, but I don't think the stairs were a secret. Years ago the servants used them."

"There's a stairway from the upstairs front hall," she said.

"But their rooms were up in that end of the attic."

"Were they? We saw there were quarters up there, but someone besides the servants has used it since." She led Daniel into the pantry and stopped before a particular cupboard. The cupboard door opened like any other, but the cupboard itself, as Daniel knew, was on wheels and swung on a hinge to reveal a landing from which one steep staircase led up into the attic and a second flight led down to the cellar. "I've never seen anything like it," said Mrs. Cutler, as if she didn't entirely approve. "My boy found it. He thought it would lead him to treasure for sure."

Daniel peered up the dark well. "You say someone's been up there?"

"The bed in the northwest room's been used, not so long ago, and there's been fires in the grate."

"It would be hard to tell whether someone slept there yesterday or four years ago," suggested the lawyer.

"I can tell," she said without the least bit of doubt in her powers. "We heard someone up there, which is how we found it. You said not to bother with the attic, but when we heard someone clunking and scraping—trying to frighten us, I wouldn't wonder—I tore up the front stairs in no time."

"You should have left the house or at least sent for me," said Daniel.

"Gory, Mr. Plainway, I had my broom. But he was down these stairs and out through the cellarway before I was halfway up to the attic, I swear."

"Did he leave anything behind?"

"Not that we could tell."

"You did say 'he.'"

"It wasn't where a woman had set down, I could tell that." It seemed that she could tell a great deal without empirical evidence.

"This house is haunted, isn't it, Mr. Plainway?" said one of the girls.

"Hush, you!" said Mrs. Cutler, then to Daniel: *"I am sorry."*

Daniel shook his head, casting a bland expression over the disquiet he felt. *"What makes you think so?"* he asked the little girl.

"We heard her," she replied. *"Mama says she wouldn't do any harm and to pay no mind."*

"I think your mother is right."

"I saw the pretty lady on the stairs," came another voice, and Daniel was then aware of Mrs. Cutler's youngest child, Harry, whom she had been nursing when Bertram Linnett was born. Harry was a block of a five-year-old now, with piercing blue eyes and hair so blond it was white.

"Harry!" said his mother.

"She was on the stairs."

"I've told you about telling stories, young man."

"She was sad when she saw me, I think. But I smiled at her, and she smiled too. Then she left."

The mother rolled her eyes, but clearly she didn't entirely discount the child's tale. *"We cleaned everything in Miss Linnett's room,"* she said, thereby changing the subject somewhat, though perhaps not so gracefully. *"We put everything back where it was, as you said."*

"Thank you, Mrs. Cutler."

"And you found the little boy," said the woman.

"I did, with the help of the gentlemen who'll be coming here."

"Land alive! Wherever has he been these years?"

Daniel told Bertram's tale, but briefly, to a pantry full of wide eyes.

"The poor bud!" pronounced Mrs. Cutler. *"But what'll he ever do with this place, Mr. Plainway?"*

"That is a question." As a matter of form Daniel took in the rooms downstairs, nodding and voicing his approval while the big woman followed him about. Coming out of the front room, where once hung the portrait of Nell Linnett, he met the older Cutler boy, who was descending the stairs.

The boy, about eleven or twelve, asked him, *"Do you want me to lay wood for a fire in that room?"* and he pointed to the right front room upstairs, which had been Miss Linnett's.

"Yes," said Daniel, after a moment's thought. *"Yes, please do. Thank you."* He must be sure to pay a little extra for the children; they were hard workers and cheerful kids, and he liked them.

"We didn't touch much up in the attic," said Mrs. Cutler, who hung back, for some reason, when he began to mount the stairs.

There didn't seem to be much point in continuing his inspection for her sake if she wasn't going to follow him, but he had committed himself to the appearance of the thing, so he continued up the stairs. He had hardly ever been on the second floor—only a time or two when the old man was ill—and he had never seen Nell's room, not even since she and her grandfather died. He touched the knob of her door when he reached it, and it swung open.

He could see his breath in the air. The curtains were pulled back, but the light of this particular day did little to dispel the shadows. The furniture was ornate; frills and furbelows embellished the bedcovers and the drapes that hung between the bedposts. Flowers populated the wallpaper; fairies and haloed devotional figures were poised within heavy round frames. The chiffonnier, the commode, the vanity, and the bed were pearl white with highlights of pink and red and gray. A brush and comb and a silver-mounted hand mirror lay in a static arrangement upon the vanity. (Nell had never left them like that, he thought.) A single chair stood by the door, like a guard, and a fainting couch lay beneath a south-facing window.

From the west windows one could look out over the rolling fields of the estate, beyond which lay Clemons Pond. Out of the vast white encasement of snow, Daniel could see the gnarled limbs of an apple grove struggling toward the sky. There, perhaps, Nell was first seen with Jeram Willum. She might have seen Jeram from this window and gone out to him.

He imagined her restless night after her grandfather had told her that Jeram was not welcome at their home. He tried to imagine the thoughts that led to her disastrous liaison with Asher. He considered the whereabouts of the gems that old Ian had hoarded in his last days; he recalled Ian's cryptic words: If he's as big a man as I am—the boy, that is—he will see where it's been put in his mother's eyes.

Certainly Edward Penfen, alias Eustace Pembleton, had never discovered the jewels. Daniel was sure of that; otherwise the man would never have gone to such lengths to kidnap and retain the boy.

Strangely, standing in Nell's room, where the memory of her young life and the sadness of her premature death might have been most painful, Daniel experienced another emotion, itself not without a pang, that blunted the lingering effects of the Linnett tragedy. Looking out over the grounds from Nell's window, he thought of Charlotte Burnbrake, of her kind face and her eyes when she smiled.

It had been an awkward departure that Monday afternoon. He had not wanted to leave, and he had half believed that she had not wanted him to. Now, with time and distance working their pragmatic forces upon him, he thought the notion absurd. They had known one another all of two days by the time he left Hallowell. She had thanked him warmly, giving him her hand, the impress of which he could still imagine.

"You must have a card," she had said, and he complied with the request. The other day he had received a letter from her, warning him that her cousin might be somewhere in Hiram; the notion seemed absurd, but he had stayed up half a night composing a reply that revealed nothing, except above his signature where he penned his fond regard. The phrase had haunted him since he had entrusted the letter to the postman. He blushed to think of it.

Daniel could see his reflection in the vanity mirror when he turned. Beyond the mirror and the vanity the Cutler boy stood in the doorway with his arms loaded with wood, and Daniel had been so lost in his musings that he had not heard his approach. "Excuse me," said the boy, sensing that he had stepped into a private moment.

"Come in, come in," said Daniel. "You're not afraid of a ghost then, are you?"

"Not by day," said the young fellow, dropping the wood as carefully as he was able into the box by the hearth. "Some fellows I know were up last Halloween . . . well—" He stopped, wondering if he had admitted to forbidden knowledge.

"It's all right," said Daniel. He'd been young once himself. "What happened?"

"Well, they saw a light in the house."

"Did they?" Daniel thought of the intruder in the servants' quarters. "Gave them a bit of a turn, did it?"

"You should have seen them running, Mr. Plainway," said the boy. "Me and the other fellows were down by the pines, waiting for them, and I don't believe any of us stopped till we reached the town square." Daniel chuckled, sad as it made him feel. "I think I remember Miss Linnett," said the young boy respectfully. He paused again in his stacking of the kindling on the bricks. "I remember thinking she was awfully pretty."

"I do too," said Daniel.

52. Lullaby

If the baggage car hadn't been accidentally left on a side rail in Standish, Sundry Moss would not have arrived at the Linnett house alone, but he had waited at the station for their bags, while Mister Walton and the Moosepath League went to Daniel Plainway's house, and an hour or so later Sundry pulled up to the empty house with a sleigh filled with their bags and the portrait of Eleanor Linnett wrapped in oilpaper and a blanket.

The horse seemed almost to know the way as they found the outskirts of Hiram and drew up before the stone columns that marked the carriage drive. The moon had ridden halfway to its zenith; but the drive had been well traveled the last week or so, and there was no way for Sundry to know that he was the first to arrive.

He turned the horse's head between the columns and entered the woods that guarded the estate. The great pines stood back from the drive at first, deferring to the middle-aged maples and oaks Ian Linnett had planted long ago; but soon the softwood closed in, and by the time the sleigh crossed a small brook, the evergreens darkened the path like cloaked figures, limned in pale light and hardly more than shadows themselves to the eye. There were bells on the harness, and these sounded unnaturally loud among the snowy trees. The pines ranked the path till it came to a low-lying wall of hedge on either side, and Sundry peered into the dark for a glimpse of the house.

He was surprised when he realized that it stood before him and that not a single light burned in its windows; the eminence of its three stories stood against a moon-illumined cloud and seemed almost to lean over him. He hopped down from the sleigh, his boots crunching in the snow. The vapor of his breath passed like a ghost, and something above a breath itself stirred in the pine boughs.

Sundry looked back into the black wall of trees beyond the hedges and considered returning to town to find Mr. Plainway's house; obviously Mister Walton had meant for him to do that very thing, and the young man had simply misunderstood their plans.

I should leave our bags now, he thought, *and then we can all come in the sleigh*.

He stood beside the horse and stroked the animal's neck. Sundry was not of a very superstitious nature, but a dark house—an empty house!— filled with the memory of tragedy and possible murder was not a welcoming abode on such a still night, no matter how indifferent he had seemed when speaking of it in Mister Walton's parlor. Even the portrait was a strange, unsettling presence in the sleigh.

The door will be locked surely, he thought, and he mounted the steps, his movements sounding loud in his own ears. With a vague shudder he took the handle of the front door and turned it.

It was not locked, and his heart made a small leap. The darkness in the hall beyond grew as the door swung open, the curtained windows barely letting a sliver of pale light onto the carpeted floors. A movement of air from within met him like a presence—cold, wakeful, and curious. He looked back to consider the horse and rig. Perhaps, he thought, he might just toss the bags into the hall.

He hadn't been using a lantern to drive by—the moon shone upon the snow like a beacon—but now he retrieved the lamp that hung from the front of the sleigh and after a moment's search through his pockets produced a lucifer to light it. With one of the bags, he mounted the steps again and stepped just inside the front door.

How easily are logic and disbelief put aside when our senses have too little information to feed them! The dark forms of stalwart furniture seem to move; the shadows stir with breath; the single lamp magnifies strange silhouettes and the contrast between the light and the darkness.

The broad staircase was a black ramp; a mirror in the room beyond the hall caught the smallest glint of his lantern and disturbed him. He lit another lamp on a low table in the hall, and this set off a softer, wider glow as he considered his surroundings, trying rather too successfully to imagine Eleanor Linnett descending the stairs.

In three or four more trips he had the bags in the hall; then he went out for the portrait. The horse had moved, backing the sleigh away from the house several feet, and Sundry had a brief, almost panicky notion that the animal was going to bolt and leave him. He talked to the horse, stroking its muzzle, then found a hitching post by the front steps and tied off the reins.

Sundry stood by the staircase with the portrait wrapped in its oilpaper and considered where to put it. With the lamp glowing in the hall, the front parlor was not quite a black pit, but the amorphous shapes of its furnishings mingled with their own shadows and rose into the dusky gray light like noiseless creatures thrust out of the ground. *This is foolish*, he thought. *If I catch my reflection in a mirror, I'll probably die of fright.*

In the parlor he lit another lamp; kindling and wood were built up in the hearth, ready for a fire, and he decided that he might as well begin warming the place before he left. It was strange how the snap of the flames bothered him at first, as if he were giving away his presence in the house. He thought of what his mother would say—*if there were any ghosts about, they'd know you were here by now*—or some such comforting opinion.

The room took on more natural proportions as the light increased. The walls drew away from him; the furnishings became less shapeless, losing the life his imagination had ascribed them. He put the portrait on the sofa and, before thinking what he did, stripped the paper from it.

What did I do that for? he wondered, considering the lovely face of the young woman: her soft smile and gentle eyes. It occurred to him that Eleanor Linnett's face was now seen in that house for the first time in almost four years, and he was startled by the thought. He remembered the moment when Mister Walton discovered the portrait in the tunnels beneath Fort Edgecomb and the moment following when they realized the striking resemblance between the young woman and Bird.

He thought, *If I knew what rooms we were taking, I could light the fires upstairs,* and went to the hall to peer up the broad flight of steps. The dark-stained oak of the stair banister and the balustrade that lined the stairwell glowed in the warm light of the hall lantern. The darkness in the front room, where the portrait had once hung, seemed like a physical thing, and he shut the door.

The stove in the kitchen was ready to be lit, and soon he had the cast-iron contraption ticking as the firebox rumbled. The sound of the fire in the parlor and the low roar of the stove in the kitchen made it seem as if the house were waking.

Carrying his lantern, he climbed the stairs, the shadows of balusters sweeping against the opposite wall. Two portraits looked down at him from the stairway, and a mirror atop an ornate dresser at the head of the flight spun refracted light. The stair runner muffled the creak of his progress, but he was within a step or two of the landing before he heard the sound from one of the second-story rooms.

Even as he stood upon the stairs, he recognized the loveliness of the voice that drifted like a faint breeze from the forward end of the upper hall. He should not have so nearly dropped the lantern or felt the touch of ice at the base of his spine, or that was what he would tell himself on another day, far from this place. The sound was wordless, almost tuneless, but carried with it the peaceful intent of a lullaby. He hardly dared step down, and when he did, the creak of the tread raised the level of his fear and the hair lifted from the back of his head.

He did not know which was worse, the faint melody or the cessation of that sound, for as he haltingly continued down the stairs, he had the uncomfortable sensation that someone had stepped into the dark hall to see who had interrupted her song.

Sundry felt out of breath, but he must have had some gust left since he was able to shout when he threw open the front door and a face appeared there before him. The face itself opened its eyes wide and let out a terrific yipe, then called out, "Cloud cover clearing by morning! Wind veering to the north, temperatures declining."

"High tide at fifty-seven minutes past eleven," came a second.

And "It is thirty-five minutes past the hour of eight," voiced a third.

Ephram, Eagleton, and Thump had only just managed not to tumble one another from the top step like a trio of human dominoes.

A second sleigh stood alongside Sundry's own, and Mister Walton was beside it, helping Daniel Plainway with several packages. The whole lot of them gaped at Sundry's startling appearance on the porch; Mister Walton smiled; Daniel Plainway frowned a little. Sundry was ashamed to be seen in such a panic, but he let out a whoosh of relief nonetheless and said, "Gentlemen, I am very glad to see you."

"Good heavens, Sundry!" said Mister Walton. "What has happened?" The portly fellow clumped up the steps. "I thought you were going to meet us at Mr. Plainway's."

"I misunderstood your instructions," said Sundry.

"We thought you must have, so we came along. Goodness' sakes, my friend, you look as if you've seen—" Mister Walton did not finish the thought, but lowered his spectacles and considered Sundry in the light of the lantern that Daniel carried up to the porch.

"What is it, Mr. Moss?" said the lawyer.

"Nerves, I should say," said the young man.

"You don't strike me as the nervous sort," said Daniel, the frown still occupying the better part of his expression.

"I'm sorry," said Sundry. "I thought I heard someone upstairs."

Daniel looked as if he suspected a bad joke but realized, when he thought about it, that Sundry was above such gross behavior. "Houses make noises," he said, and looking up, he saw a tendril of smoke against the moonlit sky. "You started a fire?"

"I hope that was the thing to do," said the young man.

"Of course," said Daniel, his expression softening. "Probably air exchanging in the flues."

"Yes," said Sundry. "It could be." He understood how upsetting the idea of a ghost in this house would be to Daniel Plainway. If nothing else, the man had probably prayed many nights that the spirits of Eleanor Linnett, of her grandfather, and of Jeram Willum were at peace.

Daniel Plainway nodded and stepped past them into the hall. It had given him a turn, when they approached the house, to see the slivers of firelight playing around the perimeters of the curtained windows.

Ephram, Eagleton, and Thump wandered in behind the lawyer, remarking on the beauty of the house, though still a bit shaken by their startling welcome.

Mister Walton came last, saying in a low tone, "Are you all right?"

"Yes," said Sundry with a rueful laugh. "I think so. But I am very glad you arrived."

53. Someone Coming Back

Ephram, Eagleton, and Thump had learned enough of the Linnett history to form their own sense of the house's hauntedness, however metaphorical; they entered the hall with a respectful stillness, but also with a curiosity that they had not the artifice to conceal. With their hats in their hands, they gaped as if expecting phantom women to appear upon the stairs and the hall portraits to wrest themselves from their restricting frames and shout *Boo!* Thump's eyes in particular appeared wide, staring from his hirsute features.

"I shall show you to your rooms," said Daniel Plainway. He stepped past the small congregation and led the way upstairs.

Mister Walton, Sundry, and Daniel took quarters above the kitchen, while the members of the club were given three of the four rooms in the body of the house. The fourth room, Nell's room, Daniel left without resident; that door was shut, and the members of the club considered it with nearly as much mystery as Daniel had considered the locked door in the house of the five sisters.

The fires were lit and there was good cheer and bonhomie as their rooms took on a rosy glow and the vapor of their breath disappeared. Sundry stood in the doorway to Thump's room, which lay opposite the empty bedchamber, and did his best to confront the recent memory of that strange voice, trying to convince himself that it *had* been the wind in the eaves or the exchange of air in a warming chimney flue.

"Quarters are first-rate," proclaimed Thump, who was inclined at times to a nautical hue in his language.

"I should say," said Ephram.

"Marvelous," said Eagleton.

They stood at the doors to their respective rooms and beamed at one another; the mysterious prospect of the house seemed to have evaporated, like their visible breath, before the comfort of the crackling hearths.

In the parlor Daniel regarded the portrait of Eleanor Linnett with a jumble of emotion. The orange-yellow firelight warmed the face of the lovely young woman and appeared to cast shadows from it, as from the real person. The first sight of that face had given him a turn, from which he was recovering when Mister Walton hesitated in the doorway.

"I thought I would never see her again," said Daniel, not otherwise acknowledging Mister Walton's presence.

Mister Walton considered the portrait and the remarkable likeness it shared with Bird. "I promise you," he said, "as long as her son is alive, she will never be truly dead."

They agreed it would be wise to take the picture from the room where they would be sitting; beautiful as Eleanor Linnett was, her portrait had a melancholy effect, which Mister Walton had felt even before he had known her sad tale. They took a lamp to the front room, across the hall from the parlor, and Daniel set the picture upon the hard sofa there. "I shall hang it in the morning," said the lawyer, indicating the place above the cold mantel.

Though Daniel was looking away, Mister Walton simply nodded, and when the lawyer turned to see why there had been no audible response, he found the bespectacled fellow pondering the image that hung on the wall opposite the hearth.

It was not an unusual picture to be hanging in the front room of a Victorian house, when tastes ran (and minds brooded somewhat) on matters considered morbid in later days. It was the tinted photograph of a tomb. Flowers stood before it, as well as a wooden cross. The picture was a characteristic product of the age: muted, a little ugly in its blunt purpose. The sky had been tinted a foreboding gray; the trees behind, skeletal and dark. Across the lintel of the tomb was the name Linnett.

What was once meant to remind the onlooker of mortality now seemed almost cruel, and Daniel would have taken the picture down, then and there, if such an acknowledgment of its power had not seemed like a form of surrender.

Mister Walton too was chilled a little by this scene, which the portrait of Nell Linnett must have watched in other days. Sundry and the Moosepathians were waiting for them in the parlor. Thump was trying not to look hungry, and all of them were glad when Mrs. Cutler arrived with dinner.

The woman arrived with her youngest child, Harry, who considered the men at the dining room table with undisguised wonder and amusement; the boy looked on Thump (or rather his beard) with something like shock.

Mrs. Cutler had set the table before leaving that morning, and as the meal was already cooked, she had but to warm the viands before presenting them. "There are those who wonder what you're to do with the place, Mr. Plainway," she said in the kitchen. This wasn't gossip but the sort of information that might be helpful in a close-knit community.

"Do they think I'm moving in, Mrs. Cutler?" Daniel knew that some less charitable individuals had hinted at the clever manipulations he had employed to secure the house for himself and that he was only waiting for the seven years to be up since the disappearance of the boy to make it his own home.

"Anyone you care about knows better, Mr. Plainway," she said. Mrs.

Cutler, unafraid of anything but the appearance of idle talk, expressed her sentiments without whispering. "There are those, of course, who say your guests are spiritual folk, come to lay the old man to rest."

"If anyone lingers, Mrs. Cutler, it isn't Mr. Linnett," said Daniel.

"I do know it," she said matter-of-factly, and if she had seen Daniel's face, just then, she might have been a little taken aback by the grimness of his expression, but she was going at the goose as if it might get up and run away before she had properly carved it.

For the men, the presence of a woman, not to say a child, did much to balance the atmosphere of the house. Mrs. Cutler was a good soul, if a little unsmiling, and she was gratified to see her work fall to such appreciative appetites. The goose and its trimmings, the potatoes and cabbage and turnip and preserved beans boiled in pork scraps, the sourdough rolls and butter could not have met with better-prepared stomachs or finer sensibilities. There were tea and coffee and cider to wash it down, and apple pie and cheese designed to send them all into a glorious postprandial narcosis.

Mrs. Cutler clattered about in the kitchen, adding to the sense of domesticity, and even Sundry relaxed beneath her practical agency. The conversation ran to interesting courses, touching upon the amusing rather than the sad, and was led expertly by Mister Walton, who was happy to remember some of his and the Moosepath League's best adventures since he returned to Maine the previous July. It was enough to draw even Daniel Plainway from his darkened mood.

Sundry's recent experience still troubled him, however, and he was conscious of their voices as they must sound in nearby (and presumably empty) rooms. He had the notion that the house itself must be alert to their negligent words and that quiet presences in dark corners must wonder who had roused them from dreams of past evenings and celebrations, echoes of which might answer the conversation at the table if the living but stopped to listen. Normally a gregarious fellow and also a hungry one, Sundry found neither the talk nor the meal making much of an impression upon him.

The wind had risen with the moon, and for Sundry this complicated matters; the house now spoke with a dozen voices, and he was conscious of every groan and creak.

Mister Walton was aware of his friend's preoccupation and wondered that Sundry, who so willingly pounced upon an armed man back at Council Hill, would be unnerved by the quiet lullaby from a restless spirit. He himself was more concerned than frightened with a soul that had not found peace—if the entire affair had not simply been the wind in a flue.

The fire in the parlor was cheery and warm; Mrs. Cutler and her son went home, and the Moosepathians were of a camplike spirit, as if they were in the deep woods, picking the day's game from their teeth and telling rough-hewn tales. Eagleton in fact was telling of his attempt to ride a rented bicycle and explaining how it was that he ended, feet up, in a flower seller's cart.

"Being Eagleton," assured Ephram, "he reimbursed the flower lady very handsomely."

"I was distressed when I detected tears on her face," said Eagleton.

"Though she sounded as if she were laughing," added a still-puzzled Ephram.

"Some ladies react to difficult situations in this manner," said Thump sagely. The memory was a confounding one. They had been dutiful in their attentions to the woman but were forced to quit their usual prognostications of the weather, time, and tide since these announcements seemed to excite her hysterics. Eagleton had returned the bicycle.

But the excitements of the day and their magnificent meal, not to mention the hypnotizing light of the fire and the warmth that it imparted to their sated forms, had its effect. Ephram, Eagleton, and Thump took turns, for half an hour or so, waking one another with the odd unexpected snore, till Mister Walton, himself drowsy, suggested that they call it a night.

Sundry banked the fire in the parlor while Daniel tended the kitchen stove and the dining room hearth. They were climbing the stairs when Daniel said to Sundry, "The house has a good many noises in the wind, but Mrs. Cutler says there was someone staying in the attic till she and her family showed up to start cleaning."

"Do you think he would come back?"

"I think *some*one might come back."

54. Parley's Plan

Parley Willum wasn't so drunk that he couldn't keep an eye on his cousin Mathom. Mathom Beasely had taken an interest in the old horse collar that hung rotting from one of the trees in front of the house, and Parley was more than a little sure that Mathom intended to leave with it. What Parley did share with his cousin was an acquisitive and jealous nature, and though he had called upon Mathom and several other relatives to go with him to the Linnett house, he didn't have to trust them in the meantime.

He watched Mathom from his shadowy eyes and his shadowy corner. George Beasely was deep in his cups and growing louder and fiercer with every draft, till one might think, listening to him, he killed bears with his bare hands. Parley's boys—Asher was not among them—were allowed but a pint apiece, Parley growled at them when they came back for more.

But Parley Willum himself had drunk enough to take the edge off his fear. He'd been up to the Linnett place once since Jeram died, with two of his boys and his middle girl, and what they had seen through the window, in the night, while the house was empty, he didn't like to think about.

The place was empty then, he told himself. It'll be lit up when the lawyer comes back with the boy.

Word had spread that Plainway had found Parley's grandson, Asher's son, and that the lawyer had hired the Cutler people to ready the house for a homecoming. Parley was convinced that the boy would be coming and that Plainway intended to set himself up as the kid's guardian, in which position he would be able to get his hands on the Linnett fortune, which everyone knew lay buried somewhere on the grounds or stashed in a secret drawer or cubby.

But Plainway wouldn't get so far without the boy, who was Parley's grandson. Possession was eleven points of the law, and once he had the boy in hand Parley would have a means of haggling.

"I don't know why that boy of yours isn't here," said Parley's brother Moses.

"What boy?" said Parley, glowering. For some reason Jeram's face had come to mind, and this nettled him.

"The young rip that got the brat to start with, who do you think?"

Asher was not around; they hadn't seen him in fact for a year and a half, and there were rumors that he had fled the county to get away from a man whose wife he'd insulted over in Steep Falls and who had offered to give Asher a fish-eye view of the village namesake. Parley didn't care to have his son involved with this business; there would be enough hands in the pie when the kid was taken, and certainly he didn't care to have someone who had more claim than he.

"Asher's done his part," said Mathom crudely and with enough emphasis to raise a chortle from several others among the men who sat about the table. Parley wished they wouldn't drink so much as he raised his mug to his lips.

"I might know a man who'd give something for that horse collar you've got hanging out there," said Mathom.

Parley was surprised; he had not been expecting Mathom to raise the subject. "I just bet you do," he said into the bottom of his mug.

"I'd split what I got, if you were to let me take it over to him. Fellow over at Kezar Falls."

Parley figured he'd never see a penny out of it. "They've got horse collars over Kezar Falls, I expect," was all he said.

"It's a mortification seeing it rot out there on a tree limb," said Mathom, and he was going to say more when Parley stood up, bad rum like fire in his brain.

"It'll rot too, for all you'll get your hands on it!" he shouted.

Berne Beasely, who was almost asleep, fell backward in his chair. George and Mathom stood, defensive and tense with the hint of violence in the air.

Mathom shouted back at Parley, calling him a fool and a liar and some things less polite, and Parley wondered why he didn't break his mug when he slammed it on the table.

Elizabeth Willum threw the curtain aside from the bedroom behind, and two of the younger children poked their heads down the open trap above the kitchen. Parley began to recite a litany of debts that Mathom owed him and threw in several items that had disappeared on previous occasions of Mathom's visiting, most of which Parley had acquired by other than usual means. Mathom began to shout back and wave his fists above the table.

Then the front door was thrown open, and Morrel Willum barged in, shouting something that couldn't be heard until the general din receded.

"He's back," said Morrel, who was Parley's boy and thirteen. "They've lit the place up like a barn dance."

The disagreement between Parley and Mathom was immediately laid aside, disagreements being neither rare nor hard to come by in that household.

"Who's they?" said Parley.

"He had four or five fellows with him."

"How about the boy?"

"I didn't see him exactly."

"What does that mean?"

"The place was pretty dark when the first sleigh came, and I couldn't make out too much, even with the moon out."

"He's there," said Parley. He went to the fireplace and took the rifle down from its place above the mantel.

The other men had guns in the corners or propped beside the table, and they began to collect these.

"We'll head up and look the place over," said Parley. "We might even get the boy before they know it, but we won't flinch at touching someone's nose with the barrel of a gun if it comes to that."

There was an odd mixture of fear and bravado apparent in the room. Elizabeth Willum turned her back on the kitchen and let the curtain fall as she retreated to her room. A third face had appeared in the open trap. The men were shouldering themselves into coats and pulling hats over their ears. Mathom banged Morrel on the back.

"It was cold, waiting out there," admitted the boy. He looked to the table hopefully, but there were no scraps left behind, not even a corner waiting in his father's mug.

The door was opened again, and the night rushed in as they blustered and bounded down the steps. Morrel went with them. Dogs barked outside. The door slammed shut. "I saw a man outside the house," Morrel was saying.

55. Expected Sentries Sleep

The kitchen adjunct to the Linnett house was more properly termed a wing than an ell, and large enough to accommodate four small rooms in the second story. The very far right room, when one was coming from the front of the house, was the smallest, some space taken up to house the stairway that ran from the pantry to the attic. The remaining three rooms had been furnished for guests, and though they were large enough for only a bed, a commode, and a chair, they were cozy little chambers, each with its own coal grate.

The fire in his room gave enough light for Daniel's purposes, and he blew out his lamp. He had felt in an odd humor ever since arriving tonight, ever since Sundry had greeted them with a shout and the assertion that he had heard singing in Nell's room. Daniel was not a credulous man when it came to portents and haunts; but as a true Yankee he was loath to throw *anything* out, and the charge to "take it with a grain of salt" counseled one to be skeptical, not dismissive—a distinction that other generations might fail to recognize.

But it was the night of the winter solstice, when the Northern Hemisphere was veered into the colder reaches of space and the sun remained hidden from the windows of the Linnett house longer than any other night of the year.

Daniel had never thought very much about this annual darkness, the silent cold hinge by which the door to summer would slowly open once again. Ian Linnett may have thought of it, for the old man had something of the Old World in him. Ian had marked the day with the evergreen from the forest and helped drive back the long night with the scores of candles upon his tree. Other visitors from the woods protected the house. The clinging ivy marked devotion to God, and the sharp leaves of the holly drove away witches and evil spirits. Many people, decorating their homes, did not know that they were creating a fortress against the influences of winter's long dark night.

Daniel wrapped the comforter from the bed around him and sat in the chair by the door. Shadows waxed and waned in time with the dull glow from the coals. He wondered that he wasn't more apprehensive, waiting alone in the near dark for some sign of those who had passed on, but strangely enough the thought of Charlotte Burnbrake eased his heart. What would she think to know that he sat in the length of that night thinking and dreaming of her? As he watched and contemplated the middle distances of his recent memory, he fell asleep as easily as a boat, unguided, might drift upon the tide.

He did indeed dream, but his dreams were shadowy without darkness, slow and filled with possibility rather than incident, and something might have moved through the room while he slept, willing to say good-bye but for a single bit of tidings.

Mister Walton, who led the way upstairs, found himself roused somewhat by the time he was in his nightshirt and snuggled beneath the crisp sheets, so he sat up in bed and turned up his lamp, by which light he found his place in *Nicholas Nickleby*, which he was rereading. Nicholas and Smike had just left the acting troupe of Mr. Crummles and (Mister Walton knew) were on the cusp of meeting the Cheeryble brothers. Here were the books' heartiest and merriest moments, and he threw himself into it with great relish, chuckling at the good-natured badinage between the kind-hearted Cheerybles.

The wind blew a little bit, rocking the windows in their sashes and piping softly at the eaves. He got up once to throw a coal or two upon the fire and warmed his toes while he stood there reading.

The wind came around to the northwest, and the sound in the eaves changed. Mister Walton lifted his head from his book and his elbow from the mantel. *Was that what Sundry heard?* he wondered. He listened but was not convinced. Sundry knew a tune when he heard one.

It was then that Mister Walton had a strange sensation that he was not alone in the room. He stood by the fire with the book open in his hands, looking from corner to darkened corner, half believing that some shadow in the room was not moving with the others. He felt a thrill up his arms and at the nape of his neck, but it was not entirely unpleasant.

For long minutes Mister Walton waited, listening to the wind and the thin occasional crackle of new coal on red embers and watching the shifting silhouettes of the furnishings and himself. Then it was gone, as if some curiosity not tethered to any physical thing had briefly visited him and, finding itself unsatisfied, left with as little warning or evidence as it had come.

Mister Walton returned to his bed then, pulled up the covers, and found it difficult to return to the legal offices of Charles and Edwin Cheeryble. The conceit that he had been attended fleetingly by something feminine led his thoughts to Phileda McCannon and the hapless manner in which he had conducted his friendship with her. It was difficult to think of Phileda, he being an optimistic soul, without warm feelings in close escort, and he was the second in that wing of the house to close his eyes and dwindle to sleep.

From his pillow Sundry Moss regarded the soft glow of the coal fire in his room upon the ceiling and listened to the sounds of the house around him: the song in the eaves, the breath in the chimney, the creaks and snaps of a seasoned dwelling in the dark and the cold.

He remained doubtful about the nature of what he heard earlier that evening but was hoping to perceive a comparable note that he might recognize and identify. He started out of a doze and sat up, expecting someone to be watching him from the foot of the bed. The face that entered his imagination, however, was not that of Nell Linnett (or her portrait) but of the young woman, Priscilla Morningside, whom he had met the previous summer and whose face had often accompanied him into sleep.

A little comforted by this separate apparition, he settled back onto his pillow. The strangeness of his present circumstances demanded his attention, however, and he fell to contemplating that voice again. He was not aware of drowsing, and contrarily the sounds of quiet creeping in the attic touched him like the unconnected elements of a dream.

56. A Solstice Carol

In the ivory light of the westering moon (and in that same light reflected from the snowy grounds) the Linnett house paled against the dark evergreens, a white face peering from a dark hood. The surrounding fields gleamed like silver, and perhaps only a fox cast a moving shadow down by Clemons Pond.

The house itself was strangely disturbed, shamming slumber.

In their separate rooms Ephram, Eagleton, and Thump drifted, but there was in the atmosphere the vague sensation of movement, and Thump in particular had the impression of being on a boat with water moving all about him.

Ephram listened to the wind rise.

Eagleton drowsed, the evening's grand meal warming him like an extra comforter. He thought of his mother and Christmas Eve. He'd had a pleasant, tranquil childhood that did not at all hint at the marvelous adventures he would experience as a member of the Moosepath League. He thought his sweet mother would have approved, however, though she would have been concerned that he dressed warmly. He did not remember his father very well; but there had been a host of uncles and aunts, and he had been provided for, even doted upon.

His mother had been a graceful blond woman, with elegant, long hands that ran across the keys of the piano like laughter. Her pale, beautiful face glowed in the light from the hall when she kissed him good night. Even when he was perhaps too old for such a treat, she would sometimes hum a lullaby at the edge of his bed and he would pretend to drift to sleep. He heard it now.

"Yes," said Eagleton, "I always pretended to sleep, so that I would hear the song, but then I really would fall asleep and—"

He awoke with something heavy on his heart. He had fallen asleep. He had always fallen asleep before she finished, and he had never felt the weight of her leave the side of his bed, or heard her soft footsteps reach the hall, or seen her backward glance as she closed the door.

There was something at his window. Eagleton raised himself up on his elbows and listened. He thought it must be the wind, but then it came again, like a cat pawing at a threshold. He was a little afraid but confusedly thought that his mother was just in the next room, and with this to embolden him, he swung himself out of bed and approached the curtains. The sound came again, more insistent than before.

He peeled the curtain back, and the cold air trapped against the glass touched him like a breath. He could not see the moon, but its light upon the snow made a great shadow of the owl sitting in the tree beside the window. The bird turned its head and blinked at him, startling him; then it flexed its wings in such a way that they brushed the cold panes. Eagleton dropped the curtain, and the room returned to near darkness, in which compass he was aware of someone singing softly.

He opened the door to put his head into the hall. The sound was a little louder. "Thump?" he said, in such a whisper that no one who wasn't standing beside him could have heard it. (Since no one *was* standing beside him, the thought of someone's hearing him filled him with a disquieting palpitation.) "Ephram?" he said in an even quieter tone; the delicate strain of melody was louder than his voice.

It was then he noticed that Ephram's door, opposite his own, was open. Eagleton didn't feel comfortable crossing the hall in his nightshirt, so he stumbled back into his room and pulled on his trousers and a pair of socks. He stopped in the midst of dressing one foot, one leg poised in the air, and listened for the song. It was like a voice on the wind, and now the wind was almost gone, and the voice with it. *Good heavens!* he thought. *Ephram must have gotten up already to investigate!* "Ever in the fore!" he whispered admiringly.

When Eagleton peered into the hall again, he thought someone might be downstairs or that the fire in the parlor hearth had caught again, for there was a flickering glow ascending the stairs. On tiptoes he crept past the landing to Ephram's room and spoke his friend's name into the darkness beyond.

It is a lullaby, he thought before he was hardly aware of hearing the voice again, like his mother's voice—a woman's voice surely, lovely and sweet. It drifted over his shoulder like a word of endearment, and he was more fascinated than afraid. "Ephram?" he called, stepping further into the room. The moon was yet on that side of the house, and the faint slivers of light that fell across Ephram's bed revealed the lack of an occupant.

Good heavens! he thought. *Thump! I must rouse Thump.*

But to do so, he must pass the room of the late Nell Linnett, and he hesitated near the head of the stairs till he saw that Thump's door was open. What could it mean? He pointedly did not look toward the *empty* chamber as he hurried to Thump's room, which also proved to be without its guest.

Eagleton blinked at the empty bed for some moments before he could be convinced that both his friends had gone somewhere without him. The voice, the melody, so strange and sublime, seemed to be coming from below now, and even as he became aware of this, he was touched by a new perception, that of an added (and unexpected) space in which a voice or song might echo.

My word! thought Eagleton. *Someone is going about opening all the doors!*

Indeed, the door to Nell Linnett's room, which he had *not* looked at before, was open as well, and when he bravely approached this third threshold, he was cognizant of a new sound, like the intermittent hum of machinery from a distance or the buzz of a bee.

Eagleton stepped into Nell Linnett's room with as much a tremor of impropriety as of fear. He hadn't been in a woman's boudoir since he was a child, and he was both curious and apprehensive about the accoutrements within. After a terrific start, however, he was more curious and apprehensive (and astonished) to see Thump sitting in a chair by the door.

"Thump?" he said in another whisper. His heart was racing, and it was a moment before he had his breath again. He leaned close to the man and spoke his name again but without response.

What time is it? wondered Eagleton. *What has been happening while I was asleep?* He was sure that he had been asleep, though it seemed as if they had all just retired. He leaned close to the man, ears straining, and when Thump let out a short snore, Eagleton gasped and nearly fell over backward. A secondary sort of snore followed from Thump's bearded visage, and Eagleton leaned close to examine the sleeping man.

Why was he sleeping here? How had he got there?

What has been happening? Should I wake him? he wondered again. *And where is Ephram?*

There was another bone-rattling snore from Thump, and Eagleton didn't have the heart to wake him, he seemed so pleasantly unconscious. It was all very peculiar. "Mister Walton," said Eagleton to himself, "and Mr. Moss, and Mr. Plainway." With these names on his lips and in his head he decided to look for the men themselves but thought that the narrow hall leading into the ell looked awfully dim. From the doorway he peered into the pitch black.

The faint light from below indicated to Eagleton a more prudent direction, and was encouraged, as he crept down the stairs, by the sense (rather than the sound) of people conversing in the parlor. The lullaby was coming to the end of a cycle, and he could hear, as he approached the door to the parlor, a voice saying, "What is that tune?"

Eagleton couldn't understand how the light had appeared so faint from the hall, for when he stepped into the parlor, he was dazzled by the myriad candles upon an enormous evergreen. The entire room sparkled with garlands, silver and gold, and greenery covered the lintels and the mantel. The tree was heavy with bright wooden figures and shiny glass ornaments. The air itself seemed to shine, and Eagleton had the impression that he was looking at a brilliant, if hazy, photograph. The tree swam before him, and the people about the room appeared to be at separate distances (some very far away, in fact), though they might be conversing with one another.

He was entirely in the room now, and all fear left him in his confusion, and all his confusion left him in his amazement, and even that emotion retreated before the power of absolute delight.

Then he saw her walking toward him, eyes shining with hope, and she moved slowly as if the light between them were water. He gasped as her face fell into focus; there was a breath of cold wind and bright, warm light, the light of fir boughs, and the thought of a hand reaching silently. The young woman took Eagleton's shaking hands in hers and by some act of tacit will made him lift his eyes so that he was looking into the portrait of Nell Linnett.

"If only my boy were here," she said, and Eagleton found it suddenly difficult to breathe.

"Your son," he said, barely hearing himself above the pulse in his ears.

"If only I could see him once more," she said. "If only I could know that he was kept safe."

"Oh, ma'am," said Eagleton.

"What have you done for him?" she said, a smile glistening through her tears. It was not an accusation, but a discovery of Eagleton's kindness to her little Bird.

"Not what others have done, I am sorry," he said. Where were his friends? Where were Ephram and Thump? They could explain. They were much better at this sort of thing, and—

"Do they love him very much?"

Eagleton was thinking of Wyckford O'Hearn and what he had suffered for the little boy, he was thinking of Mollie Peer leaping into the dark waters of the Sheepscott River to save him, he was thinking of Mister Walton and Sundry Moss, he had a glimpse of Ephram standing beside four-year-old Bertram Linnett on the grounds of Cliff Cottage, and he could hear Thump saying a prayer at the side of the child's bed.

"I have something from him," said Eagleton. He was reaching to the back of his neck, and with surprising deftness he had the delicate silver chain and the tiny silver cross. He pressed them into her hand. "It is from a son to his mother," he said, "who has seen your face and knows how much you loved him in so brief a time." Eagleton didn't know where these words came from; it was as if Mister Walton were beside him, directing his thoughts.

He didn't know, either, how he could really put it into her hand, but it was gone from his suddenly, and he looked up. Her beautiful, tear-streaked face disappeared behind the mist in his own eyes.

Someone was passing a punch around. There was laughter.

They were singing another carol. They were singing *the* Carol. Eagleton had never heard it before, and it was gone from his head, one note after another, as they followed in beautiful succession.

Is it Christmas? he wondered.

57. What They Didn't Know Inside

The president of the Broumnage Club had long ago lost his initial requisite for membership, but he was known for not wearing a hat, and his followers could pick him out of the night while the moon shone on his bald pate. He was wrapped in a heavy overcoat, however, and seemed to relish the cold. The young men didn't know why he was there with them tonight but expected that more than surveillance was on the docket.

"Where is he?" asked the old man, and several blond men glanced nervously in the direction of the pond for a glimpse of their fellow who had followed the boy.

"Why do you suppose he was watching the house?" wondered one of them.

"Sir, there's a light downstairs," said another.

They were all surprised to see a sudden glow from a parlor window of the Linnett house, but it faded as quickly as it rose, and they were left with more questions.

"What was that?" said someone.

"Do you think it was a signal?" wondered another.

The old man was considering that very possibility, and it was troublesome that such a seemingly simple pair as this Tobias Walton and Sundry Moss might prove so deep. He wondered what Adam Tempest had told Walton and also who else among their order was having some crises of scruples.

But of course, they had found what they had come for, after all, at Council Hill. Nobody would withdraw now who suspected the final acquisition of their society's goal. But what had Tempest let out?

"It's Edgar," came a hiss from several yards away.

A dark figure could be seen against the snow as it topped the rise. One of the men hurried to meet Edgar and direct him to the old man. Edgar arrived out of breath and gasped something about being followed. The old man didn't wait to hear more but moved to the head of the slope, where he could look down at the gray surface of Clemons Pond. For a man of his age, the president had notoriously good eyesight, and he scanned the open slope as if his gaze might strike down anyone in its path.

"Whom do you see?" he demanded in a hushed voice.

The slope was barren of life. In the moonlight they had command of every square foot from the Linnett house to the clumps of alders near the pond.

"I was sure there were men behind me," said Edgar apologetically.

"What was that light, do you suppose?" wondered someone again.

"Perhaps the fire flared up," suggested another, but the old man didn't think it likely.

"Where is Arthur?" wondered the old man. It provoked him that these men couldn't simply keep their posts and not gravitate to him whenever there was the smallest question in the air.

Edgar sensed the old man's pique and quickly offered to locate Arthur, who had been with two or three men along the carriage drive. He kept one eye on the imposing bulk of the Linnett house as he crossed the snowy grounds. The carriage drive was invisible till he was upon it, and the trees beyond seemed even then like a solid black wall against the sky. As he passed the hedges and entered the woods, Edgar's eyes adjusted to the new level of night, his own shadow darting in and out of the stationary silhouettes of the surrounding trunks.

He actually passed the prostrate form before he realized that it was not simply another shadow. "Arthur?" he said, feeling a sudden clutch in his stomach. "Arthur?" Edgar knelt beside the figure and turned the man over. It was one of the other fellows, not Arthur, but where—

The man groaned.

"Did you hit your head?" wondered Edgar, and he looked up to see what object might have fulfilled this possibility. That was when he realized that several other figures had simply melted out of the woods and surrounded him.

"I think that lawyer has more friends than you suspected, Parley," whispered Cousin George. From the cover of the woods they could make out at least a dozen men between themselves and the house.

"They're not friends, I warrant," said Parley, his pale eyes shining in his unshaven face.

Mathom was suddenly beside them, the flare of enmity between him and Parley forgotten in the interest and excitement of their present occupation. "What are they doing?" he asked.

"They're watching the house," said George.

"They're watching for us," said Parley. "They think we're coming up the meadow."

"Those fellows we took won't tell us what they're up to," informed George.

"We are getting that boy," said Parley. He watched the group of men outside the wood, his mouth half open, the tip of his tongue riding back and forth on his lower lip. Parley had what has been termed *animal patience* and had once taken three hours to creep up on a wild duck and throttle it. (Asked why he hadn't shot the creature, he answered, "I couldn't sight him in 'cause I was drunk.") He could wait all night if he chose and hardly move a muscle more than was needed to blink.

"They're going to notice their fellows are gone," said Mathom. Parley shot the man a glance, and he added, "They're down the brook a ways." He chortled softly then. "They think we're working for that lawyer."

"I told you they weren't friends of his," said Parley to George.

"Look!" said Mathom, and the other two men barely caught what he had seen. Some twenty or thirty yards from Parley and his cousins, one of the men nearest the perimeter of woods had suddenly been jerked off his feet and disappeared without a whimper.

"I think Benjamin is enjoying this," said Mathom.

"Let's grab another one or two," said George, as if encouraging Parley to go out in the boat again and fish some more.

Parley didn't want Benjamin to get them all, that was for sure, and it looked as if two more were being sent after the fellow who had come looking for the first three.

"All right," said Parley. "While they're sneaking down the drive, we'll come out behind them." Then some centuries of strange knowledge—instinctive and learned—faded into the shadows between trees as they slipped after their new quarry.

"Can't let Ben get them all," came George's voice out of the dark, like a ghost.

It turned into something of a battle on the other side of the woods from the Linnett estate. The road before the carriage drive became the center of concentration, and the Willum party was not daunted when the Broumnagians proved to be armed.

Parley and his clan had captured seven of the blond men before the president of the Broumnage Club realized that a simple retreat had been cut off. He had misgivings that Mister Walton and the Moosepath League (the president had been suspicious of *that* appellation from the start) were after the same goal as his own society, and now he was certain of it. He couldn't imagine that the portly fellow and his seemingly stumbling companions had tricked them into thinking they were in the house, but certainly the small force picking off his men could be no other.

The president—a veteran of the Great Campaign against the South—led his troops down the middle of the carriage drive with guns aready. Parley and his family were not interested in exchanging fire, however, and continued to snatch stragglers, and even a front-runner, from the pitch-black trail, carrying them into the woods, where it was discovered that these gentlemen were fancily decked out with gold watches and fat wallets. The original plans of the Willum party quite fell by the way.

The president himself fired the first shot, well out of hearing of the Linnett house, while its inhabitants were fast asleep. The pistol flash lit the end of the carriage drive like a bolt of lightning, and all the president got out of it was an iceball aside the head. More guns were fired, in several directions, till someone suggested that they might as likely hit one of their own who were being held out in the woods as the silent enemy.

Mathom Beasely thought it funny to let out some theatrical screams, followed by a delighted "You missed me!" Someone took a shot in the direction of the voice and was answered by deep laughter.

The carriages waiting for the Broumnage Club were useless, of course, the horses having been cut loose. Parley began to live up to his name by suggesting a means to reach peace, the burden of which lay heavily upon the blond troop.

"This is outrageous!" declared Arthur of the Broumnage Club. "We will not put up with this indignity!"

Then Parley himself took a shot and clipped Arthur's hat. Arthur and several others nearby threw themselves to the ground. The president meanwhile wondered if the men in the woods were indeed the Moosepath League. He hadn't expected them to be simple highwaymen. His bald head was the plainest thing in the lowering moonlight, but he refused to cower.

"Come out and we'll parley!" he shouted in a commanding baritone.

This, for some reason, was greeted with more laughter.

Daylight was all the Broumnage Club could hope for at this point, and like the redcoats marching from Lexington, they kept close ranks on their way to the center of Hiram and the railway station. Their tormentors were not of such murderous intent as the Lexington men of 1775, however; the occasional club member, snatched from the perimeter of their formation, would return in time, a little less weighed down by worldly goods and spouting retribution, but as a gray dawn lifted its face, the Willums and the Beaselys drifted back to Clemons Pond to count their spoils and recount the hilarity of the engagement.

The Broumnage Club boarded the first train to Portland, where they would lick their wounds and plot vengeance—once they figured out who had attacked them and after they had gained untold riches and power in their expedition to the lost city of Norumbega.

58. More on Several Related Points

"I remember now what Granny said about owls," said Emmy when she appeared in the kitchen.

"Do you?" Lydia had known all along and very well what her mother-in-law had said about owls.

"She used to say they were people coming back to visit."

"She had some queer notions," said Lydia, knowing that Emmy was thinking of her father. "I'd like to think I could come back as something other than an owl," said the mother. Her daughter sat at the table, where Lydia had a bowl of pancake batter and a slab of bacon waiting for the skillet to heat.

Emmy looked like a child, her face filled with apprehension. "I heard it again last night," she said. "Remember you and Wyck said you had heard it the other night?"

Lydia made a noncommittal sound.

"Was it the night after you hung the picture of Bird's mother?" asked Emmy.

"Good Lord, Emmy!" said Lydia. She turned toward the stove with the bowl of batter in her hands. "You're a Christian woman, not a superstitious heathen! And I heard it *before* I hung the picture."

"Oh."

"And it wasn't singing." Lydia didn't say that she first heard the owl the very night before she hung the picture in the parlor, as her daughter might make something of that.

Ephias stepped into the kitchen and cast his eyes about before settling by the stove to put on his boots.

"There was an owl outside my room," came another voice. Bird stood in the doorway, looking thoughtful.

"There is one hereabouts," agreed Ephias. He sent a meaningful glance in his wife's direction, which told Lydia that they had discussed the significance of owls already and that Ephias wasn't keen to discuss it any further. Emmy looked innocent and proceeded to cut the bacon.

"He looked at me when I went to the window," said Bird. He came into the kitchen and sat between Emmy and Ephias.

"This morning?" said Lydia. It was strange if an owl was sitting outside the house with the sun recently up.

"Last night," he said. "I heard him at the window, and I went and looked under the curtain."

"You shouldn't be getting up in the middle of the night," was all that Lydia would say. "Didn't Wyck hear you?" She could hear her son's out-of-balance tread coming down the stairs and decided that it was time to change the subject. "I see you have your moose badge on this morning," she began.

Bird fingered the little tin shield pinned to his shirt. There was the image of a moose hammered into the badge like a crest, marred by the crease of a bullet. The badge had been given to the boy by an old clockmaker while Bird was in hiding, and it had proved something of a talisman. Lydia knew he wore it whenever he was thinking about the Moosepath League, whose members had done their best to shelter and protect him.

"I want to take something over to Mrs. Partout this morning," said Lydia. "She and her husband have both been under the weather. A shame so near Christmas."

"I'll get some boughs when I'm out to the acres," said Ephias, meaning the woodlot.

Lydia was surprised; she knew that Ephias had never entirely approved of celebrating Christmas but that he had resigned himself these past years to her love of it. Nothing from past Christmastides had prepared her, however, for his actual involvement in readying the house for Christmas Eve.

"Thank you, Ephias," she said, realizing then that he was probably thinking of the boy; the perception didn't make her like her son-in-law the less. "You should go with him," she said to Bird, and he looked as if he might like to, though his present concern was with Wyck's whereabouts.

Wyckford had come down the stairs but had not entered the kitchen, and returning to the stove, Lydia wondered what he was doing, and where. It was like machine work how everyone came downstairs each morning and settled in the kitchen.

By the time Lydia was nearly finished with the pancakes, she and Bird were not the only ones to wonder where Wyck had gotten to; Emmy went to the stove and without subtlety took over the cooking. Lydia went into the hall and listened for a moment, then was startled when she passed the parlor door and caught sight of Wyck standing in the middle of the room, looking at the portrait of the young woman.

"I almost think she knows about us," said Wyck when Lydia had stood in the doorway for so long that she thought he hadn't heard her.

"I think we should put that picture away. There are thriving imaginations in this house."

Wyck laughed softly. He had been thinking about the Moosepath League since he woke, was thinking about them even now. His big frame shook and his shoulder hurt. His mother raised one quizzical eyebrow. "I was thinking of Mr. Eagleton," he said, "and the dog that ran off with his hat."

"One of the gentlemen who took care of Bird," she said, remembering them from Wyckford's account.

He chuckled again. "Well, they did their best." He felt kindly toward Ephram, Eagleton, and Thump, though their stewardship had very nearly ended in disaster.

"Kindness counts for a great deal," she said.

"I think I can ease up on things, Ma," said Wyck, almost fearing to say what came to his mouth. "I think he's here to stay."

Lydia had not her son's sense of assurance, but she put on a bland face and nodded, not wanting to harm what might be a fragile construct. The letter they had received from Mr. Plainway had been full of assurances, but they had not met the man yet, nor had he met Bird—or should she be thinking of the little fellow as Bertram? She returned to the kitchen and shook her head when Emmy cast a glance her way.

After breakfast Wyckford insisted that Bird go with Ephias, and Lydia was surprised that the boy seemed confident enough in Wyck's well-being to do so. When they had gone and Emmy had taken a horse down to the Partouts' with a basket of things to eat, Lydia could hear the arrhythmic blows of the ax behind the barn.

59. One Final Scoundrel

It was hardly more than the sound a mouse would make in the woodwork, but Sundry heard it, and his eyes opened to the dusky light of the predawn. He was rather surprised that he had slept at all and wondered what had wakened him; it might have been Mister Walton turning over in the next room or a subtle change in the direction of the wind. Then the soft noise came again, toward the main body of the house and above his head, and in another minute Sundry was half dressed. He eased himself across the floor of the bedroom and tested the door; a narrow fellow, he did not have to open it very wide before he was able to squeeze himself into the hall.

He carried his boots and moved softly in his stocking feet, taking his time to tread the back hall, hugging the wall, where the floorboards would be less apt to complain. In the front hall he listened at the door that led to the main attic stairs, and hearing a tread grumble there, he retreated behind the door to the ell.

The first hint of daylight had hardly glimmered over the rim of the world, and the details of wallpaper or the shapes of furniture had not risen from the obscurity of night. Sundry felt blind in the windowless hall of the ell, and when his mind formed bits of white haze or warping folds of darkness where there was nothing to see, he closed his eyes and listened. Was there another creak of a tread and the unintended rattle of a doorknob? He never heard the door to the attic open, but he thought he had remained hidden so long that the unknown prowler must have changed his mind or be a ghost.

When Sundry peered into the front hall, he was surprised to see the attic door open and the top of a head disappearing down the main stairwell. Before he reached the landing, Sundry knew who it was, and he considered how many stairs he might clear at a time, and how many leaps it would take to reach the man and knock him down. Or perhaps he could conk the fellow in the back of the head with a boot.

Then at the foot of the stairs the wild-haired man in the voluminous coat experienced a moment of clairvoyance and turned to look up the flight at Sundry. The wide-eyes grew wider still, and the mustache-covered lips parted in a startled gasp. With one hand on the newel-post, Eustace Pembleton (known to Daniel Plainway as Edward Penfen) had pivoted toward the back of the hall when a strange noise, a sort of groan or cry, came from that quarter.

Matthew Ephram was half stumbling in his white nightshirt from the kitchen, where he had inexplicably found himself sleeping by the stove, and with a great yawn he seemed to Pembleton like a mournful ghost. Sundry leaped down the stairs with one hand on the banister, clearing four steps at a time, his boots clattering after him. Pembleton let out a frightened grunt and turned to the front door, which he had half opened when Christopher Eagleton stepped out of the parlor, not a yard away from the man, and himself in the throes of a powerful yawn.

This second noise sounded as mournful and frightening as the first; Pembleton's response was more a cry than a grunt, and he left the half-opened door to charge into the drape-darkened front room. A terrific shriek of fear (encouraging similar feats of vocalization from Ephram and

Eagleton) fractured the first light of day, and Pembleton reeled back into the hall, clutching at air, and falling with a crash onto his back into the rectangle of light from the open door.

With his hand gripping the bottom post, Sundry cautiously bent over him, and when the wild-haired man did not move or even seem to breathe, Sundry felt for a pulse at Pembleton's throat. The thrum of Pembleton's life was sturdy, if a little erratic, and no sooner was this registered than Sundry crept to the door of the front room.

Several cries of surprise and concern came from above, and Daniel Plainway, Mister Walton, and Thump came together at the head of the stairs. "What is it, Sundry?" said Mister Walton, half in a whisper. "Good heavens! Mr. Pembleton!"

"Penfen!" said Daniel.

Sundry was keen with the memory of the voice he had heard the night before and not so keen to peer beyond the threshold of the front room, but he eased his head and shoulders slowly past the jamb and considered the dim room. A quick jolt in his frame was visible to those above, and he stepped back into the hall.

"What is it, Mr. Moss?" asked Daniel Plainway, hardly daring to move.

"Poetic justice, I think, Mr. Plainway," said Sundry. He considered the man at his feet. Ephram and Eagleton inched closer to the prostrate form, and the three men from above hurried down the stairs.

Ephram, Eagleton, and Thump met one another with many questions and declarations. "Good heavens, Thump!" cried Ephram, "I found myself in the kitchen this morning!" and Thump replied, "I was sitting in a chair in the room opposite!" Eagleton had less to say, but he peered into his empty hand, then lifted the hand to his throat.

"Was it that then?" said Daniel, standing at the door to the front room. The portrait of Nell Linnett looked out from the sofa, where he had placed it the night before. In the darkness of the room the skirt of the couch might have been the edge of her petticoats; Daniel felt a tremor sympathetic to what Pembleton must have known.

"He's fainted dead away," said Mister Walton. He was leaning over the man. The cold morning without had gripped the hall, and Sundry was reaching over the prostrate form to close the door when Pembleton let out another terrified scream, shouting, "I don't have him!" and appeared to vault to his feet without benefit of hands or knees. They would not have credited his bony form with such explosive strength, but Sundry and Mister Walton were knocked back by the wild man's violent movement, and before anyone could react, Pembleton was charging out the door, screaming, "Tell her I don't have him!"

Sundry barely avoided collision with Mister Walton as he caught hold of Pembleton's coattails. Pembleton had enough of a start to get himself across the piazza: but he tumbled down the front steps, and Sundry, after a stride or two into the cold air, nearly went with him.

Pembleton was struggling out of his large coat when Sundry landed beside him and caught the man by the collar. Pembleton swung around as if to hit Sundry, but the two men froze in deliberation of each other. Pembleton looked like a creature from some ancient tale, the troll from beneath the bridge or the hermit from the cave; he looked absolutely mad, and he gaped from his bearded, dirty face with such fear and astonishment that Sundry would have liked to let him go then and there.

Mister Walton too felt a measure of pity for the man as Sundry ushered Pembleton back inside. "Every soldier is someone's son," an old major had told him once, when Mister Walton was very young. Now he tried to imagine what Eustace Pembleton—if that was his name—had been like as a child and what sort of life had led him to this ragged end.

Daniel Plainway saw only the man who had taken Nell Linnett's child.

The remainder of the Moosepath League were congregated in a nightshirted trio at the foot of the stairs. "Good heavens!" Eagleton said several times over. He searched for his journal, but his nightshirt had no pockets (the journal was in his coat), and while he watched the proceedings, he conducted a roundabout exploration, without entirely realizing what he was doing.

Ephram caught sight of Eagleton's unconscious search for his journal, and the impression of a man chasing a flea was so strong that Ephram wondered if he didn't feel an itch himself.

"Do you know what you're going to do with him?" wondered Sundry.

"He's as much a danger to himself as anyone," said Mister Walton softly. "At least, with the authorities, he'll be decently fed and clothed."

Thump, who was feeling a little peckish himself, couldn't help wondering where the remainder of the goose was being kept.

"There's a kidnapping charge for him to face," said Daniel, not ready to entirely relinquish his anger. "You shouldn't have come back," he said to the man, "though I guessed you would."

"It's somewheres about," Pembleton growled.

"It hasn't been found if that's what you mean," said Daniel.

The man glared at Daniel. "It's in her eyes," he said. "The old man said it was in her eyes."

Daniel shivered. "That's not exactly what he said, no."

"He said it was in her eyes," repeated the man. He had lost some of his terror, and he looked less wild. Nonetheless, the Moosepath League afforded him a wide berth as he preceded Sundry into the parlor.

Ephram was now chasing an imaginary flea about his chest and shoulders and Eagleton watched him with curiosity. Not realizing that he had instigated Ephram's belief in a flea, Eagleton began to feel an itch himself.

"I'll watch him while you gentlemen dress," said the young man.

"Right," said Daniel. "Mrs. Cutler will be here soon enough to make breakfast."

This was reason enough for Ephram, Eagleton, and Thump to quit the front hall, and they hurried up the stairs with as much terror as if Mrs. Cutler were rushing out of the kitchen even now to catch them in their nightclothes.

Eagleton, when he returned to his room, was sure that something was biting him, but he left off chasing the phantom itch when he was washed over suddenly by the sentiment (rather than the memory) of a dream.

"What do you suppose I was doing in the parlor?" he wondered when they were dressed and Ephram and Thump met him in the hall once again.

"It is an extraordinary thing," agreed Ephram, "for I woke in the kitchen with my feet on the oven door."

"I was asleep in the young woman's room," said Thump, abashed to divulge this information. "In a chair," he added. He had been rather startled by his circumstances when he was wakened by Pembleton's shouts.

"Do you know, Thump?" said Eagleton. "I believe I saw you there on my way to the parlor, but I haven't the slightest idea what I was doing."

"We saw no ghosts, at any rate," said Ephram with a wink and a nudge.

"Oho!" said Thump, with great good nature. "And its being the longest night of the year. We shall have to tell Mr. Burnbrake that his hypothesis has yet to be proved."

Ephram laughed as he imagined joking with the nice old fellow about his solstice ghosts.

"Though perhaps," said Thump, "he would be disappointed."

"That's very thoughtful of you, Thump," said Ephram. "Of course you're right."

"Ah, well," said Thump philosophically. "We were asleep, weren't we? Is everything well, Eagleton?"

Eagleton looked like a man who knew he was missing something, though he knew not what. "Do you know?" he said, "I remember having something around my neck."

"Was it a nightmare?" wondered Thump, who was concerned.

"Not at all. Strangely, I have very good feelings about having it and also about having given it up somehow, but I can't for the life of me remember what it was."

"It?"

"Whatever *it* was, you know."

Thump hadn't the slightest idea what his friend was talking about, but he was fascinated. He nodded, giving Eagleton a mistaken impression of his understanding.

"It's very odd, isn't it, Thump?" said Ephram about Eagleton's situation. Ephram understood only enough of Eagleton's perplexity to be perplexed himself.

"Very much so," agreed Thump. "I should certainly say."

"I had no idea how exhausted I was," said Ephram.

"Does one tend to sleepwalk when one is exhausted?" wondered Thump.

"It would follow."

Eagleton still looked as if he had lost something. It wasn't till several months later when he perused his journal that he came across his notes on the incident with the unpleasant cabbie and the French-speaking woman and how he had come into possession of the little silver cross, but he would never remember very clearly what he had done with it.

"Was it a collar you were missing?" wondered Ephram.

"I don't think," replied Eagleton, but obviously he was not very sure. "It is very difficult to remember something when it's missing."

Thump smelled bacon cooking, and Eagleton and Ephram too lifted their heads, one after the other, as if fallen under a spell.

"Perhaps we shouldn't keep Mrs. Cutler waiting, the good woman," said Ephram sagely.

"Exactly, Ephram!" said Eagleton.

"Thoughtful," said Thump. "Very thoughtful."

60. One Possible Answer

"It's somewheres about," said Pembleton again, though by now Sundry realized that the man was talking not to him but to himself. Whatever madness that possessed the man did not curb his appetite, however, and when Mrs. Cutler offered breakfast, Pembleton was willing to break bread with Sundry in the parlor.

"Goodness' sakes, Mr. Plainway!" Mrs. Cutler declared. "What has been going on about the place!"

"We've snagged Edward Penfen, Mrs. Cutler. Or rather, Mr. Moss has snagged him. I believe he was the man you sensed in the attic rooms."

"That's well and good," said the woman, "but that doesn't go a long way to explain all the traffic out in the yard."

There was a lot to do and think about that morning, and the six men took shifts eating and watching Pembleton and strolling the grounds to ponder over the welter of tracks that covered the grounds before the evergreen woods and trailed in all directions along the carriage drive.

"It's in his mother's eyes," said Pembleton when Daniel came back inside.

"That's not what he said," said Daniel softly. Sundry and Mister Walton were sitting within a quick reach of the man, and Ephram, Eagleton, and Thump stood about looking uncomfortable whenever the wild man's gaze fell upon them.

"Have you got him, Mister Walton?" asked Sundry.

"Yes, I think so," said the bespectacled fellow.

Sundry went to the door, where Daniel stood, and asked quietly, "What was it that the old fellow *did* say?"

Daniel turned into the hall, and Sundry followed him. "He said, 'He'll see it in his mother's eyes.'"

"There was something else, wasn't there?" wondered Sundry. He wanted a rendering of the man's exact words.

"Yes," said Daniel, "'If he's as big a man as I am—' he said, 'the boy, that is—he will see where it's been put, in his mother's eyes.'"

Sundry went into the front room, and Daniel followed him. The young man looked about the room and pulled a frown; then he took the portrait of the lovely Nell Linnett from the couch. "Something else that you said has put me to thinking," he told Daniel.

Daniel smiled. From recent experience he had grown to respect Sundry's process of thought, and it pleased him to see the young man at work like Sergeant Cuff.

Sundry brought the portrait to the mantel and after a try or two hung it by its wire to the hanger on the wall. "I remember your telling us about the day Miss Linnett's grandfather was in here, looking at her picture—"

"Yes?"

"And how you caught the reflection of Pembleton—you think of him as Penfen, of course—in the glass before the portrait."

"I did."

"Was Mr. Linnett very much taller than I?" wondered Sundry.

"I wouldn't say," said Daniel, intrigued.

"And he was standing?" continued Sundry.

As best he could remember, Daniel expressed to the young man where old Ian Linnett had been standing that day.

"Here then," said Sundry. He considered the portrait above the mantel. "Do you know what I can see when I look at her picture, when I look at her eyes?"

Daniel stepped up beside Sundry and craned his head a little to make up for the few inches' difference in height. "What are you looking at?" he asked, feeling the muscles in his back contract with something like alarm.

"I don't think you have to be such a particular height," said Sundry. "It's the picture on the other side of the room."

Daniel let out a stunned "Oh!," then turned on his heel and viewed the tinted photograph of the Linnett tomb directly. He would have discounted such a macabre solution out of hand if the entire affair had not already taken so many twists. "The tomb?" he said, and without thinking, added, "What would *that* mean?"

"Indeed," said Sundry, for he couldn't say for sure, or else didn't like to. He followed the lawyer up to the picture, and they looked more closely at it, as if more clues might be apparent.

The more that Daniel considered the picture, the more certain he was that Sundry had hit upon the answer to Ian Linnett's riddle. Why did such explanations seem so obvious when they were pointed out? "Of course that's what he did," said Daniel aloud, and Sundry nodded, a little ashamed to have pointed out what seemed to be so melancholy a fact.

BOOK EIGHT

Christmas Eve – Christmas Day 1896

61. Through the Kitchen Door

Sundry was conscious of being followed, so when he got to the corner across from the Grand Trunk Station, he ducked into the side street and waited. He hadn't counted three heartbeats before he heard them running, out of breath, and he sensed that they were alarmed to have lost him.

It was growing dark, and lazy flakes of snow drifted between the buildings. Sleighs jingled past, and Sundry could hear carolers on the hill behind him. He was trying to pick out the tune when the first of those following him stepped beyond the corner. Sundry waited, hardly believing his luck when the second one passed by and didn't turn his head. When the third stepped into sight, he was more than suspicious, and just as they turned as one upon him, he let out a shout and threw the snowball he had been saving.

The boys shouted with glee and pelted him in return. Several other pedestrians either laughed as they walked through the flurry of snow or looked dismayed and made a detour around the battle. At a certain point, however, it was clear that victory was in numbers, and Sundry conceded defeat with a laugh and a cry of "Uncle!"

He was still laughing when the half dozen or so boys charged off with a great cheer. *Now if only the members had been with me,* thought Sundry wryly. He might have hired a carriage or a sleigh to come to the railhead, but it was this sort of thing on the Portland streets on Christmas Eve that he didn't want to miss, though his bags were beginning to weigh upon his shoulders.

A sleigh full of strangers trotted by, bells ringing on harnesses, people waving and shouting the best of the season. A cabbie drove by, his tall hat decorated with holly and a red ribbon. Along the wharves the prows of ships were garlanded, and lamps were lit in every cabin window. Sundry was well out of the business district by now, but the store owners had outdone themselves in the art of decoration, and many a business window was marked with the hand and nose prints of children old and young. Carolers strolled everywhere.

An older man stumbled at the edge of the sidewalk and would have lost his small mountain of packages if Sundry had not dashed up and caught several of them (dropping some of his own in the process). He offered his assistance and walked across Commercial Street with the man to the station, whereupon he carefully stacked the bundles in the man's arms and bade him Merry Christmas.

Here the cabbies picked up and dropped their trade and folk waited for late arrivals. A group of boys ran by, chased by a happy barking dog. Sundry could hear singing from inside the station, but his attention was taken by a tall blond man, who seemed to be monitoring his approach.

Sundry tipped his cap to the fellow as he neared him, then slowed his pace as it was obvious the man had something to say.

"Merry Christmas," Sundry said.

"Leaving town won't change matters," said the man. There was the hint of a sneer in his voice and in the movement of his upper lip.

"I don't believe I have . . . the pleasure," said Sundry.

"I do know you, however," said the man. He was a tall, imperious sort of fellow, with curly blond locks and piercing blue eyes.

"Found what you thought you were looking for up on Council Hill, did you?" said Sundry.

The man seemed startled. "As with knowledge, Mr. Moss," he informed, when he had recovered himself, "a *little* cleverness can be a dangerous thing."

"I will bow to your experience in this matter." There was something precariously overwrought about the man, and Sundry glanced about them to see that they were well lighted and not solitary upon the walk. Sundry's previous adversaries were striding past the station, looking for mischief, and he caught the eye of one of these boys. The man was conscious of the little gang as it settled nearby and watched the two men speak.

"You may think that you have outdistanced fate, Moss," said the man, "but there are those who have not forgotten your interference in their affairs." He was visibly shaking now, though whether from anger or some other fight within himself, Sundry could not know. "And you should be more careful whom you befriend. You may tell Mr. Plainway that *I* am not finished with *him*. And you may tell Mr. Covington and his wife that their attempts to preempt the goal of the society have met with disappointment."

"Do you refer to the other rock on Council Hill?" said Sundry, who was surprised but, from the reference to Daniel Plainway, pretty sure he knew who the man was. He felt that a moment of danger had passed, and he was ready to walk away from the man. "The runes your club found there?"

"The runes Covington did *not* find." The blond man turned to leave. "Good-bye, Moss. I doubt that *I* shall see you again, but someone surely will."

"Oh?" The implied threat snapped at Sundry's heart, and he felt a nasty qualm.

"Indeed. Someone will surely see you *and* Mister Walton, though you may not see them." The man gave a sneer over his shoulder, the threat implied very much unveiled in his wolflike expression.

Sundry's brief fright twisted into a flash of anger then, and if he had intended to warn the man about the curse (if indeed he had believed in the curse), the vileness of that expression and the absolute danger of that threat toward Mister Walton stopped the words in his throat.

"Mr. Noble," said Sundry when the man had reached the snowy drive.

The man turned his head, surprised, and considered Sundry; it may have bothered him to see a look of absolute fearlessness on the young man's face.

Sundry stood with his arms crossed before him and said simply, "I have but one thing to say, sir." Sundry glanced to the boys and gave them a brief wave as he stepped around the man to continue his way to the station door.

"Oh?" said Roger Noble, the newest member of the Norumbega Club; his lack of interest dripped from his voice.

Sundry gave a wink and almost a sincere smile. "Tell your friends not to believe everything they read." Sundry swept the boys with a nod. "Gentlemen," he said, which amused them. "Merry Christmas, Mr. Noble," he called back before stepping into the station house. *There*, he thought, *I have done my duty, and it is warning enough. But I was right the first time, and I still* don't *have the pleasure.*

Sundry hadn't intended to go home for Christmas; but Mister Walton had insisted, and Sundry was pretty sure that he wouldn't be needed. Mister

Walton was glad that his young friend and employee would be visiting his family in Edgecomb, but also a little melancholy to be without Sundry's company when his situation with Phileda McCannon seemed so vague.

Sundry seemed cheerful all around, however, when Mister Walton saw him off from his front door at Spruce Street, and the portly fellow did his best to appear jolly as he waved from the stoop.

It was snowing on Christmas Eve, all up and down the coast of Maine. It was dark by four o'clock and absolute night by five. A man with a tin whistle piped up some carols as the train progressed from town to town. Sundry had a bag of brightly wrapped gifts in the seat beside him, and he occasionally prodded through them to recollect what he had gotten for whom.

Wiscasset was wrapped in snow, and the air was filled with flakes that seemed to be blowing up the steep hill of Main Street from the Sheepscott River. The streetlights gave off haloes of descending and swirling points of white and the streets were rutted with the traffic of Christmas Eve. After the train had dropped Sundry and several other people off at the county seat, they could hear singing from above them. A large crowd was gathered on the courthouse lawn, joining in the music of the season. Sundry hired a horse and sleigh, piled his things into the back and covered them up with a blanket. In the brief time it took him to cross the Sheepscott, he and the blanket were covered with a layer of snow.

His family had no idea he would be home for Christmas, and even as he realized how very much he missed them, he grew giddy with imagining their surprise. He wondered if his twin, Varius, would be home.

The ride along the perimeter of Davis Island and down the shoulder of the Boothbay peninsula did not take long, in fact not long enough for Sundry, who was relishing the anticipation of his homecoming. The closer he got, the more acquainted he was with the houses and the more he could guess from the lights in people's windows as he passed. He turned off the main road beneath a knoll, and a quarter of a mile further on he turned again toward the Cross River, where the land descended in a series of fields. He passed one house where a single light burned in a parlor window, then drove through a stand of hardwood and along a stream till he came to a clearing and the dark forms of buildings punctuated by several lighted windows.

He and his horse had been driving almost by instinct till now, but Moss Farm gave off enough light so that he was able to draw them up beside the barn. He heard a low noise from within and thought, *The dogs must be abed.* The only thing that kept him from waking them was the sound of the wind and the sift of the snow, drowning his approach.

The farmhouse stood above him, and he could hear voices. Someone was laughing, one of his younger brothers, he thought. He climbed down and threw the reins over the limb of his mother's plum tree. He picked up the great sack, feeling like St. Nick himself, stealing up to the house.

He paused halfway to the door. He could see, through the panes of the kitchen door, his mother at the sink. She was washing dishes perhaps or preparing some Christmas treat. She was looking at the window before her, out at the darkness or perhaps the reflections of her loved ones. She was smiling. Sundry heard his father's voice, and his mother laughed at something. Snow fell between. There was something about the moment that he did not want to break.

"I'll get it!" he heard someone shout: almost certainly his younger brother Bowdoin on an errand. "I'll get it!" The kitchen door was flung open, and thirteen-year-old Bowdoin came dashing out. He let out a gasp when he was aware of the shadow on the path between the house and the barn and skidded to a halt.

"Boo," said Sundry.

62. Two Mysteries

Daniel Plainway wondered if his life had been made richer for having known Charlotte Burnbrake or inadequate for being without her. It was always with a sharp plunge of the heart that she came to mind, yet that sadness, that longing seemed more like living to him than had the undeviating standard of his previous existence. He had known her for three days, and by way of a single letter that he had with him even now, and it was strange how important she was when viewed alongside his forty-odd years. That he would ever see her again, he knew, was unlikely.

Beneath it all, he was eager to meet the O'Hearns and curious to see the boy once again, anxious to see the living testament to Nell Linnett. It was that anticipation that allowed him to open the envelope containing Dr. Bolster's report, since he expected that whatever was painful in that work was best read now, when the promise of the Linnetts' most important legacy lay ahead of him.

He had asked the doctor to write a statement of what happened on the twenty-third of December 1896, in the cemetery at Hiram, and for several reasons: Of course there were obvious legal issues involved in disturbing a place of interment, but Daniel also wanted the matter on record to discourage future fortune hunters. Most important, he wanted an account that would explain to Bertram Linnett, when he was old enough to understand, what had happened. Daniel himself had been absent.

The long envelope was tied with twine, and Daniel set these aside when he had the papers out. The doctor's hand was meticulous and even handsome, contrary to what is commonly observed in the species, and in the miles between Waldoboro and Rockland, Daniel perused the account, which had the feel of a formal narrative.

On the first page were yesterday's date and the day of the week, which was Wednesday, followed by the sentence *An account of the investigation of the burial tomb of the Linnett family, Hiram, Maine; most specifically, the chamber and casket containing the remains of Eleanor Linnett, who died in the month of April 1892; as witnessed by Sylvanus Arcade Bolster, M.D., of Hiram, and verified by Constable Ralph Haig and Deputy Constable Hiram Pleat of Hiram.*

This seemed enough for the first page and all Daniel had asked for and perhaps more. The account itself began on the following page.

In the months preceding April of 1892, several events led to the birth of one Bertram Willum, known also as Bertram Linnett, and the subsequent death of his mother, Eleanor Linnett, over which circumstances, good and bad, I presided under the eye of God and the Auspices of His Will.

Daniel Plainway, a lawyer of Hiram, was also present at the mother's death, and being an adviser and friend of the Linnett family, he continued to observe the progress of the boy. It will be for others to make account of the events that followed this child's birth, but important to this narrative is the evidence that Bertram's legacy is largely involved in a small cache of precious gems and that his great-grandfather Ian Linnett, since deceased, has hidden them from the common knowledge of men.

In this meticulous style, the situation and evidence that led Dr. Bolster, the constable, and his deputy to the Linnett tomb were laid out, and the approach to the cemetery was described.

The party above mentioned, as well as Mister Tobias Walton of Portland and Mr. Sundry Moss of Edgecomb, whose own recent stories have been entwined with Bertram's, arrived at the Hiram Cemetery, where an uncommon depth of snow, for December, blanketed the grounds and made walking between the stones somewhat difficult. A shovel was brought to clear the way to the Linnett tomb, and the cemetery keeper, George Oakum, unlocked the door. Messrs. Walton and Moss stood at some distance away, filling the office of seconds, in case there arose the need of further work or corroboration.

The darkness and expected cold touched us as we paused upon the threshold of that resting place, in which stone walls the remains of several men and women await the last trumpet. Mr. Oakum waited at the head of the stairs while we three pressed forward with the proper tools and lanterns.

We first made a thorough and exhaustive search of the area around the niches and the central dais upon which stood the casket of Eleanor Linnett. Against hope, we did not find what we looked for, and so the decision was made to move to the next stage of our search. We were surprised to find how easily the lid of the coffin was lifted, and it became obvious to us that it had been lifted since the young woman's burial.

As a doctor Bolster took some interest in what they found there, and though Daniel passed over this section of the narrative, he caught the gist of the doctor's continued surprise when the *mortal remains of Eleanor Linnett offered no sign that she had passed from this sphere more than four years before.*

Her loveliness was undimmed, and had I not known her in life I would have still believed whatever good and sweet that was said of her. There was a look of potent peace upon her brow, and even the constable was moved near to tears.

Beneath her folded hands there appeared a small painted box of about six inches long, by four inches wide, by three inches deep, and the other two men left it to me to slip it gently from beneath her lovely fingers. Upon inspection, a catch was discovered, and with the lid raised, the gems representing the last wealth of the Linnett estate were revealed. A quick scrutiny of the inside of the casket provided no other anomaly, and the only piece of jewelry left with the mortal remains was a small chain that was held between the hands and from which depended a tiny silver cross.

The work had taken the better part of an hour, the final stage of which gave us the labor of no more than ten or twelve minutes. With renewed sorrow for the lovely Eleanor Linnett, we resealed the casket, and Mr. Oakum locked the tomb behind us.

We stepped into the snow outside the Linnett tomb and were very glad to see Mister Walton and Mr. Moss, as if they were come from the land of the living to retrieve us and bring us with them back across the river. They were amazed, but very sober, when we showed to them what we had found. . . .

Daniel tried not to think about it, but he found the image of Ian Linnett visiting the tomb of his granddaughter difficult to shake. Had he gone there only the once, or had the gems been brought to her, like offerings, as Daniel delivered them to the old man?

What had Ian been thinking? Perhaps it had been a form of penance for his pride and his anger to place the worth of everything he had ever worked for and loved beneath her still hands. Like some last adherent to the customs of ancient civilization, he had sent her on her journey with the fare to take her wherever she might care to be.

Daniel changed trains in Brunswick, and at Rockland he took a steamer to Bucksport, where he picked up a third train after dark. All the while he felt a growing awkwardness about his destination; he knew that there might be little to say to the O'Hearns, that it would be as awkward for them to host a stranger on Christmas Eve, yet his sister had insisted that he go, and here he was, two or three miles outside Bangor and perhaps only three-quarters of an hour from the station at Veazie.

There was a great deal of cheer in the car, people boarding and leaving would wish Merry Christmas to all, and many miles had been taken up with one carol or another or a good tale being told. Daniel found himself easily distracted, however, and he made a game of enumerating the events he had experienced with Miss Burnbrake, as if he were recalling the chapter headings of a favorite book.

When he recalled the evening spent with the five elderly sisters, he was reminded of the locked door and of his letter to Mr. Edward Grimb, the ladies' attorney, and this—very naturally—led to his recalling the letter from Mr. Grimb that lay unopened in his coat pocket. He had received it that day by post but had been so concerned with packing and wrapping presents that he stuffed it in his pocket and promptly forgot about it.

He couldn't find the letter at first but eventually had the envelope before him. It looked like a typical bit of business, from one lawyer to another, and he wondered that Mr. Grimb might simply request that Mr. Plainway respectfully mind his own business. When he opened the letter, however, he found it of a completely different, if formal and old-fashioned, tone.

Dear Mr. Plainway,

I received your query of the 15th and very much esteem the measure of your concern as well as the extent of your discretion. The locked door at the estate in question represents a conundrum for this writer, and if you in your wisdom can comprehend a better plan concerning it, I would be obliged for your instructions.

The deceased, whose daughters now reside at the house, was a man of importance in both the world of trade and politics, but more important, he was a man who doted upon his wife when she was alive and whose grief was plain and painful to his friends when she died.

Two or three years after his wife's passing, the husband began to spend more time away from home, and the bills that I handled for him ranged between the cities of Bangor, Portland, and Boston. These were mostly hotel accounts, however, and I thought little of them till the man himself had passed away.

When I came to the house upon his death, the man's personal effects were given over to me till the will was read, and in a cursory tour of the estate, I was puzzled when the sisters told me of the locked door. Having on my person the father's keys, I inspected the room and was astonished and dismayed by what I found there.

It seems that the father, in the well of his loneliness following the death of his wife, had developed an extraordinary fixation upon a certain actress who was at least fifty years younger than himself and who divided her time between the stages of the aforementioned cities. The room was a shrine to this personage: Her portraits covered the walls, newspapers praising her powers and charms filled several notebooks, and one table-top was covered with playbills. Wreaths of dried flowers adorned the room, and I was driven into a fit of sneezing by the overpowering per-fume that permeated the room's atmosphere.

You can be sure that when I left the room I locked the door again and that I extended the sisters' banishment from the chamber while I weighed the situation. It seemed cruel to reveal the secret of their father's last years to his daughters; they are so devoted to the picture of their parents as singularly constant to one another, which (I repeat) was the case while they both lived.

I considered hiring someone to remove the articles of their father's obsession, but it would have been difficult to get all five of the sisters out of the house, and in our tightly knit community I feared that word about what had come out of that room would eventually return to these inno-cent women.

What I did discover, during the weeks while I honestly dithered about the situation, was that the sisters seemed enlivened by the idea of the locked room's mystery and indeed honored to be guarding their father's secret, even if they did not know what it was. In short, I decided to leave things as they were, and from the tenor of your letter, I think you will understand this resolution.

I thank you, on behalf of my clients, for your unselfish concern and for the trouble you have already taken in their regard. I am sure I shall hear about your visit the next time I drop by to see them. Again, if you see the opportunity for another solution, please feel free to advise me.

With all due thanks and regard,
Edward Grimb, Esq.

Thoughts of the five sisters made Daniel smile, and the letter itself gave him an unexpected level of contentment, since it presented an excuse to pen Miss Burnbrake. He knew that the mystery of the locked door had been of great interest to her, and he believed in her discretion as much as he wanted a reason to communicate to her. He thought he might begin the letter now, but decided instead that he should be preparing himself for his meeting with the O'Hearns and little Bertram Linnett.

Crossing the river and making the stages through Bangor took less time than he had imagined, and he felt he was mentally scrambling to be ready when the station at the head of the conductor's litany was Veazie.

The train had been surging through light snow since leaving Bucksport, and as they braked into the Veazie station, Daniel looked out his window to an idealized picture of Christmas Eve as the lights of the buildings glowed through the falling snow and the few vehicles waiting for passengers were decked out in bells and greenery. Daniel caught the glimpse of a tall man and a small boy standing together by a team of horses and a sleigh, and he craned his head to one side to keep them in sight, but the corner of the station fell between them.

"Merry Christmas, sir," said the conductor when Daniel stepped down from the train. The fellow touched his hat.

"Merry Christmas," returned Daniel.

"Visiting family?" asked the conductor with unfeigned interest.

Daniel hesitated, then said, "Yes, in a manner of speaking."

Further good wishes were traded as Daniel gained purchase upon his bags and wandered uncertainly toward the station.

They were there then, the tall man and the boy, watching for someone, and Daniel gave a reverse nod that they marked.

"Mr. Plainway?" said the man; he was, as advertised, a large redheaded fellow with a broad, pleasant face. He held his left hand stiffly toward Daniel, and Daniel took it carefully, remembering that the man was still recovering from a terrible bullet wound. "Wyckford O'Hearn," said the man. Then he directed Daniel's attention to the wide-eyed brown-haired little boy who stood beneath his protecting arm. "This is Bird, whom I think you have met."

Daniel stood amazed. Eleanor Linnett's four-and-a-half-year-old son stretched out his small hand and raised to the lawyer a pair of clear, serious eyes. He had some of the robust carriage of his ne'er-do-well father, Asher, and Daniel could see how the child was recognized as Nell's son, but he was most struck by how much the boy looked like his uncle; it was as if by some accident of Asher's, by some act of will on the part of Eleanor, and by the singular grace of God, Jeram Willum had been given a renewed destiny among them. Daniel was filled with gratitude to see something of that brave young man before him, and as he took the boy's hand, he lowered his head, ashamed at the tears that coursed down his face.

He had not realized what an odyssey of the heart he had experienced, and if his hopes and fears had not traveled a mythic twenty years, they had ranged through at least as many dangers of the imagination.

Of course, he thought, *I've thought of him all along as Bertram Linnett when he's the very Willum that Ian thought might someday make good, though here he is a hundred years before the old man would have predicted it.* "Bird," he said quietly. The little boy looked concerned for the distress in Daniel's face, and the man braved a smile through his tears. *If Nell did not know why she did what she did,* he thought, *perhaps God Himself has given her a reason.*

Daniel took a breath and lifted his head. "I am so glad that you have such a wonderful family now," he said to the little boy, and to Wyck he said, "I am so grateful."

63. Hat in the Ring

"Where'd you get a fine hat like that, Henry?" wondered Minnie Weitenkarl. She folded her round forearms on the bar and fixed an all-encompassing smile on Henry Hamblin; Minnie was pleasant to all the young men who patronized the Weary Sailor.

Henry lowered the tankard from his lips and brushed the foam away with the back of his hand. "It's my good-luck hat, dear," he said. He had garnered many a compliment since trading Doc Brine a dozen oranges for the homburg.

One wouldn't have guessed that since 1851 there was a standing law against the sale and consumption of liquor in the state of Maine. The tavern at the sign of the Weary Sailor was fit to burst this Christmas Eve, and Henry had to drink standing up. Behind him a dozen men were singing

"Silent Night" at the top of their lungs and giving a fair imitation of a cat fight.

"You look like someone important," admitted Minnie through the noise. Leaning against the counter on her forearms, the cut of her holiday blouse was conducive to some interested stares, and she leveled her own bright blue eyes on several men at the bar, each of whom suddenly found great fascination in Henry's new hat.

"Good luck, is it, boy?" said one old salt.

"I wore it tonight," informed Henry, "and my girl said she'd marry me."

The level of noise in the immediate vicinity rose at this news, and two or three patrons who actually knew the young lady in question were quick to sing her praises. Minnie, rather paradoxically, made this the occasion to call Henry up to the bar and give him a large kiss. One grizzled old man stood from his stool and maintained that he had been engaged several times that day himself, whereupon Minnie threw a wet bar cloth at him and he fell over.

Another tankard was thrust into Henry's grasp, and his health was cheered. A good portion of the tavern's population had no idea what this new celebration meant, but they joined in with a roar. The singers had stumbled over the third verse of their song, so they returned to the first, declaring that "all is calm, all is bright," in the midst of this uproar.

"I thought I'd see Tommy in here tonight," said Henry to Minnie.

The woman pointed to the back of the room, where several backs were huddled over a card table. "I hope his luck has changed or he's learned something about the game," she said.

Henry had a bad feeling about this, and with a nod, he left the barside to thread his way through the tables. His cousin Tommy had been seen more and more at the cards these days, and he'd already forfeited wages he had yet to earn to Colin Kinross, who was the sharp here at the Weary Sailor.

Colin was sharp in every sense of the word: the way he dressed, the way he walked, the way he looked at you over his cigar. He was a good-looking man, tall and strongly built, but not particularly likable. He concentrated his powers and his energies on making money without the appearance of spending either his powers or his energies. He was good at his chosen pro-fession—that is, gambling—like a magician really, and not the least of his talents was the ability to draw victims into his range without once pretending to be anything but what he was. Henry was a little afraid of him.

Tommy was afraid of Colin as well, the way a moth fears the flame, and Henry could almost hear his cousin's heart beating as he stepped up behind him. Two or three pairs of eyes recognized Henry, but Colin never looked up.

"How long do you intend to work over at the rope factory?" Colin was saying evenly.

"I've got a good position there, Colin," Tommy replied, his voice shaking. "I'd be a fool to leave now, when I'm so close to running the floor."

Henry felt his stomach fall to hear Tommy lie. There was a large pot in the center of the table, and at least one player's hand was already folded.

"You'd be foolish," agreed Colin, "considering you owe me the next three months of your life."

"You've been real understanding, Colin."

Kinross was unimpressed with the praise. "It's funny, though, Tommy," he drawled, "Eddy here thought he saw you over to Sawtooth Sally's just this afternoon. Didn't you, Eddy?"

Eddy shrugged.

"They must close the rope factory on Christmas Eve, I guess," said Colin. "Is that what they do, Tommy?"

"Some of us got some time off," Tommy began. "For the holiday, you know."

"They really like you up there," said Colin.

Everyone within hearing knew what was up and where it was going. Henry wondered if he could pull Tommy away from the table before Colin lived up to his reputation for deadly speed with a knife. He'd seen a man who had purportedly been cut by Colin Kinross, and the recollection froze in Henry's blood.

"I had the impression," came Kinross's quiet, smooth tone, "where the rope trade is slow in winter, that maybe you'd been let go."

"I'll get the job back in the spring," said Tommy, barely loud enough to be heard.

"And here you are trying to earn your debt back from me, and losing to boot."

"What's he owe?" said Henry. His head was reeling with the two beers he had thrown down so quickly.

"Sixty-seven dollars and thirty-five cents," said Colin Kinross as if he had a ledger opened before him. The man did not look up from the table and otherwise did not acknowledge Henry's presence.

"What are you doing, Tommy?" said Henry.

Tommy looked as if he was most distressed to have his cousin there to see his predicament. "It's all right, Henry," he said, hardly daring to look away from Colin.

"I am glad to hear you say it," said Kinross, and there was such a note of hazard in the man's voice that talk at several tables nearby came to a halt.

"Mr. Kinross," said Henry, his normally jovial air shaken by pounding nerves, "I'll stand for Tommy on this one and promise you'll get your money, and he won't be back to the table—"

"Do you have sixty-seven dollars and thirty-five cents?"

Henry didn't. The most of his money was tied up in capital at the store and he had a wedding to be thinking about and a wife after that. "I don't," he admitted.

Colin Kinross raised his head for the first time and locked a pair of dark eyes on Henry. "I'm not sure what you're promising then."

Henry tried to speak. A hush spread throughout the tavern like a visible thing, touching one table after another and freezing their inhabitants in attitudes of interest and apprehension. Henry's voice was working, but his mind wasn't providing the necessary words.

"It's all right, Henry," said Tommy again, but with the voice that a man might use to comfort his loved ones on his way to the gallows.

"There must be a way of making this right, Mr. Kinross."

"Do you think?"

Henry nodded. It was simply a test of how badly Kinross wanted to punish Tommy.

"What day is it?" said Kinross to Eddy, who sat to his immediate right.

"It's Christmas Eve, Colin," said Eddy. He was considering the cards in his hand.

Tommy flinched as Kinross's arms came up from the table, but the man was only putting his hand behind his head in an attitude of repose. He leaned back in his chair and looked at Henry carefully for the first time. "Where'd you get that hat?" he asked.

Henry felt more afraid than ever to have the man's attention turned solely on him. "Took it in trade," he said.

"That's a nice hat," said Kinross. "Isn't that a nice hat, Eddy?"

Eddy thought it was a nice hat.

"It seems to me that Tommy here doesn't belong at the table," pronounced Kinross. "Wouldn't you say, sir?"

Henry nodded, but barely.

"Tommy?"

"Yes, Colin?"

"Wouldn't you say?"

"Yeah, Colin, I'm not good at this."

"I tell you what, seeing as this is Christmas Eve, and I do one good deed on Christmas Eve, I'm going to let Tommy go clear on the whole deal."

"Oh, Colin, thanks!" blurted Tommy. He was in tears now, and he didn't know whether to sit or dart away.

"It's decent of you, Mr. Kinross," said Henry.

"But!" said the man, and he let this single syllable hover in the air before adding, "I want that hat."

Henry reached up and touched the brim of the homburg. He took it from his head and considered it, thinking: *My lucky hat*, then: *Of course! What better luck could it bring than this?* He held the hat out over the table, but Colin Kinross did not reach for it, so that Henry was obliged to lay it upon the mound of money and chits in the center of the table.

"Don't let me catch you gambling again, Tommy," said Kinross, who'd returned to his cards. The smoke from his cigar greatly obscured his face. The other players returned to the game as if nothing had happened. "With anyone," came the sharp's voice as Henry led Tommy away from the table. The room was coming alive again. The band of men by the bar, pleased with their rendition of "Silent Night," tucked into "Hark the Herald Angels."

"Merry Christmas, Mr. Kinross," said Henry over his shoulder, but he thought the good wishes were lost in the sudden noise.

64. Confession in a Christmas Kitchen

From the dark end of the wharf district to the grand houses overlooking Deering Oaks and the humbler homes of laborers and craftsmen on Munjoy Hill, the city of Portland knew how to keep Christmas. A light snow fell among the streetlamps and brightened houses, and song and celebration might be heard as a person drifted along the sidewalks.

Henry and Tommy went to Tommy's mother's for a cup of eggnog and a bowl of oyster stew, and Henry deliberately swung the conversation away from recent events at the Weary Sailor, reminiscing on the Christmases of their youth and marveling about his fiancée. Tommy promised to purchase his cousin a new hat.

Along the way they passed Mrs. Plaint's boardinghouse, where Gemma Pool's little boy, Jeremy, was sleeping peacefully. Gemma was up late; she had unraveled an old sweater and had been knitting the yarn back into a hat and scarf for Doc Brine, who she was sure had saved her son's life. The old salt who lived across the way had carved a whale from a stray piece of wood and given it to her boy that evening, and the crudely fashioned beast was even now clutched in Jeremy's sleeping hands.

Not far away Doc Brine was laying hands on the bay mare at Sporrin's Livery. The animal nickered quietly in her stall, and Doc was satisfied that she was on the mend. The owner had pressed on Doc Brine a twenty-dollar gold piece that seemed to Doc all out of proportion to what he had accomplished. Doc considered a visit to the Weary Sailor or the Crooked Cat, but his second thought was that winter had just begun and Jeremy Pool and his mother would run out of oranges and good food quick enough. He pocketed the coin and went home in the snow, a little worse for wear. The shakes were visiting him again, but he whistled as he moved down the sidewalk. Pearly Sporrin called a "Happy Christmas" after him.

Just up a side street Lincoln N. Washington lay in a clean bed at a boardinghouse. He'd paid his room in advance from some of the money he'd been given by the men he'd attempted to rob. The next day he had tossed the pistol overboard and gone to the Thump and Chaine Atlantic Corridor Shipping Firm with the card that one of the men had given him. He'd been put to work in a back room immediately. That night he had a dream about his mother.

Gemma Pool looked up when she heard Doc Brine come in the front door and climb the stairs. She hoped she could finish the hat before morning.

Henry and Tommy filled up on eggnog and oyster stew and got laughing, telling stories of childhood pranks. Tommy cried he laughed so hard or perhaps simply because he wasn't a child anymore.

Through the snow, through the music and good wishes, climbing from the wharf district to the higher elevation of Spruce Street, one would pass all manner of happiness and sorrow, but the city of Portland knew how to keep Christmas, and no more so than in the brick Federal-style house on this avenue. The songs were loud and clear in the parlor of the Walton home; Matthew Ephram, Christopher Eagleton, and Joseph Thump blended their voices as though they didn't belong to separate churches.

Charlotte Burnbrake played the piano while her uncle Ezra and Mr. and Mrs. Baffin and Mister Walton listened with pleasure to the hearty words and bouncing melody of "Good King Wenceslas." When the final notes died together, there was applause and delighted laughter. Ephram, Eagleton, and Thump looked everywhere but at their audience: at the ceiling, at the fir tree, at the piano legs. Their faces reddened, and their chests swelled a bit.

A sudden gust drifted snow against a window in the near silence that followed. It was like someone tapping to be let in, and though he knew it was only the storm, Mister Walton pulled the curtain aside and peered out.

He was sincerely pleased with the gathering; the season suited him, and he beamed with its spirit, though the joy of the holiday passed through him without entirely leaving a trace upon his own heart.

"I miss Sundry," said Mrs. Baffin, who knew what was foremost in Toby's mind.

"Yes," agreed Mister Walton. "I trust he is having a nice evening with his family." How grateful he was for these friends, and how wise he thought himself to have met such fellows—such men of simple kindness—as Ephram, Eagleton, and Thump. He missed his family, of course, all of whom were gone before, save for a sister, who (the last he knew) was in Africa with her missionary husband and who would have delighted in this company. He had never spent a Christmas within these walls without someone of the same name and blood.

He did miss Sundry too, but Sundry was coming back. There was another, of whose attention he could not be so confident. He wondered—a little hurt, and not for the first time—that Miss McCannon could not have postponed her work at her aunt's house in Orland. Over the past weeks he had chided himself for his clumsiness, for he was sure that some blunder on his part had kept her away, and coupled with Charleston Thistlecoat's manifest interest in Phileda, his own inexpert courtship gave him little hope of a happy outcome.

There was a renewed round of hems and haws as the members of the club deliberated with Miss Burnbrake on the next selection. "God Rest Ye Merry, Gentlemen" was decided upon, and there was some tugging at vests and straightening of collars as the three friends prepared to do justice to this enthusiastic song.

"Is that a carriage pulling up?" wondered Mister Walton. The curtain had not fallen back into place, and he caught the shadow of a cab and horse slowing before the house.

The song was stalled before it began, and it was Miss Burnbrake's turn to smile from the piano stool.

"Do you know," Eagleton was saying to her, "that I met a gentleman last October who has nothing but piano stools about his dining room table?"

"Yes," said Mister Walton, who had his face close to the glass. "The driver is getting down." He was pleased with the idea of unexpected guests on Christmas Eve and recalled that the Covingtons had intimated that they might stop by.

"They may be adjusted for anybody's height," Eagleton explained.

Mister Walton excused himself and hurried from the parlor. In the hall he opened the great front door and peered into the night.

The storm had increased, and the trees and bushes were white; the sidewalk had accumulated a layer of frost and down. The streetlight at the nearby corner dazzled through the falling snow. Mister Walton heard her first, before his eyes adjusted to the dark. Then she was hurrying up the steps with a man behind who was loaded with packages.

"Phileda," he said, almost in a whisper.

Her smile inhabited every corner of her face, but most especially the little lines around her eyes that Mister Walton had come to love so dearly. He half expected she might embrace him again, then startling himself with the thought and the fear of presumption, he stiffened himself and raised a hand to shake hers.

But she stepped through his guard to embrace him, and the packages she was carrying tumbled all about them. The man behind her made a low sound and turned his back, discreetly, to consider the snowy night.

In Phileda's purse was a letter from Sundry Moss, wishing her a Merry Christmas and hoping, just by the way, that Mister Walton wouldn't be lonely on Christmas Eve without the normal quota of friends about him and its being his first Christmas in his family home without family.

Phileda had known of course what Sundry meant—one couldn't even say that he had been *hinting*. She was frustrated with Toby's overcautious manner of courtship, however unfairly, and a little frightened by Charleston's lack of caution. Her instinct was to retreat, yet she was first and foremost Toby's friend. If there were any danger of his feeling lonely on Christmas Eve, she would add whatever solace she could. Her cousin could wait for her in Orland.

Interestingly enough, Charlotte Burnbrake had in her own purse a letter with similar handwriting, wishing her and her uncle a Merry Christmas and mentioning, just by the way, that the writer was concerned for Mr. Plainway, whose recent melancholy experiences must necessarily weigh upon him when he took leave of the O'Hearns on Christmas Day and conclusively left Eleanor Linnett's child behind. The trip home to Hiram would perhaps be long. Charlotte had been thinking about her mother as of late.

For a man who could be so subtle, it would be said later, Sundry Moss was a master of frankness.

Christmas punch of a legal variety was raised in toasts in the parlor, which was bursting with people by now. Phileda and Miss Burnbrake played together at the piano and laughed whenever they found themselves at cross-purposes. Enchanted, Ephram, Eagleton, and Thump stood back and admired the ladies.

From his chair Mister Walton had the opportunity to watch Phileda unbeknownst, and a thrill ran through him as something very exposed and vulnerable showed upon his face. She turned unexpectedly and caught his abashed gaze, the light of her smile not subsiding. When the toast was over and she had finished her glass, she rose and advanced upon him with an expression of serious intent.

"I am pleased that you are enjoying yourself," he said, shaken to be caught watching her with such obvious interest.

"*I* am pleased to be enjoying myself, myself," she replied with all due wryness. Miss Burnbrake was just then watching them discreetly, but with a smile.

"May I get you something more to drink?" wondered Mister Walton, who felt, in Miss McCannon's company, cast adrift from his usually adroit abilities.

"Something warm would be nice," she said, meaning that he must go to the kitchen and heat the teapot. But when he excused himself, she took his arm and went with him.

If Mister Walton had possessed more hair upon his head, he might have felt it lifting with pleasant apprehension. The walk to the kitchen seemed to take longer than it should, and during the journey Phileda did nothing to help his state of mind, choosing only to answer his questions and remarks with wordless concurrence or disagreement.

Once in the kitchen, he found comfort in activity, busying himself with the teapot and the stove. He offered her a chair, but she chose to stand with her back to the Hoosier cabinet on the other side of the room. She looked very puckish, with her pursed lips and humor-filled eyes.

"It is an extraordinary thought I just had," said Mister Walton as he paused over the stove with the teapot. "Save for the Baffins, there isn't a person in the next room whom I knew before last July!" Then he turned to consider Miss McCannon. "Or even yourself, now that I consider it."

"It just *seems* that we have known certain people all our lives," she said.

"I can hardly remember a time when I *didn't* know Sundry," he answered. "Mr. Ephram, Mr. Eagleton, and Mr. Thump are like my oldest friends. And yourself . . ." His voice trailed off.

"Am I like an old friend, Toby?" she asked mischievously.

"Yes," he said frankly, "though I am ever conscious of all the years that I *did* not know you."

"I understand you all too well," she admitted, her humor having evolved into something less conscious, something more graceful and dreamlike. "You might not have thought much of me when I was young," she said, the most fragile hint of near-forgotten pain coloring her voice.

"I can't imagine it," he said. He was thinking that *he* had been something of a blockhead as a young man and fell to wondering if in the intervening years he had changed all that much. "You must have always had friends," he added.

"I have been blessed all my life with fine people," she said, "my family included," but there was, in her acknowledgment, the implication that this perhaps was not quite enough.

"You have your admirers, certainly," he continued.

"Do I?" she asked, her impishness returning.

Mister Walton found his tongue advancing before thought. "Certainly Mr. Thistlecoat could be counted among them."

The opinion sounded like the clunk of a leaden weight in the charged atmosphere, and Mister Walton perceived that a level of jealousy had both disarmed and betrayed him.

"Do you *think* he admires me?" she asked.

Charleston Thistlecoat was the last person Mister Walton wanted to be discussing while he and Phileda had a few minutes alone, yet he must answer. "Yes," he said, feeling stupid and regretful. "It seemed to me."

She didn't know why she let herself wax indignant at this, but she said, "Perhaps it is true, for he's asked me to marry him."

"Oh," was all he had the power to say in the wake of this intelligence.

Phileda in turn watched him, almost without expression; what emotion there was in her face was unreadable. Her bright eyes flashed enigmatically behind her round spectacles. Mister Walton was uncomfortably conscious of the soft place at the base of her throat. Her neck was long and lovely; her chin was up.

"Oh," he said again. He made another, less articulate noise and looked down at the floor. He fiddled with his spectacles. With his head down, he was in the metaphorical position to bull forward, unmindful of the danger to his heart and his dignity. "I must confess," he began, "that I had hoped for some opportunity to—to pursue"—he was attempting to find the euphemism that would sound like friendship and hint at something more—"to pursue—" His voice drifted to silence. He had no words.

Then she said, "You don't imagine that I said yes, do you?"

His head came up, his eyes wide. "You didn't?"

She seemed to think this was a silly question.

"He *is* an accomplished gentleman," said Mister Walton absently.

"Do you think so? He would be obliged to you for helping him press his suit."

Mister Walton felt his heart lurch. "Phileda!" he said, with every suggestion in his voice that he had more to say, though with absolutely nothing in thought or voice to follow her name on his lips.

"Am I very mysterious?" she asked finally. Her pique had dissipated, and she could only remember how she had missed him these past two weeks.

He was laughing softly, looking down at the floor again.

"I should like to be thought mysterious," she said lightly.

Still, he had no voice.

"I am quite jealous of your adventures," she continued, "and think I must be made a member of your club so that the next time you run off to rescue someone, I can come along with you."

"Do you think?" he said. "I mean, Phileda—my thought was, I mean, my heart—" He took a breath and started again. His face was crowded, and his eyes clouded with emotion. "I hadn't imagined that I'd—or that *you'd* known me long enough—" He looked across the kitchen at Phileda, and she was determined to be absolutely no help to him. He could not read her expression. "I think," he said, "no—I *do* love you, Phileda."

Neither of them moved; neither breathed, the space between them bonded by a whip of electricity. Mister Walton was astounded to see one lone tear course its way down the plane of her right cheek.

"Well, Toby," she said rather breathlessly, "that is something that Mr. Thistlecoat did *not* offer."

"I have been thinking of Miss Simpson," said Eagleton. He was *often* thinking of the young woman (Ophelia was her Christian name) whom he had met only the once, the previous July.

"Have you?" said Ephram. They were admiring the fir tree in Mister Walton's parlor. "I was thinking of Miss Riverille," he added, "so our thoughts are not so far apart." Sallie Riverille was a best friend to Ophelia Simpson, but Ephram had been fortunate enough to see Miss Riverille as recently as October.

"'Think pleasant thoughts,'" said Eagleton. "I had an aunt who said that to me."

"Very wise," said Ephram.

"I think we are safe to say we follow her directive."

"I think you are correct." It was wonderful how often they were of a mind. They smiled at the room. "Thump?" said Ephram.

"Hmm?" Thump seemed to be lost in contemplation. He had someone on his mind as well but was perhaps more melancholy in the memory.

"'Think pleasant thoughts,' Eagleton says."

"My aunt," said Eagleton, giving credit where credit was due.

"Ah, yes." He didn't know Eagleton's aunt, but it was Christmas, and he was sure he could think pleasantly about her.

"I believe the punch has made me thirsty," said Thump. "Perhaps Mister Walton wouldn't mind if I found myself some water."

"I am sure he wouldn't," said Ephram. "Eagleton?"

"I believe our friend is right, Thump."

Thump nodded; he put his head in the direction of the hall and walked to the back of the house and the kitchen. As it happened, he took a fall at the kitchen threshold, not unlike that which he had taken at the Shipswood the night the Covingtons had had dinner with them. He'd never before seen anyone kissed in a kitchen.

65. Lightly I Toss My Hat Away

As midnight neared, triumphed, and passed, the noise never diminished at the sign of the Weary Sailor. An extraordinary chorus of several carols, sung at cross-purposes, confused the ear, and the fumes of beer and rum befuddled the mind. Harvey Shorthind performed a jig on a table to the accompaniment of a fiddle and uilleann pipes, and St. Nick arrived to great cheers. Minnie caught the bearded fellow beneath the mistletoe and kissed him for good luck.

At the back of the room Colin Kinross lifted his head, as if only now realizing where he was. He was used to quieter surroundings when the game grew serious and the players had been whittled down to a single table and the moneyed few. To the surprise of the other participants, he gathered in his winnings and retrieved the homburg from the back of his chair.

"Calling it already?" wondered one of the men at the table.

Colin did not reply. Some deed or feat at the other end of the room brought a roar from the crowd. He put the newly acquired hat on his head for the first time and was pleased to find that it fitted him perfectly.

"That's a fine hat," said somebody.

"What do you plan to do with it?" asked Eddy.

"What do *you* do with a hat?" returned Colin, but never waited for a reply. He threw his coat over his shoulders and snatched up the hat he had worn into the Weary Sailor. The crowd parted for him as he made his way to the door.

"Merry Christmas, Colin!" shouted someone. Again he did not respond but stepped out into the winter night and weighed upon the moon, which, diminished to its last quarter, floated a degree or so above the house across the way.

Alone, Colin Kinross moved west down Madison Street, and he had not gone very far before he was almost startled by a figure standing beneath an oak in the yard of a boardinghouse. It was not the presence of the form but its inhuman silence, and as he drew near to the figure, he realized that it was also a cold silence.

Colin stood for a bit and considered the stony eyes and the frozen mouth, the odd red nose. The stick arms were pitiful and thin compared with the rounded abundance of the white body. The cardsharp peered up at the darkened windows of the boardinghouse and wondered what humble dreams of Christmas played therein.

He laid his old hat on the cold pate, then stopped, his arm outstretched, his hand still gripping the crown. He could hear the sound of revelry even here, though the Weary Sailor was gone from his line of sight. A lonely breeze wandered among the bare branches of the oak.

The gambler made a strange low sound, almost a laugh, and he took back his old hat and laid upon the snowman's head the newly acquired homburg. There wasn't a better-decked-out snowman in the city, he was sure. He thought of the kids when they came down and found such a fine bit of headgear decorating their frosty companion. He brushed the snow from the band of his own hat. He settled the hat on his head and walked back to the street.

Soon the snowman was alone again, if better dressed.

The children who had made him, however, would never see the hat, as a wind came up with the morning and took the homburg from its cold resting place and danced it down the street in fits and starts, till it reached Anderson Street, where a contrary current took it up like a kite.

66. Spheres in Transit

Look at you, thought Daniel Plainway. He sat on the edge of the bed and watched the little boy sleep as he pulled on his shoes. Christmas morning shone through the windows, cold and clear, the night's snow dusting the roofs and surfaces of the O'Hearn farm.

The boy stirred in his sleep, and Daniel wondered if you could wake somebody by watching him. He had been given Wyck's bed and had slept, against his own expectations, like a child himself. There had been something exhausting about the evening, though the O'Hearns couldn't have made him feel more at home and though he had reached a satisfying end to an otherwise tragic business.

In fact, Bird (Daniel had begun to think of the boy as Bird) was that satisfying end, and the lawyer sat on the edge of the bed and watched the child stir so that he might revel a little bit in something so unexpected and fortunate.

How will he think of himself? Daniel wondered. *Will he be Bird or Bertram? A Linnett, a Willum, or an O'Hearn perhaps?*

The sound of pots on a stove rang from the kitchen below. Bird's eyes came open, and Daniel watched him watch the ceiling. The little boy frowned slightly and fished around beneath the covers till he produced a figure of yarn and scrap cloth that was supposed to represent a cat. Bird then realized that Daniel was there, and he sat up.

"Merry Christmas," said Daniel.

"Merry Christmas," said the child. Life at the O'Hearn farm might still seem a little unreal for Bird, after growing from one to four years in the ragged company of Eustace Pembleton, and certainly he did not know what to think or expect of Christmas Day. He caught sight of the stocking at the foot of his bed and leaned near it cautiously.

"St. Nick's been here," said Daniel.

Bird's mouth hung open in astonishment. Daniel had delighted in adding some items to the stocking the night before and been pleased and warmed at the generous offerings from the other adults in the house, particularly Wyck's brother-in-law, Ephias.

There were footsteps on the stairs and a knock at the door. Wyckford stuck his head in and wished them a Merry Christmas. "What have you there?" he wondered.

"St. Nick," said Bird simply, holding up the bulging stocking, and a bright smile lit the little fellow's face with such energy that Wyck was a little taken aback. He was not accustomed to seeing Bird look so very much like a kid.

"Well, dump it out and see what he brought!" declared Wyck, and he and Daniel sat by and watched as the boy sifted through the toys and trinkets and sweets.

Bird often exhibited an understanding of what others might be feeling, and Daniel was startled and moved when the boy took his hand on the way downstairs for breakfast. Greetings of the day went all around, and even Ephias, looking unconvinced, mumbled a Merry Christmas when they arrived. Breakfast was a large affair, and coffee was had in the parlor where small gifts were exchanged. Daniel was not forgotten, nor had he come unprepared. It was quiet and pleasing, and the greatest gift to Bird was without a doubt the scene itself with Lydia and her family taking up the warm parlor and a full stomach and a crackling hearth. Daniel watched Emmy disappear into the kitchen, and he wondered if she was herself with child. Then he turned to Lydia, and from her expression of love and concern, he knew it was so.

Daniel was satisfied. By the goodness and courage of others, his duty to Eleanor Linnett was fulfilled. In his heart he was finally saying good-bye, and some portion of him that had remained dormant was ready to look for new life and new cares.

The day went swiftly enough, and he stepped into the yard of the O'Hearn farm weighted down with boxes and bags of Christmas goose and squash and apple pies and canned mincemeat and assorted gifts for his sister and himself. The air was filled with sincere directives to visit anytime and promises to bring Bird to Hiram. Bird and Wyck took him to the station and helped him juggle his things out of the sleigh.

"Well, you're a big fellow," said the porter when the boy handed him a particularly heavy box. "What's your name?"

The little fellow said something that was difficult to hear.

Smiling, the porter glanced up at Wyckford. "Bird?" he said.

"Bert," said the boy.

"Well there," said the porter as he pushed his loaded dolly toward the baggage car, "Merry Christmas, Bert."

The train was not leaving the station for some minutes, and Daniel insisted that Wyckford and the boy not wait. "You must get back to your family, this being Christmas." He shook Wyck's hand and hoped he hadn't given it too hard a pump. "Thank you," he added simply.

"Good luck to you, Mr. Plainway," said Wyck. He felt inadequate to the moment, sensing that the spheres of two worlds had briefly grazed one another and that those two worlds were once more drifting apart into the uncertainty of the future. He would have liked to be Daniel Plainway's friend and didn't know how to bring that about.

Daniel nodded awkwardly a couple of times and said good-bye. The two from the farm—the big redheaded man and the little brown-haired boy who looked so much like his mother and so much like his uncle—turned as awkwardly away and climbed into the sleigh. When they were gone, Daniel was regretful that he had pressed them to leave. He didn't know why he'd made such a fuss about it. He stood at the platform, worn out and unnerved; he hadn't expected to be on this end of the matter so suddenly. *It's been a long haul,* he thought, *and I haven't had the opportunity to think what it means.*

What it meant, he knew, was that he was back to his life as he had been living it since he came to Hiram.

The train made sounds that indicated it would be leaving soon. The conductor appeared, looking at his watch. The porter who had taken his bags nodded to Daniel as he passed. Some people were coming out of the station house, having been warming themselves by the stove there. One of them, a lovely woman of about Daniel's years, paused at the top step and surveyed the yard till she caught sight of the lawyer standing by himself. She smiled. Daniel was astonished and looked it, and her smile grew.

Charlotte stepped down from the station, preceded by her outstretched hand, which Daniel took. "Mr. Moss said you would be coming back to-day," she said.

"He did?" said Daniel.

"After all you've told me," she explained, "I thought that seeing the boy might be difficult, in its way, and that you might care for some company on the train."

Look at you! he was thinking. Her gloved hand was still in his, and he said, "I can't express, Miss Burnbrake, how very thoughtful you are."

Charlotte's head was spinning a little, she couldn't believe that she was forging ahead with such courage. She did not let go of his hand but said a little playfully and a little pointedly, "I will be Charlotte, Mr. Plainway, if you will be Daniel."

And she dropped her hand from his only when he said, "Charlotte."

"I'm not so very thoughtful, Daniel," she said, taking his arm. "As you will see, I am in need of company myself."

As they passed the conductor, Daniel felt as if he were walking on air. He tipped his hat to the man.

The conductor smiled at them, saying, "I hope you and your wife have a very Merry Christmas, sir."

There was a hesitation in Daniel's step, and he was about to turn and say something when Charlotte gave his arm a squeeze and gently pulled him toward the boarding platform.

67. Number Six in an Ongoing Series

Ephram, Eagleton, and Thump had been thinking.

It was Ephram who instigated this activity, for it was he who first announced that he was thinking. "I have been thinking," he said, and Eagleton could believe it, for the expression on Ephram's face was reflective.

"Have you, my friend?" said Eagleton.

"Yes," said Ephram.

They were on their way to Thump's, and that worthy was not long in the cab before Eagleton passed on this intelligence. "Ephram has been thinking," he said.

"Has he?" replied Thump.

"Yes," said Ephram.

Naturally, Eagleton and Thump were curious regarding the subject of Ephram's rumination, and as soon as he told them, they were thinking as well.

"I have never thought of it!" said Eagleton.

"It has only just come to me," admitted Ephram.

"It is troublesome," said Thump.

"But must it be?" wondered Ephram.

"That, I think, is what makes it troublesome," thought Thump aloud.

"Good heavens," said Eagleton. It would never have occurred to him.

"I wouldn't have thought," said Ephram, but there it was.

"Christmas!" said Eagleton, suddenly. "Merry Christmas!" And this put an entirely new light upon all matters.

"Of course, of course!" said Ephram. "Merry Christmas!"

"Merry Christmas!" said Thump. "High tide at forty-five minutes past the hour of two."

"Continued fair and cold," said Eagleton. "Wind in the northwest. Expected to break above freezing this afternoon."

"It's twelve past nine," said Ephram. They were going to pick up Mister Walton now, then head for breakfast at the City Hotel with Miss McCannon and (they thought) Miss Burnbrake and her uncle.

"Ephram has been thinking," said Eagleton when Mister Walton entered the cab, but no further elucidation was tendered, and Mister Walton nodded and smiled his approval.

"Merry Christmas!" said Thump.

Sundry Moss, had he been in Portland on Christmas Day, might have discouraged anyone (himself included) from accompanying Miss McCannon and Mister Walton to breakfast and their subsequent walk, but he would probably have been mistaken in his reasoning, for Phileda and Toby had no notion of shutting the door behind their newfound affinity and, on the contrary, were eager to share each other with the world.

With as much resolution between them as they dared presently to ask for, Mister Walton and Miss McCannon were able to lend their thoughts to other things for a time, and this morning they found themselves most interested in Charlotte Burnbrake's absence from their circle at breakfast. Ezra Burnbrake had been pleased to profess ignorance in the matter, and coupled with the light of humor in his eyes, this served only to add to their curiosity. It was the topic of some conversation as they commenced their walk.

The day was clear and brisk; the dusting of the night before skirled in the streets and glistened in the sun as it took the air, and those gemlike sparks of reflected light seemed almost as bright as their happy faces. The smiles of the people they met were in concordance, and the livelier denizens of the city accompanied them along Congress Street in the direction of Munjoy Hill and the Eastern Promenade, where many new sleds and toboggans and vehicles unnamable of every shape and size were making their maiden runs.

As it happened, Miss McCannon and Mister Walton enjoyed a certain degree of privacy on their walk; the members of the club were not used to sustaining such brisk movement and were besides slowed down by the sights, prone to stop and engage fellow pedestrians with more than a "Merry Christmas" or "Season's Greetings." The subject raised by Ephram's earlier thought processes also gave the members cause for continued cogitation, and deliberate thought is not generally conducive to a swift pace.

"I have been thinking," said Thump, and his friends were glad to hear it. Seldom did it fall out that Thump bent his cognitive powers to a problem without divining a clear and cheerful solution.

"I sincerely hope that I did not complicate the day by raising such a question," said Ephram, who had been the first among them to think this morning.

"Not at all," said Eagleton, but with a frown of concentration upon his brow. (Up ahead of them Mister Walton and Miss McCannon, arm in arm, were laughing happily about something.)

"I *have* been thinking," began Thump again, "that instead of"—and here he shrugged elaborately—"we might," upon which two words he made a very generous and all-encompassing gesture.

"Good heavens!" said Eagleton.

"My thoughts, exactly, Eagleton!" said Ephram.

Thump made some inarticulate sounds, fearing that he had overstepped in the realm of imaginative possibilities.

"It's brilliant!" declared Eagleton.

"My *very* thought!" agreed Ephram.

"Do you think?" said an astonished Thump.

"Can we do that?" wondered Eagleton.

Thump raised a single eyebrow.

"Is it in the rules?" wondered Ephram.

"There are no rules!" Thump reminded them.

"We are writing the rules!" added Eagleton aloud.

"It is rather like saying there *is* no rule," thought Ephram aloud and with some astonishment.

"We have been very good at avoiding rules altogether," said Eagleton, and his hair almost stood on end when he said it.

"My good man!" shouted Ephram and Eagleton to Thump, loud enough to arrest the attention of their friends ahead of them. Mister Walton and Miss McCannon turned to see Ephram, Eagleton, and Thump shaking hands with one another.

"Is it unanimous then?" wondered Ephram.

"We are yet shy by two votes, but I can nearly guarantee them," said Eagleton. "Brilliant!" he said again, and Thump looked abashed.

By this time they had reached Mister Walton and Miss McCannon. Other folk, out for a walk on Christmas Day, or heading toward the Eastern Promenade, looked with interest as they passed. "I believe we have missed something of importance," said Mister Walton, whose eyes glinted with humor behind his spectacles.

"We have had a vote," explained Eagleton, and he took his hat off to bow to Miss McCannon. "A vote that has been unanimous among the three of us, and I daresay will be approbated by the remainder of our club." (Eagleton did not mention that the "remainder" of the club consisted solely of Mister Walton and Sundry Moss.)

Ephram doffed his hat and bowed. "If we are not presumptuous," he hastened to add.

"If you will do us the honor," said Thump, and he too lifted his top hat and bowed.

The absolute truth was that they were fearful of losing their chairman, and Thump had hit upon the happiest of solutions.

"We would be very pleased, Miss McCannon," said Ephram.

Phileda, who was already pleased without knowing about what, only smiled delightedly.

"If you would accept our invitation," said Eagleton.

When this did not seem to clear things up, Thump said, "To join our membership in . . . the Moosepath League!"

Ephram, Eagleton, and Thump were a little confounded since Miss McCannon put her hand to her mouth, even as tears came to her eyes. She seemed, however, to be laughing. Mister Walton was most definitely laughing.

"Is it too much?" wondered Ephram. He felt very responsible, since he had been the first to think that morning.

"On the contrary!" declared Mister Walton, even as he continued to laugh. "It is grand!"

"I am honored to be part of such a good and forward-thinking society," said Phileda sincerely, and she offered a firm handshake to each of them. She finished off by shaking Mister Walton's hand. Thump, who had seen the conclusion of events in the kitchen the night before, blushed to such a degree that it could be seen past his beard and mustaches and bushy eyebrows; it looked like a forest on fire.

But they were not finished with surprises yet, for when they were passing the end of Anderson Street, they heard a cheery "Heigh-ho!" rising from behind them, and watched as three familiar fellows clambered from a cab. The nearly complete membership of the Moosepath League were pleased to see the complete membership of the Dash-It-All Boys (all three of them) drawing near.

"It's the Bearhead Lodge!" declared Durwood.

"They're wearing hats," corrected Waverley.

"Gopherwood Club," said Brink.

"Do you think?" said Durwood.

"Gentlemen!" said Ephram. He and Eagleton and Thump put themselves in the fore of the receiving line, and the Dashians looked a little unsure about offering their hands to the inevitable agitation.

"Merry Christmas!" was the general cry from the Moosepath League, and this seemed to engender a start from the Dash-It-All Boys.

"Good heavens, is it?" said Durwood.

"How very fitting that you should be here on such an occasion!" said Eagleton while he pumped Brink's hand enthusiastically.

"Exchanging presents?" wondered Brink.

"We have just voted Miss McCannon in as a member of our club," explained Ephram.

"Drat!" said Waverley, a little indelicately.

"I beg your pardon?" said Thump.

"We were going to nominate her at *our* next meeting," said Durwood.

"Good heavens!" said Eagleton.

"We had no idea!" said Ephram.

"We didn't know you knew Miss McCannon," said Thump.

"I don't know if we do know her," admitted Durwood, but he shook her hand briskly. "But someone very much like her, perhaps."

"You would have done very nicely," assured Brink as he shook her hand.

Phileda barely allowed a smile. "It is good of you to say so, Mr. —"

"These fellows have clearly gotten the lead of us," admitted Roderick Waverley.

"It's a good thing we acted when we did," whispered Eagleton to Thump. They couldn't imagine Miss McCannon in another club.

"Mister Walton," said Humphrey Brink.

"Gentlemen," said Mister Walton, "we are heading for the promenade where Sundry and I first met you."

"Ah, yes," said Durwood. "I seem to recall."

"Would you like to come with us?" wondered the portly fellow. "Miss McCannon and I were hoping to join a toboggan on the hill."

Ephram, Eagleton, and Thump thought this an extraordinary idea. Durwood, Waverley, and Brink considered it with more gravity, however. "We appreciate the invitation," said Durwood, upon visual consultation with his fellows, "but it took a lot out of us the first time we watched you."

"Of course," said Mister Walton with a chuckle, and he instigated farewells. Handshakes went all around, but the Dash-It-All Boys, who might have been suffering from the previous night's revels, bore up manfully. It was Durwood (in the act of shaking with Mister Walton) whose attention was suddenly taken by something dark sailing in the air above them.

At first they thought it was a bird, then a kite.

It's too small for a kite, thought Mister Walton. It seemed to be descending directly toward him.

"Am I very much deceived in thinking that the object above us, just now, is a hat?" said Aldicott Durwood.

EPILOGUE

The Occupied Pocket
New Year's Day 1897

As the eve of the New Year fell upon a Thursday [*wrote Christopher Eagleton in his journal on the morning of January 1, 1897*] the Moosepath League was free to combine its customary meeting with a celebration of the extraordinary months behind us and the promising days ahead.

The Shipswood was a marvelous place to be, and this writer, for the first time, greeted the New Year in a wakeful state. It was an exhilarating moment when the hour of midnight was announced, although there was some confusion. Mr. Moss had been describing the manner in which his uncle customarily jumped into the New Year from the seat of a chair, and Thump was much taken with the idea. Unfortunately a waiter was passing by our table at the stroke of midnight, and Thump leaped into the man's arms, surprising everyone. The waiter, unprepared for this activity, dropped himself and Thump into the next table, and there was an engrossing commotion. . . .

Eagleton peered from his study window and considered the day without. A new thought occurred to him then, and he fell to writing again.

An unusual item in the papers this morning gave scant details about the disappearance of a large group of men in the western part of the state. One of the names attached to this troublesome business seems to be that of Miss Burnbrake's cousin Roger Noble. . . .

Matthew Ephram was winding his clocks and setting his watches, an appropriate activity, he thought, on the first day of the year. Someone had told him that the operator on the telephone would inform a person of the time, if asked, and he tried this with some success, although the man on the other end seemed to be a minute or so fast.

"If you ever are in need of the time," said Ephram to the operator, "never hesitate to call." He was a little flustered, however, when the man asked for a number, so he called Joseph Thump (of the Exeter Thumps), who was in the process (one might say, the ceremony) of laying to rest another year's *Almanac and Tide Calendar*. Thump thought of his almanacs as old friends and kept them in the tray of an old travel trunk at the foot of his bed.

Thump assured Ephram that he had suffered no permanent damage from his leap into the New Year. He was preparing to visit Mr. Rhume, the waiter, who was recovering at his aunt's, as a matter of fact, and it was while speaking with Ephram on the phone that Thump absently reached into a coat pocket and felt a small card there.

"What an extraordinary year it has been!" Ephram was saying.

"Hmm?" said Thump, more in reaction to the card in his pocket than to Ephram. Ephram repeated the assertion even as Thump pulled the card from his pocket and considered it. The first side said nothing, but when he turned it over, he was stunned (quite physically startled) by the name written upon it. "Hmm!" he said, a response that was not easy for Ephram to understand.

"Yes, well," said Ephram cheerfully.

Thump turned the card over several times, and every time he came back to the second side the name of Mrs. Dorothea Roberto was still there, and every time it gave him the same extraordinary shock. He had never really gotten over the circumstances of their meeting, having unintentionally provided a landing site for the beautiful widow during her Fourth of July parachute drop from an ascended balloon and then (that very night) having danced with her at the Freeport Ball.

"Would you like some company when you visit Mr. Rhume?" asked Ephram.

"That would be very nice," said Thump, hardly hearing his friend.

"I'll call Eagleton," said Ephram, and he rang off.

Thump stood with the earpiece of the phone against the side of his head for several minutes while he considered the card.

What could it mean? he wondered. He didn't remember having asked Mrs. Roberto for her card, nor did he recall her giving him one. *I was never wearing this coat in July!* he thought. He continued to turn the card over and to peruse it more closely, but there were no further clues to its history or purpose. *Clues!* he thought, and pawed through his pockets. There was nothing else to be found, however, and he decided to get out his summer suits and look through those.

An hour so later, having appointed to meet with Ephram and Eagleton, he was walking down the sidewalk of India Street. Several times during his progress he stopped and pulled the card from his pocket and considered the fine handwriting there. *What could it mean?* he wondered for the hundredth time. Before he had a better idea, however, he decided to say nothing to anyone about the unexpected card.

It was a brilliant day. Already they were experiencing something of a January thaw. He tipped his hat to an older woman who passed by and nodded to a boy, who stuck his tongue out at him.

Thump glanced back at the boy. *What did that mean?* he wondered. The very notion of sticking one's tongue out was strange to him and he practiced it tentatively (and to be truthful, half consciously) right there on the street corner.

Another walker—one George Selby of Danforth Street—was passing by at the time, and Selby wrote in his journal (dated that evening, January the first, 1897), *"Walking to my sister's this afternoon, I encountered a well-dressed man with a remarkable beard who stood at the corner of India and Congress Streets with his tongue partially protruded. He had a piece of paper in his hand and he seemed to be concentrating with some force."*

So, George Selby (by all accounts a cautious man) gave wide berth to the man with the remarkable beard and crossed the street. *"When I turned back, a minute or so later,"* continued Selby in his journal, *"I could not see him past the holiday traffic."*

❧ AUTHOR'S NOTE ❧

In the fall of 1953 several newspapers in the northeastern United States were host to the following learned query: *"For a book on secret societies: Requesting information—substantiated or anecdotal—regarding the disappearance of a group of men known as the Broumnage Club in western Maine in the winter of 1896–1897."*

The address given was that of a small midwestern college, and the scholar making the request was a professor whose fascination with secret societies (and the Broumnage Club in particular) stemmed from his involvement with a WPA project in Cambridge, Massachusetts, in the summer of 1939. It was then that the brownstone that once housed the base of operations for the Broumnage Club was converted into an apartment building and a small trove of the order's papers was discovered in a trunk in a corner of the attic.

Henry Irvine, then working his way through college, rescued these documents and kept them at his parents' home in Springfield, Massachusetts. Irvine's work on this (admittedly esoteric) subject and his formal education were interrupted by a lack of funds, then by the war, but after returning to the States in 1946, he finished his degree on the GI Bill. His pet project continued to be delayed, however, for the sake of teaching and family. After his unexpected demise in 1964, the "Broumnage Papers" were inadvertently destroyed.

For our purposes, however, the above query says it all, and one cannot help wondering about the efficacy of a thousand-year-old curse, written in

Norse runes upon a stone in Skowhegan, Maine. Any good Yankee would tell us to "Take it with a grain of salt," or perhaps "Just because it's carved in stone . . ."

Another document tells a different story entirely. It is a letter, dated July 5, 1906, and runs thusly:

> Dear Dad,
>
> The celebration here at Hiram was fine. I joined in several events, including the three-legged race with Mr. Plainway, which we won. The prize was the biggest watermelon. I thought that Mrs. Plainway would burst she laughed so hard, and Mr. Plainway grinned like a young boy when we returned to our place at the picnic, though he was out of breath. Nothing seems to please him more than what pleases her. I had a moment to watch them together, sitting on a blanket overlooking the village and the river, she in her white dress and hat, he in his white suit, and very little could be more ideal, with the flowers in the field and the two of them laughing. Their love for one another is so keen and so conspicuous that I would have been embarrassed if I didn't love them so myself.
>
> Today we went to the cemetery and the house . . .

The letter does continue at some length and includes the writer's *"strange sensation of walking into the scene of a play or the page of a book, but certainly not into a place that had affected my life."* The envelope enclosing the letter is addressed to Wyckford O'Hearn; the return address bears the name of Bertram O'Hearn.

Wyckford Cormac O'Hearn did play baseball again, though he never returned to the glory days of his past and never again played in a professional capacity. His greatest accomplishment may have been forming some of the earliest boys' baseball leagues in the towns of Veazie and Orono. Of interest to readers may be one of the last lines in Bertram's letter. "Tell Mom and Grandma that I have presents for them. (And one for yourself.)"

If in the preceding narratives, Bertram (that is, Bird) seems something of a cipher, then it is in keeping with the observations of those who knew him. Though well liked and admired throughout his life, Bird (as I like to think of him) became a man of few words and occasional surprises. Always a good and loyal friend—and that to many—he was perhaps only truly known by Wyck and one other person. In later years he reappeared in the annals of the Moosepath League in a very different role.

Eustace Pembleton (his real name was none of those by which he was known in this story) spent twenty-two months in prison for his role in Bird's kidnapping as well as other charges but was released for humanitarian reasons and boarded in a private hospital for the mentally ill. His care and room were paid for by an anonymous benefactor. As a young man, Bird visited Pembleton at the hospital at least four times a year (except in 1918–1919) until Pembleton's death in 1924. Mister Walton did visit with Bird once and was impressed with the young man's kindness and Pembleton's amicable responses. Bird always brought Pembleton popcorn balls and *dime novels*.

As stated in the narrative, Christopher Eagleton did not recall the business of the silver cross until he stumbled upon the December 5, 1896, entry of his journal months later. He and his fellows were much amazed by it all.

In Moosepathian circles, the events of that December are variously thought of as "the Adventure of the Holiday Haunting," "the Adventure of the Three Legacies," and "the Adventure of the Mother's Eyes." It might also have been called "the Adventure of the Three Clubs." The twenty-first of December is always the league's tree-decorating day in memory of this exploit. St. Nicholas's Day is also observed, so if you ever see boots outside a hotel room on the eve of December 6, they are not waiting for the bootblack.

To my knowledge, the Broumnage Club was never heard from again.

In the years to come, Aldicott Durwood, Roderick Waverley, and Humphrey Brink—the Dash-It-All Boys—occasionally deviated into the path of the Moosepath League, and something worth noting always seemed to occur from these encounters. In 1920, the year of National Prohibition, a club called the Dash-It-All Boys was formally founded in nearby Falmouth, coincidentally dissolving in 1933, when Prohibition ended. The minutes of their meetings are difficult to read.

The false card placed in Joseph Thump's coat pocket by Aldicott Durwood had extraordinary consequences for the Moosepath League, though the possible (if imaginative) implications of that article did not fully accumulate in Thump's mind till the following May. In the resultant bewilderment, the Moosepath League would meet the half-mad and thoroughly engaging Benjamin Granite Gunwight, and the brief era of the club's beginnings would end in the wake of a letter from Mister Walton's sister. Rumors concerning Ephram, Eagleton, and Thump and "the woman in room 12A" are universally considered capricious. This page in the history of the league is generally styled by Moosepathian historians as "the Adventure of the Pasteboard Card," though some in the league prefer to remember it as "the Adventure of the Startled Ascensionist" or "the Adventure of the Widow's Brigade."

Someday it may be told.

I have had letters from folks who ask for a bibliography, and with that in mind I shall list some of the books that most affected this and the two preceding narratives. To my knowledge the following are still in print and highly recommended: *Coastal Maine* by Roger Duncan; *Dawn over the Kennebec* and other works by Mary R. Calvert; *Maine in the Making of the Nation 1783–1870* by Elizabeth Ring; *History of Ancient Sheepscot and Newcastle* by Rev. David Quimby Cushman (reprinted by the local historical society); *Sermons in Stone, the Stonewalls of New England and New York* by Susan Allport; *A Day's Work, a Sampler of Historic Maine Photographs 1860–1920*, annotated and compiled by W. H. Bunting; *Portland*, edited by Martin Dibner with photographs by Nicholas Dean; *Along the Damariscotta*, compiled by Dorothy A. Blanchard; *No Pluckier Set of Men Anywhere, the Story of Ships and Men in Damariscotta and Newcastle, Maine* by Mark Wyman Biscoe; *Old John Neptune and Other Maine Indian Shamans* by Fanny Hardy Eckstorm; *Wake of the Coaster* by John F. Leavitt; *Benjamin Browne Foster's Down East Diary*, edited by Charles H. Foster; *Magnificent Mainers* by Jeff Hollingsworth; *Saltwater Foodways, New Englanders and Their Food, at Sea and Shore in the Nineteenth Century* by Sandra L. Oliver; *Ancient Sagadahoc, a Story of the Englishmen Who Welcomed the Pilgrims to the New World* by E. J. Chandler; *Christmas in America* by Penne L. Restad; *Madame Blavatsky's Baboon, a History of the Mystics, Mediums, and Misfits Who Brought Spiritualism to America* by Peter Washington; *The Perpetual Almanak of Folklore* by Charles Kightly; *The Wordsworth Dictionary of the Occult* by André Nataf; *Rhyme's Reason* by John Hollander; *A Field Guide to American Houses* by Virginia and Lee McAlester; *The American Language* by H. L. Mencken; the Oxford and Bartlett's books of quotations, the *American Heritage Dictionary*; the *Oxford Universal Dictionary on Historical Principles*; almost the entire range of Peterson guides to nature; and the Bible.

Many of the authors to whom I owe a debt are (to my knowledge) out of print, and these include: *Romantic and Historic Maine* by A. Hyatt Verrill; *Mysterious New England*, edited by Austin N. Stevens; *Clipper Ships and Captains* by Jane D. Lyon; *Captains of Industry* by Bernard Weisberger; *Maine Beautiful* by Wallace Nutting; *Confederates Downeast* by Mason Philip Smith; *The World of Washington Irving* and subsequent volumes on

American art and literature by Van Wyck Brooks; *A History of Secret Societies* by Arkon Daraul; *Going Fishing, the Story of the Deep Sea Fishermen of New England* by Wesley George Pierce; *The Secret Country* by Janet and Colin Bord.

Add to these the town historians whose works fortify the State Library and the writers (many anonymous) who contributed to the newspapers and almanacs of the day.

It hardly needs to be said that any errors or magnifications in the annals of the Moosepath League are purely my own.

Continued thanks to my agent Barbara Hogenson and her assistant Nicole Verity, as well as Jody Lipper. Continued good wishes, also, to Sarah Feider. Thanks to everyone at Viking Penguin who has worked on Cordelia, Mollie, and Daniel, including of course my editor Carolyn Carlson, and her assistant Lucia Watson, publicist Linda McFall and her assistant Hillary Thompson, and designer Jesse Reyes. Best wishes, also, to Michael Driscoll.

This past season I was a guest at numerous bookstores and in particular I would like to thank the folks at Port in a Storm in Somesville; Sherman's in Boothbay and Freeport; Bookland in Brunswick and South Portland; the Kennebunk Book Port in Kennebunkport; Thomaston Books & Prints; Bear Pond Books in Montpelier, Vermont; Odyssey Bookstore in South Hadley, Massachusetts; Borders in Framingham; Bickerton and Ripley in Edgartown; and the Owl and the Turtle in Camden.

Most especially, thanks to Jane and Mark Bisco, Susan and Barnaby Porter, Penny and Ewing Walker, Pat and Clark Boynton, Joanne Cotton, Devon Sherman, Johanna Rice, Frank Slack, Hester Stuhlman, and Trudy Price and all my friends at the Maine Coast Book Shop in Damariscotta.

Thanks to the Georgetown Historical Society and the Damariscotta-Newcastle Rotary Club.

Thanks to everyone who has communicated by mail their interest and encouragement. I hope that all you folks who have written from other parts of the country come to Maine soon, and please drop by and say hello at the Maine Coast Book Shop.

Regards and appreciation go out again to Michael Uhl, Nick Dean, and Jim Nelson.

Thanks to family and friends, and a terrific set of in-laws for their abiding support and good thoughts.

If all my efforts were to be dedicated to a single person, it would be to Margaret Hunter—Maggie—scientist, wife, mother, first-line editor of the Moosepath Chronicles, and patient sounding board for bouts of authorial angst. She does all these things well, rarely complains about being married to a writer, and remains an island of calm throughout. As growing *codicils* (if you will) to this dedication, may I add Hunter and Mary, who help keep things in perspective with laughter, innocence, and unbounded curiosity.

The injunction to the writer is often to "write about what you know," and I have done so. The historical context, of course, is equal parts research and intuition, the geographical context is my home, the human context is my life. I have been blessed to know people who are as good and kind and wise as some of those in this book and its companion volumes. I am grateful, then, that I can write about what I know and in the process write about the generosity of spirit, the strength of compassion, and the gladness of laughter that I have endeavored to exemplify in Mister Walton, Sundry Moss, and the members of *the Moosepath League*.